Die Trying

ELEANOR BARKER-WHITE

Harper
North

HarperNorth
Windmill Green
24 Mount Street
Manchester M2 3NX

A division of
HarperCollins*Publishers*
1 London Bridge Street
London SE1 9GF

www.harpercollins.co.uk

HarperCollins*Publishers*
Macken House,
39/40 Mayor Street Upper,
Dublin 1, D01 C9W8, Ireland

Published by HarperCollins*Publishers* Ltd 2026

Copyright © Eleanor Barker-White 2026

Eleanor Barker-White asserts the moral right to
be identified as the author of this work.

A catalogue record for this book is available from the British Library.

HB ISBN: 978-0-00-858697-3

This novel is entirely a work of fiction. The names, characters and incidents portrayed in it are the work of the author's imagination. Any resemblance to actual persons, living or dead, events or localities is entirely coincidental.

Set in (Sabon LT Std) by (Amnet)

Printed and bound in the UK using 100% Renewable Electricity by CPI Group (UK) Ltd

All rights reserved. No part of this publication may be reproduced, stored in a retrieval system, or transmitted, in any form or by any means, electronic, mechanical, photocopying, recording or otherwise, without the prior permission of the publishers.

Without limiting the exclusive rights of any author, contributor or the publisher of this publication, any unauthorised use of this publication to train generative artificial intelligence (AI) technologies is expressly prohibited. HarperCollins also exercise their rights under Article 4(3) of the Digital Single Market Directive 2019/790 and expressly reserve this publication from the text and data mining exception.

10 9 8 7 6 5 4 3 2 1

*For my parents - Wendy and Andrew -
and for my sister, Faye.
There from the start, for every roll of the die.*

'God does not play dice with the universe'
Albert Einstein

PART ONE

You've got a die. Everyone has a die.

In a dusty drawer full of old batteries, paperclips and instruction manuals for appliances you don't own anymore, or hidden at the bottom of a stationery pot at work. You might wonder how it got there. Leftover from an old board game, perhaps, an old maths set, or a drinking challenge, the pips starkly playful against the drab minutiae of your life.

Here's the thing: you haven't found it by chance. It's been waiting.

You might pick it up, roll it in your palm. You don't know what it means, so you replace it in the dusty drawer or the stationery pot, unchanged.

But there is another choice. A chance to change your destiny.

Let it fall. You won't be able to resist looking, and then you'll wonder: why this number? Why now?

There's nothing random about it.

1= *Connection*
2= *Do nothing*
3= *Discomfort*
4= *Truth*
5= *Confrontation*
6= *Wild card*

Die Trying

Once a roll is cast, the order must be obeyed. No rerolls for the same question.
You are the die; the die is you.
Play safe.

CHAPTER ONE

Adam

I met my wife on the train from Manchester to Bristol. She was sitting in the seat I'd reserved – the one by the window – wedged in place by a stack of bags which took up the entire vacant seat beside her. Normally, I'd keep walking and try to find somewhere else to rest for the next few hours, but having already trudged the length of the carriage to tuts and sighs as I knocked legs and overhanging elbows, I resigned myself to what I thought was the lesser of two evils: confrontation with a stranger.

'Sorry – excuse me. May I sit here?'

She said, 'Yes. Sure!' And then began an awkward production line of bags being passed from her to me to place in the overhead compartments; as all the while I swayed unsteadily towards her armpit, her honey-scented hair, her chest. I tried not to look at her too closely. As soon as I finished and lowered myself into the seat, I realised she was staring at me – or more specifically, the tattoo on my wrist. 'What's that?' she asked. 'Sorry, I know I'm being nosy, but that's – what is it? A shell or something?'

'It's a Fibonacci sequence.'

I've learnt from experience that most people don't like making small talk about mathematics. They prefer stories. So I told her about how the spiral represented patterns of numbers which could be found everywhere, all over the world: in space, animals, architecture, even art and music. 'And nature. If you look at a sunflower head, how the seeds are all tightly packed together, or the curl of rose petals—'

'Mansplaining much?' she laughed. 'I know what a Fibonacci sequence is.' Then she told me she'd studied Art History at Manchester University and what I had on my wrist was definitely *not* that.

'Ok,' I admitted. 'It isn't. It's actually a lizard's tail.'

She laughed again – harder this time. 'You're fucking with me?'

Fucking. She said fucking.

My body felt too big suddenly, the brush of her arm too close, the smell of her perfume – melon-sweet, a hint of vanilla – too strong. I said she was the first person who'd called me out on it, and observed her properly then: the coral curve of her lips, the playfulness dancing around her eyes, the spidery black-widow lashes which hinted at dangerous promise. I'd intended to get some work done on the train, but she started telling me about her life. She was done with men. Done with being messed about. She was coming down south to see a friend in Wales and enjoy some long-awaited R&R.

'What are you doing, then?' she asked.

'Right now?' I gestured to the closed lid of the laptop in front of me.

'No, in Bristol. That is where you're going, isn't it?'

'Yes, I'm heading home. I was only in Manchester for an IT conference. All very boring.'

'You don't *look* boring.'

What was I supposed to say to that? 'Well,' I managed, eventually. 'I'm not... *all* the time.'

It wasn't supposed to be a joke – although it was a lie, because I am – but she laughed. And then, after clearing the misted-up window with a swipe of her burgundy jumper, she looked at me for a little too long. 'I'm Jemma.'

'I'm Adam.'

By the end of the journey, she'd asked for my number.

'Play again, Daddy!'

'Again?'

'Pleeeassse?'

'One more time then – *after* I've made a cuppa. I'm parched.'

Toby's hopeful expression dissolves into one of shocked amusement. 'You parped?'

'I said parched, not parped.'

My son lets out a squeal of laughter. We've played Snakes and Ladders (or Sakes and Ladders, as Toby insists on calling it) three times already and I need to stretch my legs. I leave Toby humming to himself and wander into the kitchen.

We moved here soon after we married, mainly because Jemma's trademark enthusiasm sold it to me far better than the estate agent ever could. The suited young recruit shuffled behind us in what I presume was uncharacteristic silence as Jemma flounced into every room and furnished it with animation. 'Oh my God, a *wine* rack! Adam, look at the space under here. Look at the *windows*.' She touched and stroked random objects – a bedroom radiator, the curve of the porcelain sink, a wooden crest on the bookshelf in the lounge – and proceeded to open and close cupboard doors with all the wonder of a child on Christmas morning.

We put an offer in the following day.

Now, the cupboards are adorned with Toby's pictures: huge, crude circles with dots for eyes and stalks for limbs, as well as a gold star award from his pre-school for good behaviour and a smear of what I hope is chocolate spread. I give the cupboard door a quick wipe and run the kettle under the tap. Upstairs, Jemma's hairdryer roars to life.

Die Trying

'Snake goes "ssssss",' I hear Toby say, in the next room.

I can't decide whether to cook chicken pasta bake – Toby's favourite – or wraps for tea. Jemma's out with friends tonight, so it'll just be me and...

What *is* that?

I close the fridge door. There it is again; louder this time – a furious buzzing, coming from behind the fruit bowl. A wasp?

'Mummy,' Toby calls.

I move the bowl aside. Before I can even wonder what Jemma's phone is doing here, the screen lights up with a new message:

```
I'm so hard for you it hurts Xxx
```

Two messages, in fact, stacked one above the other with a cartoon speech bubble in one corner:

```
How much longer, sexy? Xxx
```

There's an attachment, an image of some sort which thankfully I can't see. At least, not without unlocking the phone.

The kettle clicks off; the furious bubbling subsides. I rummage in the cupboard and pull out a packet of fusilli. '*Mummy*,' Toby calls, more insistently this time. 'Will you come and play with me?'

I push the phone back into its hiding place. 'I told you Mummy can't come and play, Tobes. She's getting ready to go out. I'm just coming.'

Coming.

It's got to be a wrong number. Or her friends perhaps, messing around. I've never quite figured them out, and if I'm being perfectly honest, they terrify me. When Jemma's with them, her voice rises several octaves as she talks about our sex life, her private parts and Toby's toilet habits in a singular tone of exaggerated amusement, while the others gawp and gasp and giggle before regaling tales of Rob and Paul's manhood – or lack of, in Paul's case. 'What?' Jemma laughed once when I had to leave the room. 'It's funny.'

It wasn't funny, though. I pointed out that if *I* were to talk like that with other men, comparing her breast size with that of her friends, she'd rightly see my behaviour as sexist and misogynistic. Not that I have any male friends to talk to. Our neighbourhood is the kind of place where people exchange nothing more than polite pleasantries, and it's not been as easy as joining a gym or getting a hobby, or any of that agony-aunt stuff people suggest – I'm often stuck at work until 7 or 8pm, and on the rare occasions when I do get away by five, all I want is to get back home and see my wife and son.

I'm so hard for you it hurts.

No. It's a mistake; a wrong number. It has to be.

I carry my tea through to the lounge, bumping into Jemma in the hallway. She's wearing tight black jeans and a patterned black bra, her hair falling in damp waves around her shoulders. Is that fake tan? She doesn't normally look that bronzed.

'Have you seen my phone?'

'Your... yes.' There are smoky-grey clouds nestled behind her eyelids; an impending storm. I maintain eye contact. 'In the kitchen. Behind the fruit bowl.'

'Ok.'

She doesn't even blink.

CHAPTER TWO

My parents were restless souls. Especially my father. He was always searching for something more, something new, something *better*, I suppose. Mum called it wanderlust, although years later she dropped the 'wander' bit and replaced it with something unrepeatable. Every Saturday morning, he'd bounce into my room, commanding me to get up because we were going on a road trip.

This spontaneity was rarely as exciting as it sounds: we moved house thirteen times before my twelfth birthday, and holidays were – as far as I could tell – decided on the flip of a coin or the random stab at a map. A year after I was born, Dad got a work transfer to Sheffield, and no sooner had I completed my first year at primary school than we moved to Uttoxeter, Dudley and then Cardiff.

'We've got each other,' Mum said cheerfully, when we relocated for the tenth time and I complained that we never lived anywhere long enough to put down roots. 'You'll make new friends.'

I didn't make new friends. I didn't make any friends. The other children at school had different accents, different hairstyles, different habits. They'd already formed alliances and forged bonds, and I couldn't see the point in establishing connections with my peers only to be torn away from them again. Instead, I focused on the one thing that remained constant in my life: numbers. I scribbled furiously at sudoku sheets and usually completed maths challenges long before anyone else had turned the first page. During one pairing-up exercise, I tried explaining my enthusiasm to the boy sitting beside me. 'Sometimes the answer slowly appears in my head, like joining the dots. I don't even need to calculate it.'

He didn't ask to sit by me again.

It wasn't just school that made me feel lonely. Dad wasn't always the carefree, charismatic character one might expect him to be, and I got the sense that Mum and I were never enough for him. Occasionally, his boredom would translate into something manic and unpredictable so he'd play at wrestling, throwing me into the furniture and then pinning me to the floor with the solid mass of his muscular frame until I couldn't breathe. I would feel my eyes bulging from their sockets in terror, and then he'd lower his bony forehead and press it hard against mine, challenging me to tap out. I tried to withstand it, gasping in the sour, stale-coffee odour of his breath for as long as I could bear until a film of stars clouded my vision and then I'd reach out and thump the floor, like a flailing, dying animal. Dad always released his grip immediately then. Sometimes he would make a remark about what a good game it was – particularly if Mum came into the room to see what we were up to – but most of the time he'd just walk away with a triumphant smile.

When we moved to Bristol, Dad had acquired a position in a new company which required him to work longer hours, and the spontaneous weekend road trips slowly fizzled out. I'd joined the local comprehensive school – and even dared hope that, this time, we might be able to stay put for a few years – when Dad started mentioning a work colleague called Kim. He dropped her name into conversation sparingly at first. Kim's performance review was excellent. Kim had some great ideas around the merger. Kim had a bag just like Mum's.

I don't know what happened at the company barbecue. All I remember is Mum coming home in tears. Doors slamming. A charred, acrid smell, folding into my throat. An electric toothbrush landing with an inexplicably loud thud at the bottom of the stairs. 'I knew it,' Mum kept saying, in a voice heavy with pain. 'You must have thought I was stupid, but *I knew*.'

Kim was younger – and, I hate to say it, prettier – than Mum, with long dark hair that she continuously stroked and smoothed over one shoulder, as though petting a spaniel. Every Saturday, Dad would pick me up and take me to her house on the outskirts of Bath, where I slept in a tiny room that doubled up as an office, on a blow-up mattress that wheezed and groaned like a bagpipe every time I turned over. I couldn't wait to get home to Mum, even though 'home' was now a flat above a chip shop in Brislington. In a way, this tiny space drew us closer. During the evenings, we'd snuggle on the sofa and watch TV together, and on a Friday night we'd play board games and music to drown out the sound of drunks stumbling outside. Sometimes Mum would dance with me, pressing me to the prickly fabric of her dressing gown while singing Nickelback songs at the top of her voice.

'I love you so much,' she'd say. 'What would I do without you?'

I often wonder where we'd be now, if Mum and Dad were still together. If Mum's spirit wasn't broken by the men that followed. If she hadn't got the job in the charity shop.

If she hadn't brought home the polished-glass die.

Still, it's impossible to predict what we set in motion through seemingly random choices. Perhaps everything unfolds exactly as it's supposed to.

That evening, I do what I can to be a good father. I play two more games of Snakes and Ladders, cook Toby's pasta and then, after a quick and messy bath where Toby managed to somehow soak me *and* the floor yet avoid getting a drop of water on his head, I put him to bed. I don't mind doing any of this because it's a distraction and a novelty – usually Jemma's the one sorting out the house and tending to Toby's needs. That might sound sexist, but we talked about all this before Toby was born, and Jemma wanted to be the one to bring him up, not send him to spend his formative years with a weary, overwhelmed childminder. She'd struggled to get work in one of the Bristol museums and, as her temping job didn't earn anything near as much as mine, it made sense for me to be the one to carry on working full time. But she never seemed happy. When I got home from work, Jemma would complain that she hadn't had any 'me time', that she needed a break, she didn't feel like herself anymore. *'Do you know what it's like to spend the entire day singing nursery rhymes?'* she'd spit. And no, of course I didn't, because my day usually comprised of analysing network traffic and fielding sarcastic barbs levelled at me by Spencer, the office prick. So, when Jemma got talking to a mum who tutored at a local college, the seed was sown. She wanted to enrol on a Level 3 course in Sports Massage. She'd be able to work around Toby's school hours when he started school next September, and the extra money would come in handy.

I was baffled. It couldn't be more different as a career choice than Art History. 'You think?' she said. 'You don't think the body is a canvas? I'll be looking at the present and future, instead of the past. And anyway, I won't just be observing; I'll be *interacting*.'

My wife. She has an answer for everything.

Now, with Toby at school three days a week, this is what she does. Painting her nails. Putting her hair up, revealing that luscious expanse of neck. Zipping those black trousers against the gentle curve of her thighs.

Is she happy? Or rather, is she happy with me?

I stroke the plump warmth of Toby's cheek. He's fallen asleep sucking his thumb, and now it falls from the puckered 'o' of his lips.

I creep out of the room and pull the door gently closed behind me. Now what?

I head downstairs and pour myself a glass of water. There *is* more that I can do for my wife. Jemma has been nagging me for ages to fix the porch light and fill the holes left by the hallway coat hooks. Relationships aren't really all that different from complex networks: you need to understand what's missing in order to troubleshoot arising issues.

I can fix this.

Jemma comes home at midnight. I'm still awake, having ushered Toby back into bed following a nightmare about sharks, and the house feels cold and still. Quiet. I hear the taxi's engine idling through our open bedroom window, the lilting *thanks* of Jemma's goodbye, a slam, the car disappearing up and away from our cul-de-sac. The porch light clicks on; her key scratches noisily against the lock. In a minute she will stumble up the stairs and fit the pieces of her body against the puzzle that is mine, the way she always does when she's had a few drinks.

I am warm now. I wait.

She stays downstairs for what seems like an eternity, on her phone. I can't make out the words, only the low tone of her voice, talking in urgent whispers. And then – eventually – she comes upstairs.

'It was ok,' she says, when I ask her how her night was. After dropping her clothes in a puddle on the floor and slipping into an oversized t-shirt, she doesn't cuddle into me, but shuffles downwards against her pillow in a caterpillar-like manner, yawning theatrically when I lean towards her for a kiss. 'Thought you'd be asleep. I'm knackered.'

I reach out again; she recoils. 'Did you notice that I fixed the porch light?'

'Don't start.'

'What?'

'You were trying to make a thing about how late it is. Just don't start, ok? I'm tired.'

'I'm not making a thing of anything.'

'No, of course you're not. You never do. Just this passive aggressive shit all the time. What do you want – a medal for fixing a stupid light?'

'Why are you being like this?'

'I'm not *being like* anything. If you don't like the way I am, you don't have to stick it.' She sits up, suddenly. 'Why don't you ever go out or do anything? It's weird.'

I don't reply, even though I could tell her that it's even weirder to hide your phone behind the fruit bowl. Or to get a message saying… No. I won't think about that. I want to tell her that the reason I don't go out with friends is because I chose to live here, with her, hundreds of miles away from mine. That when it comes to a choice between a drink with a bunch of smug arseholes from work or doing nothing on the sofa cuddled up with my wife and son, my family will always win, hands down.

In the end, I say nothing. I don't want to wake Toby up. I don't want a row.

Jemma tugs aggressively at the sheet and then rolls away from me, her body a small island silhouetted beneath the covers. The porch light continues to shine, too brightly, through the thin bedroom curtains.

CHAPTER THREE

The office where I work is a drab grey building, with a revolving door and lifts which never seem to be properly cleaned: the buttons to the third floor bear the ghostly whorls of dozens of fingerprints. I jab at it with my elbow and stare vacantly at the vertical line of the closed doors as the lift begins its ascent. I've been working for Smithson Wealth Management for the past two years and enjoyed it until the reshuffle – or 'streamlining', as our ex-manager put it – just before Christmas, when they replaced almost every member of staff I'd built a rapport with. Now, we're a 'family', according to Seb, the office manager. A family expected to attend bingo once a month, lunch together every Friday and stay on until at least 7pm most evenings.

Jemma, when I first told her this, was furious. 'Family? Tell him to go fuck himself – you've got a family, and you'll leave at 5pm, because you're not paid after that. Jesus.'

How could I say that, when everyone else – mostly unattached, mostly child-free – seemed happy to enjoy the perks of the new management? Not only that, they were fearful of the rumours swirling: that there might be another round of redundancies. I didn't attend bingo or lunch. I tried to compromise on the time I finished work, sliding out at 5.30 or 6pm, and consequently disappointed everyone in the process.

'Fuck me, you look rough,' says Spencer, as I walk in. He's manspreading on the corner of Katya's desk, swinging one leg as though it's a second penis. I move over to my own desk and lay down my briefcase. 'Morning.'

'Hot night with the wife, was it?'

Katya sniggers.

I don't bite. 'Did you get the Actisoft account?'

'I'll take that as a yes.' Spencer laughs and touches Katya's shoulder before jumping from the desk. 'Certainly did. I can't get my shitting laptop to work for long enough to set up the contract our end though – take a look at it for me, would you?'

Spencer may think his balls are bigger than mine just because he's Seb's favourite employee, lapping up bingo, free lunches and 8pm finishes like a corporate terrier, but he's still in here with the rest of us. Sometimes I fantasise about winning the lottery and coming in here the morning after my win, taking a piss all over his desk and watching the hot yellow liquid trace a path through the mess of paperwork, soaking into the components of his laptop. I've fantasised about picking up my stuff and walking out too, but now that Toby's getting older there seems to be no end to the additional expenses. Trampolining club. Toys. Dress-up day and summer fete for pre-school. Clothes. Food. More clothes. More food. Not to mention the mortgage and bills.

'I'll take a look at it tomorrow, if that's ok? I've got some connectivity issues to sort out with staff who are working from home. They haven't got—'

'It needs to be done today, or Seb won't be happy. We're talking major impact here.'

Why didn't you give it to me earlier, then? I sink onto my chair and start setting up my own laptop at the desk beside the window. 'Bring it over and I'll do it during lunch.'

'Thanks.'

Spencer switches his attention back to Katya and I try to zone out her flirtatious titters as his self-obsessed rambling continues. In the kitchen, the microwave pings and a few seconds later, Chloe from HR drifts across the office, carrying a mug of something foul-smelling. I want to focus on work, but my mind keeps pulling me back to Toby. Or, more specifically, how Toby pushed me away this morning as I tried to kiss him goodbye. A swirl of sweaty blonde hair, one sticky finger jabbing at the Snakes and Ladders board. *Your turn, Mummy.* His squeal of macabre delight as Jemma landed on the head of a snake, slithering all the way to the bottom of the board. 'Bye, then,' I said to them both. 'Love you.'

Nothing. Not even a backwards glance.

I spend the next few hours fixing issues and then take a break while running a debug check, watching through the slatted blinds as people scurry about on the pavement outside: a grey-haired man shouting into a mobile phone, the jogger who steps into the road to avoid two women with pushchairs, a couple of men wearing high-viz jackets, laughing at a joke I can't hear. My feta sandwich tastes of dust. The office is quiet now; most of the others have gone out to lunch. I can't tell if it's my nagging headache that's causing the pain, or my jaw. I must have been grinding my teeth again last night; there was blood on my pillow when I awoke.

I drop the rest of the sandwich in the bin and open up Spencer's screen.

I try to call Jemma on my way home. She doesn't pick up. The car has trapped all the heat of the day and the air conditioning seems to be broken; it's circulating thick, soupy air which rushes out when I open a window. I'm relieved to be getting away from work early for once, but I need to talk to my wife.

I'm sorry, the person you are calling...

Is it my imagination, or does the recorded voice sound more apologetic than usual? I hit the 'end call' button on my caller display and swing out of the car park. Perhaps we could get a takeaway. Not that I'm in the mood for one, but it would make Toby happy, as well as give us a break from cooking. I picture his face, lighting up at the suggestion of 'getting a Donimoes'. The cheeky clasp of his hands. And then he'll position himself at the window, firing off a relentless set of questions: *how long 'til the lilivery man gets here? What is he wearing, Daddy? Shall I give him some of mine?*

It's only when I reach the end of the street that I see another car reversing off our drive. It's a black BMW which emits a throaty growl as it spins around and then accelerates past me, so quickly that I'm almost forced onto the pavement.

'Some idiot almost took me out,' I tell Jemma, when I go indoors. She's standing with her back to me, putting clean plates back into the cupboard. Her hair is tied up in a loose knot and several long dark tendrils have fallen free, clinging alluringly to the narrow ledge of her shoulders. She starts babbling that Toby's upstairs having a nap; he's been a little monkey today, she didn't manage to get anything done. She does this when she's nervous.

Or lying.

I think of the takeaway I'd been planning. The three of us snuggled on the sofa afterwards, watching *Spiderman*, the scent of warm dough still rich in the air. Yet, for some reason, I fuck it all up by asking the question: 'Was that him?'

'Mm?'

A pause, fat and heavy, strains against the brief silence.

And then, from Jemma, a sigh. Not '*who?*' Not the immediate bewildered denial that I was hoping for. She turns around, and her eyes drift to a point somewhere over my right shoulder. 'Oh. Yes.'

I can feel something stretching inside me, like the corners of a mouth pulled too wide. Her slim fingers are still resting gently on one of the plates that were bought for us as a wedding present. She looks so irritatingly beautiful. It dawns on me that the flush of her skin, the endless new clothes she's been buying 'for work', the renewed interest in jogging and healthy eating weren't borne of a desire to 'be a better person' – they were for him. The arsehole in the BMW. She turns; moves her fingers to my arm. They feel like spider's legs.

'Ad—'

I pull away. 'I'm going to check on Toby.'

CHAPTER FOUR

His name is Dan Bretti.

I don't want to know this, but Jemma tells me anyway. She met him at work when he came in to buy a voucher for his sister. He's ex-forces – of course – with a *huge*... brief pause, as Toby calls for her to tuck him in... collection of photos from the places he's been all over the world. She tells me all this when I'm getting ready for bed. She can't stand the silence or the secrecy anymore, but she didn't want me to find out this way. She feels *terrible*.

'You haven't slept with him.' It comes out as a statement, not a question. When she doesn't reply straightaway, I add a plea. 'Have you?'

'No, of course not!' Jemma half-laughs at the very suggestion. 'Do you know what? I'm actually glad it's all out in the open now – I just hate living like this. Our marriage...' she sighs. 'I'm not happy, Adam.'

I line up my pillow with the headboard. It's part of a bed set she bought online. Red flowers, a tangle of something green. Anything but look at my wife, who is beautiful and hideous all at once, a kind of Cleopatra-Medusa hybrid. My insides have already turned to stone.

'I think... I just *thought* I was,' she goes on. 'We've got so settled, haven't we? Things are stale... everything is just so *dull*, and you know that's not me. We're such different people. And all the stuff I used to do – the holidays, the road trips... I don't know... being fucking spontaneous – I miss that.'

'Life *is* dull most of the time when you've got a mortgage and a small child, Jem. Don't forget your pillow.'

She takes it from my outstretched hand. She's offered to sleep in the spare room tonight, and so she should. I wish I'd asked what had actually happened between them. I want to know, and yet at the same time, I don't. Who was it that said all truths are half-truths; that all half-truths are lies? My brain is scrambling to fill in the gaps, and right now my head feels like it's Swiss cheese.

'I'm sorry, Adam.'

I pretend to mess with my alarm clock. 'Yeah.'

After she leaves the room, I lower myself onto the bed and fold my legs mechanically beneath the covers. Dan Bretti. I resist Googling him, only because seeing his face would make him real. Instead, I try to console myself with the knowledge that it won't last. I'm her anchor, solid and dependable, that's what she told me before we married. The one person who stops her from drifting into dangerous waters.

What has she done? How could she, when we have Toby? When we have *us*.

The grinding will be worse tonight; I can already feel the twitch in my jaw. That's if I sleep at all. My legs have started to jerk of their own accord – I can't get comfortable – and before I know it, I'm half-smothered between Jemma's pillow and my own. My mind is offering me an intimate, private viewing: Jemma's fingers on Dan's body, kissing hungrily. His hands, on her. It's repulsive, and yet... the images send a rush of energy, stinging at my groin. How am I *aroused*?

Disgusting. I am disgusting.

'Alan, isn't it?'

'*Adam.*'

Sebastian Wiggin peers at me. He's in the middle of eating a breakfast baguette which has fallen open in front of him on the desk: the bacon is hanging out like a bleeding tongue against a slush of half-chewed egg.

'I wondered if I could talk to you. Spencer asked me to take a look at his PC due to performance issues; I've performed a clean-up several times. It's just that I've uncovered something, well...'

Sebastian lifts the baguette to his mouth and I wish I'd left the door open. The smell of egg is overpowering.

'I thought it needed reporting, from an ethical point of view. It appears there have been a number of searches made to websites during work time that are of—'

I break off as Sebastian begins a furious coughing fit that sends particles of meat and egg flying in all directions. He wheezes dramatically, thumps a fist to his fleshy chest and then flaps a hand to indicate that I can carry on.

'Well, the nature of the content was pornography.'

'Sorry?'

I didn't need to open the links to know what Spencer had been looking at: the titles – *Up for Anything*, *Barely Legal* – showed exactly what kind of man he was. The kind who thinks nothing of objectifying other people's daughters, sisters, mothers, wives. The kind who uses valuable work time to indulge in perverted misogynistic fantasies. 'Porn.'

'Oh.' There's a long pause. Sebastian seems to be digesting what I've just told him, and his mouth twitches into a faint smile. There's a string of bacon caught between two of his top teeth. 'Oh dear.'

'I've cleaned his device, although I did keep a print-out of all the websites and the times they were accessed. But I'm not – it's not my intention to get him into trouble. I just wanted to pass the information on because, well, not only will he keep having technical issues if this isn't addressed, it just seemed like the right—'

'Can I have these print-outs, please?'

Die Trying

'Yes.'

They're in my laptop bag. I tug the four sheets free and pass them over. Sebastian doesn't look at them, but slides them close to the baguette. I feel an overwhelming urge to lean over and throw it in the bin.

'Thank you, Alan,' Sebastian says, crisply.

What did I expect? He was hardly going to reprimand Spencer on the spot, but I'd hoped he might express some concern or suggest a meeting to discuss the company's core values. Namely, integrity.

'Was there anything else?'

A photograph on his desk catches my eye. Sebastian has a young child. How has a man like him kept a family together? My mind slides back to this morning: Toby giving me the run around as I tried to get him dressed; Jemma upstairs on the landing, a smile tugging at the corner of her lips as she tapped at her phone. The image I'd had as I pulled away, remembering how she used to hold our son up at the window to wave me off to work, and how his legs would thump excitedly against her. This morning, the narrow wooden blinds remained half drawn. There was nobody behind them.

'No.'

'Alright.' Sebastian reaches for the baguette again. 'Send Chloe in, would you?'

Sebastian is positively jovial at the team meeting, showering Spencer with praise for smashing the projected months' sales targets and suggesting that the commission he'll earn on repeat business alone will be enough to pay off a sizeable chunk of his mortgage. There's no mention of his unethical internet searches. Pizza boxes are pushed across the tables, and beside me, Katya keeps topping up her wine glass. Afterwards, when most of my colleagues peel off for an extended lunch at a nearby bar, I log into my laptop and Toby's grinning, toothy smile appears. He's wearing the t-shirt that one of Jemma's friends bought, one he grew out of in no time at all: *50% Mummy, 50% Daddy.*

0% Dan Bretti.

Have I done the right thing in reporting Spencer? Perhaps I over-reacted – Sebastian hardly seemed concerned about Spencer's searches, and now I'm wondering if I'm the bad guy here. The snake. Did I do it because I imagine Dan to be exactly the same kind of arrogant arsehole as Spencer? *I'm so hard for you it hurts.*

I open my emails and scan them quickly. There's an invite to a work party in three weeks' time to celebrate fifteen years of Smithson Wealth Management – `respond ASAP please!` – a few programming queries and several spam messages which I delete without opening. And then, without thinking, I log into Facebook. I need to check that the Jemma from before – the Jemma who used to stroke the soft cleft at the back of my neck and say that every bit of me was perfect – was ever real.

I comb through the photos, right back to the early ones of us together. The selfie from the boat at West Country Waterpark, where we're both grinning huge open smiles into the camera; I can still feel the touch of her fingers as she rubbed sun cream into my back. We'd gone to buy ice creams afterwards and I remember thinking how strange it was that she'd ordered vanilla, because she wasn't a vanilla person at all. She was popping candy, cherry fusion, honeycomb flakes and toffee sauce.

I ended up ordering vanilla too.

I scroll down. Jemma in sunglasses and sandals, on Weston-Super-Mare beach. Me, holding a milk-filled bottle towards the open mouth of a goat at the petting zoo. Jemma again, this time sporting a tight black dress and red-and-black wig for Halloween that made her look vamp-like and even more sexy, if such a thing were possible. Whose party was that? Some friend of Jemma's with young children – I can remember them crying upstairs as a violent beat thumped from a speaker in the cramped kitchen. Jemma had downed shots with the girls as I hovered near the other men, trying and failing to join in with their banter, until someone vomited down my back and we made our exit into the cold night, Jemma clutching and stumbling against me.

It was about three months after that party when she found out she was pregnant. 'I was so sick, the morning after,' she reminded me with a groan. 'The pill doesn't work if you're sick. My God, a *baby*. Can you believe that? An actual miniature human. What do I do? We're not ready to be parents, are we?'

I told her it was her body; she should do whatever felt right. We talked, sometimes late into the night, about different outcomes. Would we regret it if we did? Would we regret it if we didn't? When she told me she'd made up her mind, it still didn't feel real – not until we went for the first scan and I saw our son's oversized head, an arm moving in the blackness of Jemma's womb. The rushing gallop of his heart.

I cried.

I told myself I would be a better father than mine ever was. I would be there for my son, every step of the way.

We sped up our wedding plans, and five months into the pregnancy, we became man and wife. For better for worse, in sickness and in health, we would remain faithful to one another.

For as long as we both shall live. Those were our vows; I meant every word.

I still do.

CHAPTER FIVE

It occurs to me, after trawling through our Facebook memories, that Jemma and I haven't had a date night for a while. I consider booking The Lofthouse for old times' sake, but when I Google the restaurant to make the booking, an epiphany strikes. *Surprise your partner*, the homepage screams.

All of a sudden, it makes sense. This is exactly what Jemma has been asking of me, I just haven't been listening. I need to show her that I'm willing to take myself out of my comfort zone.

I leave The Lofthouse page and spend a few minutes scrolling through activity days that we could do together instead. Bungee jumping is out of the question, but I could probably manage off-road driving, or a Segway. The photos depict smiling couples, armoured in knee pads and helmets, rolling through a sun-dappled forest. It looks ridiculous. Jemma will love it.

This, then. This is the fix.

I run my credit card through the payment page and hit print.

Jemma messages me to let me know that she's taking Toby to a friend's house after work, giving me the chance to tidy the house and put a wash load on. I tell myself I'm not playing music in anticipation of her return but for me alone, smiling to the songs I know she loves. Did I mention she's obsessed with Abba? I can't hear *Dancing Queen* or *The Winner Takes It All* without thinking of the way she danced on our wedding day – arms aloft, face aglow – just like I can't listen to *Green Green Grass* without thinking of Toby singing tunelessly along, over and over again. Sometimes he still asks me to put nursery rhymes on in the car, which fills me with a sense of helpless dread, as though a sharpened hole has opened up inside.

Humpty Dumpty sat on a wall,
Humpty Dumpty had a great fall.
All the king's horses and all the king's men
Couldn't put Humpty together again.

Jemma comes home just after eight. There's a red flush around her slightly swollen mouth and chin, and her hair looks like it's been in one of those fairground candyfloss machines. 'We've been playing, haven't we, Tobe?' she says, by way of explanation.

'Archie's mum gave me fish fingers,' Toby says, wriggling his small body to allow Jemma to free his arms from his light summer jacket. 'I eated them all.'

'Ate,' I correct. 'Good boy.'

I wonder if this is how drug addicts feel when they get a long-awaited fix. The house is suddenly transformed with colour, sound and soul. I feel my nerve endings relax, and turn to Jemma. 'Did you have a good day?'

'Busy,' she says, dropping the keys on the kitchen side and moving to open the oven door. She smells musky. Another odour too: sour and slightly sweet. 'What's this?'

'Peri peri chicken. I wasn't sure if you were going to eat while you were out, so...'

'I have.' She slams the oven door closed.

I don't get a chance to show Jemma the tickets until I've bathed Toby and read him a story. When I come back downstairs, I'm careful to close the hallway door behind me – our son is like a bulldog on steroids at bedtime and has a habit of bounding downstairs for hours afterwards – and if things go well, I'm hoping to show her the affection I am sure she feels has been missing from me. Whatever did or didn't happen with Dan Bretti, he was the symptom, not the cause. We won't just wipe the slate clean: we'll strip and revarnish it, paint it in gold.

I can't see Jemma in the kitchen, or the lounge. At first, I think she's gone out, but then I find her in the conservatory, tapping at her phone. The box of Playmobil at her feet is scattered all over the rug beside the coffee table and I feel a fleeting twinge of annoyance – she was supposed to ask Toby to pick that up.

She looks up. 'What?'

'He's in bed.'

I step over the discarded plastic toys to reach the sofa and hold out the folded paper. 'I've got something for you. Well, us. I know you said things have been boring and I'm prepared to try and work things out.'

She puts her phone down. 'You want to do Segway?'

'Not me. *Us*.'

Her laugh isn't cruel, more pitying. 'It's not exactly you, is it? *Or* me.' She laughs again as the paper drifts gently onto the sofa cushion. 'Those things look like Zimmer frames on wheels.'

The tears rise without warning, clouding my vision.

'For fuck's *sake*,' Jemma says. 'Are you seriously crying because I don't want to do a Segway?'

'It's not... I'm *trying*, Jem. You said you weren't happy, you said you wanted to do something spontaneous. I don't want to lose you. Or Toby...' I stand up. A plastic toy bites into my foot. 'Please. I can't... we can work this out. I'll do anything – we can try counselling, or... I don't know – *tell* me! Tell me what I need to do.'

She's turned off the music and now it's too quiet. I had it all ready; our wedding song was on this playlist. Track three – two minutes, fifty-eight seconds. I didn't know how to dance properly so I'd followed her lead, moving across the wood-polished floor and watching the patchwork of coloured lights reflect off the back of her white dress. She was so close it was as though we were one person. Looking back, it feels like we were in some magical, psychedelic version of Heaven.

I reach for her. 'Jem…'

I don't mean to grab her top.

I don't mean to pull her back.

She stumbles on a piece of upturned Playmobil, clutching frantically at the air as she pirouettes wildly, then falls. Her head hits the coffee table with a crack. A heavy silence follows, and then I'm beside her, scared to touch, frozen speechless by the drops of blood spreading like rose petals across the white Ikea rug.

'Jem.' I place my hand on her shoulder. '*Jem.*' She lifts her face. The flesh above her eyebrow is already swelling around the oozing thread of broken skin. 'I need to get you to hospital. Shit. *Shit.*'

'What the fuck, Adam?' Jemma sits up. 'I'm… look at the rug. Get me a cloth or something.'

I run to the kitchen and dampen a wad of kitchen roll. My hands are shaking so much I drop it into the sink, and that's when I see that Jemma's blood is on my hands. What have I done? I do not want to go back into that room – I *cannot* go back – my feet are suddenly immobile, and I feel as if I'm going to be sick. What a piece of shit. My wife has seen straight through me, because there is nothing to see inside. I am not good enough. I have never been enough.

The kitchen roll is still dripping when I return to the lounge. I press it to Jemma's face and apologise repeatedly before asking if she is able to stand. 'I need to get you to the hospital. Can you stand? Jem, I'm so sorry – we should probably—'

'I'm not going to the hospital, Adam. Look, it's stopping now.' She lifts the paper away and I can see that she's right –

the blood has dried onto her face; the wound is no longer seeping. It doesn't look as deep as I first thought.

'Don't you think we should at least get it checked out?'

She stands up and moves over to the mirror. 'You know what? Maybe we should, and I can tell them I "fell into a coffee table". It's not going to look good, is it?'

'I'm sorry! I didn't mean to. But if you need to be seen...'

We both fall silent. Toby is staring at us through the closed glass door.

He looks terrified.

CHAPTER SIX

Jemma

I watch Toby hang his coat and lunchbox on the peg, then run to join a small red-haired boy at the window where his keyworker – Jenny – is pointing at something outside. There are miniature chairs beside miniature tables, a rainbow-coloured rug in front of a spotless whiteboard, clusters of toys inside plastic trays, coloured letters and drawings tacked onto the display board: *In our class: We make good choices. We are hardworking. We are positive. We are honest.*

Honest. We assured Toby that everything was fine. So, no, we are not honest; not with him or ourselves. I've brought him to preschool early in the hope that I could drop and run, but Margo wants to talk to me. She's the manager, and her short stature and girlish, high-pitched voice fool many into thinking she's a pushover, but they couldn't be more wrong. I've heard the steel in her voice when the children misbehave – it's enough to send chills down *my* spine. Today, she has her dark hair pulled back with a brown scrunchie; a few wiry strands of silver appear to have worked their way loose, and she's talking about how advanced Toby's numerical skills are for his age. 'Remarkably so,' she says. 'It's not just the counting – he can associate and combine numbers in a way that's quite unusual.'

'Wow. That's... really great to hear.'

Die Trying

A queue is forming behind me. I've brushed my hair over the bruise, and attempt a nod while tilting my head at an angle. Could the injury be considered a safeguarding issue even if my child isn't hurt? How do these things work? I imagine Margo or Jenny interrogating Toby, asking whether Daddy hit Mummy. I'm still mortified by them showing me Toby's drawing a few weeks ago – *My Mummy's job* – where he'd depicted me as a stick figure standing beside another stick figure lying naked on a bed, even adding a cartoonish penis and testicles. Margo had laughed, but of course she was curious. I told her I wasn't a sex worker – God, no! – although it was a shame my client yesterday didn't get the memo. He seemed nice enough at first, folding his t-shirt and jeans neatly onto the stool and talking passionately about his wife and kids until halfway through the massage when he asked if I offered 'extras'. As if eighteen months of training in soft tissue injury and rehabilitation equalled giving random horny strangers a hand job. I told him to get dressed and get out, then went home feeling disgusted and disappointed. Maybe I would have been kinder to Adam if *that* hadn't happened, because the accident wasn't his fault, but sometimes he can be so crushingly intense that I find myself fighting for air. Sometimes, I think that, if I make Adam small, he might let me go. When I tried to break up with him a year ago, his eyes immediately became dark, fluid-filled discs of sorrow. 'You can't,' he said. 'I can't live without you. Toby can't live without me, Jem. I'll do better.'

And he *did* do better, just like he always does. Buying me gifts, giving me lifts, serving my every need. 'Mr Perfect', my little sister Hannah calls him. She's still in Manchester, close to Mum and Dad and all the friends I left behind when Adam insisted we could offer our son a better standard of life here.

There's a crick in my neck now. I'm about to straighten – fuck my swollen cut, let them see – when Margo tells me to have a lovely day, and I'm free to go. I hurry back along the corridor, waving hello to some of the mums I would normally stop and chat to, leaving the display of neon-coloured children's handprints fluttering in my wake. Outside, I collide with Frankie at the corner of the building on the way back to my car. 'Have you dropped off *already*?' she says. And then, as the wind makes a mockery of my attempts to hold my hair in place and her son Blake starts tugging at her hand, 'What happened to your head?'

I hadn't wanted to see anyone today, but I've known Frankie since the boys started at nursery, and she's the only person I've spoken to about Dan. She admitted to having had an affair shortly before splitting with the father of her eldest child, Matty – now a teenager – and I appreciated the way she listened without judgement. *I* would have judged me. I never used to understand people who had affairs and always wondered why they didn't just leave, but now I can see it's not always as simple as that. Maybe they tried. Maybe they decided to stay for other reasons, nothing to do with love. Maybe they were unable to ignore the chemistry with the one person who made them feel truly alive, truly *seen*. Maybe they couldn't escape the painful knowledge that something was deeply wrong in their marriage.

Frankie tells me to hang on, and I wait in my car until she emerges without Blake ten minutes later, sidestepping the puddles in her heels, long coat flapping in the breeze. She climbs into the passenger seat beside me and glances at the clock on the dash. 'I can't talk for long, I've got work in half an hour,' she says. 'You look really upset. Are you ok? What's going on?'

'It was an accident. Sort of. Adam booked some stupid Segway experience, and I – I don't think he meant to grab me, but I ended up stepping on one of Toby's Playmobil tractors and—what?'

'He *grabbed* you?' She pulls a face which makes me feel the need to defend Adam. What I call 'being nice', Frankie calls *love-bombing*. She rolls her eyes every time we go out for a drink and Adam arrives to pick us up, always earlier than arranged. I always thought it was sweet he cared so much about my safety – previous boyfriends have never been that bothered – but Frankie doesn't see it as sweet, she says it's a violation of my time and privacy. I pull Toby's monster toy from the footwell and throw it into the back, where it lands on his car seat. 'I lost my balance and whacked my head on the table. I just wish Toby hadn't seen. We assured him it was fine, but… well, it's not, is it? It's all such a fucking mess. I've told Adam he can't stay in the house anymore.'

'Bet that went down well.'

'Actually, I think he felt so bad about hurting me that he would have agreed to anything. I've tried to frame it as a great opportunity to test how we feel about each other during a trial separation, you know? I said it might be fun for Toby to have sleepovers with Daddy every weekend, and we'd both get a bit of space to decide what we want.'

'Jem, you know how he feels. You know what he wants.' Frankie pulls that face again. The one Mum used to pull when I'd forgotten my school lunchbox, or said something moronic. 'You. It's always you.'

'Yeah, I know. Don't make me feel worse.'

'Where's he going to live? With parents, or—'

'No. His mum's dead, he doesn't speak to his dad.' The irony isn't lost on me that his parents split up when his dad cheated, something he's never forgiven him for. 'I don't even know if we can afford to live apart – I'm going to call Citizens Advice this afternoon. Have you got any rental flats or bedsits that might be worth a look?'

'Yeah, I'm sure we do. I'll send some links when I get into the office.' Frankie tugs at the bottom of her coat, where it's trapped in the door, and I catch a burst of Chanel perfume. She glances at the clock again. 'Sorry, I'm going to have to go. Are you working today?'

'No, day off. I desperately want to see Dan, but not looking like this. And I think it's important to sort things out between me and Adam first.'

She says she'll call me later and gets out of the car, and I try to put all thoughts of Dan out of my head on the drive home. His face. His body. The roughness of his palm, scraping up and down my naked shoulder, bringing me to life.

A fucking mess.

Toby; that's who I should be thinking of. His World Book Day costume, paying for the *Wild Things* visit, ordering a new preschool sweatshirt, because I somehow managed to shrink his current one in the wash and his spare has gone the same way as odd socks and lost change.

I unlock the front door and swat a damp cloth around the kitchen surfaces. While I'm unloading the dishwasher, a new Facebook notification pops up from my sister, Hannah. She's shared a picture of her and Mum in the garden with Dad. *To one of the strongest men I know. Happy birthday, Dad!*

He looks so tired. Tired, brown as he ever was – Dad loves sitting out in the sun – yet somehow reduced, like a teabag with all the liquid squeezed out. A generous smattering of sugar on top, because Dad has never lost his hair, not a single strand, despite his cancer diagnosis two years ago. Two pelvic operations have left him with a limp, reliant on a cane for walking anywhere further than the top of the street.

And I'm not there for his birthday.

I should have ignored Adam's protests and taken Toby out of preschool for a few days to go up to Manchester. What harm would it have done? I feel heavy under the weight of Adam's piety. *He can't miss preschool Jem, it'll set a precedent.*

A precedent. A fucking precedent.

In the lounge, there's the unmistakeable trace of a dark spot on the rug where Adam scrubbed and scrubbed at my blood last night, far longer than he needed to.

It's going to take forever to dry.

CHAPTER SEVEN

Adam

Over the next few weeks, Jemma spends most of her free time talking to her friend Frankie and Googling rental properties on my behalf. I've been trying to avoid the subject, skimming conversations with the lightest of touches, hoping that her enthusiasm for our separation will fade along with her yellowing bruise.

It doesn't. If anything, she's more passionate than I've seen her for a long time, thrusting her phone under my nose and describing grey tomb-like bedsits as 'cute', 'cosy', 'quirky'.

In other words, you couldn't swing a limbless cat in them. Not only that, they're expensive. We just about make ends meet now – how could we possibly afford to pay a mortgage *and* rent on a grubby little broom cupboard?

Jemma assures me she's looked into it and the extra help she'd get from the government as a single mother will cover the bills. 'It's a trial separation,' she reminds me. 'We both need to sort our heads out. You'll still be able to come back in the evenings and give Toby his bath and bedtime story.'

'What about…' I can't bring myself to say his name. *Dan Bretti*. 'Him. I don't want you to see him. I don't want him in our house.'

'Ok,' she says. 'Fair donuts.'

We're sitting side by side on the sofa and, even though her cut has now faded to a silvery underscore, I can't look at her. I'm such a fucking idiot. A fool. I've told Jemma what happened was an accident, it will never happen again, and there's so much more I want to say, but a voice keeps reminding me that I don't deserve to stay.

I am ugly and inadequate. I am a nobody.

Yet there's a powerful sensation, like pain, spreading across my ribs. I can't help it. I have to ask the question.

'What if I say no? What if I refuse to leave?'

'I'd make your life fucking intolerable,' she says. And then she laughs, to make out she is joking.

I know my wife. She isn't.

We've told Toby that I'll be going on an adventure for a little while. Jemma even manages to get Toby excited, deploying her used-car sales technique as effectively on him as she did with me: 'Just think, Tobes. You won't just have one house, you'll have two! It'll be so cool – you and Daddy can have sleepovers together.'

Now, standing in the kitchen of the cramped rental bedsit, the only thing that seems cool is the draught coming through the rusted hinge of the second-floor window. Without Jemma here, the place looks drab, uninspiring and absurdly small. A room which once would have served as a lounge or dining room is split squarely in two, with the kitchen taking up one half, living room the other. I dump the last box onto the mouse-grey carpet beside the two small settees. Am I really doing the right thing? It doesn't feel like it. I'm not just talking about the time we've shared together, but our future, which previously I'd been able to envisage, clear as the tattoo on my wrist. Jemma and I with another child – the sibling that Toby keeps begging us for. The two of us; older, greying, arms intertwined on the deck of a ship, watching the setting sun. All of Toby's milestones and achievements – dropping him off for his first day at school, watching him run like a wild dog on sports day, cheering him, consoling him, loving him, even sharing a first pint as he turns eighteen – are now shrouded in mist, vague and unclear.

How can it be this easy for things to fall apart?

There's something arresting about silence, bordering almost on the malevolent, when you're not used to it. Our home is characterised by noise: the tumble and thump of the clothes in the washing machine, Jemma's ringtone chiming, Toby singing along to the *Racers* theme tune, the thud and clatter of doors being closed, cutlery laid, plugs being pulled from sockets. Without Jemma, without Toby, who am I? Am I even really here?

I step around the boxes and move to the window. The curtains are white with pale grey streaks – the colour of pigeon shit – and smell faintly of mildew. Outside, on the other side of the car park, an empty Tesco bag flutters against the gutter.

It's not for long. My tongue probes at the flap of bitten skin inside my cheek. I'm about to turn away from the window when an old couple comes into view. They are holding hands, moving slowly across the car park before disappearing around the row of garages on the other side. I wonder if they have ever fought, physically. I wonder if either of them has ever cheated.

It's a funny word, cheat. As though love is a game.

Perhaps it is.

And then I see the ladybird, climbing up the inside of the glass: red, shiny as wet paint, with three black spots on each wing. I wonder if I brought it in with me, or whether it came in through the window. There was an article I read a few years ago about a species of aggressive ladybirds that had swarmed the U.K. and – astonishingly – carried sexually transmitted diseases, threatening our native species. I can still remember the conversation I'd had with Jemma about it. '*Seriously?*' she said. 'That's too funny. Promiscuous ladybirds? Must be nature's way of warning us not to fuck around.'

Seems ironic I should think of that now.

I spend the early part of the evening unpacking my few meagre belongings, hanging up my clothes in the wardrobe and watching crap on TV. At 6pm, I call Jemma. She doesn't pick up. I wonder if she's in the bath. We used to share baths, in the early days. She'd wrap her painted toes around my shoulders, giggling, as my back rubbed against the cold taps.

There's no bath in the flat, so I take a shower instead. I allow some of the hot water to trickle in between my parted lips and imagine Jemma soaping my chest, moving down lower, giggling as our naked bodies slip and slide against the glass. Yes. Yes, Jemma.

But when I open my eyes, all I can see is mould stippling the grouting, like dozens of tiny black pips. I keep rinsing myself, rinsing and rinsing until the water has taken away my shame, sluicing it down the plughole.

It's getting dark now; I can hear cars revving in the distance, the occasional police siren, music from one of the nearby flats. People will be getting ready to go out to bars and clubs, hook up for casual sex, or relax for the weekend with a takeaway or video game. I don't want to do any of those things. I towel myself dry, change into fresh boxers and a t-shirt and try Jemma's mobile again. It's engaged.

I wait a few minutes, thinking she might be trying to get through. It's something that used to happen all the time when we first got together. 'How spooky,' she'll say, when we finally connect with each other. 'We must have literally been thinking the same thing!'

She doesn't, though. My phone remains silent.

I get up again, peer out at the darkening sky. One of the streetlights is flickering, periodically illuminating a dark shape sticking out from the side of the garages. It looks like it could be human, but upon closer inspection appears to be nothing more than a rusted bike beside a couple of binbags disgorging their contents. A lamp goes on in a flat on the other side of the car park. A woman in a dressing gown appears, opens her fridge and removes a bottle of wine. The light clicks off again.

Is Jemma on the phone to Dan Bretti?

I wonder if she's reaching for a bottle as she talks, preparing for a cosy night in without me. What will they talk about? She gets loose-tongued when she drinks, and horny. Or at least, she used to.

Dan Bretti. All of this started with Dan fucking Bretti. Jemma has not been herself since she met him. Neither have I.

In the mirror, my skin looks pale. Dark eyes, strawberry-blond hair just like my half-Scottish mother's – or rose-gold, as Jemma flatteringly calls it – a body I've always thought of as muscular, especially during my twenties, now slightly on the heavy side. How big is Dan? I picture him as a Goliath, or a Wolverine perhaps: huge, all-powerful, other-worldly.

I vowed I wouldn't do this. I am not that kind of man – jealous and bitter – but when I return to my laptop in the living room, I find myself wondering whether to set up a fake Facebook account to find Dan Bretti. It might be easier to try and log into Jemma's profile; Jemma uses the same password for everything, despite me telling her how unsafe it is. But logging into her account would be inappropriate, wouldn't it? A breach of trust.

Despite everything she's done to me.

I try a Google search instead – Dan Bretti – and it presents me with over 100,000 hits, although, on closer inspection, many of them are Daniel *Brett*. He could be a player at Bedminster Down Football Club, who earned a brief mention in The Gazette Series two years ago, or one of several results on LinkedIn. I click on a couple of matches on Facebook where

I can only see limited information without logging in. The first has a profile picture of two men in wedding suits, their arms clasped around one another. Not them.

The second is a bald-headed man wearing sunglasses, holding a small brown dog in his arms. It could be him. It could also be the one with two laughing boys for a profile picture, or the one holding a giant spliff to his lips, eyes wide with exhibitionist anticipation. It could be the man kissing the mouth of a dark-haired woman.

I'm getting nowhere.

In any case, what does it matter? They haven't slept together. And Dan Bretti didn't hurt Jemma, did he? That was me.

I'm so hard for you it hurts.

My fingers begin tapping a four-bar rhythm against the window.

I don't even realise I'm doing it until I see a dog walker look up and then hurry away, into the night.

CHAPTER EIGHT

When Jemma opens the door to me the following afternoon, she's wearing the cream top she knows I love, accompanied by a ton of make-up.

'I thought I saw your car,' she says. 'Toby's been so excited.'

I open my mouth to speak, and inhale a mouthful of perfume. Black Opium. The scent she was wearing when we first met. 'Are you ok to drop me off in town on the way to yours?' she asks over her shoulder. 'I'm just getting ready to go out with the girls for dinner and was going to get a taxi, but...'

I follow her inside, into the lounge. 'When? Now?'

Our conversation is aborted by Toby, who barrels into me with a cry of delight. 'Oops,' he says, stepping back as I recoil from the impact to my groin. 'Sorry, Daddy. Sorry.'

'It's ok,' I gasp. 'Don't worry. Have you been a good boy at preschool today?'

He nods furiously. 'Yes. Jackson didn't share and then he hit Livia over the head and got told off.'

'That wasn't very nice.'

'Give me ten minutes,' Jemma says. 'I'm just going to change my shoes.'

'Daddy?'

'Yes?'

'Can I see your new house?'

'Soon. We just need to wait for Mummy first.' I glance up at Jemma. Is this effort for me, or her friends? I should have tried harder. Aftershave. That quarter-zipped polo shirt that she always used to run her fingers inside, turning me into liquid and solid all at once. I watch her leave the room, and then turn back to Toby. 'Shall we bring a game?'

'What game?' Toby is sitting on my lap now, pressing a toy car into my neck.

'Snakes and Ladders?'

'Yes!'

'We can play it when we get back to the flat, if you like.'

'Ok, Daddy.' He tips his head back so that I can see the small white studs of his teeth. I love my son's laugh. It sounds like the popping of bubble wrap.

'Go and get it then, silly.'

'No, you're silly.' Toby repeatedly pokes a finger into my cheek until I ask him to stop. It feels strange that this is my house, but – for the time being – not my home. We've moved the coffee table to the corner, and although I can no longer see any trace of Jemma's blood on the rug beside me, I know the ghost of her DNA is there somewhere, twisted into the fibres. I can't be in here without thinking about what happened and every time I do, my stomach stiffens, as though bracing itself for impact. Toby learnt to crawl on this carpet.

He pushes his car in a wild circuit around the rug, before flipping it onto its roof. 'Crash.'

He breaks my heart, by doing nothing at all.

'You look nice,' I tell Jemma, on the way into town. Being this close to her makes me feel nervous and slightly bilious, as though I'm coming down with something.

In the back seat, a trumpet sounds from Toby's iPad. Jemma flips down the passenger mirror and runs a finger over her teeth. 'Turn that down, Tobe.'

'So, is it just you and Steph meeting tonight?'

'I don't know. A few others might come and join us.' She snaps the visor back up. 'You should go out sometime.'

'I've actually been invited out on Saturday, but it's only a work do.'

'Oh?'

'And it's fancy dress.'

Jemma tilts her head and laughs. The gold necklace glitters around her throat. 'You *have* to do that. It sounds amazing.'

'What's fancy dess?' Toby asks.

'It's like dressing up, for adults,' Jemma says. 'It's fun.'

'I thought you didn't like me doing things like that,' I say, as if I'd entertain the idea.

'No, why wouldn't I? You absolutely should. Get out there, live a little. God, it's busy for a Thursday,' Jemma remarks, her eyes scanning the bars and restaurants as we pass. She's right, people are sitting at outside tables, walking arm in arm along the pavement, spilling across the courtyard in a wash of colour. I indicate and pull into the dropoff zone before the traffic lights.

'Is Frankie meeting you here?' I ask. 'I can wait.'

Jemma unclips her seatbelt. 'No, it's ok – she's inside.' She opens the car door to kiss Toby goodbye, and reality rushes in: the sound of car engines, chatter and music, a stink of spices and hot fat. 'Thanks. Bye. Bye, Tobe. Love you!'

I want to tell her to be careful, to make sure she keeps her drinks close and to call me for a lift at the end of the night, but she moves around a group of twenty-somethings and quickly becomes swallowed in the throng of bodies. Dressing up for adults. For a mad moment, I imagine stamping on the pedal and towards the crowd. *Here, I'm being adventurous. Is this what you want?*

I wouldn't do that, you understand. I'm not a violent man. I'm not crazy.

Although sometimes I wonder how much I really know myself at all.

CHAPTER NINE

There's an old bike tyre in the overgrown patch of grass on the way into the estate. Toby stares at it as we drive past. 'What's that?'

'A tyre.'

'Why?'

'I don't know. Maybe the owner doesn't want it anymore.'

'Why not?'

'I don't know. Maybe it's got a puncture.'

'What's a puncher?'

The questions keep coming, even after I park up and get him out of the car.

'What's that?'

'Somebody's doorbell. Don't touch.'

''S broken.' Toby peers at the Sellotape-covered unit hanging loosely from the side of the flat. 'What's that man doing?'

'Fixing his car. Look, my flat isn't here – it's on the other side. Come on.' I turn around and beg silently that he won't make any further observations.

'Why's his bum out?'

'He...' I lower my voice to a whisper. 'His trousers are just falling down a bit, that's all.'

Toby wants to play out here. He wants to know who the barking dog belongs to. He wants to know why there is a lady sitting outside her house with no shoes on. I push the key in the lock and encourage him inside, up the stairs.

'Smells funny,' Toby says.

His rucksack thumps against my leg as I follow him up. It's a relief to get inside and finally lock the door behind us. I was worried that things might be awkward here without Jemma, but maybe my son has inherited his mother's sense of optimism because – apart from a comment that the bedsit is small – he takes it all in without complaint. The plastic pot plant on the kitchen windowsill is pretty. The blow-up mattress on the floor beside my bed is *brilliant*.

Yet still I can't shake the shame. I've failed him.

I make Toby a cup of squash and eventually we settle down on the sofa with the bag of popcorn I bought on the way into town. As Spiderman swings across the TV screen, my mind drifts back to Jemma. What is she doing right now? Is she drunk? With alcohol – as with everything else in her life – there are no half-measures. What's her motto again?

Go hard or go home.

I hope she goes home. Or more specifically, I hope she calls me for a lift home. Maybe she'll ask me to come in, because she's too inebriated to look after Toby. On the day I moved out, I asked her if she still loved me. She said I had given her Toby, and she would always love me for that. *Soul mates*, I thought. We were meant to be together; this was a test of our relationship, that was all. We had both failed. I told her I would always be there for her, and I hope she remembers that tonight. She'll tell me this was all a mistake; she can't live without me. I look down at our son, our perfect son, fidgeting on the sofa. I remind myself that I'm doing this for him.

For all of us.

After the film, Toby becomes tired and restless, jumping on the blow-up mattress, poking his finger in a hole in the wall and opening and closing the main door. I check my phone, alarmed to see it's gone eight. Still nothing from Jemma. I turn to ask

Toby if he wants a bedtime drink before his story, but he's gone. I find him in the bedroom, rummaging through one of the boxes I haven't yet had time to open.

'Can I do some colouring?' he says, holding up a pile of paperwork.

'Toby, don't just— what is that?'

A handful of payslips from past jobs, the lease agreement on the one-bedroomed flat I rented in Little Stoke after leaving university, old bank statements going back to 2015. All from my pre-Jemma days – she must have pulled it from the loft. 'I'll get you some paper you can draw on quickly, ok? It's nearly bedtime.'

When I come back, Toby is leaning so far into the box his head and upper body have disappeared. The cardboard is crushed, sagging in on itself. And before he straightens, I remember what's in there. A small pearlescent box I thought I'd left behind.

'Toby—'

'Look!'

He's removed the die and is holding it in his palm as if it's a tiny planet, his mouth agape. It's hard to describe the beauty of it – solid glass, surprisingly heavy, roughly three times the size of a standard die. On sunny days, it used to scatter light across the room and I would sometimes see a wedge of rainbow-coloured light projected onto the chair or splayed across a corner. Darkness told a different story. When Mum first brought it home from the charity shop where she worked, she said she 'just had to have it'. As if the decision wasn't her own.

'Can I play with it?' Toby says.

'No. I just found some paper and pens, Tobe. That's what you asked for.'

'But I want to *play* with it.'

'Well, you can't. Because it's—' I have to stop myself from snatching it from his hand and saying the word. *Dangerous.*

Toby stares at me, upset by the raised pitch of my voice. *Don't cry*, I think. *Don't start demanding to go home.* I can imagine Jemma's voice: 'Oh Adam, please. Are you seriously telling me you couldn't deal with a tantrum? Not even for one night?'

Toby raises his fist to his face in a valiant attempt to remain brave. Four. He's only four. A bitter, soapy regret pools in my mouth. Is it really dangerous? What happened before…

I can't think about that.

'Why don't we have a quick game of Snakes and Ladders?' I offer instead. 'Fifteen minutes, then bed. Let's—'

Toby's not giving up the die that easily. He nods, keeping it gripped in his tightly curled fist. I collect his rucksack from the lounge and when I return with the board game, finally, he puts it down. I shake the counters from their plastic housing. 'Red or green?'

'Green.'

'Ok. I'll be red.'

We play using the cheap plastic die from the box, and Toby makes me smile by cupping and thrusting it either side of his face, like a cocktail shaker. 'One, two, three.'

'You're beating me! Pass the die, then.'

'It's *dice*, Daddy. Die is when you fall down dead.'

I force myself to focus on Toby, not the glass die beside him. *Dead.* 'Die is singular. One die, two dice.'

'We got two dice,' he says. 'See?'

'Don't— ok, give that to me, please. Now.' I take the glass die and put it behind the clock on the bedside cabinet, out of sight. Toby sucks in his cheeks, then slaps a hand to his mouth when its plastic counterpart lands on six. 'Uh-oh.'

I've come across this snake before. I slide down the patchwork body, back to number seven. It's 9pm now, and when I tell him we need to stop, he complains that we haven't finished. It isn't fair, he doesn't want to go to bed.

He looks just like his mum when he's angry. And, just like I always do with Jemma, I relent. He can roll one more time and, if it's evens, we'll play for five more minutes. If it's odds, we have to stop now.

To Toby's delight, he rolls a four. *Truth*. I banish the thought, and we play on. This time he climbs another ladder, storming sixteen spaces ahead. I miss a turn. On the second roll, I gain five spaces only to be returned to the head of the snake. I slide down with an exaggerated groan. 'Not my lucky day, is it?'

Toby laughs at that, as though it's the funniest thing he's ever heard. And as we're packing the game away, I think: this will be ok. We'll be ok.

It's only for a few months, after all.

'Daddy?' Toby says a few minutes later, while I'm squirting toothpaste onto his brush. 'I don't want you to live here forever.'

'I won't,' I tell him. 'I'll be home with you and Mummy soon, I promise.'

I wake at 2am with a start. Toby must have crawled into bed with me during the night; his sweaty head is pressed against my chest, one bent knee pushed into my groin and his monster toy taking over half my pillow. I ease myself back and reach for my phone.

Nothing.

I messaged Jemma last night with a photo of our sleeping son accompanied by the caption: Got him to bed without a fuss! X

Why hasn't she replied?

Beside me, Toby sighs. It's too hot in the bed, but I can't bring myself to climb out. Instead, I lie still, poking my tongue into the hole in my cheek where the pain from the bite is still fresh. A separation, Jemma had called it – I hadn't really examined the words before. Like oil and water. Or eggs. She is the yolk; I am the albumen.

Die Trying

I cannot sleep. Not now.

I'm about to put my phone back on the bedside cabinet when I see the die, peeping at me from behind the clock. Three black spots.

I stare at it for a while, listening to the irregular hiss of my son's breathing, thinking about Will and our college days, the games we used to play. I can still see Will's mouth, a tunnel of surprise. 'Man, this is crazy. Are we in control of the dice, or are the dice in control of us?'

There is a truth, knocking at the base of my skull, trying to get in. I usher it away. *You are not welcome.*

Outside, a siren screams.

CHAPTER TEN

The following morning at work, something seems off.

I don't notice it at first – I've just dropped Toby at pre-school and my mind is now on the data recovery job that a remote worker has sent through – but when I go to the kitchen and ask Katya if she'd like a tea, she abruptly rejects the offer and hurries out. My other colleagues have never been overly friendly, but today when I make my way back through the office, a hush falls as they all bend their heads to their monitors in unison.

I sit at my desk and sip my tea. Beside my elbow, my phone pings, and I look down at Jemma's response to my message:

`Dad goals! Amazing, thanks X`

I read the message twice. I've been feeling jumpy since using the die this morning, but this is all the confirmation I need that it *wasn't* a bad idea. It wasn't a compulsion either. I'd just had one of those moments where I genuinely couldn't choose between two shirts to wear, and the longer I stared at them, the harder the choice became. Nothing like it was years ago, at college. And if I hadn't, I would probably have been late getting Toby to school.

I delete a couple of spam emails, then turn back to Jemma's message. The kiss at the end is significant. At the start of our relationship, she'd get annoyed if I forgot to add an X to my texts, asking if I was upset with her and telling me that one kiss was the bare minimum anyone would expect from a partner.

Die Trying

She was laughing when she said it, but laughing in that 'I'm being serious but making out it's nothing' kind of way. Paula once shared a work email which was a jokey translation of how women and men communicated differently, using words and phrases like 'fine' and 'do whatever you want', and how with women it meant they certainly weren't fine and you should never, ever do whatever you want. Nothing illustrated this better than our second Valentine's Day, when Jemma insisted that she didn't want anything as a present. 'We've just had the new bathroom put in, save your money,' she said. So I bought nothing, not even a card, only for her to round on me in righteous indignation. 'Oh my God, Adam, I didn't mean *literally* nothing,' she fumed. 'You could have used your imagination.' In that moment I felt, suddenly, as though I'd been dropped from a great height. *Wrong decision.* Dad always used to tell me I didn't get it. 'What the hell did you do that for?' he'd rage, when I tried to wash dog muck from my shoes in the kitchen sink. He said the same thing when I used a knife in the toaster to remove my smoking slice of bread, terrified it might start a fire. He said it so often I developed a sickening lurch, like turbulence, whenever I was called upon for answers. I stopped putting my hand up in class. I struggled when people asked about my favourite colour, sport, or food. I didn't realise it was a question you couldn't get wrong.

For the next few hours, my phone remains silent. At lunchtime, Spencer says he's off for a 'liquid lunch', and all but a few colleagues from the other end of the office follow. From the window, I watch as they cross at the lights towards College Green. They could almost be a single entity, a congealed moving mass of coloured limbs.

I turn my attention back to my laptop. Would it really be so wrong to log into Jemma's Facebook account?

Yes, of course it would.

Her friends list is hidden, but as a browsing guest, I can see most of the things I already know about her: the schools and university she attended in Manchester, her places of employment, check-ins, music preferences, favourite films and pages she's liked.

This is where I strike gold. She 'liked' a company by the name of *Bretti Rocks* a few months ago. I click on the page, and it opens up details of a rock-climbing business at Cribbs Causeway, just a fifteen-minute drive from our home in Bradley Stoke. They offer climbing courses, kids' parties, events and competitions, as well as something nauseatingly described as a 'fun wall'. I open the *News* tab, to be confronted with a headline by the Bristol Post: *Local Rock Stars*.

I skim enough of the article to learn that the company has organised various fundraisers in the community – for children's charities, domestic abuse survivors, retired forces veterans – then return to Facebook. This time, I find him. In his profile picture, he's hanging from a plastic boulder, long blond hair tied back, revealing a sinewy tanned shoulder. I almost laugh at the cliché. He's the sort of person Jemma and I might have made fun of if we'd been lounging on the sofa together, watching a documentary about people in the grip of a mid-life crisis. 'Look at him,' Jemma would laugh. 'Attention seeker or what? Obviously pays for muscles like that at his age. What a clown.'

Or maybe she wouldn't. How well do I really know her, after all?

Even if this man wasn't pursuing my wife, I still wouldn't like him. It's not just the arrogance behind his smile – *look at me, doing good for charity. Look at me, with my successful, award-winning business* – or the long hair, unbefitting of a man his age. Or the tan that comes with too much time spent at leisure. He looks older than me – than both of us – and I reassure myself that he probably doesn't look that good in real life. Social media is a human shop window, after all. Nobody puts their true, broken, trampled souls on display. Dan doesn't know Jemma's burgundy leggings, the ones with whipped swirls of colour that serve as a weather vane for her 'fat' days, or the way she hums along to Abba when she's cooking dinner. He doesn't know she's terrified of frogs and hates fine rain because it makes her hair go frizzy. He doesn't know that she cried when our baby took his first steps.

You can't fake those things. I know my wife.

Or at least, I did.

I stare at him for a bit longer, then press my pen against the screen, into the dark cracks of his eye sockets.

Spencer, Katya and Chloe come back to the office soon afterwards with our two sales associates, Miles and Jake. When I head into the kitchen for a top-up of coffee half an hour later, I hear Kat's voice drifting through the open door. She's talking to Paula from accounts. 'It's disgusting. I actually thought he was cute. A bit shy, or quiet maybe, but cute. I had no idea he was an arrogant, sexist prick.'

'I don't know what it even means. Hungry for *power*?'

'Just because I want a promotion. Spencer said he's heard him make other comments on the phone too, about 'dogs in the workplace'. Us, apparently.'

'Adam said that?'

'Yep. I heard him make the remark about being hungry for power – Spencer definitely isn't making it up.'

'Horrible,' Paula says. 'Just goes to show, you don't know people.'

I wait on the steps. There's a clank of cups; the fridge door closes. No one can see me from here. I have the sinking sensation that I know exactly what has happened: Seb's raised the issue of Spencer's inappropriate browsing, and he has taken revenge by twisting a remark I made about his laptop battery when I returned it. '*Bit hungry for power, considering.*'

The kettle is boiling now, drowning out the rest of their conversation. Considering it's a new device, that's what I meant.

But my colleagues seem to believe Spencer's angle: that I was talking about them, that I'm a covert misogynist who doesn't believe women belong in positions of power. It's so glaringly obvious that the opposite is true, I feel like storming into the kitchen and telling them they're wrong, they're wrong, that I was talking about Spencer's laptop and only made the comment in the hope that he would take the hint and realise his search history had left deposits on the machine that hadn't been easy to clean – in the digital sense, of course.

I don't storm into the kitchen. I don't say anything. I take my mug back to my desk and stare into the bitter remains of my cold coffee.

CHAPTER ELEVEN

Jemma

'Have you always wanted to do this? Be a sports therapist?'

Sports therapist! Dan's so sweet. Not a masseuse (there's something so vaguely sexual about that term), not a massage therapist, but a *sports* therapist – which, of course, is what I am – but most people overlook the speciality of my work. 'No, I actually studied Art History at college. I wanted to be a museum curator.'

'That's a swerve of career.'

I squirt a shot of ylang ylang into my hand and rub it between my palms. 'I know, but it's such a competitive industry there aren't many positions available. You have to volunteer for a long time to get a shot at something like that. I did about six months of voluntary work when I lived in Manchester, but then I met Adam and fell pregnant and... well, I thought I'd try something different. Something that meant I could be my own boss, sort of. And human bodies *are* like art, in a way.'

'And history?'

'Yeah – exactly that. You wouldn't believe how much tension and stress is held in the muscles.' I glide my hands across the flat, strong planes of his back, where he's entirely hairless. 'Tattoos, piercings, stretchmarks and scars, they all tell a story.' Don't I know it. The cut above my eye has left the faintest thread of pink, which I'm not sure will ever disappear completely. 'Even climbing injuries like yours. Is that painful?'

'No.'

His eyes are closed, his head tilted to one side, hair fanned out like a sail across the pillow. God, he's gorgeous. It's the second time I've been in his bedroom, and both occasions it was my suggestion – partly because I promised Adam I wouldn't bring Dan to ours, and partly because Dan's house is fast becoming a secret retreat, my happy place. It's filled with new things, not the familiar clutter of mine. Its bold feature walls, spare room stuffed with paperwork I don't have to sort, and vaguely mysterious climbing equipment are all a playground to me. There's a huge conch shell nestled into an alcove at the bottom of the stairs, sumptuous sofas and not a trace of sticky spills or upturned Lego bricks anywhere. 'There are when she comes over,' Dan said when I pointed this out, and perhaps that was the moment I might have started falling for him, because my heart did a sickening, unreasonable lurch when I saw he was nodding to the framed picture of a woman and small child on his bookshelves. 'My niece, Olivia,' he explained.

A whoosh of relief flowed through me. Champagne into glass. Followed by the dirty, oily stain of guilt at the imagined future of me and Dan together as a blended family. I'd even asked about kids: Dan didn't have any, although he'd thought about it with his ex. 'I guess if I *were* to have any now, I'd be considered an old dad.'

'At thirty-nine? No way. More like a hot dad.'

I found myself telling him about Dad being nine years older than Mum, but it never mattered because they were so perfect together. *Like us*, I almost said.

I love that Dan was so respectful and not the slightest bit flirty the first time I massaged him, even though there was a weird current running between us. I thought it might have been one-sided, or that I'd imagined it, but the following week when he came for his session – to ease his rotator cuff injury from an old climbing fall – there it was again. An undeniable connection I'd never felt with any of my other clients. But I'm a professional, so of course I didn't act on it.

Until I saw him in Subway that Wednesday a few months ago when I forgot my lunch. I never go to Subway, so it felt – weirdly – like fate. I can't even remember what we talked about now, only how good it felt to be sitting opposite him, laughing at the same jokes, relaxed enough to gently poke fun at each other in a subtly teasing way. Then he asked if I was single.

'No,' I admitted. 'I'm married.'

'That's a shame.'

I'd flushed at his honesty. He didn't want to be a marriage-wrecker, so that was that – or so I thought. But then I saw him again a month later on a night out, loose with alcohol, and I told him I wasn't happily married; I wasn't happy at all. We ended up kissing close to a window that looked out onto dark fields, and when we finally broke apart, I thought someone was looking in at us, before realising it was my own reflection.

The guilt, especially after I've been with Dan, is all encompassing. I somehow manage to drag myself through a day at work, but my back hurts and not one but two of the clients have clearly forgotten the requirement for showering before an appointment. After collecting Toby from preschool and giving him his tea, I pour a glass of wine and call Mum and Dad. It rings and rings. Probably just up the garden – they spend hours watering a colourful multitude of potted plants and hanging baskets which can be seen from the top of the street – but I can't help wondering if they're at the hospital. They don't like to worry me. I don't like to worry them, either; it's why I haven't told them yet that me and Adam have separated. They wouldn't understand why I'd gamble my marriage away on a *whim* – Mum loves that word – even though it's more than that.

It's so much more than that.

Die Trying

Toby hurries back downstairs, completely naked. He wants to talk to Adam, and I'm half hoping *he* won't pick up, because he always makes promises to Toby he can't possibly keep – *I'll be back soon, buddy* – but of course he answers on the first ring.

CHAPTER TWELVE

Adam

'Hey! How are you?' Jemma says.

Her voice brings to mind a cathedral choir, soaring notes from an organ, Christmas carols. It makes the hairs on the back of my neck stand to attention. I wonder if she's also been waiting all day for this moment. 'Good, thanks.' I'm so thrilled to hear from her, it sounds genuine. 'You?'

'Not too bad. Thanks again for taking Toby last night – he won't stop going on about what a brilliant time he had.'

'That's ok. We had fun.'

'Good. I'm glad to hear it.'

The game of Snakes and Ladders is still on the bedroom floor in the corner by the wardrobe. I think of Toby's chubby fingers moving the blue counter along, square by square, as I edged ever closer to the head of the snake. His squeal of excitement as I slithered all the way down to the bottom of the board. At the other end of the room, opposite the mirrored wardrobe doors, the die is resting beside my glass of water. The outwards-facing single pip is magnified through the liquid, a looming black eye. One. *Connection*. 'Do you miss me?'

A pause. 'I still care about you, Adam – you don't spend five years of your life with someone and just switch off all emotions. I'm pleased you're... well, you're doing ok, aren't you?'

'Not really. Had a bit of a shit day, to be honest.'

Die Trying

'What happened?'

It is always Jemma I have reached out to in times of crisis. In the early days of our relationship, when a man jumped onto the tracks in front of me at the station, I called her straightaway and she was with me three hours later, lying by my side on the sofa in my rented harbourside apartment, combing her fingers through my hair. 'You couldn't have done anything,' she said, her words as comforting as her touch. 'There are people in this world too damaged to be saved.' But this is the thing about our 'trial' separation – we are not in the relationship, or out of it either. I don't understand the rules. I cannot share the humiliation of Spencer's rumour, and my colleagues' apparent willingness to believe it, because honesty is something we apparently no longer trade in. And if I did tell her, she'd probably only respect me less.

I'm saved from responding, because there's a rustle on the line and Jemma suddenly announces that Toby wants to talk. I imagine her opening a packet of chocolate-covered raisins, the sort we used to share while streaming a film or lying in bed together – *they're fruit, Adam, so* technically *good for you!* – and a bolt of sadness passes through me like a live current. The TV clicks off, followed by the snap of a door closing. Another rustle follows the jovial *plink* of what sounds like a plastic cup or bowl falling to the floor. Jemma's voice is replaced by Toby's, and he meanders between tales: counting numbers from a whale's belly, the cat with one white paw they saw on his way home from school, and 'The Thing', which turns out to be the new book he was given to read at home.

'You've had a busy day,' I tell him. 'Be good for Mummy. I'll see you tomorrow, ok?'

He passes the phone back to Jemma.

'Well, whatever you did with Toby last night worked – Miss Potter said she was going to give him the gold star sticker at school today, but he was on the reading bus after lunch so she'll give it to him on Monday. You're a good dad, Adam.'

'So let me come home!'

'You've only just moved out. And this is kind of the *point*,' Jemma says. 'It's too intense… I just… I meant it yesterday when I said "live a little". You could find an interest, or get a hobby…'

I say nothing. Through the bay window, I can see a bus disgorging passengers near the garages: a man in a tracksuit, followed by a woman with a trolley bag, who shuffles slowly onto the path as the bus roars away, almost knocking her down in the process. I can't help thinking of Dan Bretti, caught beneath the wheels.

'Sorry. That sounded harsh, and I didn't mean… I'm just tired.' Jemma's voice drops an octave. 'I'm not ready for you to come back yet, and we'd have to pay the tenancy agreement anyway. Let's just do this the way we said we would, and go from there.'

'Fine.'

A pause. I can hear Jemma breathing: in, out.

'I *am* sorry, Adam. I didn't want all this to happen.'

When she hangs up, I feel porous. I close the bedroom door and head back into the kitchenette, where I put a lasagne in the microwave. Six minutes. It judders and hums before falteringly turning the plastic container, round and around. Of all the appliances in the kitchen – of which, admittedly, all are dysfunctional – the microwave looks most in need of an urgent upgrade. There's a triangle of rust bubbling from the top right-hand corner, and the light inside the glass flashes on and off intermittently, like a strobe illuminating a beating heart. It reminds me of the futile attempt I'd made to talk to Kat and Paula earlier, before the others arrived, when we were all trapped in the meeting room together. 'Is everything alright?' I'd asked, looking not at the women but the motivational poster on the opposite wall: *Don't wait for opportunity, create it!* There was a muted 'mm' from Katya, an outrageously insincere 'yeah' from Paula, and you could have struck a match on the hot, heavy silence that followed.

The first mouthful of lasagne burns my mouth, the second is cold as bone.

Live a little.

Jemma doesn't know that I used to 'live a little'. More than a little. She doesn't know that someone ended up dead. She doesn't know that's why I gave it all up to be *this* man instead: someone who wouldn't cheat, lie or steal. Someone who wouldn't do the right thing only when people were watching.

And here's the irony: she doesn't want someone like that. Not anymore.

I scrape the red-streaked, flabby remains of the lasagne into the bin, where they cling to the sides of the liner like degloved skin, and head back into the bedroom. I'd forgotten how good it feels to rub the die in my palm, to feel the edges of the polished glass change from cool to warm; a transfer of energy. To scuff the padded flesh of my thumb against the pips. A hobby, then. I could go for a run in the howling storm. I could join a gym. I could go for a swim or hire a bike from Cycle the City and do just that.

I could visit Bretti Rocks.

Don't think, just do, Will used to say.

A rattling shiver dances across my shoulders. I throw the die without pausing to consider the consequences, and it bounces once on the polyester carpet before landing face up.

Three.

CHAPTER THIRTEEN

I arrive at Bretti Rocks twenty minutes later.

The unit is on the sprawling site of Cribbs Causeway, an out-of-town complex boasting a huge shopping precinct, cinema, food outlets and soft play. During the drive here, our wedding song came on the radio – *Take a Chance on Me* – and I turned it up, tapping the steering wheel and humming along until a black Polo in front of me slammed on its brakes and jolted me back to the present. Jemma has always said that we need to look out for the signs. A butterfly landing on a tombstone, white feathers, rain falling from a cloudless sky. 'And sometimes there might be things that just make you go *oh yeah*. This is not a coincidence,' she said. 'It's serendipity.'

The bushes around the car park are waving wildly. I reverse into a tight parking space between a Land Rover Discovery and a maroon-coloured Qashqai, despite there being plenty of other spaces available. It will be easy to drive straight out again, back to the flat, if necessary. Because now I'm here and our song has finished, I'm not quite sure I can go through with this. I want to see Dan Bretti in the flesh, but what if he recognises me? What if he calls Jemma to tell her I'm here? What if I am ordered out of the building and marched, humiliatingly, back to the car?

As the wind rattles around me like a malevolent spirit, I can't help thinking of Will. Because I felt it earlier. That sense of anticipation, fear and connecting with something *other* while waiting for the dice to land. Serendipity. Will called it 'the occult', although later admitted it was just a joke. Of course the die wasn't tapping into some predestined version of fate. 'Life doesn't work like that,' he laughed. 'Everything is down to chance.'

Still.

I scroll through my contacts. There he is – *Will* – languishing at the bottom of the list, when he was once always at the top of my recent calls. Will King. When I first met him at college that blisteringly hot day in September as he sank into the vacant seat beside me in Maths – late – I envied the way he delivered his name 'for the class'. Will King. Just like that; two decisive bullets.

Later, when he invited me to his house to study, I envied him for his home, too: a three-storey house on Hanbury Road with an olive door and large silver knocker, like something from one of those house-swap documentaries Mum used to be so obsessed with. Inside, there was a wide hall, painted in cream, with four doors leading off to a dining room, lounge, kitchen and study; rooms I caught only a glimpse of as we ascended the stairs. Will's bedroom took up the entire width and breadth of the third floor, an attic conversion with tall windows looking out to a sky slashed with orange scars, so close I felt I could reach up and touch it through the open window. Mum and I had moved from the flat above the chip shop to a two-bedroomed mid-terrace house by then, and I hated myself for feeling embarrassed when Will asked to come back to mine. I was ungrateful, superficial, unkind. Mum had worked hard for what little we had. She worked hard for me.

But Will didn't seem to notice that it would have been possible to fit my entire house in his neatly mown front garden. Our front door opened straight into the lounge, where he spotted the die almost as soon as we walked in. 'Man, this is incredible,' he said, lifting it from the open box on top of the fireplace. 'Like a sculpture or something. Do you use it?'

'What do you mean?'

'For dice play. Like the book.'

I had no idea what he was talking about.

'*The Dice Man.*'

Mum was using the whisk in the kitchen to make batter for home-made tempura chicken, and I had to keep leaning forwards to hear him properly. Every time I did, I noticed something new – the patch of scale beside his right ear, the slight twang of a cockney accent that rounded off his vowels, how his eyes looked brown in the light, gold in the shade. 'It's about a man who uses a dice to make life choices, and it gets *dark*,' he laughed. 'It's quite old now. My Dad's got a copy of it at home – I'll lend it to you, if you like.'

Don't think, just do. I haven't spoken to him for years, but I really could do with a friend right now. I hit the call button, and look up at the glow of letters, black against a sharp yellow background, as it rings. *Bretti Rocks.*

Bretti Rocks.

Bretti Rocks.

Bretti Rocks.

It continues to ring, and eventually clicks to answerphone. Maybe Will doesn't want to speak to me, and after everything that happened, I wouldn't blame him. Maybe he's changed his number.

Maybe he's dead.

I push the phone into my jacket pocket. The owner of the Discovery is back, and as he climbs into the car beside me the wind catches the door, making a *crack* against my own. He lifts his hand – *sorry!* – then shoots out of the space before I have the chance to get out and check for damage, pulling his seatbelt on with one hand as he drives away.

And a moment later, I discover there is. A thin white scratch I can dip a fingernail inside, the sort people say can be repaired, polished over – like a smudge on a painting – but never looks quite the same.

Die Trying

I look up again at the building. Above the sign, the clouds are heavy with unspent rain. No point going back to the flat now. The die has issued a command; I need to see it through.

Bad things happened when we didn't.

The place looks like the inside of a Quality Street tin. The kidney-shaped 'rocks' studding the walls are painted in bright colours – purple, yellow, orange, green – and in another area, a couple of children are dangling from ropes against bold space-and city-themed backdrops. Music from unseen speakers is being largely swallowed by the echoing clatter of buckles and the squeak of rubber shoes hitting the walls. 'It's not exactly you, is it?' Jemma had said when I raised the suggestion of doing Segway. She's right; it's not. Neither is this.

There's no sign of Dan Bretti on reception, only a boy of seventeen or eighteen – Joshua, according to his name badge – and a woman with several nose piercings and hair plaited into tight red cables. The unit is huge, loud and windowless, scented heavily with the sweat from damp bodies, and I'm so busy scanning the oddly-angled walls spanning up to the ceiling for Dan Bretti, I don't notice that Joshua is smiling at me.

'Can I help you?'

'Oh. Yes.' I return the smile. 'What, er, what do you offer?'

'For yourself?'

'Yes.'

'Well, if you're new here, I'd recommend bouldering.' The door marked *Staff Only* opens behind him and I stiffen in anticipation, but a bald man emerges. He grabs a water bottle from the shelf, then disappears back inside. Joshua's still talking. 'We can loan you some climbing shoes. We'll just need a quick signed disclaimer and safety brief, then you'll be good to go.'

'Great, thanks.' I take the iPad Joshua slides towards me. Where is Dan, anyway? I imagine him pressing his lips against my wife's face, parting her legs and reaching up inside them with hot, insistent fingers. *I'm so hard for you it hurts.*

'You alright?' Joshua asks.

The stylus is trembling in my hand. Joshua taps at the screen. 'Just there.'

He thinks I don't understand how an iPad works. I'd felt sorry for him before, assuming he was being exploited by Dan Bretti, enslaved on minimum wage and forced to work unsociable hours, but now I don't. I give him a look, and tap the details in as quickly as possible.

Not *my* details, obviously.

A few minutes later, I'm standing on the crash mat wearing shoes that feel horribly thin on the sole and uncomfortably tight around my toes. The first few boulders are easy to grasp and I pull myself up steadily, keeping my body close to the wall, using my feet to feel for studs, which are rougher than I expected. There are only two other people in this area – both men – one tackling the purple boulders, black bag dangling from his waist, and his long-haired mate, who keeps returning to the mat to rub chalk into his hands. I keep one eye on the reception area, hoping that Dan will walk in, but after a while it becomes difficult to do this and focus on the task in hand. The boulders become increasingly vicious, biting into the callouses already forming at the base of my fingers, and as I scramble higher, I imagine Jemma bringing Toby here. I imagine Dan kitting up my son with ropes and harnesses and helping him to ascend the walls. The three of them, drinking hot chocolates in the café afterwards, erasing me brusquely, like the chalk on their hands.

My thighs are throbbing. I swing myself above the next kidney-shaped rock, and there's something about the way my biceps swell and burn against the sleeve of my t-shirt that feels like retribution.

I'm nearly at the top now. Up here, the boulders are smaller, so widely spaced apart that I'm struggling to gain purchase.

Die Trying

My breath comes in wet bursts and firm, sharp fingers of pain are jabbing all over my body. I lift my sleeve to wipe the sweat from my face, but then my foot slips from its anchor and I'm wheeling, cycling the air for a second, until I land with a thump on the mat below.

CHAPTER FOURTEEN

The following morning when I awake, I feel as though I've been mauled by a large dog. My chest is sore when I breathe, and the act of walking to the bathroom makes my calf muscles sing. Even though the discomfort reminds me how I sometimes felt the day after one of Dad's 'play' fights, it isn't an unpleasant sensation. I slept better than I have for months, despite dreaming that I'd been back home, hacking at the seats of the lounge sofa, convinced that Jemma had taken the die and hidden it in a place beyond reach. 'Where is *what?*' she said, in that tone of voice so familiar to me these days. 'What are you talking about? What die?' And then, in that way that dreams make a nonsense of reality – or perhaps it's the other way around – she morphed into Abbie, Will's girlfriend from college.

I wait for the clock to switch from 8.09 to 8.10, then climb out of bed. Unsurprisingly, Jemma hasn't hidden the die inside the fabric of our sofa – it's right there, on my bedside cabinet. She sent a message last night, asking if I wanted to meet her and Toby at Jubilee Green Park this morning – with not one, but three kisses – and I can't help feeling as though she might be having second thoughts about our separation. Maybe she's lonely. After all, she did apologise yesterday, and said she didn't want any of this to happen. *'You don't spend five years of your life with someone and just switch off all emotions.'*

No, Jemma. You don't.

Die Trying

Under the shower, with the water beating down on my sore muscles, I imagine that she'll come running up to me in the park, the way people do in films when they've just missed their flight to be with the love of their life. I imagine taking in a mouthful of her hair as she hugs me and laughs, whispering 'sorry' over and over again. I'll forgive her for whatever it was with Dan Bretti, because we have each other and we have Toby, and maybe we needed this test; we needed to miss each other to find ourselves again.

It doesn't happen like that.

Jemma's on her phone when I get there, wearing jeans and a startlingly bright yellow t-shirt, her hair scraped back from her face, and she offers me a slight wave of acknowledgment as I walk across the green. The sun is high in the sky, sharp as a sting. I checked the weather earlier, and it looks like there'll be more rain coming in, but not until later – something most of the other park-goers must also be aware of, because it's busier than usual for a Saturday. I locate Toby, who is digging in the sand pit like a frenzied terrier, and we chat about his buried dinosaurs until Jemma joins us a few minutes later.

'Hey, you ok?'

I stand up, brushing sand from my jeans. I want to ask who was on the phone, but of course that's none of my business.

'Do you want a coffee or anything? I got this from that little pop-up shop over there,' she says, gesturing towards a mobile unit a few hundred metres away, and I can't help thinking of the comment she made when the drinks trolley came around on the train, the first time we met. 'Wonder if they've got anything stronger,' she winked, then grabbed my arm, taking me by surprise. Later she told me she just knew the universe had placed me on *that* train, at *that* moment, for a reason. 'Everyone comes into our lives for a reason, Adam.'

'I'm ok,' I tell her. 'Unless they've got anything stronger.'

She frowns. 'Aren't you driving?'

'No, it's just a... don't worry.'

'Oh. Ok.' She plucks at my top, and she's so close I can smell the hint of spiced cherries in her perfume. 'This is nice, is it new?'

'No.' Jemma's sister bought me the polo shirt two Christmases ago. It's the sort my dad might wear, with chunky blue-and-white stripes and a wide-open collar, the sort favoured by rugby players and men of a certain physique. I'd thanked her before tucking it back into its wrapping, thinking I'd never wear it. But there it was on the left-hand side of my wardrobe this morning, along with a River Island t-shirt and a couple of other tops I'd forgotten I owned. It seemed essential I got my choice of clothing right. And not just the clothing: the scent, the hair, the watch – Fitbit or Bulova – because, despite the fact we were meeting at a children's playground with our son, it felt like we were embarking on a first date. So yes, I used the die. No big deal. I would have been late otherwise, paralysed with indecision, doubting myself.

We stay in the park for almost an hour, and to anyone watching, we are just a normal married couple enjoying a normal Saturday outing with our son. Jemma goes back to the van to buy an ice cream for Toby, and while she's waiting in the queue, my phone rings.

My phone never rings.

'Daddy,' Toby calls from the climbing frame.

I wave at him absently, then return my gaze to the screen. It's Will. His name seems to bulge and pulse before my eyes. I slide my finger across the glass. 'Hello?'

'Adam.' The voice is crisp and deep; unmistakably Will's. 'Long time! I had a missed call from you last night.'

'Yes. *Yeah*. It has been a long time. How are you?'

'I'm ok. How are you?'

'I'm good.'

Die Trying

There's a brief silence, which Will eventually fills by telling me it's a relief to hear, because he thought I might have been calling with bad news.

'Oh no – nothing like that, thankfully,' I tell him. 'Sorry. I found the die recently, that's all, and I started thinking about you. *Us*. All the stuff we did, back in the day.'

'The die? I thought you threw it away!'

'So did I.'

'We had a crack with that thing, didn't we? I always laughed when you said it was guiding us towards fate – or karma, or whatever it was you went on about, but there was always that weird energy, wasn't there?'

Jemma's heading back now, both hands full with ice cream cones, an ice lolly tucked under one arm. I take a few steps back and press three fingers to one ear, trying to block out the electric squeals of children at play. 'I know we said we wouldn't do it again, but I've given in. Only a few times.'

'Say that again? You sound like you're in a theme park. Or the dental clinic from hell.'

'I've *used the die*,' I hiss. 'Just a few times.'

'Oh.' He laughs. 'I'd be lying if I said I hadn't been tempted to play over the years, but every time I think about it, I feel like an alcoholic contemplating just the one beer. Mad isn't it, how addictive it became?'

'I know.'

Jemma almost collides with a couple of children playing tag. She's looking straight at me.

'...partner and stepdaughter now, if you can believe it.' Will is saying. He wants to know if I'm married. Any kids. Where am I working? I fire out responses – yes, one, Smithson – eager now to wrap up the conversation, because it feels wrong, having him and Jemma taking up the same space like this; he is the past, she is the present. Or possibly not. Will asks if I want to meet up soon, because it's difficult to chat properly like this, and I find myself telling him yes, that would be great. He thanks me for getting back in touch, and by the time I end the call, I realise I have wandered off the path, far from the row of rocks Jemma and I were sitting on just minutes earlier.

'Who was that?' Jemma asks, when I return. She's taking bites from her ice cream the way she always does, nibbling at the edges as though it's a slice of pizza, instead of licking it. My cone is lying on a napkin on the rock beside her; there's already a small yellow puddle forming around it.

'Just a friend I used to know,' I tell her. 'Sorry about that.'

'You were supposed to be keeping an eye on Toby.'

'I was. I did. I could see him the whole time. Thanks for this.' I pick up the ice cream, and she gives me a small, intimate smile, as though she's about to share a filthy joke.

'Male or female?'

'Sorry?'

'The "friend".'

Her eyes are wide, crimped with curiosity. Is she jealous? 'Male,' I tell her. 'Will. We used to go to college together.'

'I've never heard of him. Was he at our wedding?'

I almost burst out laughing. Will, at our wedding? He would probably have slept with the bride of honour – Steph – embarrassed and entertained Jemma's family with drinking games and revelations about our college escapades and been unconscious by the end of the night. 'No,' I tell Jemma. 'I'm pretty sure he wasn't.'

She licks the edge of her napkin then presses it, without warning, to my chest. 'Small drip.'

'That's no way to talk about your husband.'

It's a terrible joke, a 'Dad' joke, and it's one of those moments that could go either way, because although I *am* still Jemma's husband, I feel like a fraud for saying it, and half expect her to snap that I don't have to keep going on about it. But she laughs. Thank God, she laughs.

Die Trying

'I'm so glad you're getting back in touch with old friends,' Jemma says, removing her fingers from the swell of my breastbone and staring into my eyes with such intensity I almost forget about Dan Bretti and Will and Spencer and all the terrible, terrible things that have gone before. Almost, but not quite. 'No, really, I am. It'll be good for you.'

CHAPTER FIFTEEN

That's how I end up meeting Will the following Saturday, at the 360 Café on Clifton Observatory. I don't roll the die to decide, although I do consider it, thinking it might be a funny and fitting excuse. *'You'll never guess why I can't meet you today.'* Deep down, I suppose I wanted it to happen, and not only because I'm curious about his life now, or because Jemma approves.

He's the only one who understands.

I sit close to the main entrance, opposite a couple with two large black dozing retrievers. The irony of leaving sleeping dogs to lie is not lost on me, especially when the bigger one with flecks of grey keeps opening one eye and staring at the door every time it opens. The owners – a couple in their late thirties – are agonising over colours for their kitchen refurbishment. 'Not the midnight blue,' the man says, shaking his head so vehemently that some of the cream slides over the side of his mug. 'Too dark.' When they get up to leave, I consider doing the same. Will is fifteen minutes late, and the waitress has already been over twice to see what I'd like to drink. I've told her I'm meeting someone: I'll wait. But there's only so long I can sit here watching people come and go without it getting creepy.

I could roll to decide. And just as I'm considering it, reaching into my pocket and feeling the blunt, reassuring solidity of the die in my palm, Will walks in.

Die Trying

I don't expect him to look like the same dimple-chinned eighteen-year-old that he was when we last saw each other, but it's still a surprise to see that his face has thinned with age and his hair is darker now, teased into thick, soft waves that go some way to covering his high forehead. As he narrows his eyes and scans the room looking for me, he looks almost angry.

'Will.'

'Mate!'

I stand, and we clap each other on the back. I've always been at least an inch taller than him, but for some reason it seems we're now almost equal in height. Then I realise why: I'm wearing brogues, he's wearing trainers. 'Sorry I'm late.' He points at the space on the table between us. 'Do you want a drink?'

'Yes, I'll – I think the waitress will be back in a minute.'

'It's fine, I'll go up.' He slides a phone from the back pocket of his jeans. 'Coffee? Tea? Anything to eat?'

'Coffee would be great, thanks. Milk, no sugar.'

I watch as he goes up to the bar and leans gently over it, pointing at the board and laughing in response to something the barista has said. The last time I saw Will, I fully intended to tell him that I rolled the die that night. We'd finished our A-levels by then and both been questioned and released by police. It was three days before my eighteenth birthday and I felt that something between us had shifted. They say that death either brings people closer together or pulls them apart, and as we sat in his garden – painfully beautiful where the border of flowers between the patio and the lawn was in full bloom – he told me the truth. His truth.

'She's going to bring it over,' Will says, clumsily tugging out the chair opposite mine. His mouth is now almost consumed by a surrounding mess of facial hair, and when he opens it to speak, the shocking, glistening pinkness reminds me of a baby bird lost inside a nest. 'So come on, mate, what's going on with you? I honestly couldn't believe it when I saw your missed call.'

Mate. Jemma's right – this will be good for me. No-one's called me that for years. 'I honestly don't know where to start.'

'You're married, aren't you?'

'Yes, with a son. Toby's four.'

'Mad. I've got a thirteen-year-old stepdaughter, Molly, and – maybe even more mad – me and my partner Claire are trying for a baby.' Will pauses as the waitress lowers a tray with two coffees and a toasted teacake onto the table between us. 'Look at us both, doing the stable nuclear family gig. How's your mum doing? Is she still living locally?'

'No. She died.'

'Oh man, I'm sorry. Jesus. How did she... if you don't mind me...'

'Pulmonary embolism. When I was at uni.' I take a sip of coffee and set it back on the saucer. 'It's fine. I mean, it isn't, but you know. Long time ago now.'

'What about your dad? Do you still see him?'

'No, not for years.' Not since the night it happened, although I don't tell Will that. He takes a bite of his teacake and I steer the conversation back onto safer terrain by talking about the jobs I had after leaving uni, then meeting Jemma and working at Smithson. 'It's ok, I'm just an IT guy – it pays the bills. What about you?'

'Well, it's funny you called when you did – I was living in London until recently, and only moved back to Bristol because I met Claire and got a new job here doing consultancy. And house prices in the capital are insane. Help yourself.'

I shake my head at the plate: no thanks.

He leans back, resting one elbow on the chair behind him. 'I haven't been able to get all the dice stuff out of my head since you called. Remember the time we followed that Eddie Stobart lorry all the way to Edinburgh?'

'Was that the time we slept in the field with the cows?'

'I think so. It must have been, because the lorry park was next door.' Will looks thoughtful. 'I still wonder sometimes what might have happened if we'd followed the yellow car instead.'

'The one with the blacked-out windows? I had a bad feeling about that. Maybe we wouldn't be alive now to tell the tale.'

As the last word leaves my lips, I realise what I've just said. *Abbie. Abbie isn't here to tell the tale.*

Will has a new partner now. And yet, he'd said Abbie was irreplaceable; the first and only girl he'd ever loved. I'd spent many sleepless nights after her death worrying not only that he might find out what I'd done, but also that he might take his own life. That day in the garden, he'd hinted at it: a Russian roulette last throw of the die.

'And liar's day?' Will says. 'Remember that?'

I'm warming to the memories now, because we'd become fully fledged disciples by this point, and the die always evoked a terrifying thrill. On the day in question, we had to spend an entire twenty-four hours telling lies: Will calmly explained to customers in a queue at the bus stop how he'd just set his house on fire, spoke for almost an hour to a local shopkeeper about the history of the town and its fictitious pagan connections, claimed to a lecturer that he was half Caribbean and that Rihanna was his little sister. Will's comfort zone – like his confidence – was always far broader than mine. I told him I hated him, and he curled a bubble of muscle around my neck in a momentary display of camaraderie. It *was* a lie, but my feelings for Will were always complicated; a cocktail of envy, admiration and fear. 'How could I forget?'

We finish our coffees. I order the same again, then for the next half an hour we talk about our jobs, kids, and how strange it is that so much time has passed, when it feels like none at all. Will goes to the toilet and when he returns, he's smiling. 'Have you been in there?'

'No.'

'Spotted tiles, like dice. Must be a sign.' He laughs at this, because it's the sort of thing I used to say. *It doesn't feel right, it happened for a reason, it's fate.* And Jemma believes it too – she sends fireworks fizzing and popping through my bloodstream when she speaks like that. 'Actually, maybe you're right and I've been wrong all this time. Have I told you yet about the podcast series I've been making?'

'I don't think so. How do you have time for all this?'

'I make time because I love it, although the one I'm doing at the moment, *Chaos,* has pretty much run its course. I've gained a decent following from that and a YouTube channel I set up a few years ago, but...' He puts both elbows on the table. 'I'm ready for something new now, and I really think a livestreamed dice podcast could be huge. Especially one about all the insane stories from our dice days. Imagine how *brilliant* that would be.'

Is he insane? Has he forgotten what happened? I look past his shoulder, to the customers lining up behind the till, so he can't read my eyes. A short woman with a cluster of tattoos beetling up her neck is standing in front of an older lady, mustard-coloured jacket folded primly over her thin arms. Like us, Abbie would be thirty-three now. What would she have done with her life? Would she have married Will, or someone else? Kids? In my mind, she is exactly the same: dark hair exploding from a tortoiseshell clip, those high, fleshy cheekbones that seemed to pull her eyes up into a permanent smile. The smile that seemed to drop only when I was around.

'Come on,' Will persists. 'What do you think?'

'I mean, obviously it's up to you, but it wasn't really a happy ending, was it?'

'I know.' For the first time since he got here, he looks solemn. 'I'd obviously want to honour Abbie's memory, not diminish it. I still think about her a lot. But things only started going wrong when we went on a quest to dismantle everything we were and excuse shitty, immoral behaviour. *I* did, anyway. The podcast would be about the good stuff we did, and maybe using it to have some fun, like we did in the early days.'

'You'd want *me* involved?'

'Of course I would! Do you have it with you?'

'It's in the car.'

'Think about it then. Or roll to decide.' Will downs the last of his coffee and cracks another smile. 'Anyway, I should get back. We'll have to do this again sometime. Maybe we could meet with our better halves next time?'

I stand up, pat my wallet in the front pocket. 'It would be great to meet your partner. And I'd love you to meet my wife and son, it's just… we're on a very temporary separation at the moment.'

'Oh mate, I'm sorry.'

'It's fine.'

'I guess it's easy to lose sight of each other when you're wrapped up in the needs of a small kid. Claire's been stressing out lately, because it hasn't been happening for us, and she keeps… ah, it doesn't matter. Just got to keep focusing on what's important.' Will slides his chair back under the table. 'The devil's bones were good for that at least, weren't they? Shook us up, made us see what mattered.'

We walk out together, through the glass doors and into the mid-afternoon breeze. Will stops at a puddle of golden leaves lying at the foot of the nearby horse chestnut tree. Another clap on the back. 'I'm that way. It's been so good to see you, mate.'

'You, too.'

I watch him walk away, then stretch out the taut muscles of my back, pulling my elbows sharply behind me, feeling something crack. Someone has spray-painted the word FUCK on the wall opposite.

Fuck, indeed.

CHAPTER SIXTEEN

'Everyone comes into our lives for a reason,' Jemma always says, and I can't help wondering if the same is true of the die as I drive back along Observation Road with music playing and the Clifton Suspension Bridge looming in my rear-view mirror. Do *things* also come into our lives for a reason? Will said we could use the die to have some fun like we did at the beginning, and admittedly, it *was* exciting at first. We used it to decide on different hairstyles and choices of clothing. We took different routes home. We went to the library and allowed the die to choose a book, then had to sneak a sentence of its choosing into conversation with teachers. We became, by turns, joyful, tedious, complimentary, arrogant. It didn't come naturally, but that was the point. Will assured me that everyone was acting, all the time. 'I'm not the same with you as I am with my parents,' he said. 'And your mum will be different with her new boyfriend from how she is with you – in private, anyway.'

I didn't doubt it. Her new boyfriend – Paul – had been mowing the grass when I came home from college one day, and never really left. If I'd known he was going to be different from the others, I would have been kinder to him. It wasn't long until Mum seemed suddenly to be finding fault with everything I did. I'd find them cuddling in different rooms around the house – a kiss on the neck here, a hand on the buttock there – and they'd both stop and regard me with a polite smile, making feathery conversation, as if I was a waiter arriving to collect their cold dishes.

Around the same time, the dice permitted Will the courage to talk to the object of his affection – Abbie Reynolds – which he'd previously been too inhibited to do. I was convinced she wouldn't be interested in him. It wasn't that he was unattractive – he wasn't – but we both acknowledged that we were different, and I was sure the fact that he was wearing his shoes on the wrong feet when he approached her for the first time would result in an instant rejection.

But it didn't. Unlike myself, Will seemed able to adopt the roles he was assigned with ease, and when the die ordered him to cross the refectory to tell Abbie that he was in love with her, he rose from his chair and immediately performed the task. We'd been using the die for around eight months by then, and it had forced us to wear so many different masks, I wasn't sure there was anything left underneath. Even though most of the choices had revolved around daily decision-making and harmless challenges, the games got under my skin to the point where I couldn't pick which clothes to wear or what to eat without first consulting the die.

Will stayed at the girls' table so long his baked potato was going cold. I picked at my own as the chatter around me rose to a din that was almost unbearable, crushing rational thought. I resented the die that day. It had ordered me to wear a long-sleeved t-shirt and trousers, while Will, by contrast, was dressed in blue shorts and a white t-shirt with sunglasses that – despite the shoes – made him look like an airline pilot from a Hollywood film. He returned to our table shaking the die in his fist. *Result*.

Nothing changed that much at first. Will and I continued our weekend adventures, travelling by train to Oxford, Brighton and Bath, talking to strangers about imaginary friends and relatives we were going to visit, or medical treatments we were undergoing. We dressed up in superhero costumes and pretended to fight each other. Nobody else knew about the die. To the outside world, we were just being typical, hedonistic teenagers. I thought Abbie would quickly tire of Will's unpredictability, but far from being deterred, she seemed to find it appealing. When the die ordered him to cancel plans at short notice, he countered with exuberant demonstrations of affection.

'Don't you mind?' I asked him. 'We *can* stop doing this.'

In truth, I wasn't sure if we could, even though a part of me wanted to. I was feeling permanently exhausted all the time, on edge, bristling with expectant energy. Will kept reminding me that the die gave us freedom and the chance to do things we wouldn't otherwise, and it was hard to argue with that.

Over time, Abbie became a third wheel on our lunch table. Occasionally, she'd bring her best friend Elisha – a pretty, petite brunette with a laugh that managed to sound both dirty and uplifting – and I often found myself slipping off to use the die to decide how to talk to her.

'She likes you, mate,' Will said. 'Abbie told me.'

Was he lying? Will and I used the die for so many untruths and twisted realities that recently, I'd found myself questioning everything he said. 'Ask Abbie, then!' he protested. 'She said you're invited to her party. Mate, you're in.'

As it turned out, he *was* telling the truth, but I didn't want to go to the party. If Elisha and I were to be together, I wanted to do things properly, with flowers and a meal, not shouting to be heard over heavy bass music, with drunken students stumbling into us, slopping drinks from plastic cups.

The die told me to go.

It was late June by then, and everyone seemed to be tanned and hairless, the smell of sun cream, coffee and smoky, barbecued meat swelling the air. We took a bottle of vodka from Will's parents' alcohol cabinet – the lesser of five other evils – and arrived to find the party in full swing. Abbie took Will by the hand and I followed behind him to the kitchen, where Elisha was standing in a short black dress, generously cut into a V around her breasts and studded with so many sequins she glittered like a disco ball every time she moved. She stepped forwards to hug me, then gestured to the rows of vodka, gin, wine and foreign spirits with unreadable labels, set out on a long table beside a variety of glasses and straws. 'Help yourself,' she shouted. 'I'm going for a piss.'

Abbie and Will had already gone to the garden; I could see them from the kitchen window, rocking gently on a wooden swing beside Elisha's summerhouse. Other students I vaguely recognised from college, as well as older young adults I'd never seen before, wandered in and out, pouring generous measures from the bottles and delving their hands into the bags of crisps and nuts open on the side. I kept sipping my bottle of beer, wondering when Elisha would come back. Eventually, she returned, accompanied by a girl wearing a blaze of red lipstick, who proceeded to take all the mixing bowls out of the cupboard to make fishbowl cocktails.

'Can you believe he's single?' Elisha said to her friend, and it took me a moment to realise she was talking about me. Then she was on me, pressing against my body, sticky as papier mache. 'You're the hottest boy at college, did anyone ever tell you that?'

Her eyes were bloodshot and she was swaying slightly. She smelled of alcohol and something marshmallow-sweet – a vape, I realised, when it clattered from her hand to the floor. It wasn't supposed to be like this. I want to say that, when she squeezed my groin on her way to pick it up, I told her to stop, but I didn't. Disgust was grappling with desire. The girl with the red lipstick was laughing, muttering something about getting a room, while glugging spirits from two bottles into the glass bowl. I wanted to tell her to fuck off, but before I knew it,

Elisha was pressing a glass in my hand, straw to my mouth. 'Try it,' she said.

It reminded me of something from childhood. Strawberry sweets, melted into a hallway rug. Sticky hands. Empty bottles. Air freshener. By the time I'd finished, the kitchen was a whirl of colour and people, Elisha a singular glistening diamond. Outside, the swinging seat was empty, Will and Abbie nowhere to be seen.

The die told me not to sleep with Elisha that night.

But we kissed and hugged, and the more Elisha drank, the more she pressed against me, twerking to the music and rubbing herself against my clothes, until at some point during the evening, I found myself being led to a poky downstairs bedroom with soft lighting and a bed that squealed when we sat on it.

'Don't,' I said, when she took off her top, but my voice was swept away by the music, along with the rest of my resolve. In just a few seconds, I'd spilled myself inside her.

After that, the problems started.

I desperately wanted to explain, but for the following three rolls, the die ordered me to ignore her messages. On the third – several days later – it ordered me to apologise, prompting an angry outburst from Abbie. 'Leave her alone,' she fumed when I saw her at Will's later that evening. 'You don't want her, you just want to mess with her head.'

I didn't want to mess with her head, but I was relieved when the die rejected any and all suggestions of a date – trying to save me from hurt, it seemed, even though I hated myself for it. I hated that I could be the sort of man to do what my father did to me and my mother.

And I hated the fact that Abbie stirred something in me Elisha didn't.

CHAPTER SEVENTEEN

On Monday morning, I arrive at work and grab a coffee before the team meeting starts. By the time I pull open the door, most of the seats in the conference room are taken, and I find myself squashed into an awkward non-space between Miles and Paula, who move their chairs, grudgingly, to accommodate me. The room stinks of shit, sweat and stale coffee. Seb remains standing as he runs through a number of new contracts, enquires about the progress of existing ones, then reminds us about the forthcoming social, at which he hopes to see as many of us as possible. 'Distribute the notes to the team, please, Katya,' he says, stiffening his spine self-importantly.

And then we're dismissed.

I check my emails, responding to the ones I can deal with quickly, then open a new webpage. I can't listen to anymore of Will's podcast series while I'm at work, but the first episode of Chaos was surprisingly entertaining. Will talked about family life in such a tender, funny and brutally honest way that I found myself laughing out loud. His guest speaker, Danny – a fellow podcaster, by all accounts – revealed that he'd become a completely different person as a result. 'As you know, I'd been in and out of prison,' he said. 'I got stuck in these patterns and didn't particularly care about anything. Then there was this tiny person, and he was mine, he was me, and it was fucking incredible, as though God had given me a reset button.'

That's exactly how I felt when Toby was born. Things were going to be ok; my life was finally on the right track. Jemma had come into my life exactly when I needed her, and Toby was our reward for doing things right. All those years when I'd wondered if Mum's sudden death was my punishment for Abbie's brutal end were put to rest when Jemma agreed to marry me.

We were fine. We were happy, until Dan Bretti came along.

'Not brownies,' Kat says to Spencer, heading into the office from the kitchen, carrying a plastic container full of cake. 'Blondies. I made them yesterday. Help yourself.'

'Good job they're not called gingers,' he says. 'No one would want them.'

Kat doesn't laugh at the obvious and inappropriate reference to my hair colour. But neither does she offer me one, despite handing them to everyone else in the office. I pretend not to hear and keep my face fixed firmly on the monitor until they head off for yet another liquid lunch, then close the spreadsheet I'm working on and turn my attention back to the *Bretti Rocks* climbing page. It's only when I'm scrolling through the photos, growing increasingly repulsed – does Dan need to be in quite so many of them? – that I have an epiphany.

His business information will be registered online.

Companies House records show a Richard and Rachel Bretti, *not* Dan Bretti, as shareholders. The correspondence address is listed in Penzance, Cornwall. I take a screenshot with my phone, then return to Dan's Facebook and Instagram pages. He's been tagged in two new pictures where he's standing with his arm around a tall blonde woman, their heads tilted together. To my delight, there's a baby-carrier by her side with a tiny child inside.

The chair creaks as I lean back. Does Jemma know about her? Does Dan's wife know about Jemma? I imagine delivering the news: *I'm really sorry to tell you this, but...*

Then I notice the caption below: *Day out with big brother and Livvy.*

Beth Hawkins. A quick look at her profile shows she's married to Sam Hawkins and that Dan is her brother.

Ah.

Dan isn't just a muscular sportsman, he's an *'amazing big brother'* too. I scroll through photos of them in restaurants and pubs, glasses being raised beside spotless kitchen islands, throwbacks to the two of them as children, gurning in first-day-at-school uniforms. I work my way back and click on a post from 23rd August last year, where Dan is smiling broadly and – in what I can only imagine is making up for some form of inadequacy – holding up a ridiculously oversized set of kitchen tongs. *Happy birthday Beth x* Dan has commented. His own birthday, it transpires, is just a few days before hers, which comes as no surprise whatsoever. Of course he has a birthday in the summer! He'll never know what it's like to experience the yearly disappointment of being a Boxing Day child; waking up to the stink of day-old stuffing lingering in the air, a lazy river of crumpled wrapping paper winding around the house, creeping downstairs to a tree already drooping in defeat.

After work, I drive on autopilot, listening to Will's podcast as Cabot Circus disappears from my rear-view mirror to be swiftly replaced by the open grey expanse of the M32. In the second episode, Will is asking his guest: *if you could go back and change one thing in your life, what would it be and what effect would it have right now?* It's strange to hear the voice of my childhood friend coming through the speakers like this, and as the other man speaks of longing to reconcile with his estranged brother before he died, I can't help but mull over the question for myself. What one thing would I change?

Too late, I realise I've automatically made my way home. Home, not the flat. I slow to a halt on the other side of the road beside Derrick's house, hoping he won't come marching out in righteous indignation – he takes umbrage with anyone parking outside his property, even though it's a public right of way.

Justin and Louise have finally cut their front lawn.

Sally at number thirty-seven has put her bin out on the wrong day again.

I look up at our house. Jemma must be in; I can see shadows moving about behind the windows and, a moment later, the bedroom light clicks on. Maybe she's on the phone to Frankie, or one of the other mum friends she chats to for hours – seemingly about nothing – outside preschool. There are so many of them, it's hard to believe that she fretted about missing family and being lonely before moving here. I reassured her that she didn't need to worry. Whatever happened, we'd always have each other.

But now, Dan Bretti.

He's crawled inside her beautiful head and laid eggs there.

I can feel my palms dampening in sticky desperation, because I know that, if I could change one thing, I wouldn't have left. And I wish I had the die, because then I would know what to do. I restart the engine, and Will's disembodied voice fills the car again. 'You're right,' he laughs. 'It could have been a whole other life.'

CHAPTER EIGHTEEN

I arrive at Will's house the following Friday evening after work. He lives along a tree-lined road that seemingly leads to nowhere until suddenly, there it is: a stone cottage with smoke curling from the chimney and two cars parked outside – a spanking new Mercedes and a small convertible, both in black. His n hers. As I knock and wait in front of the wide stone porch, I'm struck by the coolness of the air, lightly infused with the scent of silage.

'You found us! Come in.'

Will is barefoot, dressed in a burgundy polo shirt with navy jeans. I'm ushered into a large, square kitchen, where his wife hurriedly slams the oven door closed and comes towards me for a hug. It's so unexpected, I can't process the sudden, conflicting rush of sensations: warm arms gripping my sides, the pillow-soft brush of blonde hair against my cheek, a heavy fusion of spices and fruited wine.

'I'm Claire,' she says. 'It's so nice to meet you.'

She offers me a drink, then Will takes me on a brief tour of the house. 'Through here,' he says over his shoulder, as we cross the dark wood floor of the hall. There are black-and-white pictures of seascapes on the opposite wall, a vase of flowers with pink, oddly coiled petals on one shelf, a window looking out to the darkness beyond.

We walk through a set of sliding glass doors into the lounge, where Will's stepdaughter Molly is slouched on a leather sofa, watching *Frozen II*. 'Hey Molls,' Will says. 'This is Adam, my friend from college.'

She turns her head, fractionally. 'You've got *friends*?'

'Ha. Honestly,' Will says. 'Who'd have teenagers? Anyway, come and take a look at this.'

He takes three strides towards the patio doors. I snatch my gaze away from the huge fireplace and artfully lit bookshelves and follow, wondering how many times I can tell him what an impressive home he has. The garden is no different – there's a lush expanse of green, bordered by an array of plants and trees, and stone steps leading up to a wooden arch. Beyond that is a wooden annexe, like a huge, oversized playhouse. And it's this – not the house, not the garden, both of which are impressive – that finally blows me away. Will has *built* this. He shows me the videos on his YouTube channel of what it looked like at the beginning – a single slatted base, four panels without windows or doors. Now, it's an operational working space, with a separate kitchen and bathroom and even a fully furnished bedroom. 'Comes in handy when me and Claire fall out,' he laughs. Then he pushes open the last door.

'My studio,' Will says, proudly.

Three black leather seats surround a centre table, upon which sits a cluster of headsets and microphones. There are thick wooden blinds hanging at the windows and a deep grey, rustic-brick wallpaper, making the room look simultaneously mysterious and academic. 'Wow. So this is where the magic happens.'

'Exactly right. Mate, this is my *haven*. You could say it's today's equivalent of a man shed. I love it.'

'I've listened to a few of your episodes. They're really good.'

'Thanks.' Will brushes one hand against his jeans. He's wearing the smile I recognise from our dice days – the one that stretches his eyes into slits, his cheeks into apples. 'There's just something about putting out ideas and shared experiences and feeling that you might be making a difference somehow, somewhere, if that makes sense.'

'It does. I was listening to that one about going back in time and changing one thing in your life – it was interesting. I was thinking about my own answer to that, and it wasn't easy.'

'Good, because that's the point. It might have seemed spontaneous, but I gave Danny the questions in advance, so he had plenty of time to prepare. And if you were up for the dice podcast, we could do something similar.'

I smile. 'I do like the idea, but you know… last time—'

'Last time, we were seventeen-year-old twats. We're not the same people now.'

'True. But it *did* get addictive.'

'We'll make sure it doesn't.'

I turn around and look through the doorway at the small kitchen area: all gleaming chrome, a microwave on one shelf, kettle beside the sink. 'You seriously did all of this?'

'Yep.'

I press one hand into the soft leather seat. Jemma's right – this is good for me. I've been replaying our conversation at the park – *male or female?* – and realised her coy smile was carefully designed to hide a flicker of jealousy. If she hadn't already made arrangements to go and see her family in Manchester, I'd have tried harder to persuade her to come this evening. She would love the house, the Kings, the whole podcast idea. We could have talked on the way home about how it would be possible to have a life like theirs, without the additional expense of the flat. 'If we had a house like that, I could have my own massage room,' she'd say. She wouldn't have to put up with dickhead clients. We could give Toby the sibling he'd been asking for, before the Dan Bretti-shaped grenade came crashing into our marriage.

Die Trying

Dan. Fucking. Bretti. I can still feel the raw nub of flesh from where my teeth clamped to the inside of my cheek, waking me in the night; a thin seam of salivery blood trailing across the pillow. In my dream, I'd been throwing hard, fierce punches to Dan's head, but none of them landed. I ended up grasping at his face instead, tearing the skin as easily as if it were a sheet of paper.

'So, you'll do it?' Will asks.

I've already rolled the die; I *know* I will, but I need to be clear what I'm committing myself to. Despite being a 'tech-head' (Spencer's description, although it's entirely possible I misheard), the world of podcasting is unfamiliar. I've downloaded several other podcast series: some informative and thought-provoking, others seemingly pointless – an exercise in conversation for conversation's sake – and one was so breathtakingly misogynistic, I tore my earpods out in disgust, horrified to be associated with a gender that thought talking about women that way was acceptable. 'What kind of things would we tackle? Have you thought about themes?'

'Yes, mate. I thought we could do something funny, but then I came home from work the other day and Claire asked what I wanted to eat, and I just thought: *I'm done*. I couldn't think straight. I'd spent all day making decisions, and now there were more to make. They were stupid, minor ones, but even so, I passed them all back to her. What to eat, what to watch, what to wear. It got me thinking – are modern men… well, and women, I suppose – are they burning out due to decision fatigue? And then I thought maybe it would be better to approach the pod from a male wellness perspective.' The microphone is switched off, but Will leans down to speak into it, affecting a gruff voiceover tone. '*Join us on a journey as we leave life's energy-sapping decisions up to chance. Will the die optimise our lives, or destroy them?*'

'I like that.'

'I knew you would. So, you'll do it?'
'Yes. I'll do it.'

As we sit down to discuss logistics, I can't help thinking of the Einstein quote that always sprung to mind, years ago, when it felt as though things were moving in the right direction. *'God does not play dice with the universe.'* If Will and the die have come back into my life for a reason, maybe my separation from Jemma is also a test: *how much do you love your wife? What would you do to get her back?*

Anything. I'd do anything.

Will suggests taking the same structure for the podcast that he uses for *Chaos* – a different topic to debate every week – then asks how I feel about rolling the die live on air at the end of each episode.

I draw a sharp intake of breath. 'Risky.'

'Not really. We'd be the final arbiters, and it'll be easy to filter out anything that doesn't fit our spiel.' Will lifts one foot and places it on the opposite knee, reminding me – as if I ever needed it – that he is still in the alpha camp, relaxing in the comfort of his kingdom. He suggests a 'face your fears' week, a 'truth' week, another episode challenging our morality. 'We could delve into themes of self care, optimising performance, positive masculinity. Being vulnerable.'

This, from the man who didn't cry at Abbie's funeral. 'Are we going to include resources about gambling responsibly? And just in case... some kind of addiction support, because we both know—'

'Yeah. Most definitely.' Will grabs a notepad and pencil from the shelf behind him, just as Claire appears at the door to tell us that dinner's ready.

As he snaps off the light, I notice a small black mark, like a burn, near the top of the wall. It looks out of place against the clean, pale paintwork. And then a memory rises: the dent in Will's bedroom wall, his furious denial to his parents that he had anything to do with it, his private confession to me that the die had ordered him to throw a paperweight. 'Technically, it wasn't me,' he insisted. 'You said it yourself – we're not in control.'

In the dining room, we eat chicken with olives and roasted butternut squash. Claire asks about our 'dice days,' eager to know about the man her husband was before she met him. I give her the edited version, finding myself suddenly fascinated by a knot in the wood on the table between us. It looks like a cow's eye. Or a planet, surrounded by whorls. 'So, in *The Dice Man* book,' Will says, reaching for the pepper, 'The main character uses dice to make random decisions and detach from his identity. He was a bit of a...'

'Dick?'

'*Molly.*'

'Well, was he?'

'Yeah,' Will admits. 'He was a dick.'

'Oh,' Claire says, topping up her wine. 'Is that a good idea, to detach from your identity? Is it even *possible*?'

'Of course not.' Will shrugs. 'It's fiction. When we were doing it, we were just a pair of teenagers, having fun. Although we *did* push ourselves to do things we weren't comfortable with.'

'Like what?'

Will laughs. 'I'm not telling *you* that, Molls.'

'I'm not sure we want to know,' Claire says, and she's right; they don't. I've thought about Will over the years, and always imagined him alone, enjoying a life unencumbered by commitments. But here he is. Mature, resourceful, planning a family. Refusing Claire's offer of a second glass of wine because he wants to go for a run in the morning.

The evening wears on, and Will talks about the circumstances of how they met – in a London Costa, when Claire asked to borrow his phone charger 'just for a few minutes' and says he must have done something right, because she ended up going home with him. Claire leans towards him, her hair caressing his shoulder, and explains that the move to Bristol has taken a bit of getting used to, but they're settled now. They're happy. Molly wanders in and out, eyes glued to her phone, and we talk and laugh some more until the wine runs out. Eventually, I realise it's getting late; I should probably get back to the flat.

'Thanks for a great evening,' I tell Will at the door, while Claire goes upstairs to deal with a spider in Molly's room. The earlier pearl sunset has disappeared, leaving the moon peering at us through a sullen black eye.

'Anytime, mate. I'll set everything up and we'll do that test episode next week, if you like. It'll just be a kind of introductory chat to start with, so no need to prepare anything,' Will says. 'Looking forward to it.'

CHAPTER NINETEEN

Jemma

Frankie invites me to her house on Sunday morning 'for coffee and a catch up'. We were going to meet at a café, but she had to wait in for a plumber to fix the downstairs toilet and decided it would be cheaper and easier to meet at hers, which is fine by me, as I'm pretty skint at the moment. She greets me at the door wearing a linen dress printed with lemons, and flat sandals, then invites me through the back of the house to the kitchen, where Matty is opening and closing cupboard doors, complaining about the lack of food in the house. He seems to grow taller and skinnier every time I see him. A gangly creature: half-man, half-child.

'Matthew, you've just *had* breakfast,' Frankie tuts, then shakes her head at his retreating back as he slopes from the room, empty-handed. 'Wait until Toby's that age. They're like bottomless pits.'

'Toby's a bottomless pit now! Takes after his mother – no self discipline.' I slide onto a stool at the kitchen island as Frankie fills the coffee machine with water.

'How was Manchester?' she asks.

'Good. Well… good until Toby announced that Daddy didn't live with us anymore.'

'Oh, no.'

'It's fine. Mum gave me a bit of a lecture about making an effort, marriages have rough patches et cetera, but at least it's out in the open now. I don't like keeping secrets.'

Especially from my family. Dad looked frail, Hannah skinnier than ever – obvious even to Toby, who called her 'skeleton face', earning himself five minutes on the naughty step – and I hated the sense that, somehow, I'd failed them. We were meant to work at things. That was what we did, as a family: Mum continued turning up for her night shifts on the Covid wards throughout both lockdowns, and Dad went off, always whistling, to his job as a prison officer. Even when he got his cancer diagnosis, he told Hannah and me with a confident smile that he would beat it. Then Mum squeezed his hand and said they'd conquer it together. Love: that was the difference. They had a love that didn't leave either of them gasping for air.

Frankie slides a coaster in front of me, then places my coffee on top and sits opposite me. 'So Adam wasn't weird about you going?'

'Do you know what, I think he might finally have accepted that we're not getting back together. He's been in touch with an old friend and they've even been talking about starting a podcast—'

'A *podcast*?'

'I know. Bizarre, right?'

'Is the friend female, by any chance?'

'Exactly what I asked, because I was kind of hoping… But no. Will, I think he said his name was. And it's nice… I feel more relaxed around Adam now I know he's got other things going on in his life, because I still care about him, you know? I just don't feel remotely physically attracted to him, not at all. With Dan, it's like… God, it's *magnetic*.'

'I know. Look at your face.' Frankie laughs. 'Didn't think it was possible for good sex to make you look ten years younger.'

I put my chin in my palms. 'It's not just the sex; we're like the same person. We… this is going to sound corny as hell, but we *get* each other. With Adam, everything's so serious, and he takes things to have a different meaning, when there isn't necessarily... I don't know. I think we'll get on much better as friends than we ever did together.'

'Or not, if Matthew's dad is anything to go by. But you'll be ok. It sounds like you know what you want. You'll get through this, one way or another. You're doing the right thing.'

Rob returns with Blake soon after we finish our coffees, the two of them damp from swimming. Rob says hello, makes himself a cup of tea, then disappears into the lounge where a sudden burst of sound indicates he's put the football on. I slide my mobile into my back pocket and tell Frankie that I'd better get going.

'Off to see Dan?'

'No, he's working, which is a massive shame seeing as I've got the day to myself. It's just going to be washing and ironing instead of... well...' There's a lilt in my tone and I widen my eyes, so she's left in no doubt as to what I mean, but neither is Matty. He comes out of the downstairs study – his gaming room – with a grimace of revulsion.

When he's safely out of sight, we both laugh. 'To be fair, that's the face I pull at the thought of myself naked, too.'

'Stop it!' Frankie gives me a hug. 'He's fifteen, we're basically sexless fossils to him. Anyway, thanks for coming over. I'm so glad you're finally getting your life back.'

Getting my life back. Hasn't that been exactly the problem – the sense that my life has been taken from me in pieces? Or have I given it away? I came across my Art History books the other day and remembered how much I used to love poring over the images at uni, late at night, with a stomach full of cheap food and alcohol: *The Hunt in the Forest, Massacre of the Innocents, The Awakening Conscience.* Gothic architecture with pointed arches, large stained-glass windows and gargoyles leering from above, their ugliness believed to ward off evil spirits. Recently, while massaging clients – especially on days when my back feels crippled with pain – I think of those pictures and knead too roughly, gathering the oiled flesh in folds, leaving dark red indents from my knuckles. Because, yeah, sometimes I feel resentful. Resentful and pissed off at the way some of the clients discard their clothes like impatient emperors before lying on the bed, waiting to be served. Makes me think of Hannah's friend's brother from years ago – the piece of shit who left her with an anal tear and an eating disorder. The *expectation*.

'Don't do it, if you don't like it,' Dan said, when I told him I'd just had to massage a man so large and hairy, it was as if he'd rolled in grass cuttings. 'What would you rather do instead?'

It was then I realised I don't always dislike the job. I've got some lovely clients: there are days we have fascinating conversations, and I learn so much from their injuries that I feel honoured to be able to help. No, it's the claustrophobia of being in a dark room with a body stripped bare. The deep, cellular realisation that, somewhere along the way, I've made choices that never felt like choices at all. Like giving up on my dream of working in a museum. Like moving here. Like keeping Toby. Which sounds – fuck – it sounds terrible, and I love my son to bits; I'd never be without him and would fight to the death anyone that hurt him. But when I found out I was pregnant, Adam told me it was my body and I should do whatever felt right, but then he would show me pictures he'd found online. 'Look, our baby is the size of a pea.' And then, a couple of weeks later, 'the size of a raspberry.' When I said I wasn't sure I was ready, he talked about our baby's incredible brain and nervous system already being formed, and I panicked then, realising things were moving too fast; that the cost of inaction would soon be something huge and life-changing. I would never admit this to anyone now, but I booked an abortion. I thought I'd be able to keep the procedure quiet and pretend to Adam

I'd had a miscarriage. I meant to go through with it, but the steering wheel felt stiff in my hands about a mile up the road and at first, I thought it was just the guilt, making everything heavy. Then I heard the grind and slap of rubber. I pulled over and, before I'd even climbed out to check, a man pulled up alongside me and wound his window down to tell me my tyre was 'flat as a board, love. Too dangerous to drive on.'

Now, of *course* I'm glad that fate stepped in. I have never regretted keeping Toby. But maybe a part of me gave up when Adam asked me to marry him. I thought: *why not?* I was already in this deep. And when he said it made more sense for me to move down south, because his work was here and I'd soon be off on maternity leave and it would be better for our son to grow up in Bristol, again, I thought: *why not?* I wouldn't have to watch Dad's slow deterioration. I wouldn't have to see my sister's trauma, dressed up in baggy clothing and chunky beanie hats. It would be a fresh start.

And yet...

I put the key in the lock and step inside. Breathe. Freedom has a smell, a taste, like grated lime and mountain air. *Getting my life back.*

One step at a time.

I am. I will.

CHAPTER TWENTY

Diecast #Pilot

Diecast, **with Will King and resident host Adam Dowdell: Pilot**

I'm sitting opposite Will in one of the black leather seats in his studio. His voice sounds different as he introduces me on the podcast: confident, controlled, with only a hint of the cockney accent I'm so familiar with.

'I think it's fair to say that we're living in a time when there have never *been* so many options. Right? We're bombarded with choices 24/7: what to eat, what to wear, whether to take that call or reject it. Even which podcast to download.' Will laughs. 'By the time we get to the big decisions – at home, at work, about the *future* – we're literally fried. Modern men are expected to optimise sleep, diet, productivity, gym time, family time, and ultimately we end up spending so much energy deciding how to live, there's none left to actually *live*.'

Will points out that most of us don't burn out from one big choice, but a thousand tiny ones. 'And the worst part? We think it's *normal*. How can we demonstrate healthy masculinity when we're stressed and depressed from all these choices tugging us in different directions, every minute of the day?'

He's good at this. I feel my body relax into the cold leather. And he's right; we're *not* the same people we were at college. I saw the way he was with Claire when I first arrived, fingers sliding around her waist, a gentle kiss on the head, the way he asked if she wanted a drink and promised he wouldn't be long. Respectful. Committed. Nothing like he had been with Abbie, eyes always scouring the immediate surroundings, just in case another attractive girl happened to be nearby.

Will gestures for me to get closer to the microphone and I oblige. 'How relevant are dice in today's tech and digital age? Do you think they'll ever disappear altogether?'

I consider this. 'I doubt it. There's something about holding a physical die that tech can't replicate, or can't replicate well at the moment. I could hit a keyboard, roll virtual dice, but it wouldn't feel as prophetic as holding this one. There's an energy... powerful... like connecting with some other entity.'

'Yes. *Yes*, the energy – we'll come back to that. So, for those listening, Adam and I met at college, back when we were seventeen and knew everything.' He laughs, then explains the rules we 'lived or died by': no rerolls, no option to disobey the die's command, and the six options which remained static, regardless of the situation. We would be using the same system for the podcast – *1= Connection, 2= Do nothing, 3= Discomfort, 4= Truth, 5= Confrontation, 6= Wild card* – providing the framework for each episode's theme. We originally came up with these choices by adapting the Stoic philosophy of limiting unnecessary choices and focusing only on what was within one's control. Will isn't wrong: we *did* think we knew everything.

How wrong we were.

'We'll be choosing a different topic every week, and discussing the outcome of each during the episode that follows, and we'd love for you to participate. This is going to be an interactive show, so play along and send us your videos, messages and clips to let us know how the die has optimised your life. If we roll a six, it's over to you guys for the choices. All we ask is that you don't use your dice for compulsive or harmful behaviour, because that's absolutely *not* what we're about. And if you enjoy our show, please like and subscribe.'

My gaze drifts to the window, where a strand of cloud opens to reveal a patch of blinding sunlight, then folds itself closed, like the hand of a magician. I can't help wondering what Jemma and Toby are doing now. Are they missing me? Jemma certainly seems happier lately; she's been giving me that relaxed, flirtatious smile she always did at the beginning of our relationship – chin dipped, eyes raised – and when I told her about the podcast, she said she was 'truly happy for me'. She said it sounded brilliant. She wouldn't say that if she didn't care.

'So, with that in mind, what dice roll first really went against the grain for you?' Will says, addressing me directly. 'The one that made you feel least comfortable. Your number three.'

I'm ready for this question. I've prepared for it; I want Jemma to hear it. Forget Segway and clichéd, packaged 'date' experiences, I'll remind her of our origin story and show her that I can – and have – lived a little. I take another sip of water from the glass beside me, then lean into the metal microphone grill. 'My tattoo.'

Suddenly, I'm not in the studio anymore, I'm following Will through a glass door littered with designs printed on paper, my heart a wet sock, slapping about inside my chest. I'm staring at the black-and-white chequered floor tiles smattered with black hairs, confirmed to be the yield of a previous customer's 'back, sack and crack' wax. I talk about how the die landed on number six – wild card – for the design. 'It was random, or so I thought. The first picture in the window I laid eyes on – a lizard.'

'Why was that such a big deal for you?'

'I was about to permanently disfigure myself! It was bigger than anything I'd ever done before, and I nearly bottled it. I *did* bottle it, in fact, when the tattoo artist wasn't even halfway through.'

Die Trying

Will's laugh is genuine, not the specially prepared podcast one that sounds like he's trying to clear his throat. 'You bolted out of that chair faster than my stepdaughter through the school gates on a Friday afternoon. But you didn't fail the dice – you got the tattoo. Well, a third of the tattoo. Even if it was just the curl of a lizard's tail.'

'I know. And I eventually grew to love it, because I thought it looked like a Fibonacci sequence. I would never have got it, if it wasn't for the die. My wife said it was one of the first things she noticed about me.' The sun is pouring in through the window now, like warm honey. 'We met on a train from Manchester to Bristol. Her name's Jemma. She always says... she says...'

'You ok?'

I'm so hard for you it hurts. The heat feels like it's splitting my head in two: white hot, sharp as lightning. '*Breathe through it,*' Mum used to say whenever things got too much; her hand a circular saw on my back, round and round and round.

'It's ok, we can stop. Let's stop it there,' Will says, standing so abruptly he almost knocks the microphone from its stand. 'Mate? Do you want to get outside for some air?'

He opens the door. Light rushes in, and now I can stand; the pain is easing. Will calls for Claire, then watches as I grip the doorframe and step out of the studio. 'This isn't a dice thing, is it? You haven't taken—'

'It's not a dice thing.'

'What's wrong? What happened?' Claire appears on the grass outside, her white trousers billowing, eyes frantic with concern, and even in my panicked state, I find myself thinking: *I can't remember the last time a woman looked at me like that.* She wraps her arm around me, ushers me towards the house, this woman who isn't Abbie, and I follow her inside.

CHAPTER TWENTY-ONE

I have the urge to run. Nowhere, anywhere, it doesn't matter. What was I thinking?

I'm back at the flat now, removing my shirt and trousers, wishing the shame was a stain that could be discarded with them. Will and Claire had been kind, sitting me down with a cup of sugary tea and painkillers, listening to me talk about Jemma's rejection with expressions that cycled between empathy and disapproval, but I didn't miss the look that passed between them when I said the break was only temporary. That every relationship has its ups and downs. Claire offered to take me to hospital to get checked out and, when I declined, suggested I stay for lunch. 'It's only pizza, but you're welcome – there's more than enough.'

The die told me to leave.

I pace to the wardrobe and pull out a pair of dark blue shorts which I haven't worn since the time Jemma persuaded me to play football with Rob and the 'boys'. How long ago was that? Two years? Three? I don't remember much of the game, only that I failed to save a single goal.

I slide them over the boxers Jemma bought me that same Valentine's, emblazoned with five hearts and the words: *Excellent, would use again*, written in Comic Sans on the left thigh, with an arrow pointing to the centre.

She made me model them. We both laughed.

I'm not laughing now.

Die Trying

I feel restless. The die is in my jacket pocket, and I draw it free. Yes. *Yes*. It talks to me like this sometimes, urging me to roll. What we want and what we need often turn out to be completely different things, and often it's hard to tell one from the other until we cast the die. Some of the best dice encounters Will and I shared were the ones we feared, or those which past experience had taught us to stay away from.

Three.

Sometimes it happens like that. You get a glimpse, a foreshadowing, like when I played Monopoly with Mum years ago and knew she was going to jail. I'd felt a strange, burning sense of anticipation when she rolled a double three and couldn't stop staring at the policeman's pointed finger on the board. 'Oh no,' she said. Time slowed as the dice tumbled for a second, then third time, and as they came to rest on another double three, I had an overwhelming sense that somehow, through the power of thought, we'd both made it happen. Or maybe not. Maybe we'd glimpsed the faint shadow of a path already determined.

This time, when I arrive at Bretti Rocks, I recognise the black BMW parked directly outside. Dan Bretti suddenly emerges from the building with a younger man – in his twenties, perhaps, wearing a beanie hat, hands shoved deep in pockets. I watch him wave, and just as I'm preparing to roll again, Dan climbs into his car and the younger man goes back inside.

Dan taps at his phone with one hand as he tugs on his seatbelt with the other. Is he texting Jemma? There's a current running through me like heated wire and as I try to steady my hands enough to turn the ignition key, the die tumbles into the footwell.

I leave it there and follow him. Despite staying only a couple of car lengths behind, it's hard to keep up; Dan is a predictably terrible driver. He leaves it too late before merging into the correct lane at roundabouts, doesn't always signal and, on one occasion, drives through an amber light when he should have stopped, creating a huge train of cars between us. As we swing onto the M5, Dan glances in his rear-view mirror and I wonder if he can feel the weight of my thoughts: sulphurous and pulsing, sticky as blood. But there's no recognition. I am invisible to him.

Seven minutes later, we're heading into Patchway. Dan passes the shops, then turns into a residential street. This isn't the address registered to Companies House. I instinctively slow down and when he indicates to pull up on a short strip of pavement peppered with half a dozen houses, I stop in a lay by on the corner and wait for him to get out.

I am ready. All he needs to do is step onto the road.

My foot hovers over the accelerator. I could run him down, right now. There's nobody around apart from an elderly gentleman walking a golden retriever.

But first, the die.

It's in the cup holder, along with a toothpick and an assortment of loose change. I grip it in my palm and picture the number five, so clearly it burns behind my eyes. *Come on.*

Dan gets out of his car, holding his keys between his teeth; rucksack under one arm. The die tumbles back into place.

Two. Do *nothing*?

I almost roll again, but Dan is already walking around the other side of the car. He steps onto the pavement and hits the lock, prompting a chirp and two orange bursts of light. Then he disappears inside the second house on the left, a red-bricked semi with a large glass plaque on the wall beside the door.

Fuck. I punch the steering wheel with both fists, then wrench it to one side, hitting the kerb and making the die bounce from the holder. I don't slow down until my breathing does, and then I turn onto a side street, waiting for my piece-of-shit mobile to connect to the internet, so I can find my way back home.

Where is the die? I unclip my seatbelt and slide back my seat, feeling around in the footwell and under the mat. It must be in the car somewhere – there's nowhere else for it to go. It didn't fall into the gap between the cup holder and the seat, I'm sure of it, but I push my fingers into the uncomfortably tight space anyway.

Nothing.

I lift my phone from the seat to check underneath.

Nothing.

What the hell, as Jemma would say.

Perhaps it rolled behind me. I'm about to get out of the car and open the back door when my phone starts ringing. *Jemma*.

'Hello?'

'Where are you?'

'What?'

'Where are you? You're meant to be taking Toby to McDonald's.'

'That's not today, is it? You said your mum was having him overnight – I thought it was tomorrow.'

'Sorry – I can't... the signal's a bit...'

'Jem?'

'My mum's having him *next* weekend. Where are you?' she repeats, her voice suddenly clear. 'Toby's waiting, he's getting upset, and I'm going to be late for work.'

'Oh God, Jemma, I'm sorry. I must have...' I snap my seatbelt back on. 'I'll be straight there.'

I hang up and tap the details into the satnav. *Home*. Where the heart is. The anger has abated now and a strange, weary sensation is taking its place. I'm about to put the car into gear when I feel it: a hard nub, just underneath the clutch pedal. The die wasn't there before, I'm sure of it. I took off after Dan

Bretti like a fox on a scent and when I think about the journey now, it feels like someone else was holding the wheel. '*How far would we go? How far would we really go, without boundaries?*' Will had asked.

I'm not sure I know the answer to that.

CHAPTER TWENTY-TWO

'A gun?'

'A *Nerf* gun,' Toby says, drawing a chip from its packet. 'And a shark tooth. And a new car and a rocket.'

Beside us, a gaggle of teenage schoolgirls are stabbing at the ordering screen with painted fingernails. Saturdays are usually busy but despite having missed the lunchtime rush, there's still a queue over a dozen deep, and the only table we could find was one with an abandoned, ketchup-smeared tray on it. Toby's birthday isn't for another seven months, but I humour him anyway. 'What car do you want?'

'A Mustang.'

'Very nice, I wouldn't mind one of those myself. Do you think Mummy will buy me a new car on my birthday?'

Toby shakes his head, laughing, and I'm starting to see how his face will look as a teen. The sharpness of his teeth, now seemingly too big for his mouth. A sprinkle of freckles across the bridge of his nose. The way he keeps blinking as if it's a tic – rapidly, squeezing his eyes closed for a fraction too long before he answers a question. It breaks my heart that he's changing and I'm not around every day to witness it. 'No, because you and Mummy aren't married anymore,' he says.

'We are, buddy. We are married.'

Has someone at school said something? Or has Jemma? I want to ask, but he starts rattling off more birthday present ideas. A flying ball, whatever that is. A big white kitten like

Lewis's. A dinosaur egg. I take a bite of my double cheeseburger and thank God the die didn't command me to do anything stupid earlier. I could have been in a police cell now, not sharing lunch with my son. I was thinking about it all the way to the house, and it scared me, how close I'd come to ending Dan Bretti's life.

Jemma's only at work for a few hours, but Toby and I make the most of it. After our late lunch, we wander over to Cabot Circus where he plays with a demo Hot Wheels playset and pokes at bubbles drifting from the nearby bubble machine. There are no tantrums of the kind Jemma keeps talking about. He takes my hand as we head back to the car park and the moment is so tender, so painful, because soon I'll have to say goodbye and I won't see him for another four days. And then, just as we're about to go up the escalator, I see the pop-up flower stand.

It's bursting with colour; a beacon of hope.

'Shall we get Mummy some flowers?'

There's nothing in it for Toby; he wants to go home. But as I reach in my pocket for the die, I remind myself it's not necessary. And probably not wise, given what happened earlier. Things are happening too fast, just like they did before.

Just as I was afraid of.

In the centre of the stand, there's a striking orange bouquet that Jemma will love. She'll be so grateful that I've thought of her, she might invite me to stay for a cup of tea. And she's always saying how tired she is – I could run her a bath and take care of Toby so that she could have an early night.

I hand over a twenty-pound note and tell the florist to keep the change. The bouquet is bigger than my head, and the orange blooms are interspersed with thin, green twisted stems of foliage that look like they've come from another planet. I love that orange is her favourite colour. And I love that I can make these small gestures which say: *I know you.*

Twenty minutes later, at the house, Toby bursts in without waiting for me to knock and I follow him inside, the enormous bouquet brushing against the coats hanging in the hallway. Jemma's in the kitchen. She stops tapping at her phone when she sees the flowers. 'Wow.'

'They're for you.'

'Oh. Thanks. Why?'

Why? The flowers feel heavy, suddenly, in my hand. It's a question I have no answer to. Toby rushes straight upstairs to get his iPad and I take my time removing the Paw Patrol bag from my shoulder. 'How was work?'

'It was fine.'

'You look tired.'

'Oh, *thanks.*'

'No, I didn't mean it like that. I just thought… the flowers, you know, you said you were struggling. You always look gorgeous.'

Jemma gives me a tight smile.

'I could stay for a bit, if you need to get on with anything. I can do his bath and bed—'

'No, no. I'm sure you need to get off and, you know what, I *am* tired,' she says, taking small but not-so-subtle steps towards the bottom of the stairs. '*Toby.* Come down and say goodbye to Daddy.'

And that's how I know I've messed up. Somehow, by stupidly trusting my own judgement, I've messed up.

Again.

CHAPTER TWENTY-THREE

I'm watching TV back at the flat, in semi-darkness. When I got back from Jemma's – *ours*, I must stop thinking of it as hers – the bulb in the lounge was flickering, creating an irritating strobe effect that hurt my eyes. I turned it off, then on again, but the filament had burned out. There were no spare bulbs anywhere; yet another reminder that this place isn't home. It never will be.

I scroll through Dan's social media feed, then Jemma's. Neither has posted on the other's profile. Neither has liked the other's photos – at least, not for several weeks. Maybe the die has worked its magic. Whatever it was between them – if anything – has obviously fizzled out.

I put the phone down and try to focus on the film instead. It's the sort of thing Jemma would like: a romcom with a familiar plot which is watchable, all the same. A young man and woman both work at the emergency unit in a hospital, and the sexual chemistry between them is palpable. They share confidences and flirtations during their breaks and come close to starting a relationship, but something always stands in their way. An alarm, the sudden appearance of a colleague, her pulling away at the start of a kiss upon the realisation that a sick patient is lying the other side of the wall. And then the arrival of a new love interest, Iris, who is sexy and electrifying, but I hate her – I'm supposed to hate her – because she stands in the way of the two protagonists destined to be together.

There's a row, someone moves away, and for a while it all looks hopeless until a terrorist attack happens in the heart of the city. The man confronts the suspect, courageously grasping him by the throat then throwing him to the ground, while around them sirens scream and people scatter in all directions. In a tense moment, the terrorist pulls a knife, and in the next scene our hero is unresponsive, presumed dead, until he arrives at the hospital and... oh, I know the ending. I already know the ending, because it wouldn't work any other way. He's treated by his original love interest in her new place of work, and she's so distraught she won't leave his side for a moment, not even when her shift finishes and a superior comes to admonish her. I'm so engrossed, sitting there in the dark, that I almost forget I'm not at home with Jemma's head resting in my lap, heavy as a watermelon.

When it ends – shortly after a 'five years later' scene, when the reunited couple are embracing at the kitchen sink, looking out to their children playing on the lawn – I feel curiously uplifted. The moral of the story is clear: every relationship will face conflict, but things will work out exactly as they're supposed to in the end.

No wonder Jemma didn't want the flowers. She seems to like me best when I'm *not* making her the centre of my world, and perhaps this is what she's been saying all along – she wants a chance to miss me. To see me afresh. I think back to the park, and how she'd fingered my polo shirt. '*This is nice, is it new?*' And then, when I'd been on the phone to Will, she was curious. Maybe even a little jealous. '*Male or female?*'

I get up and instantly stub my toe on the corner of the sofa. When the sharpness of the pain subsides, I grip the corner of the sofa and hobble to the kitchen. One day, Jemma and I will laugh at this. I'll tell her about the blown bulb and how I managed to simultaneously stub my toe and kick over a glass of water, and what a fitting metaphor it seemed for my life at that point. 'Thank God we got through it,' she'll say, wistfully. 'We almost lost everything.'

I clean up the spill with a wad of kitchen roll, then roll the die.

Two. *Do nothing.* I'm not allowed to contact Jemma again tonight. I roll again. Two.

It rejects the suggestion of reading, listening to another podcast episode, watching TV or taking a shower, in favour – finally – of rearranging the flat.

It seems pointless, but after twenty minutes of shifting the sofas – carefully avoiding my feet and the wet patch – switching the cutlery in the drawer, taking out the cleaning products under the sink and moving the bed so that it's facing the wardrobe instead of the door, it's surprising what a difference it makes. The flat feels bigger, and no longer looks like the punchline to a joke about life. Or death.

Nothing bad happens. Even when I roll twice more to decide what to eat – toast and butter – and what to watch on TV in the last hour before bed, nothing bad happens. Why would it? The die only ever responded to our method of questioning, and I'm not using it to indulge in shitty, immoral behaviour, as Will admitted to doing in the past.

Is it likely to become a compulsion? Maybe.

But being myself has got me nowhere.

Over the next few days, I stop worrying about whether I'm using the die too little or too much. On Tuesday, it orders me to drink a mug of coffee with six sugars, then get dressed for work.

Black suit, black tie, black trousers. The outfit I wore to Mum's funeral.

I'm early. Seb is the only one in the office when I arrive, and he's left his office door open. He looks up from his desk, and then – probably because I haven't brought any cakes into work, as seems to be the custom most mornings – returns his focus to his laptop without saying a word. At ten to nine, Paula drifts in holding a takeaway Costa cup, followed by Miles and Katya five minutes later. And then Spencer. I've just remembered why I don't wear this shirt anymore: the top button is too tight. I'd fiddled with it continuously at Mum's funeral, virtually strangling myself as I tried to hold the Order of Service with one hand and undo the button with the other. It was only later, when I saw the redness around my throat, that I realised it had really happened. Mum had gone.

I would have chosen the same suit I wore to Abbie's funeral, had I not disposed of the hideous navy jacket and trousers the moment I got home. Abbie's parents had asked everyone to attend dressed in something bright, which just went to show that they didn't know her at all. The last time I saw her at Will's house, she'd been sitting on the beanbag in his lounge as he went to make drinks: black boots with the chunky heels stretched out in front of her, a thread from her home-knitted jumper catching on the zip as she talked. She'd eventually forgiven me for 'disrespecting' Elisha, who now had a new boyfriend – a gothic-styled weirdo called Pete, with a nose ring and hair that made a windowpane of his face – and now seemed completely at ease in my company. She shifted on the beanbag, and it made a sound like the ocean. 'It scares me,' she said, 'thinking about where we're all going to be, a few years from now. Don't you just wish time could stand still so we could stay like this forever?'

I thought I'd been the only person terrified of what lay ahead, but Abbie understood. And I was angry with Will then because, over Abbie's shoulder, I could see him in the garden. He wasn't making drinks. He was on the phone to Lily. *'Die's orders,'* he'd winked earlier, after spending the night in her bed.

I hated him for that. I hated that Abbie would have to go through the pain of his betrayal.

And I can still remember the shock at hearing her name coming from the disembodied black mouth of the home radio, two weeks later. 'You didn't see anything when you were out last night, did you?' Mum said. 'That girl from your college has gone missing. They're appealing for witnesses.'

Kat's mouth is wide open, laughing at something Spencer has said. I walk to the printer, and the expression Spencer gives me – of faint amusement, superiority – is identical to the one Dan wore when I came to the house. 'Jesus Christ,' he says. 'What are you wearing?'

I slip my hand into my pocket, where the die is resting against a folded tissue. Five. I slide my prints from the top of the machine, then take a step towards Spencer, so close I can smell his aftershave. I am the upstanding hero from last night's story, showing courage in the face of terrorism. Spencer's expression changes to one of surprise, then fear, as my hand reaches for his neck, scrunching a handful of expensive white fabric. 'Why don't you go fuck yourself?'

CHAPTER TWENTY-FOUR

'Why don't you go *fuck* yourself?' Jemma's eyes are wide. 'You actually said that?'

'I actually said that. In an American accent.'

Jemma laughs. She turns back to the bubbling saucepan and stirs the pale fingers of pasta inside. 'Not like you to bust his balls, but he probably had it coming. Good for you.'

Every week, I look forward to Wednesday. Or more specifically, Wednesday night, when I can go home and for several glorious hours, pretend we're still a family. Jemma cooks, so it doesn't feel like I'm there just to bath Toby and read him a bedtime story. She's still wearing her wedding ring. The flowers are sitting in a vase on the windowsill. I take a clutch of knives and forks from the cutlery drawer and think about how good it felt, watching the skin around Spencer's collar corrugate into reddened cords. The shock on his face.

Immediately afterwards, Spencer had muttered something about me being dead, but I wasn't – I was very much alive. He went back to his desk and I went back to mine. Seb had popped out to pick up his usual breakfast baguette from the van along the street and as soon as he returned, Spencer went in to see him. It was no surprise when I got the email from Seb half an hour later, asking me to pop into his office for a chat.

'I've received a serious allegation from Spencer Redgrave,' Seb said, using the tip of a thick finger to press his glasses upwards where they settled into a red dent at the top of his nose. 'He said that you swore at him and attacked him in an unprovoked assault.'

I wanted to laugh at how ridiculous it sounded. *Me.* Yes, of course I understood the seriousness of the incident. Yes, I appreciated that there would be an investigation. I thanked Seb – for what, I wasn't sure – and nodded gravely when he explained that I would be suspended immediately on full pay. And when I stood, looking down at the circular patch of thinning hair on the top of his head, there was a tingling sensation, like thousands of kisses all over my skin.

We eat dinner at the dining table. The die is snug in my jeans pocket, hot from the warmth of my thigh, and I find my fingers drifting to it every so often to check it's there, like a winning lottery ticket. Toby keeps sniffing: mouth closed, two sharp intakes of breath. He looks like his mother but I wonder how much of my DNA is lurking inside, because I used to do the same. It drove Mum mad. She took me to a doctor who explained the behaviour away as a tic, rather than any medical issue, and eventually it stopped. I never found out why it happened, or what caused it.

'Toby got the gold sticker again on Monday. Did you tell Daddy about that, Tobe?'

'I got it for my counting,' Toby says. 'And I got Maths monkey.'

'Well done, buddy.'

'Got Daddy's maths skills,' Jemma says, cocking an eyebrow. She has this way of making innocent things sound naughty. Is she flirting with me? *Fucking* with me?

I do not respond.

'Toby, don't you dare.' Jemma's voice hardens now. I know that tone. Toby sees it as a challenge, not a warning, and continues to attempt sliding from the chair until she erupts: '*Sit back down and eat your dinner.*'

He doesn't move. His eyes slide between us. At four years old, he knows far more than he should and controls his world the only way he can. Jemma used to get frustrated when I wouldn't get involved with discipline, partly because I didn't want to undermine her authority but mostly because I was afraid of getting things wrong. Just as I am now.

My fingers slide over the die in my pocket. One. It's a risk, but I hold up the die anyway, telling Toby that whatever it lands on is the number of mouthfuls he has to eat before he can get down from the table. 'You've hardly touched your dinner,' I add, glancing at Jemma to gauge her response. She used to complain that I wouldn't back her up in arguments, that 'sitting there in silence to avoid confrontation is not joint parenting.'

Her mouth is full, but she lifts her eyebrows in surprise. And possibly, approval.

'We can play the chocolate game afterwards,' I tell Toby, and this is all the encouragement he needs. He rolls, he eats three mouthfuls of pasta, and Jemma drops her fork onto her plate to admire the die.

'That looks like crystal,' she says. 'Where did you get it from?'

'It was in my box of old stuff from the loft.'

'I found it,' Toby says. 'And I ated my pasta. Can we play the chocolate game now?'

'In a minute.'

When we've finished, I collect our plates and load the dishwasher, then Jemma pours herself a glass of wine. The chocolate game, as its name suggests, involves a large bar of chocolate – which I bought on the way here – and a variety of props: scarf, hat and gloves, and a knife and fork. We played it at Toby's last birthday party in the Jubilee Centre, and at the time I kept looking at the clock, the hands of which seemed stubbornly to cling onto the minutes, as the screams and shouts of the children rose to a feverish pitch. The die got passed and rolled, passed and rolled, and whenever someone cast a six, the props were torn off and flung in a different direction, the chocolate chopped with the knife and fork and gorged for as long as it took for someone else to claim the prize. By the end of it, a migraine had set in. Jemma complained afterwards about the convenient timing of my 'headache', not realising the game had triggered something huge and monstrous. 'You think I like clearing shit up, either?' she demanded. 'Well, I don't. Go and hand out the party bags.'

This time, with only three people, the game is more orderly. The dishwasher rumbles behind us as we push the die around the table. Toby rolls the first six. He pulls on the hat, gloves and scarf and stabs at the chocolate with the knife, fighting to get a piece to his mouth without it falling off the fork. Jemma takes another sip of wine and laughs; she's more relaxed than I've seen her for ages. There are clothes hanging flat on the radiators – Toby's half-sized jeans and Fireman Sam pyjamas, a couple of Jemma's work blouses – and occasionally I get a whiff of Ocean Breeze leaking from their fibres. When the die lands on one, I lean closer to my wife. A three, and I turn around, toss the die over my head or through my legs. On five, I accuse Toby of cheating, and I wait for a four, so I can tell Jemma I love her.

I watch my wife and son. I relax. I laugh, because they do not know that this is more than just a game.

For the first time, I feel like everything might be ok.

Later, after getting Toby out of the bath, I sneak into our bedroom to grab a towel from the airing cupboard. Jemma's still downstairs finishing her second glass of wine: I can hear the pizzicato strings of *The Great British Bake Off* seeping through the floor. For some reason, I feel guilty being in here, even though I'm still paying half the mortgage. Both pillows are dented, as though compressed by invisible human heads, which doesn't necessarily mean anything – Jemma often rolls over to my side during the night. Below that, there's an open book, spread-eagled on top of the pillow: *Hostage*.

'Daddy,' Toby calls.

'Just coming.'

It doesn't take a minute to pull the die from my pocket. Six again. Sixth page, sixth line.

Emergency services are on their way, caller.

What the hell does that mean?

'*Daddy.*'

I put the book back in its place. I rush back to the bathroom, then I wrap my son in the huge green towel and cuddle him so tightly that, for a few moments, all I can see are stars.

CHAPTER TWENTY-FIVE

Before I moved out of the family home, if Jemma and I talked about time, it was only to lament how little we had of it. Every Sunday evening, Jemma would ask where the weekend had gone; on weekday evenings our messages to each other would be frequently peppered with requests. 'If you've got time, could you…' She spoke about it as a concept essential to our health, like air or water. There was never enough of it, and what little we had was apparently the wrong quality.

Perhaps my temporary suspension from work isn't misfortune, but an opportunity. Because now I have all the time in the world.

On Friday afternoon, Jemma rings just as I'm pulling up outside the gym. She can't see me, but I check my appearance in the rear-view mirror anyway and wipe a thin string of banana from my lip before answering.

'Hello?'

'Hi.'

'Is everything ok?'

'Toby's fine. I just wanted to talk to you about arrangements for tomorrow. Are you ok to pick him up at ten instead of eleven? Mum didn't realise she'd booked to go back on a specific train.'

'I'll be there. Where did you say you were going tonight?'

'None of your business,' Jemma says, and then laughs. 'It'll be a late one, so might see you in the morning, might not. How come you aren't at work?'

'Oh, I...' I've been trying not to think about the email I received from Seb earlier, confirming that my disciplinary hearing will be held on Monday morning. He'd attached the Company Disciplinary Procedure, and evidence of my 'assault' in the form of a lengthy statement from Spencer. There were two additional witness statements which I didn't bother opening. 'I'm at the gym. I've got the day off.'

'Oh, nice. Alright for some.'

'I can get Toby from school later, if you like?'

'No, it's fine, my mum will be here then. She'll probably want to take him out for something to eat.'

A ponytailed woman in leggings passes the car, bumping the wing mirror with her oversized sports bag. *Emergency services are on their way, caller.* 'Jem?'

'Yeah?'

'Take care tonight, won't you?'

She hates it when I say things like that. She hates it, and I say it anyway.

'I'm going now,' she says. 'Have a good workout.'

Later, back at the flat, I've just made an omelette for tea when Jemma calls again. I place it on the side, keen to tell her about my gym session. She'll laugh when I tell her about the woman on the spin bike who screamed at everyone to 'go faster,' and the girl opposite who wiped her face with her t-shirt and muttered something about not knowing they were on the Waltzers. I want to tell her about the man who stood in front of the mirror and posed with the heaviest weight available, before tripping on a curl of upturned carpet. I've been enjoying the way my belt loops easily into the next hole, watching the soft pads of flesh either side of my chin give way to a sharper, well-defined jawline, and when I caught a glimpse of my topless body on my way through the changing rooms, I realised that I no longer felt powerless.

Quite the opposite, in fact.

My heart does a small bounce as I slide my finger across the screen. I think about saying something provocative: *'you again'*, or *'missing me already?'* but I don't have time to roll the die and the standard greeting slips from my tongue, like a slipper from a foot. Easy. Comfortable. 'Hello?'

At first, I think she's in trouble. Jemma's inaudible whispers are followed by a series of bumps and scuffles, a gasp. 'Jem?' I say, then with more urgency, '*Jem.*'

And then, she speaks. 'Oh God, yeah,' she says. Her breath is coming in heavy, ragged gasps. I hear a wet, slapping sound, followed by a low groan. 'Turn over,' a male voice says.

I keep listening, even as I feel the bile burn the back of my throat. I want it to stop. It doesn't. It goes on and on, the sounds becoming louder, more frantic. Squeaking. Thudding. A slopping noise, like the stirring of too-thick gravy.

Why am I still listening? There's a tightness radiating from my neck, all the way down both arms, and my chest feels like it's slowly being crushed by a giant tyre. A monster truck, on top of me.

Oh Jemma. Oh Jemma.

I cut the line.

Steam is still rising from my omelette, glistening and slowly shrivelling on the plate. It looks like an organ. Why did she tell me she loved me, when all along…

I reach for the die. I *want* to die.

I grab my keys and head outside.

CHAPTER TWENTY-SIX

It's bitterly cold.

The water is below me, a roiling mass, moving gently. Apart from a couple walking arm in arm up the Brunel Way footpath, there's no-one else around.

Turn over.

Jemma lied. She wasn't '*out with the girls*', she was fucking Dan Bretti – noisily, hungrily – and if she's lied about that, what else has she lied about? Our separation being temporary? Loving me? What if Dan Bretti isn't just a test of our marriage, and she's supposed to be with him? Or – worse still – what if Will is right: the die is meaningless, and fate doesn't exist? If this is all mere coincidence and we are just drifting around, bumping into one another, procreating at random, passing time until reaching the black void of death, what then? What would be the point in anything?

There's a strange taste at the back of my throat. To my right, the Avon Gorge is alive with colour, the lights from the houses and Clifton Suspension Bridge making a glittering patchwork of the water. On my left, the dark tongue of the Cumberland Basin curls out of sight. I think of the footage on the news that night, ten days after Abbie went missing. Mum was out with Paul and I'd been sitting on the sofa, eating a microwaveable shepherd's pie that she'd left in the fridge with a note telling me to '*have a fun evening!*'. The newsreader solemnly talked about spending cuts and the decommissioning of an aircraft carrier, and I was about to change channels when the subject switched abruptly to footage of two police vans and an ambulance on the bridge, throwing malevolent swathes of red and blue light across the screen.

And then, the newsreader's solemn tones: '*A body has been found tonight in the search for missing teenager Abbie Reynolds…*'

A body. Her body.

I look down again. The water is lapping lazily against the concrete wall. This used to be the main entrance to Bristol docks, acting as a junction between the harbour and the River Avon – a place of transition and limbo – and it feels tragically symbolic that Abbie's life ended here.

Turn over.

My hand reaches into my pocket. Perhaps Jemma's infidelity was karma. Perhaps all of this is exactly what I deserve. *I am the problem.* I could call and confront Jemma, but I know exactly how things would unfold: she'd suggest 'a meeting' to talk about contact arrangements, formalising maintenance payments, selling our home – as if we were business partners, not a husband and wife who once promised to love one another 'til death us do part'.

Death would have been easier. Death *would* be easier.

It hurts to breathe. It hurts to see.

The wind is a claw at my hair, raking through my thoughts. If the die commands me to, I will jump.

Don't think, just do.

The concrete is uneven, and there's a moment of panic when I think the die is going to tumble into the water, but it rights itself, bounces backwards, then comes to rest against a black metal cleat.

Two.

Not tonight, then. Not here. Not now.

Not like Abbie.

The cold is driving out of the open mouth of the gorge, cutting through my clothes and making my eyes burn. I turn my back to the water and look at the empty face of the underpass. Do nothing. Withdraw. Sometimes, I hate the die, because I should have killed Dan Bretti when I had the chance. I'm tempted to throw it in the river and drive home to slaughter them both, but then I remember Toby.

The thought of my son makes a whimper escape. I get back in the car and scrub at my face with a damp sleeve before starting the engine.

The Black Dog is half a mile along the road, and it beckons to me with a swaying wooden sign. Green and black paint is peeling from the frames of the windows, and the legs of the picnic benches outside are half consumed in a patch of overgrown grass. It looks like the kind of pub where people go to find trouble, or cause it.

I step inside. The floor is sticky as I walk to the bar, my shoes make disgusting noises that remind me of Jemma's phone call. The barman takes his time drying a glass before taking my order. 'Double scotch, please.'

He points at the card machine, then turns to pour the drink without saying a word. Behind me, one of the men raises his cue to the pool table and strikes the balls, sending a gunshot-crack through the heavy thud of the background rock music. I shuffle to a table, trying not to think about my wife having sex with Dan Bretti. *Turn over.*

I down the Scotch.
Turn over.
I order another.
Turn over.
Two pints of bitter.

Die Trying

Turn over.

The light becomes harder, sharper, and it dawns on me that an hour has passed in no time at all. I swirl the ice in my glass. The pub is filling up now and I'm vaguely aware of a man with a long, dark beard and Metallica t-shirt removing a couple of the chairs from my table and taking them to the other side of the room. Conversations swirl around me: about money, the state of the country, the cunt of a prime minister who put them here, and I find myself focusing on the green-and-red striped socks of the man standing at the bar; the way his ankle moves mechanically backwards and forwards as he talks. In the toilets, the light is too bright, the floor a moving carousel, and I sway against the urinal, waiting for relief. Behind me, the door clangs shut and a man pisses beside me; great, stinking jets of yellow that rebound against the porcelain, splashing my jeans.

The soap dispenser is empty. The water emerges from the taps as a choking splutter. The hand dryer roars, then immediately falls silent. I put my hand in my pocket.

Four

'I kill...' I try to say, but my mouth isn't working properly; words feel rubbery. 'Killed. S'a truth. I got to tell you... I killed—'

'What did you say?'

I don't answer. My hands are still wet. For no reason whatsoever – perhaps from fear – I laugh.

And then I'm outside, my mouth thick with the taste of damp pennies. The die has fucked me. My wife has fucked me. And I think the barman might have fucked me, because I'm pretty sure there was another twenty in my wallet that isn't there now. I pause beside a picnic bench, wondering if I'm going to throw up. The world tilts.

I reach in my pocket for my phone, then drop it on the grass. Passcode. What's my passcode? My fingers have become huge and unwieldy, useless as mushrooms.

I slide sideways, onto the ground. It's almost a relief, feeling the cool brush of grass, looking up at the dark safety net of the night sky. The same sky that, centuries ago, Neanderthals gazed up at in wonder. All of us, pieces on the same playing board.

CHAPTER TWENTY-SEVEN

Jemma

What a night.

We went for food at Za Za Bazaar, followed by drinks along the waterfront, where we bumped into Dan's sister, Beth. I recognised her straightaway from the photo, except this time she wore huge blonde curls pinned up on top of her head, jeans and a shimmery black blouse printed with tiny red cherries. She gave me one of those hugs that leaves you momentarily breathless, then flattered me by saying I was a vast improvement on Dan's ex, before adding – less flatteringly – that she was a 'psycho'.

'Really?' I said, squashing up around the circular table as Dan headed back from the toilets. 'In what way?'

'Ugh, she was just so *needy*. Texting and calling all the time, to the point where Dan had to get a new phone and change his number,' Beth said. 'Total nightmare. And when she started leaving hundreds of fake reviews for the business, we had to get the police involved. It left him so stressed and depressed, I didn't think he'd ever trust anyone again. But here you are!'

'Here I am.'

'Well, then. Welcome.'

We clinked glasses. I wanted to say I'd been going through the same thing, but it wasn't the same at all. Adam's been happier and fitter lately, to the point where I genuinely thought he'd accepted our split (and obviously, he's never harassed me at work) so I said nothing. It was hard to talk over the bass thump of music anyway, but Beth leaned over again, beckoning for my ear. '*Neither* of us could go through shit like that again. At least, not on my watch.'

I tried to work out if there was any shard of a threat in her words, before deciding there wasn't. And if there was – so what? If Hannah ever decided to date again, I might say something similar to her partner. I lifted my glass again – in solidarity, a silent understanding – and after that, the conversation lightened. Dan's friend Steve asked if I climbed, and I told him I didn't. No, I didn't hike either, although I'd like to. Dan admitted that we had literally nothing in common, yet somehow, we worked. I put my hand on his thigh. 'Come on. You love Abba, really.'

He doesn't love Abba – he loves eighties rock, soft metal and indie bands. He loves thrillers, fantasy books and being outdoors. And yes, we worked, because Dan knew how to take the piss out of himself: admitting that his nickname at the climbing centre was Double O '*as in 007*', and loved his friends and family in a way that felt almost tribal. Dan put his arm around me from time to time, kept me topped up with drinks without fretting over my alcohol levels, and didn't keep a close eye on me in case I was stolen away. Instead, he subtly checked whether I was ok with occasional nods and gestures.

I was ok. I was more than ok. We caught a taxi back to Dan's house just before midnight, and after checking in on Mum and Toby, I realised Dan had already fallen asleep. I watched him, taking in the thin lines across his forehead, the relaxed curve of his lips, the dark pinhead dashes of stubble pushing through his chin. I thought of the way he groaned when I massaged his tight shoulder. 'So, you fix people?' Beth had asked, when I said I was a sports massage therapist. For some reason, then, I thought of Adam. *Not always, no.*

Now, someone is banging nails into the wall with a hammer.

'*Whatthefuck?*' Dan flings back the covers as though he's been stung. I grab my phone, thinking of Toby – is it Mum, has something happened? – and there are, there are twelve missed calls, but not from Mum.

Adam.

Dan is yanking on a pair of boxers, bending and stretching, too fast, the leg won't go in the hole. He steadies himself with a hand on the radiator, and then, through the letterbox, the shouting starts.

'*Fucking... kill you...*'

'Jesus Christ it's a nutter. Don't go down, I'll call the police. Is it 999 or 101? I can never—'

We both hear the words that ring out next: '*... my wife.*'

'Oh my God.' I put my hand on Dan's forearm. 'I think it's Adam.'

'Adam? Your ex?'

'Yeah.'

'I thought you said—'

'I know. He's not normally... wait, let me check. Don't go down yet.'

I move into the spare room, where Dan's laptop is propped on a desk in front of the window, and lift the curtain. If it is Adam, and he looks up now, he'll see me. Here, in Dan's house, in a lilac satin nightslip.

It's hard to tell who it is from this viewpoint. The man is staggering away from the door, and there's a streak of mud down the back of his t-shirt which I momentarily mistake for a pattern. I can't see his face. It's only when he drops something and stumbles against Dan's car as he bends to pick it up that I can make out his profile.

Die Trying

Fucking hell. 'It *is* Adam.'

Dan is standing beside me now; I can feel the warmth from his body, radiating against my shoulder. We watch as Adam lurches falteringly up the road. He reminds me of a ship navigating rough weather.

'How does he know where I live? Shall I go and talk to him?'

'I don't know. No.' I remember the look on Adam's face when he told me he'd told Spencer Redgrave to 'go fuck himself'. Like someone was pumping him up from the inside, puffing his cheeks, lifting his mouth into a grim smile.

'Shall I call the police?'

'No. No, let me... I'll talk to him.' I pick my phone up off the floor, where it's lying in a tangle of fabric with my underwear, trousers, and the olive top I wore last night. It rings six times, then goes to answerphone. 'Honestly, this really isn't like him at all.'

Dan looks worried. He could almost certainly take Adam in a fight, but I'm no longer sure of Adam's intentions, or how far he would go. Fury can create almost superhuman strength – I should know. It's precisely why I can't call the police. There's a chance they'll dig around and find that *I've* got a record, which could lead to me losing my job, or even Toby. I don't know how these things work, but I'm not taking any chances. 'Do you want me to leave?'

'No, of course not,' Dan says. 'I just... I never wanted things to be messy. Is he violent? Has he ever hurt you?'

No, never, I'm about to say, and then I remember the coffee table. I never thought that was deliberate at the time, but he *was* forceful. I repeat that this isn't like Adam at all, but perhaps it is. That tiny square of paper I found just inside the front door the other day. I'd disregarded the brief consideration that Adam might have opened my mail, thinking myself paranoid. *Had* he been better lately, or just better at operating by stealth? Happier, because he was operating in plain sight?

I carefully slide my phone from the stand and send Mum a message instead, asking her to let me know if Adam turns up. *Fuck.* Why can't he just leave me alone? I feel like something terrible is thundering towards me, and I won't be able to stop it, no matter how hard I try.

CHAPTER TWENTY-EIGHT

Adam

It takes me a while to figure out where I am.

No sheets or blankets. The sofa. I'm freezing cold.

I urge my body onto its side, disgusted at my lack of control, the paleness of my sweating skin, the feel of my lips – cracking and crusted with dribble – as I run my tongue around them. A slab of pain swells in my head.

What time is it? What happened? Where's the die?

My wallet is lying in a damp patch on the carpet next to an overturned glass of water, and I grope around it frantically. There it is. Tiny, firm, ageless. I can remember wanting to speak to Jemma, but have no idea if I made the call, or whether I mentioned what I heard her doing on the phone last night. My only memory after leaving The Black Dog is of sitting in a taxi and asking the driver if he'd mind slowing down, at which point he became angry. 'You be sick?' he demanded. 'You sick, you pay £100.'

My body feels hot and jumpy, as though full of boiling frogs. I'm trying not to think about all the double shots I consumed last night, or the sound of Dan Bretti's low, primal growl. *Turn over.*

Turn over.
Turn over.

Die Trying

I rush to the bathroom, where I throw up and miss the toilet pan by inches, spattering brown liquid all over my bare feet.

I must have gone to bed after that, because when I wake for the second time, the room is flooded with light and I'm lying on top of the duvet, still fully dressed in last night's clothes. There's a burning sensation at the back of my throat and I'm soaked through with sweat. My alarm clock is flashing 00:00, and I wonder if I accidentally turned it off during the night. Or maybe there was a power cut. And beside it, the die, pulsing with a red glow.

It's only when I peel off my clothes, disgusted by their sour, musky scent, and head into the bathroom that I remember the vomit. I scrub the floor clean using the washing up bowl and a bottle of bleach, then step under the shower and pull the curtain closed. I feel suddenly claustrophobic and dizzy, unable to see or think clearly through the stench of bleach and condensation running down the walls. I swipe the curtain to one side and in the mirror, my lip is fattened and split, with a piping of dried blood marking a route from one nostril to the corner of my mouth: *you are here*. When I reach for the towel on the radiator, my phone clatters to the floor.

It's 11.43. There are eight missed calls from Jemma and a string of text exchanges. I scroll up through the messages, which begin shortly after 1am.

Jemma: `What the hell were you doing at Dan's?`
Jemma: `Where are you now?`

I replied at 2.06am, declaring my love for her. And then, when she didn't reply, I sent a second: `Fuck off.`

After that, my messages become increasingly nonsensical.
`Ugly prick of brat.`
`There issue show you dont know.`
Jemma: `What the fuck is wrong with you?`

The call lasted one minute and twenty-seven seconds. I can't remember a word of it. Anything I said or did after the taxi ride is completely unreachable, as though the driver took us through a black tunnel and lobotomised me in the process. Jemma messaged me afterwards, saying she agreed that we both needed to get some sleep. Then there was a seven-hour gap, followed by the missed calls and four further messages.

Jemma: `You up?`

Jemma: `You said you'd still be ok for this morning...`

Jemma: `For fuck's sake, Adam. Toby's waiting, and my mum has to go. Where are you?`

Jemma: `Fine. Don't bother. I'll sort things out, as usual.`

There's a voicemail too, but I don't need to listen to know that it'll be Jemma, her fury blowing a hole through my speaker for letting our son down. I feel sickeningly sober. Did I confront her about what I heard last night? Jemma's phone clicks straight to answerphone when I try to call her back, and I dry myself roughly before heading back to the bedroom. The die suddenly looks like an ordinary glass cube, spotted with black pips. *Fuck you too*, I think. *Fuck you*. It might as well be a lump of cheese. I throw it against the opposite wall as hard as I can.

Ten minutes later, I'm walking to Jemma's, having dressed so quickly my clothes are sticking to me and my face is still flushed from the heat of the shower. I am not the kind of man who goes to the roughest pub in town and drinks spirits by the double. I'm not the kind of man who gets punched by a stranger, vomits on the floor and breaks promises to his son.

The die was meant to lead me back to Jemma, not make things worse.

Her car isn't on the drive; nor is her Mum's. I knock anyway, then peer through the letterbox just in case she's in the bath or on the phone and hasn't heard me. Toby's Fireman Sam wellies are lined up in the hallway beside Jemma's Converse, and I can smell the cherry air freshener that dispenses a no-so-discreet burst every now and then, making the house smell like a sweet shop. I wrestle my phone from the damp cocoon of my jeans pocket and try calling Jemma again.

Where have they gone? Three Brooks, perhaps. I imagine my wife crouching beside Toby at the edge of the pond, flinging seed to the ducks. One of my earliest memories was Mum taking me to a similar place, where a gaggle of geese was joined by a swan and her cygnets. The swan kept swooping towards the flock, pecking great chunks from their feathers, stabbing them with its beak. 'Be careful, it has young,' Mum told me. 'Mothers can be dangerous.'

Even at that young age, I remember being surprised; I'd always thought it was fathers. Perhaps you can't trust anyone.

Jemma calls me back just after I've taken a taxi to collect my car from The Black Dog. It looks derelict by day, the peeling paint glistening against the dark wood frame of the windows, plain white curtains pulled tightly shut. There's a sign inside the glass frame of the door: *Sorry, we are closed*, making me wonder if last night ever happened.

'Hello?'

For one ridiculous moment, I think Jemma might be relieved to hear my voice. So relieved, in fact, that she'd tell me she regretted getting physical with Dan Bretti. She didn't want to. She was drunk; he had a tiny penis, it had all been a terrible, terrible mistake. Toby needs me. *She* needs me. If I just come back...

I hear the dishwasher door slam closed. A beep. The swish and slop of water. *Turn over.* She's angry. She's upset. No, I can't come over and see him now, am I mad? And last night... last night... what was that about? How did I know where Dan lived? She knows the situation isn't fair on me and she's sorry, but Toby doesn't deserve to be punished. Tomorrow, we'll meet up and talk properly. About everything.

The sky looks dystopian, a vast grey belly of cloud hanging overhead. The alcohol is out of my system, but a swathe of tiredness has set in now, heavy as snowfall, muffling coherent thought. Everything is a disaster. I feel like the die, an object being rolled, over and over and over. Scary at first, but just like before, I'm getting used to it.

I'm starting to think you can get used to anything if you stop caring so much.

CHAPTER TWENTY-NINE

The night Abbie went missing, I was sitting in *The Raven* – a pub in Bath which served traditional food and beers – waiting for Dad to turn up. We'd had a long period of no contact, and I wasn't happy about the die rejecting Abbie's offer for me to attend a party with her in favour of meeting the man who abandoned me and Mum years earlier. But the command of the die was law; its decision was final. On the train to Bath, I tried not to think about the scent of Abbie's perfume, or how she would look in the new dress she'd been showing off to Will earlier in the week. I tried not to think about Will, either, because I knew he would also be using the die that evening.

And yet, I was curious about what Dad would have to say. It wasn't like him to reach out, and I wondered if he might have been doing some reflection. Maybe he would offer an apology for the way he'd treated me and Mum. Maybe he would acknowledge his role in my turbulent childhood, and I would have to decide whether to grant him forgiveness. The die was good for things like that. Before, I'd be racked with indecision, wondering what to say, how to behave, but with the die as my guide, it didn't matter whether my response was right or wrong – it was *something*. It even occurred to me that Dad might be seeking a reunion with Mum, especially if things with Kim hadn't worked out.

The pub was narrow, with steep stairs that revealed thinning numbers of patrons until I reached the fourth floor: the library. I

Die Trying

was the only one there. The walls were lined with old books – some dating back to the nineteenth century – and a huge black stuffed bird which peered at me as I sat down and sipped my cider. Dad turned up fifteen minutes late while I was flicking through a book titled *The White Cliffs of Dover*, wearing a black t-shirt, jeans and Doc Marten shoes. His hair was shorter, and I noted a smattering of salt amongst the peppery hair at his temples.

He wasn't there to apologise. He told me – because he thought I ought to know – that Kim was pregnant. Apart from a brief comment about how I was now old enough to drink, he didn't ask how I was doing. He didn't ask about Mum. It felt very much as though he wanted to boast about his renewed vigour, his 'second chance' and although I was polite, I was struggling to contain the swirl of emotions inside. I wanted to ask why I hadn't been invited to the wedding. I wanted to ask how I, as stepbrother, would fit into their lives, but then Dad dropped another bombshell which left the questions stagnating at the back of my throat.

'We're moving to Canada next month,' he said. 'Kim's got citizenship, so what better chance to make a fresh start and bring up our boy there? And you know me – never one to turn down an adventure.'

I couldn't stand it. I couldn't stand his grinning face. I went to the bathroom and then I rolled the die, hoping it would choose options three, four or five – a fifty per cent chance – but it landed on two.

I walked out of that pub and never saw my father again.

On the train journey home, it poured with rain, streaming up the windows in silvery ribbons, making a mockery of gravity. I thought about Abbie. I thought about Will too, and how he'd shrugged, telling me it was 'die's orders' to spend the night with Lily instead of going to the party with his girlfriend. It was still raining when I arrived back at Temple Meads, and

I'd raced to the bus stop with my coat over my head, wondering what to do next. And the die seemed to have it in for me, because how else to explain its command for me to return to an empty house and stare into the flame of Mum's candle in an attempt to reach Zen state, instead of granting the five more fulfilling options?

Abbie messaged me twice that evening. The first text came soon after midnight, asking if I knew where Will was. The second, she asked if I'd give her a lift from the party. She'd been drinking, her phone was about to die and her taxi didn't turn up like it was supposed to.

The die, the die. It definitely had it in for me that night.

When I reach Will's house twenty minutes later, it looks as though nobody is home. The convertible is missing from the two spaces outside the house, and I imagine they're enjoying a typical Saturday as a family like Jemma and I used to: shopping or a trip to the cinema, sometimes McDonald's or Greggs afterwards as a treat. I knock for a second time and then it starts to rain, plipping onto the lid of the black recycling tub at my feet.

'Oh!' Claire appears through the side gate, startling us both. 'You scared me!'

'I'm so sorry. I tried to call Will, but he didn't pick up so I thought I'd pop by and see if he was in. *Is* he in?'

'No, he's gone to B&Q to pick up some paint. It's just me and Molly here.' She frowns at me. 'Are you ok? What's happened?'

'My wife—'

'Your *wife* did that?'

'My... oh God, no. Not this.' My lip; I'd forgotten about that. 'It's a long story.'

'Oh.' Claire kicks off her crocs at the door. 'I don't think Will'll be long. Do you want to come in?'

'Thanks.' I follow her in, and she asks me to excuse a mess I can't see. Only the vestiges of family life: cups and bowls on various surfaces, kitchen roll dangling empty from a holder, a glass filled with ballpoint pens on the table. Claire offers me a drink – tea or coffee? – and folds a dishcloth over the handle of the oven as she waits for the kettle to boil. 'You don't have to tell me what happened, but do you want something for it?' She squints at my lip. 'Ice? Painkillers?'

'No, honestly, it's fine – it looks worse than it is. I think I was attacked last night.'

'I had a few drinks, and I don't normally do that kind of thing.' It seems important to make this clear. 'I very rarely drink, as it happens.'

Claire turns away to pour boiling water into two cups adorned with cherries. 'I was going to say it doesn't sound like Will's description of you. Are you going to report it?'

'No.'

'No?'

'I... well, the truth is, I went out with the die. My wife misdialled me yesterday when she was with someone else and they weren't playing Uno, put it that way.'

Shit. You're kidding? Claire hands me the mug.

There's a bubble in the centre, going around and around. I watch until it pops. 'Thank you. I'd forgotten how toxic it could get. Actually, no, I hadn't forgotten – I genuinely thought the die was my answer to getting Jemma back.'

Claire takes a sip of her drink and looks like she's going to say something, then stops when Molly comes into the room. She acknowledges me – *alright?* – then asks how long Will's going to be. She wants some sweets. She'll do her homework *later*. Claire tells her she's got exams next year, and yes, it might seem a long way off now but it'll be here before she knows it. I feel simultaneously present and not, like an outsider looking in. The smell of coffee. The strangely comforting sound of rain against the window. The calendar on the wall – a glorious colour photograph of Will, Claire and Molly; the perfect family.

Six Mickey Mouse-shaped cutters, standing in a glass jar beside the tea and coffee caddies. All of it, so *wholesome*.

'Maybe I should roll some dice,' Claire says, when Molly leaves the room. 'Give myself a day off. Forget work and household chores for a while.'

'What is it you do?'

'I'm an HR manager for a building society. They've let me work from home today because it's Molly's teacher training day, even though she's probably old enough now to… anyway, go on. What were you saying?'

'About the die? It sounds stupid but I genuinely thought it was fate.' *Shut up*, I think. *Shut up*. But Claire's fingers are threaded through the handle of the mug and she's looking at me the same way Jemma always used to, when she cared. When she wanted me. 'Jemma seemed to love the person I was becoming; even said I was looking "buff" these days. Why say that, when she just wanted to sleep with someone else?'

'Maybe it isn't the die that's toxic,' Claire says. 'You've been hurt by someone you love, and that's such a painful thing to go through, so it's hardly surprising you've turned to dice again. Anyway, maybe it *is* fate.' Claire smiles, making a dimple appear. 'Maybe there's something better on the cards.'

CHAPTER THIRTY

There is nothing better for me than Jemma. Claire's words irritated me for a moment, before I realised there was probably some truth to them. She'd gone on to talk about my happiness being important, didn't I agree? It sounded like the sort of thing Jemma would say, except Jemma was usually referring to her own happiness, not anyone else's. Jemma loved saying things like 'you only live once' and 'we should chase our dreams', at which point I would usually point out that the average human lifespan was around seventy-two years and dreams didn't pay the bills.

When had I last felt happiness without sadness also being present?

It's 2.30am, but I can't sleep. I tug the pillows around me, clutching desperately to their corners. I'd intended to tell Will that I was going to take a break from the die to prove I was in control, not the other way around, but the more Claire talked – about how things that seem terrible at the time often turn out to be for the best after all – the more it seemed that perhaps she was right. Maybe it *isn't* the die that's toxic. Maybe Jemma's just a fucked-up, cheating liar, and the die was doing nothing more than revealing her true face, although of course Claire didn't use those precise words. She was far too nice for that.

2.46am.

My thoughts switch to Abbie. Had her death been in vain? Will was certainly a better person now. He'd come home half an hour after I arrived, urged inside by Claire as rainwater pelted onto the mat, before collecting a towel, kissing his wife and finally taking a seat beside me in the lounge with a beer. 'Back in the madhouse,' he laughed.

If Abbie hadn't died, maybe he'd never have met Claire. Maybe I'd never have met Jemma. Maybe Abbie and I would be together, a thought I dismiss immediately as unthinkable, because then Toby wouldn't exist.

2.52am. I turn over, and my pointless erection scrapes uselessly at the empty covers. In just over eight hours, I'll be meeting Jemma, and it won't go well if I'm tired. It probably won't go well if I'm *not* tired either, but my headache – which was previously throbbing quietly in the background – has suddenly burst to life, as though someone has opened the door to a party. I *could* use the die. Not because I need to, but because I want to. I could put on a mindfulness podcast, the sort Jemma listens to through the Bluetooth eye mask that makes her look like a giant fly. I could read, take more pain-killers, go for a drive, call or message someone. Or I could plan further options for our meeting tomorrow. Nothing too extreme.

The moment I get out of bed, I realise how tired I am. Sleep is a tease. I've been wanting it to take me to that dark place where I can lose myself completely, but only now I've discarded it as an option does it throw the weight of itself upon me. *I will, I will. Just give me another chance.*

No.

The die slips from my fingers onto the carpet, then bounces out of view behind the beside cabinet, forcing me into a kneeling position to check my fate.

Six.

I pull yesterday's jumper and a pair of joggers over my t-shirt and shorts, then head down to the car. At least it's stopped raining. There's a freshness to the air – not petrichor, something like breath. Mirrors in puddles, secrets in shadows. It's 3am now. Three times six – eighteen minutes. No lights.

At first, it doesn't matter. There are streetlights everywhere, and apart from the odd driver who flashes me from the opposite direction, I can navigate the streets without difficulty. It's only when I reach the country roads that the only source of light comes from the lone car in front of me: a cherry red VW Up! exactly like the car Jemma used to drive when we first met. 'I had to buy this one,' she said, when we strolled back to the car park after our third or fourth date. 'Because it's got my initials on – see? JFJ. Just for Jemma.'

This VW isn't *just for Jemma*. This VW has the registration plate RTD.

Raise The Dead
Resist The Darkness
Roll The Die

Adrenalin makes me press harder on the accelerator, and I keep glancing at the time on the dashboard, willing the minutes to pass. The Up! abruptly slows, then turns off down a side road and I'm plunged into darkness.

Emergency services are on their way, caller.

Any minute now, a lorry could come around the bend – or another car, from behind – and plough into me. Perhaps *that's* how it will end. A shattering of glass, a crunch of metal. The die rattling against the cup holder beside me.

Ten minutes to go. I slow to a crawl. I'm damp with sweat, and the salt and vinegar crisps I ate before bed feel like they're burning a hole through my stomach. The road might curve, or I could slide into a ditch, and I may as well be in a different universe now, because I can't see anything but darkness.

The fuel light pings on, making me jump.

Not yet. Not yet.

And then the clock changes to 03:18. I switch on the lights, and everything comes into focus: silhouettes slinking out from hedgerows, a moss-covered gate, a flattened plastic water bottle by the side of the road. I punch the steering wheel in exultation, and then I punch it again.

It's only when I get back to the flat I realise the tiredness has left me.

The headache, too.

CHAPTER THIRTY-ONE

'Are you going to say anything, or just keep staring at your cake?' Jemma asks. We're in Brew Happy, an independent boutique café with artificial wisteria crawling across the service counter and ceiling. So much of this place feels fake, from the *'display purposes only'* range of plastic cakes sitting in a glass case underneath the counter, to the smile of the waitress and the sugar substitute that Jemma is clicking into her latte. I'm annoyed that she left Toby with Frankie instead of bringing him here today, saying he wanted to see Blake and that his presence would have been 'a distraction'. I'm annoyed with the die, too, for showing a three. I don't know what I wanted, but it wasn't that.

'I'm sorry. I am, I'm really sorry,' Jemma says. 'It must have been horrible to have heard... well...'

Yes, it was, Jemma. It really was. I fold my arms and stretch my legs under the table, but even as I divert my gaze to the serving area, with its row of glass jars filled with cookies, I can still see Jemma in the corner of my eye, fingering one gold hoop earring.

'But I'm not the only one who behaved terribly on Friday. I just... I think it's important we talk, you know? And draw some boundaries.'

'Ha! Now *that's* a great idea. We could start by not sleeping with other people!' I hate speaking to her like this – it goes against everything I cherish – yet at the same time, it feels strangely freeing. 'How's that for a boundary?'

'Why are you being weird? You know that's not what I meant.'

'I agree with you. We do need boundaries. We absolutely do.' I can't look at her without thinking of the sound she was making on Friday night. *Oh God, yeah.* She claims to be an atheist, but it's always God she calls for in the moment of climax. We watched a documentary once, when Jemma was pregnant with Toby, about how anglerfish mate. The female absorbs the male – eyes, fins, organs – and he remains attached, entirely dependent on her for survival. It was so beautifully grotesque, we couldn't believe it, couldn't stop watching. Jemma kept one hand over her mouth; I kept mine over the rounded tump of her belly. 'That's just so gross,' she said. 'I'll never sleep tonight.'

She did sleep, though. In bed, we tucked our bodies together like a pair of stacked bowls, inhaling and exhaling the same air, our hot skin fused together so that it wasn't clear where each of us ended and the other began.

'Did you open my post the other week?' Jemma demands now, dabbing a finger at the pastry crumbs on her plate.

'I didn't mean to. The addressee details were pushed up in the window, so the only thing visible was our address and I didn't know it was for you. I thought it might have been my credit card—'

'This is what I *mean*, Adam. It's overstepping, and you've always got an excuse.'

'It was only a circular.' From the estate agent's, to be precise. I tore it into pieces, just in case it gave Jemma any ideas. She tells me I'm completely missing the point, and I keep the smile in place, because it's uncomfortable. It's easy to fake emotion in a place like this. I fix my eyes on the collar of her blouse, not the movement of her lips. She's had her hair coloured again – glittering streaks of blonde keep peeking between the dark strands, like sunlight through a forest.

'Here we go. One reviver smoothie, one Oreo hot chocolate without cream,' the waitress says, placing the tray between us. Jemma pulls her elbows back. 'Oh! I think you've got the wrong—'

'No, that's right. Thank you.' I take my smoothie.

'Is this some kind of statement?' Jemma asks, when the waitress moves away. 'Just because I used to drink those, and you said they looked like Shrek vomit.'

'*You* said they looked like Shrek vomit. Not bad, actually. Want some?'

She shakes her head and folds her arms across her chest. 'No, I'm ok.'

'Sorry, you were saying...' I take a sip of the sour green sludge, and it hits the open sore inside my cheek. My teeth must have been working furiously last night – I'd woken with a stiff jaw and so much blood on the pillow, some of it had smeared on my chin and dried to crisp flakes. 'It all sounded very serious – should I call the waitress back to take notes?'

'It *is* serious! I'm mortified by what happened Friday night, but we still need to discuss it like adults. I care about you and always will, but I don't think I'm *in* love with you anymore, if that makes sense? I know that's a cliché, but it's how I feel.' She tries to make up for the brutality of the words by reaching both hands across the table towards mine and pulling an expression of deep sorrow. 'The point is, we both need to be thinking about Toby. He needs you to be reliable. He needs security.'

'Yes. Yes, he does. Didn't he have exactly that, before you made me move out?'

'I just mean... if we all know where we stand, it will be easier to move on. I never wanted to hurt you, Adam.'

'I know, and I have moved on. I'm going to the gym, I'm back in touch with a good friend, I'm doing my own thing. You said yourself I was looking great.' The waitress brushes past, carrying two waffles drizzled with melted chocolate, and the scent reminds me of the days when I'd come home from work to find Toby on a portable step in the kitchen, his hands covered in cake batter and Jemma bustling around, trying to clear the mess from the worktops. All so innocent. So much more innocent than what she was doing on Friday night. *Turn over.*

'So why did you go to Dan's house and threaten to kill him?'

'I was drunk. Sure you don't want any of this green vomit? It's actually not that bad.'

'You're lucky he didn't call the police.'

I stir my drink. 'I am. A lucky man indeed.'

Jemma doesn't notice that her hair has snagged on a piece of plastic wisteria behind her. I watch it cling on, even as she moves forwards and backwards, taking sips of hot chocolate. 'It can't happen again, Adam. We're separated. We're not together anymore, and I... well, I like Dan a lot.'

She said that about me once. Although it's very much a Jemma statement – she *really likes* a lot of things. The new season's frappe flavours in Costa. Shoes and trainers with distinct patterns. The smell of Lush *Sticky Dates* shower gel – the connotations of which I don't wish to dwell on right now. Baby clothes. Chocolate straight from the fridge. Free stuff. New stuff.

I pull out my phone. 'This is interesting – the dictionary has three definitions for moving on: *to leave the place where you are staying and go somewhere else.* I've already done that.'

'Adam—'

'*To start a new activity.* I've done that as well. In fact, I think you've got some catching up to do.'

'What is wrong with you today?'

'What do you mean?'

'I'm serious. How are we meant to have any kind of relationship going forward, if you can't communicate with me properly? Don't forget you're the one who's let Toby down two weeks running.'

The die could have chosen truth, confrontation, seduction or silence. But here I am, uncomfortably grinning like a buffoon as my wife reminds me this is all my fault. I can tell that the young couple on the table next to us, recipients of the chocolate-drizzled waffles, are listening to every word. So is the older woman waiting for her husband to come back from the toilet with their grandson. I stir the vomit in my glass, then lean back. 'What a piece of shit I am. What a piece of shit we both are. How do you *want* me to react, Jemma?'

'It's not how I *want* you to react. We need to be able to have a civil conversation about this.'

'I'm being perfectly civil.' I take another sip of my drink and shudder. 'Urgh. Actually, this is more like Hulk's piss.'

'Jesus Christ, Adam. Are you even alright?'

I consider this as the waitress bustles past with a trio of extravagant milkshakes. No, I am not *alright*. Jemma has no right to start a war like this, and still look as beautiful as she does. I could stand on a chair and announce what Jemma has done. I could clap a hand on the back of the young man beside us – barely out of his teens, surely? – and cheerfully warn him that if he wants to keep the relationship going, he shouldn't be too intense. Not too distant, either. Have boundaries, but don't be controlling. I could strike up a conversation with the old couple and ask what their secret is. I could go and press ten pounds into the tip jar. I could fold my napkin into the shape of a—

'It's not just me you're affecting with your behaviour,' Jemma goes on, pushing her drink to one side. 'Mum missed her train yesterday morning because you didn't show up, and the next one wasn't for an hour, which meant she also missed her optician appointment. Then I had Toby crying his eyes out, because he thought you didn't want to see him anymore.'

Die Trying

She'd have made a good samurai. Strike after strike, cutting me open. My pulse stages a fast and noisy protest in my ears as I try to keep an uncomfortable smile pinned in place. *Stop the fight!* 'Of course I want to see him. I wanted to see him today. I'll come round this afternoon and make it up to—'

'Sorry, but you can't just flit in and out when it suits you. Toby's only four, he doesn't understand about all-night benders and hangovers – all he sees is his Dad not turning up when he's supposed to. And… you know… I care about you, I do, but if you're struggling, please, just get *help*.' The old lady is pressing a fork to her cheesecake now, practically fishing for her eyeballs. I consider getting the die out and suggesting we roll to decide. Me, Dan, nobody or – wild card! – someone else entirely. To divorce or not to divorce. That would give the old woman something to talk about. But Jemma's getting into her stride now, happy to be thinking of ways to fix me. 'Frankie knows someone who does counselling, I'll get her number. Adam – you need to sort yourself out, if not for me, then for Toby. And get some sleep! You look knackered.'

I *am* knackered. There's a bolt of lightning zigzagging across my skull, and I rub at the back of my head, trying to earth the pain.

Discomfort. 'Do you love him?'

Jemma smiles sadly, but doesn't answer the question. And I feel like we might just be sharing a moment, but she shakes her head and pulls her handbag from the back of her chair. 'I should be getting back. Call and speak to Toby later, if you like.'

Perhaps this is how things will be from now on. She'll shower breadcrumbs of offerings amongst pieces of broken glass.

My wife, my wife.

I can't decide whether I love her or hate her.

CHAPTER THIRTY-TWO

Jemma

When I get home, Toby's Fireman Sam bowl and spoon are still in the washing up bowl, along with my coffee cup. I peer through the blinds, suddenly fearful that Adam might have followed me home, then prop my phone in the wooden stand that Mum bought me for Christmas. Adam was so *weird* – I've never seen him like that before.

But then, he did hear me and Dan having sex, a thought so mortifying I've had to blank it from my mind.

Fuck.

The shame is huge and muscular, a fattening cloud. 'You've made your bed, now you'll have to lie in it,' Mum used to say, a statement that now seems grimly appropriate. I can't lie in it with Dan anymore. He phoned this morning to ask if I was ok, before telling me it was probably best if we cool it for a while until I've sorted things out with Adam. 'I really, desperately want to be with you,' he said, 'but not if it's going to make things difficult. Especially with a kid involved.' That last sentence really got me, because he was right and also, so fucking wrong. Things are already difficult. And I get that he's been burnt before, but he doesn't understand – withdrawing isn't going to help. It'll make things worse.

Jesus.

Die Trying

I press my head against the cool, solid worktop surface. There's a high-pitched ringing sound in my ears and I wonder if a migraine's coming on, but as suddenly as it began, it stops. I'm about to send Frankie a text to say I'm just grabbing her cake tin and will be straight over, when another message pings up on my screen. I open it straightaway, hoping it's from Dan.

It's Adam:

You never answered my question earlier.

Question? I'm about to ask what he's talking about when a second appears:

Do you love him?

Why is he so desperate to know? Somehow, I'd envisaged Adam and I having the kind of break-up celebrity couples have, where they use words like 'uncoupling' and 'co-parenting' and continue to enjoy a kinship more enriching than their marriage had ever been, but this is so far from that, it's made me rethink everything I thought I knew about my husband. I start typing a lie – *No, of course not* – then delete it and reach into the units to find Frankie's cake tin instead.

A sea of mixing bowls and pans clatter to the floor. Adam used to keep the cupboards tidy, and now I wish I was that sort of person, the sort to find pleasure in order. I retrieve the tin and push the crockery back into place, then I hear a different sound coming from upstairs. Crackling. Tapping.

Adam?

I press my hand to the wall as I climb the stairs. He still has a key. He couldn't have somehow got in through the back before I arrived, could he? The sound stops for a moment, then starts again.

My bedroom window is open. I remember now, I left it like that – as I always do in the mornings – to let fresh air in, 'clear away the ghouls', as Mum used to say. Rain is spattering onto my Clare Mackintosh paperback, which is lying, half-read, on the windowsill: *pock, pock, pock*.

The *relief*. I'm jangling with it.
I wipe the book on my jeans, then close the window.

Frankie opens the door to me half an hour later, wearing jeans and a t-shirt adorned with lemons. Always lemons. Even her tea towels are covered in them. 'Do you want to come in?'

'No, I'd better get back. I've got work in the morning and haven't done washing or lunches yet. Has Toby been ok?'

'Yeah. Yeah good, no trouble. The boys had a scuffle over something earlier, but it's all forgotten now. How did things go with Adam?'

'Weird. He was... I don't know... just *odd*. And he looked like shit, which made me feel even more guilty. I think he might be having a breakdown or something.'

'Oh God.'

'I said I'd get your cousin's number, the one who does counselling, if that's ok? No idea whether he'll use it, but he definitely needs to.'

'Of course.' Frankie scrolls through her phone and, a moment later, mine pings with a shared contact: *Pure Mind Counselling Services*. 'I just... do you feel safe? I'm worried this has gone beyond normal heartbreak and into something darker. He had no right to turn up at Dan's like he did. Toby said earlier that Daddy made him sad.'

'Toby said that?'

'Yeah. I just think—' The hallway door opens and I can hear the fast, urgent pelt of rap music over the boys' excited voices. 'Sorry, I keep – *Matt*. Put your headphones in, the little ones don't want to hear that vile language. Can't bloody think straight. What was I talking about?'

'Adam letting Toby down. I'm pretty sure he wouldn't *do* anything – he's just pissed off and feeling low. But... you know... so am I. I just wish...'

I wish something would happen to Adam. I can't say it, and I don't really wish it, of course. It's just that playing the role of persecutor, relentlessly, is torturous. I hate myself for doing what I've done, but I hate Adam equally for driving Dan away and messing with Toby's head. For making me constantly check over my shoulder. I keep wondering if Dan's told Beth about what happened. *Not on my watch.*

'You wish you could wave a magic wand,' Frankie says, finishing the sentence for me. 'I know, I've been there. But things will all work out in the end, I promise. You just have to get through hell first.'

Back home, Toby plays with his iPad while I'm doing the washing and making lunches. I forward the counselling link to Adam – mistakenly adding three kisses, the way I usually would with Dan – then message Hannah, asking how Dad's been. I can trust her to tell me the truth, unlike Mum, who says things like 'bearing up' and 'coping ok', which means nothing at all.

She replies with a thumbs up. Which means she doesn't want to talk. Which means *she* isn't bearing up.

Toby's gone quiet. 'You ok, buddy?'

He's fallen asleep. I take a blanket from the pile of fresh washing and slide it carefully over him, then sink onto one of the dining room chairs. My paper and pencils are still there, together with a half-drawn sketch of a woman standing beside a window. Faceless. I add shade to the curve of her skirt, and then to the dip of her palm, held tightly against her own shoulder. I draw until my hands are black and there are graphite smudges over the tablecloth, not realising how much time has passed until Toby wriggles himself awake on the sofa and asks if he can have something to eat. I look at the woman I've drawn, looking out to a world beyond, at something in the unseeable distance.

CHAPTER THIRTY-THREE

Adam

It doesn't take long for the adrenaline to wear off. And then something else takes its place. Heavy and sour, like the tonsil stones which used to hide in the dark crevices of my mouth, waiting for a vulnerability – infection, a cold, a bad night's sleep – before the doctors agreed that enough was enough, I could have them cut out.

You can't cut out a broken heart.

'We need to know where we stand,' Jemma told me earlier, or words to that effect, so it seemed fair to ask whether she loved Dan. What I was really asking was: *do I have anything left to lose?*

Her response to that will determine what happens next.

I'm so tired. Two nights without sleep is all it has taken to cause havoc in my brain and since I got in, I've been stumbling about the apartment in a strange haze. After making myself a sandwich, I put the butter on top of the microwave. I pulled two forks from the cutlery drawer and sat down to eat, only to wonder why I was holding them. I've lost the remote control to the TV. Perhaps it's in the fridge.

Jemma's obviously not going to reply. I open my laptop and type the words *separating and divorcing* into Google to see whether I can insist on seeing Toby. The government website recommends that we reach agreement on where Toby will live, how much time he'll spend with me and how we'll support him financially, with a suggestion that we use a parenting plan or mediation to avoid court. I scroll down to the bottom, then accidentally click on the subheading *Ending your marriage*.

Jemma is smarter than me in matters like these. I imagine her dressed in the killer grey trousers and white blouse she wears to interviews, calmly explaining that I had to leave the family home because I hurt her. She thought it was an accident at the time, but now she's not entirely sure. She would explain to the court that I didn't pick up our son for contact on at least two occasions, and of course there was the drinking. The swollen lip from a fight. All things considered, I probably wasn't fit to be allowed unsupervised access to our son.

I must have briefly nodded off, because when the message from Jemma arrives, my laptop has slid halfway down my legs. I move it onto the sofa cushion beside me and the screen springs to life. *Get a divorce*, the words say, in sharp black font. Bold as anything.

Jemma's text is a cop out. She hasn't answered the question; just sent a link to the counselling service she'd been talking about. Perhaps she thinks it might even provide more ammunition in court, if it came to that. *Oh, and his mental health is poor. I have further proof of this, your honour.*

Has Jemma been playing her own game all this time?

It's only when I'm brushing my teeth before bed that I realise she's sent three kisses. Our 'love language', as she called it, when we were together. 'You get three kisses because you're more important than anyone else in my life,' she explained.

What is she doing? Is this her way of telling me she doesn't love Dan Bretti, without actually saying the words? Is she saying she still loves me?

I can't think straight. I climb into bed, and it's only as I'm falling asleep that I realise the die is still in my palm, warm as a nut.

When I get to work the following morning, the large meeting room has been set up for the disciplinary hearing. I'd hoped to slip in undetected, but Paula comes out of the toilets just as I'm going in, and without looking me in the eye, mumbles an awkward hello.

Seb loves to keep people waiting. I pour a glass of water and take a seat, wishing I'd added the option to throw it in his face. They've installed a new pot plant in one corner, or perhaps it's always been there. Green, brown, unremarkable. Designed to blend in.

I almost feel sorry for it.

'Ah, Adam. I hope I haven't kept you,' Sebastian says, bustling into the room. For a moment, I see him not as a grown man but a child pressed into an adult suit, inflated with bellows. I see him at the corner of the playground near the fence, longing for home time so that Mummy could rescue him with treats to soothe away the hurty words. 'You've helped yourself to some water, I see. I did ask Paula to bring some biscuits as well, but she's clearly forgotten.' He pulls a face, as if to say *'women'*. 'Do you want a biscuit? I can get them.'

'No, no. It's fine.'

He makes a great show of pushing the papers together, as though demonstrating the size of a small fish, then pauses to press his glasses up his nose. He's positioned directly in front of the poster on the opposite wall: *Don't wait for opportunity, create it!*

If that's not a message, I don't know what is. 'I'm actually going to save you some time, because I'd like to hand in my resignation.'

'I beg your pardon?'

'No need to beg,' I say, surprising myself. I hand over the letter. 'I've decided this company isn't the right fit for me and I'd like to leave with immediate effect.'

'I see.' Beads of sweat are pimpled along Seb's forehead, and I can tell by the way he's tapping the papers again – big fish, little fish – that he's disappointed at the missed opportunity to assert his dominance. 'Are you quite certain?'

'Yes.' The die feels like it's on fire in my pocket. Six. Finally, the wild card. I stand up. 'I'll collect my things from my desk.'

'I'm afraid that won't be possible, as you're subject to disciplinary action. Someone will need to escort you out so, if you wait here, I'll get Paula or... ex*cuse* me. You cannot—'

He hurries after me, but I'm halfway along the corridor before he's even out of the door. I reach the main office. I'm at my desk. And faith is a funny thing; I can feel it – an ice cube at the back of my neck, a prickle of heat in my palm. Not everything can be quantified with evidence. Just because you can't see something, doesn't mean it isn't there.

Something is definitely guiding me in that moment. I collect what little belongings I have from my desk drawer – a couple of notebooks and pens, a memory stick, several pound coins for the monthly lottery syndicate, a photo of my family – as Seb stands beside me, protesting that I really must leave, this is not acceptable behaviour.

Acceptable behaviour! The die has decreed that I resign and tell the team the truth about Spencer, but I don't expect to find myself in the centre of the room with my arms held wide, pockets bulging with stationery, shouting that I can talk *all about* acceptable behaviour, like allowing a colleague to visit pornographic websites during work hours because he happens to be pulling in over fifty per cent of our sales. I feel like a madman, standing naked in a rainstorm. I don't know how long the rant goes on, because I'm experiencing a similar sensation to that I had during my night-time drive: a complete diffusion of self, as though I'm nowhere and everywhere, all at once.

I'd like to say that mouths drop open and keyboards fall quiet. That when I march out of the office with my photograph tucked under one armpit, at least one of my colleagues comes racing after me to say that no-one else likes Spencer either and I was brave to take a stand. But Spencer isn't there and everyone else either doesn't care, wasn't listening or was doing the British thing of pretending that nothing was happening.

I take the stairs. I push open the doors and, when I step through them and breathe, there's a lightness inside, as though someone has replaced my organs with air.

CHAPTER THIRTY-FOUR

The details of the rest of the day are vague, because I 'wasn't quite with it', as Jemma would say. The die took me to the waterfront, where I did nothing but sit on a bench outside the planetarium for an hour watching people come and go, then to the train station where I caught the next departing train to Keynsham. I rolled, and rolled, and rolled again, striding through the skate park, the tennis court, then a small green where a couple of dog-walkers gave me puzzled looks as I passed, although I'm not entirely sure what I did to warrant them. Perhaps I doffed my cap, like a nineteenth-century gentleman. Perhaps I barked in response to their greetings. I expected the die to send me back to the flat, or perhaps to an independent café where I could browse for jobs, but whatever my purpose was, it eluded me until I reached a sign at the outskirts of the Chocolate Quarter and experienced an ominous sense of deja-vu. Had this been where Dad said he'd leave me alone to make my own way home, to teach me skills in the 'university of life'? I must have only been about six or seven at the time. Did Mum come and collect me, or was that a memory which ended up congealed with others? Shiny purple wrappers. Sandals that pinched my feet. Weak sun, fibrous clouds, like a torch shone through a baby's blanket.

Eventually, I rolled a two and after a short journey back on the train, returned to the flat. I was worn out by then, but the die wouldn't permit me to eat, despite a raging hunger twisting sickly at my insides. I had a brief look at job vacancies, and they read like the cast of a bad crime horror whodunnit: *funeral service assistant, driver required to install bouncy castles, barista, vehicle paint sprayer, life drawing model.* I thought about messaging Will, because things seemed to be getting out of hand. 'Maybe it's not the die that's toxic', his wife had said, but how would she know? How much had Will really told her about what we did back then?

The die sent me back to bed. And now I'm not sure whether it's the same day, or whether another night has passed – it must have: there's a half empty bottle of vodka on the kitchen side which I vaguely remember the die telling me to steal from the corner shop – but it doesn't matter, because it has a fresh punishment in store.

Four. *Truth*.

I'm so nervous, I drink two glasses of water to try and lubricate my mouth, then sit on the bed, furiously massaging the die in my palm. I'll have to tell Jemma about my job. Maybe it will be ok; she can hardly be annoyed with me for standing up to an organisation which didn't respect my moral or personal boundaries. *Boundaries* – her word. Maybe my resignation is even the kind of thing she had in mind when she said I should 'live a little'. She always used to complain about me not being around enough – well, here I am. I'll be here for Toby. All day, every day, if that's what he wants.

Another headache is setting in. I stumble into the kitchen and yank open the cupboard door to look for tablets, but the handle comes away in my hand, sending a screw spinning across the floor. This place. I swallow a couple of pills, then text Jemma to ask if I can come over; we need to talk.

She replies a few minutes later:

`Can it wait until tomorrow? X`

Tomorrow? A quick check on my phone screen confirms that tomorrow is Wednesday. The one day of the week when

I'm permitted to see my son. I can't wait another twenty-four hours, particularly as I won't be able to use the die again until I've fulfilled the order. *Not really*, I type.

Another message pings up on my phone:
What's it about?

Questions. Always, so many questions. I should tell her to wait and see, but that would irritate her. I send a one-word reply – *work* – and Jemma's response comes almost immediately:
Oh God, redundancy? Easier if we stick to arrangements and chat tomorrow ☺. Hope you're ok!

No, I am not ok. I have stuck to arrangements. I called Toby on Monday evening, and it almost killed me to hear the pitch of his voice, high and sad, asking why I didn't come to collect him on Saturday. I imagined Jemma in the background, relishing every moment. '*He needs security.*' When she came back on the phone, she asked if I'd called about the counselling yet, as though I could be made whole by talking with an empathic stranger. I told her no, I hadn't, and asked again about her feelings for Dan Bretti.

'I'm not answering that,' she said, and hung up.

She's not answering now, either. Her phone rings three times, cuts to answerphone, and I end the call halfway through the beep.

I pick up the screw from the floor. There's no 'messy drawer' in the flat containing paperclips, staples, pens, batteries, scuffed rubbers, a couple of misplaced tools and the odd toy from a Christmas cracker, because I have accumulated nothing. My life, and everything in it, is still at home.

I glance down at my phone. *Easier if we stick to arrangements.*
Easier for Jemma. Not for me.

I walk all the way home, hoping it might clear my head – and to some extent it does – but now I can hear Jemma's voice:

you can't come here when I'm not, Adam. Those weren't the arrangements.

Well, sleeping with someone else wasn't part of the arrangements either, and I'm only here to collect my screwdriver.

I lift the latch on the side gate. Despite all the rain we've had lately, a circular section of the lawn is a slightly fainter shade of green, as though someone's placed an enormous hot pan on top of it. At the beginning of summer, Toby begged me to blow up the paddling pool and when I gave in, spent hours dipping in and out of it, pouring water from a small plastic watering can and taking his cars in and out of the 'car wash'. We had one of the hottest summers on record, the sort that felt like it would never end, and by the end of August we were complaining that it was too much. Far too much. 'Give us rain,' we begged. No-one's saying that now.

The rest of the garden looks unkempt, weeds pushing up from between the cracks in the patio, the rose bush that I planted against the back fence to celebrate our third anniversary wilted and dying. When I open the door to the shed, I find the paddling pool deflated in one corner, squashed against the cobwebbed ruin of Toby's Megablocks city project. Old magnets, bits of wood, tubes of paint. I've kept it all for future use, never imagining that there may not be one. Where's the toolbox? It's normally on the bottom shelf, along with a variety of plastic containers housing an assortment of screws, nails, nuts and bolts – I've spent many a peaceful Sunday afternoon in here organising and labelling them all – but now it's all in disarray. A trio of tennis racquets and the deckchairs we bought from B&Q last year are pinned against the shelves by an enormous rowing machine.

That's new. Is it Dan's? Is he moving in by stealth? I can imagine the conversations: *do you mind if I leave this at yours? And this?* That's how the most successful invasions begin, bit by bit, a rowing machine here, a toothbrush there. Before long he'll be clearing out what's left of my goods and trampling the rest underfoot.

A dog is barking in a nearby garden. No-one responds. It goes on and on, echoing around the neighbourhood in the same pitiful tone: it could almost be a recording, played on repeat. *Poor thing.* I yank the rowing machine out of the way and locate the contents of my toolbox amongst the mess on the floor. I could go into the house and refuse to leave. I could go and rescue the barking dog. I could collect Toby from school and—

My phone is ringing. I pull it from my pocket, dropping it face down on the dusty floor, and when I turn it over, Jemma's name appears. I swipe at the screen. 'Hello?'

'What are you doing at the house?'

'What?' I step out of the shed. 'Are you—'

'I've had a Ring doorbell installed and saw you go down the side alley. What are you doing?'

'You're *spying* on me?'

'It's hardly spying, it's a security camera. What are you doing there?'

'Jesus, Jem, I'm getting my screwdriver from the shed. I've left most of my tools here, remember?'

'Oh. Sorry, yeah. I just wish you'd said. I panicked when I saw movement near the door. I didn't realise it was you at first.'

'I did say.'

'You said you wanted to come over to talk, not about collecting stuff.'

The dog has stopped barking. I wonder whether someone's taken it inside or it's given up. *Truth.* 'Well, as you're on the phone, you might as well know. I've resigned from Smithson.'

'Hang on, I'm just paying.' I hear an automated voice in the background advise that there's an unexpected item in bagging area. 'For fuck's sake, there's never anyone... Did you say you *resigned?*'

Die Trying

'Yes. So I'll be around more to help out with Toby until I get another job. I can collect him today if you—'

'You resigned?' She repeats. 'Why? I thought you'd been made redundant.'

'I rolled the die. Told everyone there about what Spencer was like and what he'd done, then I walked out.'

'You're fucking with me.'

'I'm not.'

Jemma laughs. She actually laughs. 'Oh my God.'

Oh God, yeah. The wind blows the shed door open with a bang, exposing the disorder inside. My toolbox, upside down on the floor. A sea of metal fixings, scattered around the rowing machine. Did they have sex in there? The hinges creak, then it slams shut again. Open. Shut. *Turn over.*

'What's that?'

'Only the wind. Shall I pick Toby up, then? I'm here, and it would save you rushing back from the shops.'

'No, it's fine. We're actually going to watch Archie doing Tae Kwon Do in the leisure centre after school. They said he can join in for a free session, if he likes the look of it. But your *job*. I mean, I'm glad you've told Seb where to shove it, but what are you going to do?'

I lean against the shed door before it can slam open again. 'I don't know yet. What are *you* going to do?'

'What do you mean?'

'You've already moved my bike out of the shed to make way for Dan's rowing machine. It's got a coating of rust around the handlebars now it's been left out in the rain, so thanks for that. Will he be taking over my side of the wardrobe soon?'

'The rowing machine isn't Dan's, it's mine! This is exactly the reason I didn't want you coming over while I'm not there,' Jemma says. 'I don't want you snooping around...'

'Snooping? It's my house too, Jemma. I'm still paying half the mortgage.'

'You opened my post. A few weeks ago.'

I explain to her again that was a mistake. The address had been pushed too high up in the plastic window – how was I supposed to know she was the intended recipient?

'Yes, I *know*, but we had an agreement—'

'On your terms. All on your terms. You want me to be grateful that I'm permitted one evening with my son during the week, *one evening,* and expect me to be ok with that? It's killing me. You've got the house and Toby, and nothing has changed for you except the added bonus that you get to fuck someone new while I continue…'

She hangs up.

Somewhere close by, a car door slams. A moment later, a text message arrives:

I refuse to be spoken to like that.

A second immediately follows:

And for the record, yes I do love him.

CHAPTER THIRTY-FIVE

My heart is beating so hard I can feel it in my cheek. It's getting louder, louder still, until I realise it isn't my heartbeat. It's a helicopter, thudding overhead.

Emergency services are on their way, caller.

The die is lying on the path in front of me, five pips facing skyward, promising resolution. We're not supposed to roll for the same outcome twice, but this is different; the context has shifted. Jemma is sleeping with Dan Bretti. He has indoctrinated her into thinking she is in love with him. The time has come for a permanent solution, and now the die concurs.

I push it back in my pocket and take my bike through the side gate, surprised not to find police waiting for me on the other side. The helicopter moves away and now the dog is barking again, a plaintive *woof* that echoes around the neighbourhood. I'm not sure how I get from the garden to the main road – my body seems to be acting of its own accord – and before I know it, I'm passing through Jubilee Green and it feels as though the trees are moving with me, waving me on. Every jab from the screwdriver in my back pocket arouses new memories: Toby, slithering from that dark place of blood and swollen flesh, a stern-faced midwife inviting me to sever the cord. The first glimpse of Jemma smiling coyly at me from the top of the aisle on our wedding day. My graduation, when the sun was a golden ball hanging above us in the sky. A factory-procession

Die Trying

of students, the brief handshake with someone I didn't know, being instructed to leave the stage to a smattering of muted, polite applause. Abbie's name spelled out in flowers on top of a pale oak coffin. Mum showing me the dice she brought home: *'Look what I picked up at work today.'*

An oak tree showers me with droplets that roll down my neck. I keep going until I come out the other side of the green and back into a housing area, passing a row of parked cars with folded-in wing mirrors. I keep hearing Jemma's voice in my head. *'Nobody collides by accident, Adam.'* It doesn't matter that I'm going to kill Dan Bretti, because tough decisions have to be taken for the greater good, and doing the right thing is always subjective. If I don't fulfil this order, worse things will happen. Terrible things.

I don't feel right. I don't feel right at all. A sour, herby taste – like sweat – congeals in my throat. A puddle of leaves stirs on the pavement ahead. There's a rushing, roaring sound, coupled with the spinning sensation of vertigo, and I push harder on the pedals, trying to escape myself. I pull out slightly to avoid a mulch of leaves, and my rear wheel skids.

I don't see the pothole until it's too late.

I'm lying face-down on the ground, trying to breathe.

'Don't move,' someone says. 'We're calling an ambulance for you now, ok?'

A car crawls past. There's a jangle of keys – or money, perhaps – then a panicked voice joins the first. 'Is he ok? I saw...'

An orange light flashes in the puddle beside my face. I feel sick. The voices merge to chime, like bells, then a hand is placed on my back. 'Can you tell us your name?'

I open my mouth, but it hurts too much to speak. I think of Mum, stroking my damp hair against hot, sour sheets. Did I kill Dan Bretti?

'Can you tell us your name, my love?' The voice changes, becomes sharp. 'Tell them he's not responding. Tell them to hurry up.'

'Dam,' I manage.

'Dan?'

What are they talking about? Where's Jemma? I need to find my bag, my phone, my die, but the pain is popping and whistling now, a silent disco. The woman at my side won't stop talking: *just keep still, love, that's it, the ambulance will be here in no time.*

The ambulance arrives, quickly followed by police – two distant wails which bounce around my skull as they draw closer. A friendly female paramedic crouches beside me and asks more questions, then I'm loaded onto a stretcher. My limbs appear as inanimate objects, splayed out around me. Colours keep fading and sharpening. 'I can't see,' I tell the male paramedic, in the back of the ambulance. 'There are spots…'

'Ok.' He shines a light into my eyes, then checks the machine above my head. 'We'll get you thoroughly checked out when we get to hospital. Have you got any family we can call?'

I attempt to sit up, but a network of wires snags and pulls at my chest 'Jemma.'

'Who's that, then? Partner, wife…?'

'Wife.'

'Really? That's my wife's name, too. How long have you been married?'

The bile leaves my body with a violence I'm not expecting, straight into the cardboard sick bowl resting on my chest.

CHAPTER THIRTY-SIX

Jemma

Adam's been taken to hospital.

Fuckfuckfuck. Get practical, Jem. Toby needs collecting, so – shit, Tae Kwon Do, he won't want to miss that. I give Archie's mum a quick call to see if she can take him, and she says she'd be happy to.

'I hope your husband's ok.'

'Thanks. So do I.'

All they've told me is that Adam's had a cycling accident and I should come up, but now I wish I'd asked more questions. *How bad is he? How did the accident happen? Was it my fault?* Logically, of course, I know it wasn't, but I can't help thinking of the last text I sent. Was he flying along like a crazy person, not paying attention? Was he hit by a car? They said he was 'stable', which is reassuring, but what does that really mean?

I glug a few mouthfuls of iced tea from the bottle in the fridge, then push a packet of Monster Munch into my bag. I haven't had much to eat today. I was planning on cooking the beef wellington for tea which Mum brought down and has been sitting in the freezer ever since. Something hearty and home-made for me and Toby; we've been eating too much junk food lately. Now, the thought of cutting open the pastry to reveal solid pink meat makes me feel queasy.

Die Trying

Adam's body. Are doctors looking at it now?

I feel like the worst person in the world. 'Karma will get him,' Hannah had said, when I raged about the police dropping her case because there wasn't enough evidence to take it to the CPS. They'd actually said that! As the infuriatingly nonchalant officer sat in our kitchen, hands wrapped around Mum's mug – the one shaped like a strawberry – I felt a rage unlike anything I'd ever felt before. So what if Hannah had been flirting with him? So what if she'd kissed him earlier in the evening? I couldn't wait for karma: I'd gone straight round to her attacker's house, less than an hour after the officer had left, and when he opened the door, I kneed him so hard, he collapsed on the floor. And then I kicked between his legs with a force I hoped would leave him forever childless. Karma delivered.

Maybe *this* is karma, for the way I've treated Adam recently.

Somehow, I drive the twenty minutes to the hospital and locate a parking space. Inside A&E, I'm buzzed through to a brightly lit area containing at least six beds, two with the curtains drawn around them completely, as though preparing for a show. On the other side of the divide, a baby is crying. An old man with two black pips for eyes stares at me as I pass, and I almost stroll straight past Adam's cubicle, because he's lying flat on the mattress, almost unrecognisable due to the two foam blocks holding his head in place.

He's crying. He tries to speak, but I can't understand what he's saying, so I whip a tissue from my pocket before realising it's actually a paper towel, one of the green ones I used to bring Toby's painted clay model home from school. 'Wait there, I'll get a tissue,' I tell him. And then, even more stupidly, 'Don't move.'

A consultant stops me as I'm about to leave through the double doors. Only now do I realise we're in Resus.

'Are you here to see Mr Dowdell?' she asks.

'Yes.'

'Can I have a quick word?'

'Of course.' My phone is ringing in my pocket, the jaunty tune at odds with the serious look on her face. I apologise, and fiddle with the settings until it finally falls silent. 'Sorry. Sorry. Is everything ok?'

'I was just explaining to Mr Dowdell that he has a couple of cracked ribs and concussion from the accident, so in that respect, he's got off lightly.'

'Oh, that's a relief. He hasn't ridden a bike since the summer when we went out with our son, so I thought it was...' I'm waffling. 'Did a car hit him? I've only spoken to the paramedics earlier, and didn't have a great signal, so—'

'No, he says he hit a pothole, which flung him into the road. A number of witnesses also said his tyre appeared to slip out towards from the side of the pavement.'

'Oh.'

'However, the scan results did show up something else,' she says. 'There's a small mass on the brain, close to his neck. It could be nothing to worry about, but I'd like to perform further tests.'

I glance over at Adam. He's gone back to sleep. 'What do you mean, a mass? A *tumour*?'

'Potentially, yes. We don't know yet if it's anything to worry about, but it's possible he'll need surgery to remove it.'

'Shit! Sorry. I just can't... a *tumour*...'

'It's not uncommon.' The consultant smiles, more warmly this time. 'To pick up other issues on a scan like this. We obviously don't know whether the mass caused him to suffer any instability which contributed to his accident, but in a way, it's a good thing. We're aware now, and can treat it accordingly.'

I tell her that Adam *has* been acting differently lately. 'I've been putting it down to our separation, because he hasn't taken it well, but could it be this?'

Die Trying

'It's possible. Has he been having visual disturbances, anything like that?'

'No, I don't think so. It's been mostly behavioural changes, although we're not living together, so I wouldn't know if he's had any issues with his sight. Will he be back to normal when you get rid of this...' I don't want to say the word *mass*. It conjures up visions of congregations in a musty church hall. Or puffy grey clouds, gathering before a storm.

'That depends on a number of factors,' she says. 'We'll know more when we've done a biopsy and further tests.'

I'm in shock. I move back to Adam's bedside, forgetting all about the tissue, and find myself dabbing his face with the paper towel. Some of Toby's paint is still on it, and I end up smearing red around his already swollen cheekbone. 'Sorry. Did you want... oh God, there's green—'

'Jem, what are you doing?'

'A bad job of face-painting.' I sit on the hideous mustard-coloured chair beside his bed, which has obviously been designed for someone with a much larger body. 'Sorry. How are you feeling?'

'Exhausted.'

'You look it.' And yet, he also looks content in a way I haven't seen for months. Years, even. When Dad took me and Hannah to visit Grandad in the funeral home, I kept changing my mind about whether I wanted to go in, thinking he would look shrivelled and horribly... well, *dead*, but he looked completely at ease. Much more than he ever did in life. His face had relaxed into an expression that said, 'finally, some peace', and Mum even joked he was probably happy not to have to listen to Nan nagging anymore. I focus on the pinpricks of light filtering through the curtain so that I don't have to look at the swollen gash above Adam's eyebrow. 'I'll bring Toby as soon as I can. Archie's mum's taken him straight to Tae Kwon Do, so I can't stay for hours, but I'll come back tomorrow. You don't have to go through this on your own. Do you think... I mean, do you think this is why you've been...?'

'I don't know, Jemma. I can't make sense of any of this right now.'

'No, I know. Ok.' I squeeze Adam's hand and tell him I'll support him. Can grief cause brain tumours? Maybe all this stress I've put him through has manifested into something ugly inside his head. The machine on the other side of the partition starts beeping, and I see a pair of feet hurrying to the bed. Tights. Flat black lace-up shoes. The machine is silenced, and there's a murmuring of urgent whispers. I want to keep talking, because words stop the maggoty thoughts from crawling around my brain, but for once I have nothing to say. Any attempts at conversation – about Toby's school work, the weather, my Mum's new glasses or the disruption caused by the changed bin collection day – will be crushed under the weight of one word. *Tumour*. What will I tell Toby? Something about hospital and being poorly; he doesn't need to know any more than that.

Adam has fallen asleep. I take my phone into the corridor, send a quick message to Archie's mum – Still at hosp, all ok? x – then call Frankie to let her know what's happened.

'*Shit*. A brain tumour?'

'Yeah. They said, well not in so many words, but they implied it was lucky he had his accident, otherwise they wouldn't have discovered it. I *told* you he's been acting weird.'

'You weren't to know. How is he doing?'

It's already getting dark. I watch a man outside the window pacing up and down, up and down. He looks distraught, his free arm tucked under the opposite armpit in a protective gesture. 'He hasn't said much. He's asleep now. I think he needs to process things, and I just... I don't know what to say to him. I'm going to have to let him come back now, aren't I?'

Die Trying

'No, you're not. Don't think about any of that now.'

'I meant letting him live back at home for a while, not actually getting back together. He's got no-one else, Frank.'

'Yeah, but that's not your problem,' Frankie says, kindly. 'Remember last time we spoke? You said you wanted to kill him.'

'Only because he let Toby down.'

'Twice.'

I *had* wanted to kill him. I'd never felt a fury like it; stiff and as real as the hairs on my arm. Adam had created this child with me – this perfect, squashy, tiny human – and promised to care for him the same way I did, yet as soon as he couldn't have *me* anymore, he weaponised his love for Toby. Or that's how it seemed.

'He did that, not you,' Frankie says. 'The tumour is a shock, and by all means tell him you'll support him, but think of yourself and Toby. What *you* want.'

'I know. I will.' A car pulls up outside and the pacing man, having ended his call, rushes to it. The female driver shakes her head several times. It looks like the end of something. Or the beginning of something.

Sometimes it's hard to tell one from the other.

PART TWO

CHAPTER THIRTY-SEVEN

Adam

It's been six weeks since my operation to remove the benign meningioma. *Emergency services are on the way, caller.* Had the die known something I hadn't? Did it make me cycle to Dan's not to kill him, but to save my life?

Or is this all part of the beautiful randomness of life, as Will would claim? I certainly *feel* different. My hair has nearly grown over the scar and, apart from tight lightning-bolt sparks of pain around the site for the first four days afterwards, I've experienced none of the nausea or headaches I was warned about. I'd lain awake at night in hospital at first, worrying not just about the mass growing inside the dark vault of my skull, but also that there might be consequences for not fulfilling the order of the die. It all feels like a dream now: dark brown tea brought to me in pale blue mugs, a cuff tightening and loosening around my arm, the steady, unblinking stare of the man in the bed opposite who shuffled to the toilet twice a day until the morning I'd woken to find his bed empty, the sheets and pillow smooth and untouched, making me wonder if he ever really existed.

And then several things happened to make me think the die wasn't seeking to punish me after all. Jemma brought Toby to the hospital – clutching a home-made card bearing a smiling yellow sun below the words *Get well soon, Daddy* – and each time I hugged him, breathing in the scent of his freshly washed hair, I was reminded of the fact that I'd almost killed a man. That's not something that can be undone.

The day after that, I was surprised to see Katya from work walking onto the ward carrying a small white rose bush. She placed it next to Toby's card and told me that Jemma had phoned Smithson 'to give everyone a mouthful', which she acknowledged as probably no less than they all deserved. 'Spencer can be quite convincing,' she admitted. 'Most of the time it's just banter. We didn't realise he'd actually make up something like that about you.'

I wasn't particularly interested in her olive branch, until she dropped the bombshell that Spencer had been arrested for drink-driving after one boozy lunch too many. 'I don't know if he'll be able to carry on doing the job if his licence is revoked,' she said. 'His role is basically driving to see customers all day long, and he had a massive bust-up with Seb about it, because he never admitted to having previous convictions on the company car insurance.'

Karma? Fate? Possibly. Possibly not. I lay in that bed for a long time after she left, observing the veins in my arms which seemed suddenly more prominent. I didn't know whether I was in awe of the die or terrified by it.

Will comes over to the flat the week after I've been discharged, carrying four cans of Guinness held together with a plastic collar. 'Old school,' he says. 'I almost went for the Kingfisher, then thought of all the times the die chose this stuff. Not sure I can drink it, to be fair.'

'Aren't you driving?'

'Yeah, but I'll be ok with one.' He follows me up the stairs into the flat, where he cracks open two cans. 'Neat little place, this.'

'You think?'

'Not as bad as I was expecting, from your description.'
'Jemma gave the place a lick of paint while I was recovering.' Perhaps she'd also been worried about karma, because she kept saying how sorry she was, and how she wouldn't have been so sharp if she'd known I had 'something going on medically'. It amused me the way she couldn't bring herself to say the word *tumour*, as though verbalising it might cause something to take root in her own head, too. She came to the flat several times a day after the operation, to prepare meals and keep me company, and I was grateful for that as well as the opportunity to see Toby without strict time limits. After they left on the third day, an extraordinary, blinding exhaustion fell over me. Jemma had been in fact-finding mode, playing the role of detective, and I knew from experience that she would keep pushing, performing costume changes with her questions. I'd seen her with friends, dissecting the minutiae of other people's intentions, turning over possibilities, analysing and probing them for meaning before arriving at a conclusion that *must* be right. I couldn't give her the answers she wanted. 'There's no genetic component, as far as I know.'

'Exactly! *As far as you know*. But what if there is?' she said. 'Toby might be at risk. Don't you think you should get in touch with your dad to find out?'

No, I didn't. In any case, I wouldn't know where to start – he lives abroad now, and I don't have his number. I pointed out that benign brain tumours could also be caused by environmental factors, injury, trauma or stress, noting the way her hand flew to her neck at the mention of the 't' word. She apologised. She wasn't trying to stress me out. But as I said, I was exhausted, and for the first time since my operation, I almost gave in to temptation. After she left, I opened and closed the bedside cabinet drawer, listening to the die rattle inside and wishing it had been lost in the accident along with the screwdriver. I fantasised about driving somewhere and throwing

Die Trying

it into the sea, or burying it in a place it could never be found. Then I thought back to those early few days of living in the flat, when it felt as though I'd been swept into deep water, my feet reaching and scraping for solid ground, finding none. The die had been my lifebuoy.

'I've cooked a couple of pizzas, which probably covers the smell of mould.' I lift one of the plates from the worktop. 'Want some?'

Will shakes his head. 'I'm ok at the moment, mate. How are you doing?'

'I'm ok.' I take two glasses from the cupboard. 'Feel surprisingly good, considering.'

'Considering someone's been rummaging about in your brain? I can't believe you watched it on a screen. The thing that gives you conscious thought! It must have been surreal.'

'It was. It really was.' The surgeon had talked me through it, seemingly in as much awe as I was. He had opened a gate to my thoughts, memories, emotions – everything that made me real. 'I didn't want to die. That was all I kept thinking: *I really don't want to fucking die!*'

'Well, you didn't. Cheers to that.'

'Cheers.' I take a slice of pizza and move into the living area. Will follows, taking a seat on the smaller settee. I click on the TV, then take a sip of Guinness. 'Nope. Still not a fan.'

'It's good for you, apparently.'

'Didn't they say that about tobacco? And marriage?'

Will laughs. 'I'm not sure anyone ever said that about marriage. Let's hear it, then, your epiphany? Claire wants to know if you saw a tunnel of light or Jesus – I told her we used to see that kind of thing all the time when we were dice-living.'

'Brought on by hallucinogens?'

'Yeah. Man, those things brought us close to God.'

God. Will always talked a lot about God, for someone who doesn't believe in him. So did Jemma, come to think of it.

What was it she said? Something about the universe being within ourselves, like one of those infinity mirrors. 'Did I call it an epiphany?'

'No mate, I'm messing with you.'

'It's just an idea I had. The die has been pretty instrumental these past few weeks, with the resignation, personal challenges and...' I haven't told him – or anyone – about where I was heading on my bike that day, only that I'd used the die. 'Anyway. I've been thinking about the podcast again.'

'Mate, there's absolutely no rush for any of that. You don't have to—'

'No, hear me out. Burnout, that was what we were talking about, wasn't it? The decision fatigue that's killing so many of us these days. I want to do it. I feel *ready* to do it. Not yet, obviously, but in a few weeks when things have settled down. The die put me back in charge of my life and this might sound mental, but I want to give something back.'

'You sure?'

I lift the remote, turn the TV down. 'I've had a lot of time on my hands, and I don't *think* I should do it. I need to do it.'

CHAPTER THIRTY-EIGHT

Diecast #1

Diecast, with Will King and resident host Adam Dowdell. Episode One: *Face Your Fears*

Will has set up the equipment as before and it looks like a film set, with a glass jug of water beside two empty glasses, a laptop and a notepad scarred with bullet points. I'm wearing a pale-blue shirt over jeans and a white t-shirt, and Will – in a teal Gymshark t-shirt and joggers – looks like he's just returned from working out. We've agreed to use the die only for podcast purposes, to avoid either of us derailing the series with missed appearances, changed schedules or poor choices affecting our performance, and it's been harder than it sounds. As soon as I awake, and then regularly throughout the day, I find my fingers twitching for the die. Will wasn't wrong when he said the temptation to dice felt like an alcoholic contemplating just the one beer.

'So,' Will says, leaning towards the microphone. 'Welcome back to *Diecast*, where we leave the tiresome task of decision-making up to chance. In this episode, we'll be looking at fear. What is it? What are men *really* afraid of?'

As he talks, I think of the surgeon, talking me through the post-operative scan and telling me it all 'looked good'. He saw inside, except he didn't. Not really.

'I'm a pussy when it comes to spiders,' Will laughs. 'But let's talk about the other fears. The bigger fears. Failure. Rejection. Inadequacy.'

Why is he looking directly at me? I smile stiffly. There's a musty, burning smell in here, like an ancient lightbulb switched on after years of gathering dust.

'Losing control,' I add.

Will points at me. 'Yeah. Losing control. Although, let me add, that's not only a male thing. My wife's pretty good at giving me both barrels.'

I laugh, but can't help wondering what Claire would think of that comment. I heard them arguing through the door when I first arrived, about how she didn't want him to spend too much time in the studio. He was trying to explain that recording didn't take long, a comment that was immediately flung back with an angry retort that she knew. Oh, she *knew*. There were also equipment checks, research and planning, co-ording socials and editing to do. Twenty minutes here, an hour there. Did he think she was sitting on her arse, watching TV, while he enjoyed time in his man shed? No, she wasn't. She was sorting out the house and Molly, and had he forgotten she worked full-time too? Eventually, when the disagreement abated to a level I couldn't hear, I knocked and stepped inside to be immediately greeted with the usual masks of politeness. Smiles. Offers of hot drinks. 'So nice to see you! How is your recovery going?'

Will offers me the mic, and I separate my back from the chair to talk about how my fears have diminished since my operation. 'Being given a second chance at life can make you re-evaluate definitions of success and failure. I don't fear rejection anymore, because it's happened. My wife left me, I've lost my job, but I'm alive.'

Here's the thing – I *thought* I wanted to die, many times over the past few months, but what I really wanted was an absence of pain. And sometimes, conversely, amplification of it, because it took me back to a place as familiar as the freckle on my left thumb. *Here you are, old friend.* Yet since my operation, the world seems to have exploded with colour and sound. I find myself staring at things at once new and familiar: a skeletal leaf stuck to the sole of my shoe, the honeyed arm of sunlight reaching across the sofa, the fizz of shaving foam as I tap my razor into the bathroom sink. In the flat, when thoughts of Jemma sneak into my head, I focus on the patch of wall where her brush has left marks and remind myself that she isn't perfect. None of us are. Perhaps the podcast will help me let her go.

'I'm alive,' I repeat. 'And although decisions feel like they matter less, when I get up in the morning I still wonder what to wear. What to eat, what to do. You know when you're standing in a shop or a restaurant, completely overwhelmed with choice? And then you eventually go for the same thing you always do – because it's comfortable, it's familiar. I think a lot of that... it's fear.'

Will takes over. We've curated our conversation carefully, so it sounds like a natural conversation between friends. 'Yeah. Even the tiniest decisions, like: how do I speak to that girl in the office, who seems to like me, but might just be one of those friendly types who flirts with everyone? Should I go to the gym, or is that dude who looks like The Rock going to be working out beside me again? So much of what we do, we have no control over, and that's what's terrifying. We constrict ourselves with expectation, insecurity, uncertainty and... well, fear. Most of us want to be the best, but what the hell is "the best"? And does it even matter?'

'You're going to say no.'

Will laughs. 'Damn right I'm going to say no! Because when you've got a die, it isn't you making those decisions. It's chance.

Or the universe, if you like. A *cosmic guide*. Which is admittedly a pretty cool way of looking at things.'

There's something comforting about listening to Will speak. He exaggerates the faint cockney accent that is almost imperceptible in everyday speech, and I find my gaze drifting from the table down to his feet, where one of his shoelaces has come undone and is drawing a lazy white scribble across the carpet. I can see why he loves doing the podcast; there's an illicit privacy to this space. But equally, I can understand Claire's frustration. Man shed. It's a nonsense, this myth about men needing space and privacy. What men need is connection. And purpose. As Will's mouth forms shapes about fight, flight or freeze responses, I wonder if the die has been biding its time. Waiting not for us to slip up, but to atone ourselves.

Will gestures towards me – it's my turn to speak – and I run through the six options once more, before reminding listeners that the die should not be used for harmful or illegal behaviour. *Or as a reason to cheat on your partner*, I think, staring directly at Will, but he doesn't notice. He's leaning down now, tying his errant lace. When he pops up again, he runs through a prepared speech about the *just do it* mentality that frees you to fulfil the will of the die. 'Don't listen to the fear,' he says. 'That's only your nervous system railing against change. Change is *good*.'

And then it's time for our first roll. We use a different die to determine who takes the challenge – I am odds, Will is evens – and it's been so long, I grip the die and savour the moment. It feels as though a million ants have been released and their tiny, skittering feet are racing through my bloodstream.

'He's ready to roll!' Will says, by way of explanation. 'What's it going to be? Don't forget to like and share and *definitely* upload your own rolls. We want to see your die challenges – this is an interactive show.'

The only way I can describe it is relief. It is only in the release when you feel something transcendal. A clarity of thought. An exchange, so powerful it's almost orgasmic. The die clatters beside the mic and stops.

Three.

Not truth, then. Discomfort.

CHAPTER THIRTY-NINE

Jemma

'I said it's too loud in here!'

Frankie grabs my arm and shouts into my ear, almost spilling her vodka and coke down my top. 'You sound old.'

I don't normally feel like this. Usually, I love the buzz, the noise, the music, but tonight I *feel* old. The top I ordered on Vinted – flatteringly layered around the waist, softly sculpted around the chest – didn't arrive in time, so I had to dash to town after work and grab a top from Zara. Cream. Paired with black trousers and some kitten heels. It looked fine in the house but now, as a group of girls in short dresses pass me through a cloud of perfume, I feel like an office manager popping for a few drinks after work.

We take our drinks through to the 'snug', an open-plan area separated from the noise and bustle of the main bar. There are three other tables here, one of which is occupied by a young couple who look at us with open hostility as we place our glasses down and take off our coats. They were clearly hoping to have the place to themselves, and I can't blame them. I'd be exactly the same if I was here with Dan.

Frankie points at my vodka and coke. 'How many?'

'How many what?'

'How many of those is it going to take to cheer you up?'

Die Trying

'Sorry.' The couple are holding hands across the table now. *Get a room.* 'Is it really that obvious?'

'Yes, it bloody is! Just try and forget about Dan for one night.'

'Actually, I've been back in touch with him. He said he was missing me.'

Frankie raises her eyebrows. 'And?'

'And... well, ok – I cracked. I told him I needed to see him. Badly. We met at the mall last week, and since then we've been taking things steady.'

'I'm happy for you. No, I am.' She lifts her glass, clinks it gently against mine. 'What about Adam?'

'Do you know what? He seems to be in a pretty good place right now. He's stopped going on about getting back together and even said something about finding *acceptance*, and... what? That's good, right?'

'Yeah... hang on.' Frankie starts scrolling through her phone. 'There's something I wanted to show you.'

She turns it around; hands me the phone. A bearded man is standing on a windswept beach, talking to the camera. He pans around and gestures behind him to an expanse of angry sea. 'I saw it on TikTok,' Frankie goes on. 'I follow this guy's other channel – apparently he's set up this new show, *Diecast*.'

'Catchy.'

'Yeah. But look at this.' She presses a finger to the screen, forwarding the video by minutes.

'I can't see anything.'

Frankie tells me to keep watching. I wonder if it's going to be one of those videos where a spider or a clown leaps out of the screen. There seems to be a small orange ball floating in the water. The beach is deserted. 'Do I need to zoom in? I still can't—'

'Just *watch*.'

After a few more minutes, a head appears from beneath the waves, followed by a body wading quickly out of the water.

'Jesus. Someone's actually been in there! It looks freezing. They must be… oh my God. Is that *Adam*?'

He reaches for a towel, then starts talking to the screen. I can't hear what he's saying. A group of three men have walked into the snug, slamming pints onto one of the free tables, laughing loudly. The music must have been turned up too, because suddenly I can't hear Frankie either. She leans forward, shouts. 'Yeah! I couldn't believe it either. He's a co-host. Adam!'

'No way. What was he doing in the sea? He's just—' I twist around to speak to the men. 'Can you *shut up*?'

'It's called having a good time, love. You should try it.'

I turn back to Frankie. 'This is mad. Adam's just had brain surgery.'

'I know,' Frankie shouts. 'But he seems ok.'

I look down at the screen again. She's right. Apart from the gleaming wetness of his face, Adam looks exactly as he did after Toby's birth: shining, shocked, positively jubilant. 'That must be the podcast he was on about. I didn't know they'd started it or that they were filming too.'

'Yeah. It's all about using a die to make decisions. "Reducing decision fatigue" they call it and, from what I can gather, it's all about male wellness. Promoting healthy masculinity, that sort of thing.'

Adam and I had a conversation last year about cold-water therapy. I'd been training for my diploma and said how amazing it would be to try, as it was supposedly so effective at reducing muscle soreness and inflammation. Adam had made a couple of disparaging noises about how these things are fads that probably do more harm than good. 'If you ever catch me doing anything like that,' he said, 'know that I've officially lost my mind.'

Has he lost his mind? I thought so when he came hammering at Dan's front door – it's no wonder Dan was nervous about taking things further after that – but I'd put it down to Adam's

Die Trying

tumour changing his behaviour. This is different, though. This is – what's the word they just used? Optimising. Adam hasn't turned up at Dan's house to threaten him since. Maybe he genuinely *wants* to change and send a positive message while he's at it. If so, good luck to him.

We order another drink. Frankie tears apart a packet of crisps until it resembles a giant silver mirror, then we pick at the greasy contents on the table between us. The conversation moves to preschool – the parents who park on zig zags, Alex and Helen, the two mums who are always early and arrive in gym gear every day of the week, how Margo seems blind to bratty Izzy Stone's temper tantrums – and I tell her that I've been fielding a few at home too, from Toby. It's hardly surprising, as he's trying to adjust to full days in preschool as well as Adam's hospital stay due to a 'poorly head', but sometimes I feel so impotent against his four-year-old fury that it feels personal. As if he's trying to punish me.

Frankie's only half listening. A notification pops up on her phone, and now she's looking at an image of a pavement, a lamppost, a patch of grass. It's only when a man saunters past that I realise it's live footage from her Ring doorbell. 'Everything alright?'

'No, it bloody isn't. I grounded Matt for swearing at me earlier, and he's just gone out.'

She rings him. He doesn't pick up. She calls Rob instead, who says he has no idea where Matt's gone; he hasn't seen him, he's still at the cinema with Blake. 'Jem, I'm really sorry, but do you mind if we call it a night?' Frankie gestures at her glass. 'If I leave this, I won't be over the limit. Just in case I need to drive anywhere later. Fuck's sake. He seems to think that now he's fifteen he can do whatever he wants.'

'That's fine,' I say, even though I'm going to have to pay the babysitter for the whole evening and I'd been looking forward to a few more drinks, maybe even a dance, so I could forget about everything for a few hours. Work. Adam. The message Hannah had sent: Mum won't tell you this, but Dad just wants to sleep all the time. He's not great, Jem.

We wait outside, shivering, for our cab. Frankie runs back inside 'for a quick pee – hold the taxi if it arrives', and I scour the street, watching groups of men and women trickle in and out of the bars. There was a time when Friday and Saturday nights represented fun and freedom, an opportunity to cast off inhibitions and throw myself into a hot jacuzzi of music, alcohol and laughter, but now – sober – it feels grubby and sinister. Snapshots of conversation: *such a bitch... I told him... rat.* Someone presses against me from behind. Garlic breath. I turn and glare, the man moves away, and when I look back, I'm sure I can see Adam's head moving amongst a crowd of men.

Is it Adam?

No, it can't be. It isn't.

He's making me paranoid.

CHAPTER FORTY

Adam

'Are you sure?' Will asked. 'An ice plunge?'

I told him Jemma mentioned it a while ago. I couldn't imagine why anyone would put themselves through that level of extreme discomfort; it seemed like a perfect demonstration of how the die could 'shake things up', as Will put it. 'Yes,' I told him. Doctors had cleared me for exercise. It was a challenge, something out of the ordinary – wasn't that what the podcast was supposed to be about? Three minutes. It was no time at all.

It was an entire lifetime.

The sea had been flat as a sheet of steel, glittering and radiant, welcoming me with all the promise and deception of a politician's smile. My feet, my ankles, my calves, my waist. I'd turned and shouted to Will, who was filming a few feet away: '*I am the Dice Man!*' It helped me disassociate. Adam Dowdell would not be wading into icy water at 6am on a cold October morning. Adam Dowdell would be in bed with his wife, or stretched out on his stomach on Toby's bedroom floor, playing cars with his son as morning light gradually poured across the carpet.

There was a buoyancy aid attached to my wrist, which bobbed up and down in the water as I became more deeply submerged. My balls retreated. My heartbeat became disordered, jumping frantically, spasmodically, inside my chest. Will raised his right wrist to demonstrate that he was starting the timer, then I closed my eyes and fought to control my body. I felt like I was being burnt alive. How long had passed? Thirty seconds? A minute and a half? I had no idea, and I couldn't remember how to coax my breathing back into a normal pattern. When I opened my eyes again, the clouds had closed ranks and huddled close, as if in conspiracy.

'How was it?' Will asked afterwards, handing me a towel and woolly hat. I couldn't speak at first. I didn't feel a high, or the famous sense of euphoria until a few minutes later, when the violent shivering subsided and a tingling sensation crept across my skin. *Phenomenal*, I could have said, because some sort of reboot was also happening in my core. Heat and light. A surge of certainty. Viewing the footage afterwards, I can't believe how different I look: crazed from shock, the dilated blood vessels in my face exaggerating my ecstasy. Will releases the footage, sharing it with his *Chaos* followers as well as the small but rapidly growing number subscribing to *Diecast*. There are love-heart, muscle and fire emojis in the comments section, as well as dozens of messages of support:

```
This is so inspiring. I'm going to give it
a try.
Well done, you two! Love your new podcast
Will, keep it up #dicelife #diecast
Can't wait to see what's in store next.
Adding to my watch list.
Fair play to you both. This is incredible.
```

I didn't realise it would have such an impact. Something as small as a forgotten conversation with Jemma has resurfaced as an order from the die, and I can't help wondering again if none of this is incidental. All this time, I've been pushing for answers, when perhaps all I had to do was wait.

A thud at the bottom of the stairs makes me start. I open the door and look down the stairs to see an orange shadow moving away from the glass. A brown envelope is lying on the mat; probably another reminder for this month's rent. I'm trying to survive on what's left of my wages, and if I don't get another job soon, I'll have to dip into Toby's savings.

Jemma doesn't know how skint I am. She was surprisingly negative about the podcast, phoning to complain that I shouldn't be discussing our split publicly like that. 'And you shouldn't be going into freezing cold water. You've just had an operation!'

'Eleven weeks ago.'

'Yes, but—'

'I rolled the dice. I had to.'

A pause. And then. 'Have you got a job yet?'

I told her I'd been looking. So far my inbox has been graced only with rejections, each one a paper cut to hope.

I collect the letter from the mat, which is resting near the scooter Toby left here yesterday. I tear it open, thinking about his tears when I told him I wasn't going back home. 'When?' he sobbed. 'When?'

I screw up the letter in my hand and drop it into the bin without even opening it, then go for a run, jamming the Airpods into my ears so tightly it hurts. By the afternoon, I've had enough of thinking about it.

I open my laptop and book an appointment with Francis Grayling, family solicitors.

Their offices are in the centre of town, tucked between the local newspaper office and a Subway. I tell the receptionist I have an appointment with Peter Berry, and she directs me to the yellow seats in the waiting area. There's a coffee machine in one corner, a stack of *Psychologies* magazines on the table, and a strange opaque glass rectangle is hanging on the opposite wall. It smells sterile in here, as though someone has been trying to scrub away the mess of bloody divorce battles and broken family parts. It's nothing like Smithson, yet for some reason it reminds me of my old workplace: tall windows, expensive furniture, the benign carpet and doors that lead off to other offices, no doubt humming with a hot tangle of manipulation, power, greed and envy familiar to so many of the corporate organisations I've worked for. I run a finger along the thin scar at the back of my head – *alive* – then relax back into the seat and load the *Diecast* TikTok page. Someone has uploaded a new video. Three brothers – one who looks to be in his teens, the other two older, possibly in their early twenties – are carrying two lilos across a sandy cove which looks like the same spot I went to when we filmed the cold-water challenge.

'Mr Dowdell?'

I look up. The receptionist tells me she's sorry but Mr Berry is running slightly behind. He shouldn't be too much longer.

'Thank you.' I return my gaze to the screen. The two younger men are in the water now, heaving themselves onto the lilos. Are those *aubergines* printed on the blonde man's shorts? The camera zooms in and I realise he's younger than I thought. Sixteen or seventeen, perhaps. He leans to one side, trying to grab the other man's lilo, but his brother has a longer reach. He pulls his arm and the lilo buckles, tilts and then flips the younger boy into the sea.

The laughter is so close to the microphone, it comes out in a burst, like a hosepipe tap turned suddenly the wrong way. I fumble for the sound as the receptionist continues to stare primly at her monitor, pretending she hasn't heard. The older brother – not that much older, I realise now, with a jolt of alarm – pumps a fist in the air and reclines onto his lilo, triumphant.

Where is he? The other boy has completely disappeared. The water nudges his abandoned lilo further from shore.

'Mr Dowdell?'

The boy rears from the water, white-faced and cadaver-like. I can't hear what he's saying. He drags his legs through the water, the aubergine print now clinging to his skinny legs, and the third brother – still filming – throws him a towel. I click the home button and get up. 'Hello.'

Peter Berry apologises for keeping me waiting and takes me into an office along the corridor. After running through the paperwork I filled in earlier, he asks when I left the matrimonial home, whether we're formally separated, whether either of us has yet filed for divorce. Yet. I press my fingers to the table and find myself focusing on the bump at the centre of his nose as he keeps talking. Property, equity, assets. Income and expenditure. Childcare for Toby, child maintenance, primary care.

I tell him I've been considering taking out a loan, or even borrowing from Toby's savings that I've been paying into since he was born, because finances are getting tight.

'Don't do that yet,' he says. 'And definitely try to avoid dipping into your son's savings – that would reflect badly if it goes to court. Let's explore what you're legally entitled to first. Can I ask why you left your job?'

'I wasn't happy. I hadn't been diagnosed with the tumour at that time, but... well, my wife certainly thinks it played a part.'

Peter jots down more notes. 'And since then?'

'Since then?'

'Have you been back to work?'

'Not officially. I've just started co-hosting a podcast with my friend and we're trying to build an audience.'

'Is that currently generating an income?'

Behind him, on the white shelves, a pair of wooden deer. Printer, paperwork, books on family law. 'Not yet, no. We're only a few episodes in.'

'Ok. From a legal perspective, unpaid or voluntary work is generally considered a hobby. Do you have any plans to return to a role in—' He glances at his notes. 'IT?'

I feel a wave of discomfort at the thought of it. 'No. Not at the moment.'

Die Trying

'Alright. Just bear in mind that if things don't work out financially, you might need to look at other sources of income.' He floats the possibility of claiming Universal Credit and some sort of single-person reduction of the council tax before relaxing back into his chair, mirroring my pose. 'If it's a struggle to manage half the mortgage, are there any friends or family members you could stay with for a while? Just until you're back on your feet?'

'There could be. A friend. I'm not sure how serious his offer was, though.'

'It's worth asking. In fact, if it *is* at all possible...' He stabs the paper in front of him with the nib of his pen, three times. 'I would strongly recommend it.'

CHAPTER FORTY-ONE

'Of course I was serious!' Will says.

'Really?'

'Yeah. You being here full-time will make things a lot easier, in a way – we can plan and practise episodes together, and it'll massively take the pressure off me. How long are you thinking?'

A bus pulls up outside, releasing a theatrical whoosh and hiss. I lean forward to close the window. 'I don't... well, I need to find out if it's possible first, but just until I'm back on my feet financially. Are you sure Claire won't mind?'

'Not at all. Like I said, it'll take the pressure off. She'll probably think it's a great idea.'

As soon as I hang up, I realise there are other considerations. Toby: where would he sleep? Would he be *allowed* to stay over, and would it be taking the proverbial even to ask?

I head into the bathroom. The tiles are spongy and uneven, soft from years of damp. The whole place stinks of shit and mould. I have to get out.

I've been given a second chance for a reason.

I spend the next few days sorting out my affairs. The estate agent confirms – with some surprise – that the landlord is happy for me to end the tenancy agreement early, given my 'exceptional circumstances', and fortunately for me, he knows someone who desperately needs the accommodation.

Die Trying

Not so fortunately, he won't be refunding the deposit.

Packing up feels like a relief. It's only when I drop the last box into the boot of the car and slam it closed that I feel a squeeze, deep in my gut. Occasionally it happens in my head, a brief, mild twisting sensation, like someone has grabbed my soft tissue between thumb and forefinger. 'All perfectly normal,' the consultant said at my check-up appointment, 'as long as it's manageable with painkillers.'

I don't need painkillers. It doesn't even last that long. Just a few seconds; enough to ground me. As if the universe is trying to give me a mental Chinese burn. *You're not in charge.*

I start the engine and stick a finger up to the flat.

Yes. Yes, I am.

I'm halfway to Will's house when it occurs to me that I should take some beers, and perhaps a bouquet of flowers for Claire. I pull into the car park at Tesco's and stand in front of the row of buckets suspended inside metal hoops, considering the display of colour before me. *Should* I buy a bunch? I have no idea what Claire likes, and they're not just flowers; they're a reminder of my wedding to Jemma, the orange blooms I'd bought before I heard her fucking Dan Bretti, the crisp white heads on Mum's coffin, pale pink on Abbie's; neat and orderly as a row of soldiers.

I stand and stare until a man leans over me to pluck a bouquet from its watery lodgings, breaking me from my trance. A bottle of wine, too. We'll raise a toast: to new beginnings, to positive challenges, to success.

The damp grass is lit up by a yellow spill of light from the windows. I can hear sounds inside: plates and cups being disturbed, Molly shouting to ask what's wrong with the WiFi, a rush of water as a tap is turned on, then off again. I imagine them as if in a snowglobe, unshaken, trapped in their perfect world. Even though the doors and windows are closed, there's a faint scent of something meaty drifting through the walls. Shepherd's pie? Sausages? It reminds me of the canteen at the hospital where I found myself soon after Toby's birth, when I'd been gripped by a ravenous hunger and realised I hadn't eaten for over twenty-four hours. Jemma was breastfeeding and I hadn't wanted to leave them, but she told me she was dying for something other than tepid hospital water from a jug. I ordered myself a plate of beef stew – with a bowl of takeaway pasta and the biggest bar of chocolate I could find for Jemma – and ate it in a seat near the window, smiling at everyone that walked past. I was a father. A dad.

Will flings open the door. When did he start wearing *cardigans*? And yet, bizarrely, the camel fabric suits him, especially now his hair has thickened to a crest and his beard has been trimmed to a thin brown apron around his mouth. 'Hello, mate,' he says. 'Thought that must be you.'

He looks like he's about to step outside, so I lift the flowers, blocking his exit. 'I bought these for Claire. Oh, and a bottle of wine, to say thanks for having me. I hope I'm not getting in the way of dinner, or—'

'No, we've finished. Er, do you want to come in?'

It would be rude not to. I follow him through the kitchen and hallway, into the lounge, where Molly and Claire are discussing something over an open laptop held in the crook of Molly's arm. Claire's face breaks into a wide smile when I offer the flowers and then she invites me to join them in a glass of bubbly, just as I hoped she would. 'Only if you don't mind. I don't want to get in your way.'

'Not at all.' She instructs Molly to put the flowers in water. Will returns with the wine glasses and the three of us sit on the sofas: Will and Claire on the three-seater, me on the huge round single cuddle chair opposite. The wine tastes of berries and the crackle of autumn nights, and it feels peculiar to be here with Will again, as if we've come full circle in the story of our lives.

'I hear the podcast has got off to a great start,' Claire says, shifting forward and making the bubbles bounce in her glass. 'Will said the responses to your ice challenge were incredible.'

'Yes. They were. I didn't expect people to connect with us the way they have, but they seem to like our message.' Will has already explained that he's been promoting *Diecast* on his mailing list and socials, and many of the subscribers and followers of Chaos have picked up our new show. 'Anything could happen, which will keep things fresh and exciting. Our next topic is a random act of kindness, and I think—'

'Oh! You've already done that with my flowers! Will, take note – if it lands on you, I wouldn't mind a new lamp for the dining room.'

'That wouldn't be very random. And also, a bit boring for the show.' He laughs, puts his arm around her proprietorially, and I can't help thinking of Abbie. Her open, curious face – *who's he on the phone to?* – and the lies she told herself to conceal the truth. Does Claire know about the girl he promised to love for eternity? I sip my drink and lean into the folds of the sofa, watching the moon slip out of view behind the *Fruits of the Forest* bouquet in the window. The conversation moves on to future episodes, how we can drive traffic towards our platforms and increase numbers of followers, then Molly shuffles into the room and perches on the arm of the sofa beside Will.

'What?' she says. Her sleeves are hanging over her hands, her long, dark hair is tucked behind both ears, and she has the hunched, slightly apologetic air of a teenager unsure where she belongs. 'I want to listen.'

'You mean, you want to get out of doing your Maths homework,' Will says.

'It's Statistics – this *is* kind of relevant. We were literally talking about the probability of rolling different numbers with dice a few weeks ago.'

It seems absurd that she's only four years younger than Abbie was when she died. 'So, you'll know that each roll is independent,' I say, twisting around in my chair to look at her. 'Or at least, that's what they teach. You have a one in six chance of rolling any number on a single die, which is a one-in-two-hundred-and-sixteen chance of rolling the same number three times in a row. It's defined as randomness, but some mathematicians believe that nothing is truly random. There's a theory—'

'Oh, mate,' Will laughs. 'I forgot you were such a massive nerd.'

Claire nudges him. '*Will.* Anyway, so what if he is? Nerds rule the world.'

I love this family.

Molly nods politely, but then her attention is captured by her phone and she clambers off the sofa and leaves the room without looking up from her screen. Claire says she may as well run through some 'housekeeping' while I'm here. She asks me to try and use the right-hand side of the space near their cars. There's no washing machine in the annexe, so if I'm desperate I can use theirs, otherwise there's a laundrette in town. The key sometimes sticks in the lock, the tap sputters a couple of times when it's first turned on, but that's all perfectly normal. If I have any trouble with the boiler or fridge, the instruction manuals are stashed beneath the cutlery drawer.

'Thanks,' I say. 'Seriously, I really can't thank you enough for this.'

An hour later, I'm at the front door, thanking them again. A security light clicks on as I head to the car to collect my suitcase, bathing me in sharp white light. I notice tiny moths fluttering aimlessly, the brush of damp grass against my trainers, and when I return to the annexe, the key doesn't stick in the lock – it glides in effortlessly, as though it has been awaiting my arrival.

Die Trying

It's so peaceful in here. I unzip my case, smooth out my clothes and mount them onto the hanging rail in the small, single bedroom. The carpet smells new, the mattress is firm and everything would be perfect if it weren't for the fact my bedsheets and pillows still carry the dank, sour smell of the flat.

CHAPTER FORTY-TWO

Diecast #2

Diecast, with Will King and resident host Adam Dowdell. Episode Two: *Random Roll of Kindness*

'Hello, and welcome back!' Will says, more cheerfully than I know he feels. He's exhausted from a busy few days of consultancy work, and this month's attempt at pregnancy has failed. 'Don't tell Claire I told you,' he said. 'She really thought it had happened this time.'

I told him I was sorry, and a short silence followed; it was one of those awkward conversations that Will looked relieved to move on from. I could have told him that I was in the dog house too, for not telling Jemma I'd ended my tenancy agreement and she'd had to find out from Frankie, but it would have been disrespectful to badmouth her like that.

Gossip. It wasn't what we did.

'Thanks to everyone who has liked and shared our first episode,' Will says. 'We've been blown away by the support and your own submissions, which have kept us entertained and humbled. Big shout out to the guys who shared truths about their mental health and relationship issues, their fears of not being good enough. We're here for you. And if you haven't subscribed yet, hit the button now. We're going to show you how the die can literally transform your life.'

Die Trying

I can't help thinking of the boys on the lilo. There have been other responses too: shared text messages sent to former partners and potential conquests, a screenshot of someone's cleared photo album and the words: *been too scared to do this until now!*, a video of a man taking a shortcut home through the woods after his night shift. And the upload that clocked up nearly 800 views – a close up of an enormous spider in the corner of a small, cluttered room, followed by a tirade of abuse directed at the die when it landed on two, then a sped-up sequence of a young man's night spent on the floor, set to a *Psycho*-style soundtrack.

Will is talking about this week's episode being all about doing something selfless. 'Which may seem counterintuitive – doesn't altruism detract from the busyness of our lives? Doesn't it give us *more* to do? The answer to that, my friends, is no, it does not. Because constantly having to make decisions is draining. It's toxic. It makes us less kind, less tolerant, less present, and we end up feeling like life is a competition we cannot win.'

Astonishing, that people will listen to these words and resonate. That the die – and we – can wield such power. I find myself leaning forward, then back, looking beyond Will to the bookcase over his shoulder stuffed with his *Doctor Who* memorabilia, several box files and an assortment of notepads and pens. My die stays on the shelf, and I don't come into this room unless we're recording, although I was tempted last night. 'Where is Toby going to sleep?' Jemma had demanded. 'I don't know these people.'

These people. She made Will and Claire sound like terrorists. I told her they'd agreed Toby could stay on a blow-up bed in the annexe with me on the weekends I had him overnight. She huffed a bit, then relented and asked if I'd got a job yet.

'Performing a random act of kindness, believe it or not, can actually *simplify* thought patterns,' Will says. 'And if you've been ground down by work, by kids, by relationship issues – hey, we've all been there! – kindness is the last thing you feel like doing. But it's the best thing to get you up and winning again. That feel-good high you experience means you can approach later decisions with clarity and positive intent.'

Will discloses his own experiences of kindness from strangers, from the very minor – doors held open or a driving courtesy acknowledged, positive comments on his podcasts and a colleague's remark that he smelled good – to the tale of a community eager to help after a neighbour's house burnt down. When he turns the microphone to me, I say it's an easy one, because I'm sitting right here, right now, because of his generosity. And then, deviating momentarily from the script, I ask why.

'Why what?'

'The kindness. You didn't have to take me in.' I'm almost certain he'll cut this from the final edit, but I want to hear him say Abbie's name. *This is atonement. This is what I do now, I make things right. She didn't deserve the way I treated her.*

Will gives me a puzzled smile. 'Mate, you're going through a rough ride. I'm sure many people would do the same, in our situation.'

Then he moves on, and the gratitude shrivels to something hard and dark; a nut lodged under my ribcage. If we're doing this in Abbie's memory, why haven't we mentioned her yet? Will talks about rolling a two, and how doing nothing means withdrawal, or resisting the urge to intervene. 'And sometimes the themes overlap. It can feel like you're being corralled down a certain path, but that's the magic of the die. It speaks for you. No need to stress out – it'll always have your back.'

The windows and door are closed. And yet there's a cold draught circling my legs. I feel my jaw snap shut and resist the urge to grind my teeth.

'…it can be something for a colleague or family member, or for a complete stranger. You can pay for someone's drive-thru meal. Reach out to someone you haven't spoken to for years,' Will says, and then it's my turn again. I run through the six static options and disclaimer like a flight attendant describing the safety brief.

And then it's time to roll.

CHAPTER FORTY-THREE

The woman in front of me at the coffee shop is wearing a flowing green dress, secured at the waist with a thick belt, and her red hair is piled up on top of her head with a brown clip. Her toddler is rocking inside the pushchair with a violence that threatens to break the straps securing him, but if she's noticed, she's choosing to ignore it. I lean forward. 'Sorry to interrupt, but I'd like to pay for your drink.'

'What?'

'Let me pay. No strings, I just want to help out.'

She looks stressed. And terrified. One hand returns to the pushchair. 'Er, no... thanks.'

I feel the sting of dismissal, acute as Jemma's rejection of me. She moves aside and I invite the elderly couple behind me to go in front, deciding to pay for their drinks instead. And a toasted teacake. And a slice of Victoria sponge.

The man pulls a brown leather wallet from his coat pocket and I try again. 'Please, let me pay.'

His partner turns around and stares at me suspiciously.

'What did he say?'

'I don't know. What do you want?' his partner asks. She's tiny and fierce-looking, with a blue scarf wound loosely around her neck.

'Please let me pay. I'm doing a random act of—'

'Are you one of those pyramid sellers?'

Die Trying

'No. I just want to pay for your drinks, I don't want anything in return.'

The machine lets out an alarmed rattle, then hisses noisily before releasing a trickle of brown liquid into a cup. The man hands a twenty-pound note to the barista. 'We're perfectly able to afford our own drinks, thank you. We are not a charity.'

I turn to Will, who is sitting on a stool at the back and filming discreetly, trying not to laugh. *Connection.* He'd talked me out of calling or sending a gift to Jemma, reminding me that this project was about doing things differently. 'Connection with *others*,' he said. 'There's nothing random about doing something for your ex-wife. The podcast, the die... it's about challenging yourself, remember?'

But this is an exercise in humiliation, not connection. Perhaps I shouldn't be surprised – people are so used to being tricked and manipulated that it must become second nature to reject an offer of kindness. Or is it me? Do I look like the kind of man who can't be trusted? Would people be more likely to accept a random act of kindness from a woman? I step out of the queue, about to tell Will this is pointless – I may as well go into the supermarket next door and buy something for the food bank – when a woman appears at my side. She's tall and ferociously thin, with cat-like eyes and short hair cropped to a crescent moon at the nape of her neck. I take a step back, assuming she wants to go past, but instead she smiles. 'Miserable bastards.'

She must have recognised us from the podcast. I start babbling – 'we're not always like this!' – but it turns out she was referring to the elderly couple, who have collected their order on a tray and are now waddling unsteadily towards a vacant table.

'You were just trying to do something nice,' she says. 'And if there's still a random act of kindness going, I'd love an oat milk latte.'

Her name is Lisa. We sit at a table three rows back from the window and as I tell her about the podcast, her face expands. 'That's *amazing*. So, you're a presenter?'

'It's Will's show really, but yes, I'm a co-host. He's over there.'

Will raises a hand. I gesture for him to join us, because it feels wrong to be talking to another woman alone like this, much as I'm enjoying her company. It feels wrong precisely *because* I'm enjoying her company. She's wearing a small gold bracelet on her wrist and it catches the light as she lifts the mug to her mouth.

'This is Will.'

'Hi, I'm Lisa. Adam was just telling me about your podcast, the whole dice thing. It sounds so interesting.'

Will holds the back of my chair, as if to steady himself. 'It's... yeah, it keeps us on our toes. We've only just got it up and running properly, but it's the engagement with the public that's really going to help things fly. I'm blurring the faces of the customers in here, at the request of the café manager, but would it be ok if I got a picture of you two together? For the socials?'

'Fine by me,' Lisa says.

Connection. I lean in, close enough to smell the coffee on Lisa's breath, almost close enough to feel my own pulse throbbing against her ear. Her jumper is hanging open and I focus on Will's hand holding the back of his phone, to avoid looking at the dark gap inside. 'What did you say it was called?' Lisa says, after we pull apart. 'Dice Cast?'

'Diecast.'

'Die. Cast.' She taps the title into her phone. 'Got it. Oh, that looks brilliant. I'm... yep, I'm following you now – Lisa Fisher. Wow. It's really nice to meet you.'

Jemma's words come to mind again then: *nobody collides by accident, Adam.* I can't help wondering if she'll see the pictures of me and Lisa together. And later, back at the annexe,

Die Trying

I wonder what she'll make of the fact that Lisa's just liked and shared the clips with the comment: hot guy bought me a hot drink today. Turns out he's the co-host of a hot new show - Diecast!

I boil a couple of eggs on the hob and eat them with toast, standing in the kitchenette while scrolling through the latest comments on our socials. Will uploaded the *Random Roll of Kindness* footage on the drive home, and we've already nearly doubled our following. There are 389 laughing emojis on the clip of me being rebuffed by the elderly couple, and a couple of listeners have responded to Lisa's comment.

Love this. Dice date?

Amazing!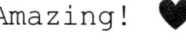

I'm going straight down Costa for some dice loving!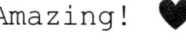

Will has invited listeners to share their stories of good deeds gone wrong, and a couple of Die Harders I recognise as contributors from episode one immediately appear online, telling us about the ice-skating date that ended with a broken arm, the birthday surprise that started a fire, the homeless person who threw a packet of sandwiches back in his face because they wanted money. They're looking forward to doing their own rolls – *will share soon, wish me luck!* Messages of support are coming in from new followers too, and I keep refreshing the page, reading them anew; it makes me feel less alone. Who are these people? I imagine them sprawled on sofas or sitting, cramped, on a train. Maybe they're waiting for a child's party to finish. Maybe they're in a damp, mouldy flat like the one I've just left, and our podcast is their only source of connection.

Well, then. Maybe we can spread some hope.

I take a closer look at Lisa's profile. She's uploaded her latest favourite reads: a horror novel titled *Remain*, and a David Nicholls novel about a couple brought together on a long-distance walking expedition. There's a picture of her with longer hair, curled into waves, wearing pink novelty glasses sporting the words *Happy Birthday*. Other pictures show a close-up of her feet inside a pair of yellow Converse trainers. A field of poppies. No sign of children, although there are photos of her with an older couple standing beside a folly set close to a long stretch of sandy beach. 'Appley Tower' the sign says.

Hot guy. I drop the egg cups and plate into the washing up bowl and gaze across the grass to Will's house. Through the window, I can see the flowers I bought Claire, still perky in their vase.

A sensation billows in my chest. I don't know what it is, but it's not unpleasant. It feels like I'm expanding, and if I don't do something to ground myself, I might float right off the floor.

CHAPTER FORTY-FOUR

It surprises me how much I enjoy waking every morning to the sound of birdsong, in bedsheets that no longer smell of despair, watching swirls of cloud that ripen and bloom against the morning sky. Sometimes, I see Will and his family behind the windows: briskly swishing the curtains open, popping up and down behind the glass, flicking lights on and off, like a theatre skit. Random, as Jemma would say. But it isn't random. Claire always goes downstairs for a cup of tea before she has a shower or gets dressed. She takes Molly to school around 8am, and on colder days she starts the engine five minutes before she's due to leave. She doesn't flit in and out because she's forgotten her bag, her phone, her sports bottle or lunch, like Jemma used to. Will usually gets up around 8.30am and starts his consultancy work before coming to join me in the annexe later in the day. Family life. I feel both connected and strangely isolated at the same time.

It was Jemma's suggestion that I bring Toby here on Wednesday evening, instead of me going home to bath him like I normally do. 'It'll be good for him to get a feel for the place before he stays there overnight,' she said, and I resisted at first, because it's not just Toby I look forward to seeing on Wednesday nights. But she had a good point – as she so often does – and after collecting him from preschool and taking him for a Pizza Hut I can barely afford, I bring him back to the annexe. He rattles my clothes on the hangers and opens and closes the drawers. He wants to look in the fridge, the shower room, the utility cupboard.

'What's in here?' he says, pressing on the locked handle to the studio.

'That's where I do my work, buddy.'

'Can I go in?'

'No, it's top secret.'

Toby sucks in his cheeks. 'Why?'

'It just is. A secret room. In a secret house, in a secret garden.'

He's like a pinball, wanting to bounce on the bed and fiddle with the thermostat. Eventually, I give up trying to persuade him to do his homework and take him into the garden to play with the football which has been rolling around in the boot of my car since the summer. The grass is damp and, much to his delight, he slips over while running. A ladder of mud appears up the side of his trousers and he tells me to watch, then tries to recreate the move, over and over again.

I don't realise how damp we've become until Claire appears like a phantom in the dark, arms folded over her thin white long-sleeved t-shirt, asking if we want to come in. 'It's freezing out here,' she calls. 'Come in the house, if you like. I'll make hot chocolate.'

We head up to the house, where I change Toby out of his muddy trousers and into the spare pair Jemma always packs in his bag. The kitchen is hot and bright, and I'm not sure if I'm imagining the sound of voices and laughter from another part of the house until Claire calls Molly to 'come and see little Toby'.

Molly appears a few moments later. Her hair is tied into two French braids that hang over her White Fox hoody, and her jeans appear too long for her legs – they cover half her socks, and the ends are a row of fraying threads. She stabs at her phone screen twice and the laughter stops. 'Oh my God, how cute. Hello.'

'Hello,' Toby says. 'Do you live here?'

'Yeah, I live here. Where do you live?'

'At home with my Mummy. Daddy lives outside in the secret house.'

'Aww,' Molly croons. She crouches down to be closer to him, and her hoop earrings rest against her collarbone. Claire pulls a face at me conspiratorially: *too adorable!* 'Do you want to look in my room?'

'Yes.' Toby puts his hand in Molly's, so trustingly that I feel hazy with love. Sometimes when that happens, I hate Jemma even more for giving me something so pure and whole, only to snatch it so cruelly away. The microwave pings, Claire steps forward, and when I blink, Toby and Molly have gone.

'Will said you've been in touch with the woman you met on your last podcast challenge,' Claire says. 'He's asleep in the lounge, by the way.'

'Oh. Thanks.' I take the mug. It's so hot, I almost drop it. 'Yes. We're just exchanging friendly messages, nothing more.'

Lisa told me she's a phlebotomist. *Or, as I like to tell people, a vampire!* I laughed at that, imagining her teeth sharpened into fangs, sinking into Dan Bretti's neck. She talked about her parents who live on the Isle of Wight, and her dog, Winston: *a bulldog with a heart of solid gold.*

'Do you think you'll see her again?' Claire asks.

I hadn't thought about that. I brush her off with a comment that I probably won't have time – the podcast is taking up so much of it – which isn't far from the truth. Between moderating comments and uploads, I've been observing with interest how listeners have been searching for common ground, seeking allies. Four men – Hamish, Trevor, Josh and Chris – have been adding the hashtag #tripleroll, asking if anyone else keeps rolling the same number. And one of the boys I recognise from the lilo following the *Face your Fears* week is back with an upload of himself picking up litter from a local park.

Die Trying

'Come through,' Claire says, and I follow her into the lounge, taking in a pair of glasses on the dining room table, a navy jacket hanging over the banister, an unopened bottle of Lucozade sitting, two-thirds empty, at the bottom of the stairs. 'He's still asleep! *Will.*'

He lifts his head from the arm of the sofa, blinking uncertainly.

'Adam's here. He's brought Toby.'

'Oh. Alright? Sorry mate, I'm shattered.' Will composes himself quickly, tugging at his t-shirt and dropping his feet to the floor so I can sit down. I place my hot chocolate onto a coaster and see a muscle in Claire's jaw twitch, before she turns and leaves the room. We talk about the podcast until Toby comes back downstairs with Molly half an hour later, carrying a Jenga set proudly under one arm. Molly helps him set up the game and we play several rounds, followed by a couple of games of Connect Four and I can't help imagining Jemma coming to pick up Toby and watching us through the windows. Bare feet. Laughter. The mimosa glow of the lounge lamps, creating a wash across the carpet.

But Jemma isn't coming, because that isn't the arrangement. 8pm comes around too quickly, and I thank the Kings again for a great evening before bundling Toby into the car. He's tired now, and sweaty, his hair sticking at odd angles to his face.

'Did you like that, Tobe?'

'Yeah.'

'Want to come back and stay at the weekend?'

'Yeah.'

He turns his head into the cushioned part of the seatbelt and yawns. I can feel the evening slipping away. The steering wheel feels cold against my hands, and I direct the fans to the windscreen, where seeds of rain have starting to appear on the other side of the glass. 'What did you do upstairs with Molly?'

'Played Boomerang.'

'In her room? I don't think you should have been throwing things indoors, buddy. Something might get broken.'

I swing onto the road. When I glance back at my son, a small crease has appeared between his eyebrows. 'I didn't *throw* anything. I played on Dan's phone first. I wanted to show Molly.'

The road is unfurling before me, like the tongue of a serpent. Toby is telling me how the game works – something about slingshots and monsters and collecting gold coins, but I can't hear him properly because there's a bloody, noisy throb pulsing through my head. I try to keep my speed steady. 'When did you see Dan, Tobe?'

'At the park. Don't like him.'

Nor do I. The momentary pleasure I get from this declaration is instantly swept away by another, darker, thought. My father's spittle, hot on my face. His hand against my back, pushing me forwards, making me trip on my own feet. If Dan Bretti has hurt my son, I *will* run him down. I won't need a die to—

'He doesn't play with me,' Toby says.

'Is that why you don't like him? Toby? Has he ever been mean to you, or shouted at you?' I know I need to be careful – if I press too hard, Toby's likely to tell Jemma I've been interrogating him. I can picture her face now: *Daddy said what?*

'No,' Toby says. 'He never plays. He just talks to Mummy.'

Does he? Does he, now? I can picture the scene; Jemma's head tilted back in laughter, one hand touching his wrist, his tricep, his shoulder, as he talks. She's a tactile woman, my wife. I imagine Dan Bretti's stupid wet gash of a smile, smeared across his face.

There's a click, a pop, and I realise I'm grinding my teeth again. I remember how I breathed through the cold-water challenge – in for three, hold for four, out for three – and half an hour later, I pull up outside our front door with no memory of how I got there. Toby's asleep now, his beautiful head bobbing, a cord of dribble attaching him to the strap.

Jemma comes out to collect him. 'Everything ok?'

I don't respond.

'Adam? What's...' She puts her head in through my open window to look at Toby. She smells of burnt orange peel. 'Is he ok? He's in a different pair of trousers. Did he—'

'He's *fine*, Jemma. He got a bit muddy playing football, that's all.'

'What's up, then?'

Confront. My wife's default setting, always. Look at you, I think. Look at you, so sure of yourself, still comfortably installed in the home we used to call ours. 'Toby said he'd met Dan.'

'Oh. Yeah. It was only... we were at the park and bumped into him with his niece. It wasn't a planned arrangement or anything like that.'

'Right.'

'Adam, it was nothing, I swear. Toby made a little friend of Olivia and played a game she showed him on Dan's phone... that was literally it. Does it matter?'

For some reason, I think of Lisa. I think of Claire, Will and Molly, the four of us kneeling before the Jenga tower as if in prayer, until I brought it crashing down. I don't have the die. I don't know if it matters.

I open the car door abruptly, making Jemma take a step back. 'I'll carry Toby in.'

CHAPTER FORTY-FIVE

Diecast #3

Diecast, with Will King and resident host Adam Dowdell. Episode Three: *Truth or Die*

'We're back for episode three, and it's going to be a good one,' Will says. 'Thanks to everyone who's subscribed, liked and shared our podcast so far, and huge love for those brilliant clips and messages. If you haven't watched our last episode yet – go back and catch up, it's golden. Adam had a bit of trouble delivering his random act of kindness, but then… Adam, mate. Tell them. It's your story.'

'I, ah…' I'm embarrassed, suddenly, despite knowing the script. 'Yes. No one wanted my free coffee—'

'And cake!'

'Yes. And cake. They thought I wanted something in return.' I mimic the old man's voice: '"*We are not a charity*". Anyway, I was eventually rescued from my shame by a lovely woman.'

'Who called you hot.'

I laugh. 'It *was* fairly dark in there.'

'It was. But mate, you *are* hot. If I were to choose a bromance with anyone, you'd be my first choice.' He laughs. 'Anyway, the die got you out there. It found Lisa!'

I'm not entirely comfortable using her name as part of our performance, but Will assures me this is the kind of thing which will drive the podcast figures up. Laying ourselves bare, making it real. And he's right – finding Lisa has breathed a small, sweet shot of positivity into my life. I'd been so angry when I returned to the annexe after dropping Toby back at Jemma's, I removed the studio key from the top of the boiler, where Will said I would find it, in case of emergency. I couldn't stop thinking about Dan allowing my son to handle his phone, where his filthy hands had been, typing obscene messages to my wife, and crept in to look at the die.

Two.

I left it alone. And then, just when I needed it most, Lisa sent me a message:

Thanks again for the coffee - it was great to meet you the other day! Love your podcast too. I've even used a die to decide on a few things this week! Funny how you realise what you want before it lands 😊

I messaged her back:

Thanks! That means the world to me.

Then I thought about asking her to please be careful, before realising it might sound odd. Instead, I messaged a single word – Goodnight 😊 – which she replied to with a red heart emoji.

'So, you've all been sending in your stories of good deeds gone wrong,' Will says. There's a laptop on the table between us, which he pulls towards him now. 'We've just had another one in from a Tom Starling. *Booked my first proper girlfriend a hotel suite for her birthday and spent all day filling it with balloons and rose petals, only for her to bail and leave early with another guy*! Ah, man, that's brutal. You never forget your first love, but that takes it to a whole new level.'

He tells listeners to keep doing the good stuff. To keep filming and sharing random acts of kindness, maybe even get a chain reaction going. 'And for all the miserable old bastards who are "perfectly able to afford their own drinks", get yourselves out there and do something for others! It doesn't have to cost anything. It can be a compliment, a free kindness. Whatever!'

You never forget your first love. I'm not sure whether Will fully comprehends the power of those words, because he's swiftly moved on to announce this week's topic – Truth or Die – and without a hint of irony, asks if there's ever a good reason to lie. He says the truth is always subjective, because we're always trying to present ourselves in the best light. We want the promotion, we want company, we want validation, we want sex. We tell lies in order to protect ourselves. To feel better about ourselves.

There's a magpie in the tree outside. It lifts its head, looks directly at me, then flies away.

We're joined online by a body language expert Will's been communicating with: Jason Puller, a self-proclaimed 'Human Lie Detector' who talks about how the classic signs of deception are often a myth. Only by closely observing someone's normal behaviour, then contrasting it with how they respond under questioning, can he spot the 'leaks': micro-expressions, changes in speech patterns, tone, movement or posture. He sounds impressive, but I've done my research: I know that scientific precision on human lie detection hovers around fifty-five to sixty-five per cent – barely above chance.

'And what if the individual has learned to lie very well to them*selves*?' Will asks. 'What if it's a lie told to protect others? Is an omission of fact the same as a lie?'

My mind drifts back to the time I lied to Jemma. It was shortly before we moved in together, and she'd used my laptop when she left her own charger back home. I hadn't expected her to have left her email page open, but there it was – all the e-receipts for her train journeys, online purchases, spam from clothing and beauty companies. I'd been meaning to log out, but just before I closed the screen, a new message appeared from Manchester Museum titled *Interview*.

I don't know why I opened it. I didn't feel well and was working from bed, curtains closed, the laptop propped open on my lap. The email thanked Jemma for her application and wanted to invite her for an online interview, asking her to accept or decline using the two buttons at the bottom of the page. To this day, I still have no idea how it happened. I lifted my arm to wipe my nose, knocking the laptop, and when I looked again, a new message had appeared: You will not be attending.

I panicked. I couldn't say anything to Jemma; she hadn't even told me she'd applied. I deleted the email, then emptied it from the trash folder, telling myself the museum would probably send another. If she asked me, I'd tell the truth.

But she never did ask me. And I vowed never to invade her privacy again.

'Accountability for ourselves *and* others,' Jason says, and it takes me a few moments to realise the conversation has moved on; he's referring to a chat show from some years earlier, where a man took his own life after failing a lie detector test. 'Our words – as well as our actions – sometimes have consequences we can't possibly imagine. That's as true of the lie as it is of the reveal.'

When the forty-five minutes are up, we thank Jason for his valuable insight and it's time to roll the die. I'm so convinced it'll be my turn again – despite the odds being in Will's favour – that when it lands on four, the microphone catches my short bark of surprise. '*Truth*,' Will exclaims. 'Adam, I'm starting to think you're right – this thing is prophetic.'

He scratches lightly at his t-shirt and I wonder if it's a leak, a tell, but then I remember him saying something about trying to shave his chest with a blunt razor: *probably Molly nicking it again.*

'Before I open up to you guys, I just want to say – sometimes, you might find the categories overlap. Discomfort, for example, might intersect with truth. Or even the wild card, depending on how you play it. And two... that can be fun. Withhold. Withdraw. You don't apologise, don't correct, don't say "I love you" back. Just smile and see what happens.'

I'm almost swallowing the microphone in anticipation as Will clears his throat and says he's going to talk about something deeply personal. Something that makes him feel guilty, less of a man, inadequate. Something that everyone assumes is enjoyable because 'you know, you're having fun in the process, right?'

Infidelity, I think. I wait for the words to come. *You never forget your first love, and I chose to sleep with someone else on the night my girlfriend died.*

But he doesn't say that. Instead, he tells the listeners about his and Claire's failure to conceive. How sex has been reduced to a clinical order to perform when a smiley face appears on a stick. How they can't do anything spontaneous anymore. The devastation he feels when her period arrives and he feels like it's all his fault.

By the end of his speech, he's even mustered a tear. He passes the last section over to me, where I remind listeners to keep listening and subscribing, but most importantly, play safe. When we've wrapped it up, Will composes himself again.

'Alright?' I ask.

'Yeah. You alright?'

'Yes. Are you staying to do edits?'

'Not now. I said to Claire I'd get straight back. We can do them later, if that's ok?'

'Yes.' My words are stiff, brittle as chalk. I want to say something else, something about Abbie, but it isn't the time.

It's never the time.

CHAPTER FORTY-SIX

On Tuesday, Jemma asks me if I can come over and bathe Toby – a gift not born entirely of altruism, as I know Toby's doing football practice after school tomorrow evening – and, for the first time, I don't spend the entire day checking the clock. *Diecast* has had a fresh uptick in followers, and we've been getting regular contributions from a small subgroup of regular contributors calling themselves 'Die Harders'. A couple of men had resonated with Will's truth bomb, saying it was a 'mad lonely' place to be.

Best of all, the interactive nature of the podcast has generated a steady stream of interest. Die Harders have been uploading footage of their 'truth' rolls, sharing photos of a family reunion, disclosing stories of community clean-ups, fast food bought for strangers at drive-thrus, the creation of micro-therapy groups for men struggling with lost loves, exhaustion, relationship neglect, the sense that life hasn't turned out the way they expected. No sooner had I told Will I was surprised by the amount of positive engagement, another tranche of responses flooded in.

'Connected' with my work colleague and she reported me for harassment.

Rolled a two, and wife called me a heartless bastard for ignoring her calls and messages!

Honesty is not always the best policy. Got the wild card and asked my parents to tell me something I don't know. Opened a whole silo of worms...

Interestingly, some contributers from the previous two weeks have performed follow-up rolls. Someone calling himself @jojenkins said he'd followed up a random act of kindness – feeding the scrawny cat up the street – by rolling a five in truth week and confronting the owner, who turned out to be desperately unwell. Been getting his shopping and sorting out care. It's been an eye-opener, that's for sure!

Why isn't the queue moving? Jemma asked me to pop in and grab a 'couple of bits' on my way home, and the only shop assistant manning the self-service checkout has disappeared to wrestle a security tag from a bottle of whisky. The woman in front of me huffs, then turns and scowls at me, as if I'm responsible for the delay. 'Faster checkout,' she says. 'That's a joke.'

I smile in what I hope is a sympathetic manner, then look down at my phone again. **@starlingtom**: Been thinking about my ex again since last episode. Rolled a six so decided to go for it... I'm going to track her down. Wish me luck, DH!

DH – Die Harders. There are a few comments underneath, mostly supportive, although **@turtlebay** has added: Wouldn't bother mate, she's a woman... she'll only screw you over again. It's his opinion – which he's entitled to, of course – but I don't agree, and it's not an attitude I want to be promoting to our followers. I make a mental note to talk to Will about moderating the content more closely, when I notice he's sent me a new message: LOOK!

There's a screenshot of a DM to our Instagram page from someone called Jon Wilkes:

Hi, I'm a journalist with *Men's Health*. Any chance we can talk about your story/movement?

'Excuse me.'

The man behind me is pointing at the vacant space where the tutting woman was. She must have scanned and paid for her trio of peppers and left, because now she's nowhere to be seen. I move to the next available till and scan Toby's fizzy teeth and Jemma's face cream, cheese dippers and carton of milk. 'You can eat here, if you want,' she'd said.

Men's Health.

Back at the car, I type a reply to Will:

`This is brilliant.`

I'm about to drive away when I realise I've left Jemma's shopping at the checkout.

'Daddy, watch.'

Toby draws water into his toy and squirts it at my chest. I wipe at my t-shirt with my hand. 'Try to keep it in the bath, Tobe, ok?'

'Look, Daddy. It's a creeper.'

My hand moves to my pocket. My phone isn't there.

I press my fingers into the other pocket.

Nothing.

Another jet of water strikes, close to my ear. 'Stop it now, Tobe. Let's get the shampoo and give your hair a—'

'Whish!'

Toby's tiny pink toes are peeping through the bubbles. He lifts the rubber toy and another jet of water spatters my t-shirt.

'*Toby.* That's enough.'

His face is pink. He drops the squidgy toy and twists to pick up one of the foam numbers instead, which are bobbing at his back, half consumed in bubbles. Did I leave my phone in Sainsbury's? I feel an irrational panic at the thought of being without it. Our followers might reach out – as they often do – with a confession, or for support. Will might need me. I imagine him, right now, in the studio working on content for the next episode, cursing me for my absence. Claire hasn't been happy with him for sharing details about their personal life. I could hear her through the walls of the house when I went to put my rubbish in the bin store last night. 'I'm sorry sex has become a *clinical order to perform*,' she snapped. 'And now people at work know I'm trying for a baby. I'm standing up there in meetings wondering if they're listening or imagining me pissing on an ovulation stick.'

'I've stopped making you wet now, Daddy. Look, number two,' Toby says, standing up to stick the number to the tiles.

'Very good, Tobe.'

He crouches down again, dunking both hands into the water. The salmon Jemma cooked for us earlier keeps repeating on me; little smoky signals of distress. I'm about to ask Toby what the number two is, multiplied by another number, when I hear my phone ringing from Toby's room. I must have dropped it in there when he was getting undressed.

'Wait there, buddy.'

Jemma has put her Abba album on downstairs; I can hear the muffled notes of *The Winner Takes It All*. I push open the bedroom door and there's my mobile, lurking beneath Toby's pile of discarded clothes. One missed call and a message from Will:

```
You're not going to believe this. Rich Logan
has invited us on to his show!
```

Surely not. Rich Logan has almost three million followers on Instagram and is one of the best-known names in podcasts, ranking consistently at the top of the charts for his forthright interviewing style and wide range of topics. Is this a wind up? I open the *Diecast* Instagram page and there it is; a DM from what looks like Rich Logan's official account:

```
Hey lads, love your Diecast stuff. Mad
concept! Fancy jumping on the pod?
```

Our latest episode now has 8630 views. **@Diecast**, **@RROK** and **@Truthordie** are trending.

There are more uploads on our podcast page. More likes and comments. A second message from Will appears – `He wants to arrange dates for us to go to London. Call me back!` – and I've started tapping a reply when I hear it.

A bang.

And a scream.

I run back into the bathroom to find Toby covered in blood. It's pouring from his nose, dripping into the water, turning it a coral pink. 'Jemma,' I shout, instinctively. '*Jem.*'

Toby's body is hot and slippery, almost impossible to grasp in my shaking hands. His blood starts running down the nape of my neck, and once I've got him safely cradled against my damp chest, he starts to scream – a sharp, thin wail of shock, straight into my ear. The Minecraft toy bobs to the surface of the water, an unsettling smirk on its rubber face. As I reach for a towel and pull it around Toby's tiny body, Jemma bursts in.

'Jesus. Oh my God. What happened?'

'He bumped his nose. Tip your head back for me, Tobe.'

Jemma rubs his back as I gently squeeze the top of his nose. The blood is already starting to clot, and with it, the liquid guilt inside me solidifies.

'Let's get you out of here.' I turn and open the door, unable to stand the oppressive, choking steam for a moment longer.

'I'll take him,' Jemma says. 'Go and get a cup of water. And the Calpol, it's in the cupboard. Get some cotton balls as well, they're in the downstairs loo.'

Toby wriggles against her, complaining that he wants his toy. I tell him I need to count his teeth, and he reluctantly opens his mouth. Nothing looks inflamed, thank God.

'You got blood on your top.' He points at my neck. 'And there.'

'I know. I'm sorry. It's ok, buddy.'

Die Trying

It isn't ok. It isn't ok at all. I rush downstairs, where Abba is still playing: *SOS*, which isn't a coincidence. It can't be. I call over the noise and tell Alexa to stop. My lungs feel stretched and raw; heavy as bricks. Water. Calpol. Cotton wool. I bring them back upstairs and present them to Jemma; an offering. Toby starts protesting as she wipes a damp cotton wool ball gently around his nose.

'Let's get you cleaned up, Mr Bump,' she says.

'Do you think we should call 111?'

'I don't know.' Jemma tilts her head to look inside Toby's nose. The knees of her jeans are wet. 'How hard was it? Did he go under?'

'I went to get a towel. I didn't see.'

'You didn't— Keep your head up, Tobe, that's it.' Jemma doesn't look at me. 'Yes. Call 111.'

And then I see the foam number that Toby has stuck on the tiles above the bath: *two*.

I can't think about that right now.

The NHS advisor asks some alarming questions: is Toby conscious, breathing, does he seem agitated or confused? Thankfully, the answer to most of them is no, and he tells us to keep an eye on him and administer pain relief if necessary. I trail a finger over the back of my head, across the scar, as he talks. A curl of salmon skin is hanging from the food waste bin where Jemma must have been in the middle of scraping the plates when I yelled for help; the open container smells pungent. I thank the advisor, hang up, then remain standing for a moment, completely still.

Emergency services are on the way, caller.

Two. Do nothing. Withdraw.

I stare out of the window into the darkness, before readjusting my focus and noticing my reflection. My t-shirt is clinging to my torso, wet and streaked with blood. I've been here before. Jemma on the floor, clutching a wedge of kitchen towel to her nose.

The people I love, I hurt. Is this karma? Is the dice evening the score?

I shouldn't be here. I push my phone into my pocket, collect my jacket and leave the house.

CHAPTER FORTY-SEVEN

Jemma

Adam's gone.

I still can't believe he just *vanished* like that. I looked everywhere, all over the house, checked the Ring doorbell and sure enough, there he was, driving off. Without even saying goodbye to Toby.

'Where's Daddy?' Toby asked, when he'd finished his KitKat and I'd helped him into his pyjamas. 'Can he read me a story?'

No, Daddy couldn't read him a story, because he was already back at his friend's house. He'd called to say he was sorry, he was truly sorry, but he had to leave, giving no fucking reason whatsoever. 'I know you're still pissed at me for introducing Toby to Dan,' I told him, 'But come on, we're both adults. You can't just disappear when things get ugly.'

It was irresponsible. Unacceptable.

'111 said to keep giving Calpol through the night, if necessary,' Adam said. 'Sorry, I should have told you that first. They don't think he needs to go to hospital. How is he? Can I speak to him?'

I couldn't believe his nerve. The cold was pressing into my bare feet from the kitchen tiles, and I was still shaking from the lingering shock of Toby's accident. 'You could have spoken to him *here*,' I said. 'Like you were supposed to.'

Toby lets out a deep sigh. He's asleep now, and although I've cleaned him up, there's still a thin crust of blood visible inside both nostrils. Normally I'd go downstairs and get ready for work with the TV on as background noise, or read a few chapters of my book, but I'm wound up, tight as a noose. Adam had repeated his apology, before saying it was the dice. I mean, seriously! 'Of course it was. Nothing's ever your fault, is it?'

'No, you don't understand. I had to—'

'No, *you* don't understand. When Toby realised you'd gone, he cried again. For twenty minutes! And even though I tried to calm him down, he kept telling me you didn't love him, you were angry with him, because guess what? Actions speak louder than words.'

I told him that if he wanted to see Toby again, he'd get a proper job. Sort himself out with counselling. Enough of this bloody podcast, enough of the die. It was time to start behaving like a responsible father, and still, I can't believe his response.

'We're just getting started,' he whined. 'We've been invited for an interview with *Rich Logan*.'

He seemed to think I'd be impressed. 'Seems you've made your choice then, haven't you?' I snapped. And then I hung up.

I head downstairs and take a sip from my unfinished glass of wine, but it tastes warm and sour, hitting the back of my throat with a sickly tang.

I pour the rest down the sink, and then call Dan.

There's a knock at the door half an hour later. Dan's brought another bottle of wine and bag of chocolate-dipped marshmallows. We've only known each other for six months, and said we'd take things slow, but we've been inseparable since we got back together. Rather than things feeling intense or claustrophobic like they sometimes did with Adam, it feels like we're building something fun and adventurous. As equals.

He's damp from the shower, wearing a Berghaus fleece over a dark-grey t-shirt that clings loosely in all the right places. I usher him into the kitchen. 'Thanks for coming. You can calm me down.'

'I was hoping to do the opposite.' When Dan presses his lips to my forehead, I feel heat of a different kind, though anger still bubbles beneath it. I've sprayed air freshener everywhere to cover the stink of fish, but I haven't had time to tidy up, and Toby's bloodstained towel is still sitting on top of the wash basket beside the machine. 'Ignore this,' I say, casting a hand over it. 'I haven't killed anyone. Yet.'

'That bad?'

'Adam's just... I can't believe he's putting a stupid show, a *die*, above his own son! Have you listened to the podcast?'

'No, but a group came in the other day and were talking about it. Caused a massive problem when one of their partners admitted they'd been throwing away their contraceptive pills. What is it? A game?'

'Something like that. He doesn't seem to understand that actions have consequences. The podcast is meant to be about reducing decision fatigue, whatever that means, and healthy masculinity, which is ironic. Honestly, I'm so done with it all. Even living here.'

'Do you want me to open the wine?'

'No. I need to keep a clear head in case Toby needs me tonight. If it's open, I'll want to down the lot. Thanks, though.' I move into the living room and sink onto the sofa with a heavy thump. There's no way Adam and I are getting back together – the thought of it now is like trying to stick a scab back on healed skin – but would it really be so wrong to start thinking about moving out? I tell Dan how much I miss my family in Manchester; how strange it feels to be so far away while Dad is ill. 'And Toby's missing out on so many experiences with his wider family. I'd never considered moving back before, because obviously it would mean taking him away from Adam. But now, with Adam behaving like this...'

'I don't know if I can be any help, because I don't have kids,' Dan says. 'But I'm a great believer in following your gut. If you're being drawn to something, there's usually a good reason for it.'

He's right. When we were apart, I felt like I'd lost a huge, important key that might unlock the next part of my life. And I know how dramatic and ridiculous that sounds – if I heard that line in a film, I'd roll my eyes and tell the actor to get a fucking grip. But it honestly felt like I needed to *do* something. When I messaged Dan to ask if we could meet, that Adam wasn't of sound mind when he threatened him and if he pulled that shit again, I'd kill him myself... yeah, I felt like I was back in control. I pull a face. 'I know. But I'd miss you too much.'

'I've never been to Manchester. I'd be up for that.'

'Don't say things you don't mean.'

'Would you want to live with me?'

'Of course I would. But what about work? Your sister?'

'There are climbing centres everywhere. My sister runs the business... she could easily find another instructor. Ah, but wait. No. No, I couldn't live with you.'

'Why not?'

'You play Abba. On speaker.'

I hit him with a cushion. 'You idiot. I'm going to play their songs all night now, just to give you an earworm.'

I don't, of course. We go to bed and test the idea of living together for signs of stress, as if it's a piece of smelted glass, too hot to hold. It's mad. Of course, it will never happen, it's just a fantasy. But he talks about the proximity to the Lake District, how I could take my sketchbooks and draw on the mountains, and I imagine the wind on my face like a scalpel, my body prickling inside layers of thermal clothing. Seeing the world through the eyes of a giant as cars and trains move like ants, miles below. *Yeah*. I want him to see the trams, the museums, the throbbing, vibrant heart of the city that has never stopped feeling like home. And then, because we're so close, I feel comfortable enough to tell him about Hannah. The piece of shit she trusted, who ended up wrecking her life. How guilty I felt for abandoning them all.

'It's not your fault,' he says. 'Some people are just cunts. Can't take no for an answer.'

We don't have sex. I'm worried about waking Toby, and Dan's exhausted. He falls asleep before I do, and I watch the rise and fall of his chest, the sweep of his lashes, the shadows pooling beneath the curve of his chin. *Some people can't take no for an answer.*

Adam's not going to like the idea of selling the house. I've never raised the *d* word – divorce – but at some point, we'll have to have these difficult conversations. He may not have liked the fact I introduced Toby to Dan either, but he was happy enough to talk and flirt with a random woman in a coffee shop, then upload the footage for content. *Truth*. It hurts, of course it hurts.

There's nothing pure or simple about it.

CHAPTER FORTY-EIGHT

Adam

I drive straight back to Will's house to be greeted with a bottle of Cava and enough enthusiasm to plug the pocket of shame. A barefooted Will invites me into the lounge, white t-shirt hanging out of his tracksuit bottoms. 'Mate, this is *awesome*. Rich Logan will help us go stratospheric.'

I keep my jacket zipped, feeling Toby's blood harden against my skin as it dries, gulping at the wine as Will continues to talk in exclamations. *Rich Logan! Reposts! Followers! Subscribers!* Somewhere around the second or third glass of wine, I stop worrying that he might be able to smell Toby's blood on me and ask where Claire and Molly are.

'Molly's upstairs. Claire's gone out.'

'Oh. Ok.'

I don't ask if they've had another row, and he doesn't tell me. Neither do I mention what's just happened with Toby. Will's in a celebratory mood, and I find myself swept along as he discusses what we can do to amplify our following. We've already added another hundred followers, and after the Rich Logan show... well, who knows? He suggests pitching for sponsorships, applying for guest slots on other wellness podcasts, buying and selling merch. 'I think we could really ramp this up now,' he says. 'Things are starting to stir. Feels like we're gathering momentum – we need to catch this wave and ride it. How about a *Diecast* meet-up? Live rolls of the die? It could be wild!'

And here we are again. The point of no return. It's intoxicating, exhilarating, unstoppable. I briefly considered Jemma's words on the way home, before realising there was nothing to be gained from them. What was the point in *counselling* when I was the one of sound mind? What was the point in stopping the podcast – if that were even possible – when we were spreading the word of the die?

It wouldn't make a difference anyway. She's made up her mind.

And Will's right; something *is* starting to stir. A movement, like the slow unfurling of a dragon's tail. The listeners, they want recognition. They all want to feel heard. Some of them have taken truth to the extreme: one has recorded himself confronting his boss, his parents – even his girlfriend – by telling them what he really thinks, while others have tied podcast themes together, admitting they cheated their random act of kindness (*gave a load of shit to a charity shop that should have gone to the tip*) or cherry-picked a fear. A growing number of followers are splintering into subgroups; adding the hashtag #RROK and filming themselves as a group, passing random rolls of kindness down a line by ordering food or drinks for the one behind, until an unsuspecting member of the public breaks the sequence.

The *Diecast* community is starting to feel like family. And it staggers me how quickly this place is starting to feel like home. Claire's flowers are still standing proud in the vase on the window, and the lounge smells faintly of the *Pink Sands* candle on the shelf above the TV. I think, fleetingly, of hot beaches. Bronzed skin. The lick of cool water on bare toes. Jemma wanted to go on holiday with me and Toby once; I can't remember why it didn't happen. Another one of those arguments that seemed to go round and around, tight as a wedding band, twisting and twisting until it made us both sore.

The wine is burning a path to my bladder. I break off our conversation to ask if I can use his toilet.

'Of course, mate. Upstairs, second on left.'

It's impossible to stand in Will's bathroom without thinking of Toby. In here, the bath, sink and taps are gleaming so that my face appears as a distorted orb inside them. Not a speck of blood. The towel, draped over the chrome radiator, is as soft as the hair of a newborn. I can't help stroking the heads of the three electric toothbrushes with my free hand and casting my gaze at the row of items scattered around the sink. Handwash, in a pump dispenser. A white flannel. Dental floss. Mouthwash. A tube of toothpaste, bent into a right angle as though it's been winded. I finish and zip up, then wash my hands.

There's nothing out of the ordinary in the bathroom cabinet. No anti-depressants or benzodiazepines like the kind Mum used to take. No sleeping pills. No evidence whatsoever, in fact, that Will ever has trouble sleeping. Just a bottle of castor oil, shampoo and conditioner, an assortment of what looks like mini-perfumes in glass jars shaped like teardrops, shaving gel and a box of folic acid tablets.

I unlock the door and step out into the hallway. I've forgotten Molly's up here until I hear the low burble of her voice through the white rectangle of her bedroom door. 'Weirdo,' she says. 'Yeah. I know. They keep arguing about it. My Dad's never fucking around anymore. Yeah. Totally messed up, and Mum just… you know, either working or talking about another baby, like – hello? You already *have* a child.'

I wait.

'Do it, then,' she says. 'Yeah, I want to. Fuck this shit.'

I don't tell Will what I overheard. It would be more than a little creepy to tell him I'd been listening to his daughter's conversation through her closed bedroom door, not to mention the fact the die reached out to me earlier. *Do nothing.*

We have another drink, congratulate ourselves on our success and, then, when Claire returns forty-five minutes later, I stumble back to the annexe – tired, a little drunk, still on a high from our podcast recognition – and peel off my jacket. All the while I was wearing it, there was no blood on my t-shirt beneath. Nobody saw; it didn't exist.

It did, though. It does.

I press the t-shirt deep into a canvas bag along with all my other dirty washing. Jemma doesn't pick up when I call, so I send her another message of apology, asking her to give Toby a hug and kiss from me. And then I spend a couple of hours trying to distract myself from today's events by reading new comments, rewatching our podcast episodes and listener footage.

@starlingtom: Reached out to my ex yesterday! Keeping faith… or will die trying lol. Wish me luck DH!

@andrewemms: So glad I stumbled across this pod! Just did my RROK and I'm sleeping rough tonight in the town centre. #Diecast #homeless #RROK #Solidaritysleepout

@gillgayner: Just rolled a one. Anyone up for a coffee over the weekend in the RWA coffee? My treat 😊.

Just before 10pm, Lisa messages:

Are you still up?

It's almost midnight when I turn off the light and plug in my charger. The last thing I see before I go to sleep is a picture of Toby, smiling at me from the home screen.

CHAPTER FORTY-NINE

Diecast #4

The Rich Logan Show – special episode with *Diecast* hosts Will King and Adam Dowdell: *Six Lives Project*

Rich Logan's building in East London looks like the inside of *Dragon's Den* – red brick and exposed steel girders, with tall floor-to-ceiling windows that give the impression of a space curated to look casually thrown together. The studio itself is a soundproofed glass box within a larger, open-plan loft. 'Wow,' Will says, taking one of the cushioned seats opposite Rich Logan's chair. 'This is definitely something to aspire to.'

'Make yourselves at home,' Rich says, pushing two bottles of water towards us. The lighting in here is warm – almost intimate – and makes him look like a waxwork figure. As he settles into his chair, I realise there's a thin sheen of powder on his face. 'Relax, get comfortable. Are you warm enough?'

I snatch my gaze away from the framed posters of achievement and the Spotify plaque on the textured acoustic panels behind him. 'Yes. I'm fine, thanks.'

'Yeah, yeah. I'm good.' Will's virtually trembling with excitement. I can tell what he's thinking: *one day, this could be us.* We've just been ushered through a small lobby with a coffee bar and shelves of merch by a young woman wearing a bright red lanyard – KAYLEE – that matched her heavy stamp of lipstick, and now, watching the tech crew moving beyond the glass, I feel like an exhibit in one of the Sealife tanks that Jemma insisted we take Toby to last summer.

Rich asks if we're ready to dive straight in and then he's off, saying how delighted he is to be welcoming two guests 'blazing a trail through the podcast scene'.

I catch Will's eye. He smiles.

'Let me ask you a question,' Rich booms, to his listeners. 'How many decisions do you make in a day? From the minute you get up, to the time you go to bed, it's relentless, right? I don't know about you, but even whether to *get* out of bed is a tough one, most days.'

35,000. That's how many decisions we make in a day. Rich invites listeners to consider a life hack unlike anything they might have considered before, and of course, we know the rest. The die. It can cure the 'constipation of indecision'. It can optimise one's life. It can energise people in ways they can't imagine.

A sound technician on the other side of the glass is looping a red cable around his forearm and, for no reason at all, I imagine myself on a tube platform, watching transmission lines tremor as a train rattles into the station. There's a pinch of pain somewhere above my right ear. A ringing sensation in my ears.

As quickly as it started, it stops.

'And here's why I think you're really onto something,' Rich says, pressing both elbows onto the desk and addressing us directly. 'People like leaders. They like decisiveness. Worse than someone who makes bad decisions is someone who can't make decisions. We've all made bad ones – I've certainly had my fair share. We can learn from them. But flip-flopping around with no opinions, always deferring to your partner or colleagues...' he puts on a high, reedy voice. '"I don't know... I can't... how do I...?" Pathetic, right? We end up sounding and feeling like losers. If you look at people at the top, they don't waste time on the small stuff. Steve Jobs. Obama. You don't see them on TV asking the interviewer what they think.'

Will leans towards the microphone. 'Yeah, I mean, it's really about simplifying life. Less perfectionism. Trusting your... well, if not yourself, then the die. And having a bit of fun in the process.'

Rich asks if we think most people simply need more discipline. Whether men aren't as good at decision-making as they used to be. 'And why is it that when women make decisions, they're called selfish? Ball breakers. Why are we all so confused and afraid?'

I don't have the answers. I feel like I did as a child, with Dad towering over me, spitting out questions like nails to hang my incompetence on. Even Will, usually so efficient in debate, appears too starstruck to formulate a coherent argument. Usually, he'd say something about the die offering practice in decision-making, which naturally leads to an improvement in clarity – the fake-it-to-make-it theory – but he's just nodding and agreeing with Rich's comments. *Yeah, too much energy is wasted on choices made by emotion.*

I'm not sure he believes that. He was quiet on the train journey here, and I know it's eating him up that he had to miss Molly's dance performance to be here today. Far from my presence freeing him up to spend more time with family, the podcast's interactive nature and growing popularity has meant more time working with me in the studio, not less. I finally told him about Jemma's refusal to let me see Toby and he stopped then, right in the annexe doorway, the wind stirring a cauldron of red and yellow leaves on the path behind him. 'Mate,' he said. 'I'm sorry.'

Neither of us suggested giving up the podcast. We both knew it was impossible.

'So, the *options*,' Rich says. 'Let's talk about that. They're set in stone, right?'

It's my turn to speak. I explain the importance of having a system to underpin the randomness of choice, otherwise the die would operate purely on chaos. 'And greed, because it's human nature to tilt towards personal fulfilment instead of self denial.' I talk briefly of the Stoic virtues that have always informed our method, and Rich nods sagely.

'Yeah, that's interesting. The balance of control and surrender. How much we give up, how much we hang onto, and the die... I get it. Yeah, I get it. It makes choices so *easy*. Ok, let's say me and my girlfriend are choosing what to watch on TV. How would that work?'

'The nightly scroll of doom,' Will laughs. 'So, rolling a one might convince you to watch the old series you used to binge when you were both happy. Two could mean turning off the TV and... uh... doing something else. Talking. Having sex. Whatever. Three could be a heavy war documentary or something like the Jeffrey Dahmer series—'

'Oh man. Did you watch that?'

'Yeah. And the whole time I was thinking: *I'm glad he never had a die.*'

We all laugh then, because it's funny. Ridiculous. Men like Jeffrey Dahmer – sick, with a grossly deformed grasp of humanity – are thankfully so rare as to be specimens of disbelief. We are good people, doing good things.

'If he did, you would hope he always rolled a two,' Rich says. 'And actually, I find two an interesting option. Sometimes, the hardest thing for a man is to do *nothing*.'

A tingling, inside my fingertips. Something acknowledged. I force myself to focus on the reassuring weight of the chair beneath me, and we talk about our previous episodes, followed by a teaser for our forthcoming rendezvous with fans: the Six Lives Project. 'We just ask that followers cast their die *before* they arrive, to decide on their persona for the evening,' Will says. He glances at me, then back at Rich. 'And, in a minute, we'll do the same.'

A man behind the glass is making a rolling gesture with one hand.

'Ok,' Rich says. 'It's been a pleasure… a *delight*, having you on the show. Thank you, Will and Adam. The table's yours.'

It's Will's turn to cast, as he undertook the last challenge. I can see Kaylee's outline hovering behind the door, clipboard tucked beneath one arm, and I feel like snatching the die from Will's hand. It all seems so performative. That hot, heady magic of rolling alone, the sense that I was tapping into something huge and mystical – it's absent now.

There's a moment of silence. The die skips theatrically across the smooth surface, pirouettes gracefully, then lands close to Rich Logan's microphone.

'Six.' Will cheers.

CHAPTER FIFTY

We catch the train back to London the following Friday, two days after Rich Logan's show goes live. Initially, we were planning to hold the fan meet and greet in a café or workspace in Bristol, but *Diecast* has blown up – exactly as Will predicted – and when a London events company offered us a last-minute space, the opportunity seemed too good to turn down.

There's just one speck on the horizon. Actually, two. For reasons unfathomable to me until I listened to more of his content, Rich Logan's team heavily edited our episode so it seemed to acquire darker undertones. His team renamed the title *Stop Thinking Like a Victim*, and inserted a long pause after Will flippantly suggested 'having sex' as an antidote to watching TV. Our laughter at the mention of Jeffrey Dahmer seemed obtrusively loud; crudely inappropriate.

'It's not ideal,' Will acknowledged. 'But it's not terrible, either. Most people aren't focusing on that – they're hooking up to the *Diecast* community, seeing what we're about. Look at the figures!'

I couldn't deny that he had a point. Wasn't this – all of it – exactly what we'd been longing for?

The train shudders to a noisy halt, and a moment later, commuters stream through the open doors and along the aisle, eyes scouting for a vacant seat. Will and I have been lucky to reserve two together, with a table, although I did have to ask a man with bright green headphones and a rucksack big enough to contain the crown jewels to move. Wild card = chaos. Anything goes. I'm looking forward to the evening until the second speck – which turns out to be more of a vulture-like shit splatter – appears, not on the horizon but staring up at me from the local news page on my phone screen. I turn it to Will. 'Have you seen this?'

He closes the lid of his laptop. 'Fucking battery keeps dying. What's that? We've hit the... oh fuck.'

When Kindness Turns Cruel, screams the headline. There's a short video clip of the couple from the coffee shop who rejected my random act of kindness on a bench inside the Galleries, looking considerably older than they did before. Within seconds, they're approached by a group of three men, one of whom immediately tips the entire contents of his takeaway coffee cup over Richard's head. 'Snobby bastards. Here's a random act of kindness,' he calls out. And then, unhelpfully echoed beneath with the aid of subtitles in bold white text, 'Smile for the podcast.'

Christine and Richard are eighty-one and eighty-three years old respectively. Their daughter, Susan, confirms that Richard has been trying to get out more, following his hip operation six months earlier, but they are now both too scared to leave the house. 'It's disgusting,' she says. 'My parents should feel safe to go shopping in peace. They've done nothing wrong.'

Will drops his head into the palm of his hand. 'We should pull the meet. The optics would be horrific. A *party—*'

'We can't cancel. It's too short notice.' I'm closest to the window; my breath is steaming up the glass. I can't help thinking of the smiley face that Jemma drew on the train, the first time we met. *We can't defy the die*, is what I'm really thinking. 'This is awful, but maybe we can use the event to drive home the message that our podcast isn't about doing harm. It's about being part of a healthy brotherhood, self-mastery, vulnerability. *Accountability.*'

'You reckon?' Will flips open the laptop lid again. 'I'll make a… ah, I can't – battery's dead. Shit, we don't need this on top of the Rich Logan slant.'

'Maybe we could…'

'What?'

I stare out at the endless green fields zipping past. Cows. Pylons. A solitary farmhouse with smoke emerging from the chimney. 'Maybe we should talk about Abbie.'

'*Abbie?* What the fuck has Abbie got to do with this?'

'She was there at the start of all this, and one of the biggest consequences of us using the die. Surely we should at least mention her name.'

Will's fingers tighten around his pen. He doesn't seem to know what to do with his other hand – it slides from the table to his lap, then back again. 'What, tell everyone the die told me to sleep with Lily that night? I don't think so. And can you imagine how her family would feel if we exploit her memory for clicks?'

'I just—'

'I know you liked her,' he says. 'As more than a friend – I know that. And what I did… I've never regretted anything more in my life. I don't want all that dragged up again.'

No. Maybe he's right. We've never spoken about my feelings for Abbie before, and the mention of them now makes me feel sullied and disloyal. He knew, and yet he kept her for himself? I press my mouth closed and try to stop the urge to grind my teeth, just like Abbie did, constantly, with a piece of gum. Sometimes I felt I was inside her mouth too, being ground to a flavourless pulp. I can't stand the thought that Toby might also become a footnote, nothing more than a fond memory, a disembodied voice, because not seeing him is killing me. We spoke last night on the phone and Lisa called me afterwards, asking why I was crying. 'I can't believe your ex would stop you seeing your own child,' she said. 'Especially after what she did to you. It was only an accident.'

I imagined Mum then, stroking my head. *Only an accident. Everything will be ok.* Lisa opened up about her experience of being cheated on too, saying you don't simply move on. It disrupts your entire sense of self. She said the die was good for helping, for healing, for changing perspective and getting out of your head, and I thought of all the other people who might be rolling, right at that moment. A bigger purpose. That's why I had been called upon: to make a sacrifice, change the lives of others, honour Abbie's memory.

And yet...

When Kindness Turns Cruel.

Sometimes, it's hard to keep the faith.

We take the Elizabeth Line across the city to Shoreditch. 'Plenty of time,' Will keeps reassuring me, so we stop for coffee and baguettes in a courtyard. It seems like the ideal place to stop and talk, until a pneumatic drill starts up in the vacant unit nearby and we're forced to abandon our seats, such is the shredding of my synapses. It feels like I'm being physically shaken, a jar of broken parts. We head out of the courtyard and into a thriving square with street artists and a maze of vintage market tents that catch our attention. By the time we find the basement space booked for our party, there's only half an hour to spare.

And there's already a small gathering outside.

'Woah,' Will says, stopping so abruptly I collide with his shoulder blade. 'Wow. Hello! This is... wow. You're here for the *Diecast* meet, right?'

Unnervingly, a few of them hold their phones up to record us by means of reply. To his credit, Will hides his nerves by moving forward and greeting them one by one. 'Amazing,' he keeps saying. 'We thought nobody would come!'

I imagine myself as an actor slipping into character. We've asked listeners to take on one of six personas for the evening, depending on their roll: the provider, the stoic, the disrupter, the confessor, the challenger or six – the wild card – meaning they can pick and choose, or switch between roles. After our slot on the Rich Logan show, Will invited listeners to decide which of us was to outsource ourselves to attendees for the evening, and the outcome was decisive.

Both of us.

The basement space has an arty feel, with wooden beams, fairy lights and portraits that resemble melted Skittles smeared across the canvas. There's a small stage accessed via three wooden steps and, after inviting guests to help themselves to a drink from the bar, Will and I give a short speech about the purpose of the meet. To connect, to be authentic. To find our energy and vulnerability but *not* as an excuse to settle scores or promote misogyny and intolerance. The group seems open and interested – not aggressive, as I had feared – and I start to relax as more people pour through the doors. There's a huge variety of old and young, smart and casually dressed. One man is wearing ripped jeans and odd shoes; I wonder if he's a disrupter or a challenger. Another is wearing a bandana, black biker jacket and the most enormous boots I've ever seen. Maybe it's his usual attire. Maybe not. There are a few women here too, standing together near the back window. 'This might feel alien,' Will says. 'But see if you can guess each other's personas. If you're not comfortable talking to strangers, all the more reason to do it. Unless you're a stoic, of course.'

We did something similar in college, just the two of us. I can't deny it was liberating, but also frightening, to rail against natural conversational instincts and interrupt, swear, make absurdly false claims. We're about to do it again now. This time, Will invites the followers to 'grab us, roll your die for us. We are literally at your mercy.'

A few drinks in, and the atmosphere changes. The music from the nightclub upstairs grows louder, punching through the walls and ceiling like a metal fist. I've been asked to describe – by a man wearing a t-shirt inscribed with the words *Porn Hub instructor*, who rolled a four – my darkest fantasy. Will, as provider, has just bought a round of drinks for everyone. A stoic is nodding at the ranting of a challenger who disagrees with his political standpoint, and if it weren't for the pressure of the stoic's fingers around the glass, the tightness in his expression, I would consider him infallible.

Outside, the sky is darkening; soon the day will be rubbed out altogether. As Will's voice grows louder, his face glossy with ebullience and inebriation, I find myself wishing that Lisa was here. She'd take me away from all of this. Two of the women are dancing now, holding up their phones and recording themselves singing, while the third…

The third is kissing Will.

CHAPTER FIFTY-ONE

Jemma

'Your ex runs *Diecast*?'

'Unfortunately, yes. Well, he's a resident host.' I honestly thought Adam couldn't sink any lower, but here he is, all over Instagram and TikTok, having a *party* – seriously! – while revealing 'his truths'. 'Hurt someone I loved,' he says earnestly, when asked about the worst thing he's ever done. 'My deepest fear? Well, I've already lost my son. I'm not sure...'

I had to stop the clip, because I thought I might vomit. Now, I'm at Beth's house, having been invited to a small gathering with Dan and a few of their friends from the climbing centre, and no sooner had I removed my coat than the subject of *Diecast* came up. Beth started it, by asking if anyone had seen the video clips from 'that' podcast. The one where the male host kissed someone last night. Better than reality TV, but what a pair of *fuckwits*. I knew what was going to happen next. I wanted to bolt across the kitchen diner and put my hand over Dan's mouth – *nonono, please don't say anything!* – but it was too late; he'd already spun around, bottle in hand, and the words were out. 'That's Jemma's ex. Adam.'

'Your ex?' Beth repeats. It's not really a question; her tone of voice suggests she's processing something in her head.

'Yeah.' I try to make light of it. 'I know, "fuckwit!"'

'So, all that stuff about his wife cheating on him – that was you?'

'Yeah, but I—'

Dan interrupts. 'Jemma's hardly responsible for what her ex-husband does.'

'She cheated with *you*, Dan. What if his followers start turning up at the climbing centre for revenge attacks? And seeing as I've been contacted by Tom fucking Starling because of that stupid podcast, I'd say it does concern me. I don't need that shit in my life again.'

'That's not Jemma's fault,' Dan says firmly. There are five of us in the room, and no one seems to know what to do. I'm grateful that Toby's run upstairs to play with Olivia. The two men leaning over the dining room chairs stop picking at mozzarella sticks; one sits, the other looks down at his phone. Beth's husband, Sam, lifts both hands from his hips, a gesture of peace: *why don't we all calm down?* I put down my glass and slide my coat from the back of my chair. 'Sorry. Maybe I should go.'

'Jemma...' Dan says, but I'm already out of the room, heading upstairs to collect Toby. I'd been looking forward to talking about the places Dan and I had seen on the outskirts of Manchester to rent, but now there's a weird atmosphere. Fucking Adam and his fucking podcast. I'm cringing at the memory of him unburdening himself on it at my expense. *Rock bottom. Not in a good place. My wife kicked me out.* I imagine them all talking about me later. *Can't believe she's the ex-wife! Didn't he have a brain tumour?*

Toby doesn't appreciate me dragging him away from his new friend, and wails all the way down the stairs. Dan's waiting for me at the bottom, wincing as Toby's shout penetrates his ears. 'She didn't mean it, Jem.'

'I wish you hadn't mentioned it. Are you still coming back to mine?'

'Do you want me to?'

'Yes. Of course I do. But... you know, I don't want you to leave early as well.'

Dan hems and haws, putting one hand on the banister. 'I'll probably stay for a bit, then. Let me come out to the car with you.'

It's windy outside. I strap Toby into the car seat and give him my phone to play with, then move around to the driver's side where Dan's standing, shivering from the cold. 'Who is Tom Starling, anyway?'

'He's an old boyfriend of Beth's. Well, not even a boyfriend, really – he booked a hotel room for their first date as a birthday present, and when she said it was too much, too soon, he got all funny about it, saying they *had* to go – he'd spent all day filling it with rose petals and balloons.' His expression darkens. 'She had no way of getting home, so she called me and I went to collect her. That was the end of it, but now the fucking worm's back again, insisting that he's rolled a die for connection and that they must somehow have unfinished business.'

'Can't she call the police?'

'No, because he hasn't *done* anything, as such. She doesn't want me to get involved. This isn't personal, you know. We've always had each other's backs, and as I had all that trouble recently with my ex, she's wary. She just doesn't know you properly yet, but don't worry. I'll talk to her.'

I climb into the car and wind down the window. 'Would it help if I have a word with Adam? I don't know exactly what he could do, but—'

'No. Honestly, Jem, this isn't your circus.' He leans down and gives me a kiss. 'I'll see you later.'

When I get home, Toby and I get changed into our pyjamas and eat popcorn on the sofa. I stroke his hair and read him four stories, thinking about how far the tentacles of Adam's podcast have reached. After the assault on the elderly couple, several people have come forward to complain about having their secrets splashed all over the internet, and there was that other man – Callum, Caden... something like that – who posted on Facebook to say he only realised how warped his mind had become after walking straight past a homeless man being beaten up 'because he rolled a two.' What if Beth's right and some of Adam's less principled followers decide to take revenge? It's probably only a matter of time before they find out who I am – Adam hasn't exactly been restrained in his criticism of me.

I'm halfway through reading *Where the Wild Things Are* when a swathe of white light penetrates the blinds. I tell Toby to wait a minute, then go into the kitchen to peer through them.

Sally from number thirty-seven is climbing out of a taxi.

'Mummy?'

'Sorry, Tobe.' I drop the blind.

This has to stop. Yesterday, I could have sworn I saw Adam on the other side of the bushes, watching me and Dan with Toby at the park. It had been a beautiful day, with leaves spiralling around us like flakes of coloured plaster, and Toby asked Dan to pursue him in a game of chase, zig-zagging across the park until he – Left-Feet Toby, Adam and I used to call him – tripped and fell in a wailing heap at the bottom of the slide. I ran over to dust him down and that's when I spotted the flash of colour: white t-shirt, dark jeans, same build. He strode briskly off, causing a pair of pigeons to flap from a puddle, and I realised it couldn't be Adam: wrong build, wrong height, and biggest clue of all, he was walking a small brown dog on a short orange lead.

I need to get away from here. As soon as possible. The sense of unease is palpable now; so close that it feels like another entity, something I could press my palm against. *Face Your Fears*; that was one of the *Diecast* episodes, wasn't it?

What if you can't name them? What if they are beyond conscious grasp?

CHAPTER FIFTY-TWO

Adam

So much for changing the course of destiny. So much for mental wellness, growth mindsets and being authentic. The *brotherhood*. Will's fucked up again, and although he said he stopped the kiss almost as soon as it began, I didn't confront him. I couldn't.

Because I was the stoic.

And now, reactions are divided. Unbelievably, some people are calling Will a lad. A legend. The *Diecast* pages are alive with speculation.

@Bibisim: Hypocritical much? Thought Diecast was meant to be about accountability and positive inspiration, but Will's married. Not ok...

@svaldez: These two are my guilty pleasure.

@RSpyder_88: I was there, and she definitely started it. She was a disrupter, he was a provider... what do you expect lol. Not sure he stopped it that quickly though 😜. Thanks for an amazing night, lads!

When I got back to the annexe, I couldn't sleep. There was a new message from *Men's Health* telling us that 'due to recent news coverage about the podcast' they were sorry, but they'd need to cancel the interview next month. To my horror, when

Die Trying

I refreshed the page, Katya had left a comment beneath the Rich Logan footage: `Used to work with Adam and felt sorry for him after everything he's been through. Now... not so much!`

Others piled in, saying Will was full of himself and I was about as useful as a punctured condom. Our defenders were just as visceral, responding that the 'slippers and sandals brigade' should shut up and get a life, because they'd 'obviously never had a night to die for'. The following morning, Will rejected my plea for him to come down to the annexe – urgently – to discuss strategy, saying he needed to be with Claire; he had a lot of making up to do.

I read the words until they blurred before my eyes. And then, because I needed to get away from the hex in the room next door, I drove into the city and walked without purpose; passing mannequins in windows, lumpen shapes in shop doorways, a solitary woman, hunched and limping. When I reached McDonald's, I experienced a wash of despair, thinking of the last time I was there with Toby. Somehow, I'd found myself back in the place where I began, going round and around in circles. And then, as if the universe were trying to prove my point, I heard a slap of laughter and saw Spencer amongst a trio of suited men heading towards me, blue lanyards swinging from their necks. I pulled the hood of my jumper up and darted into a side street until they passed by.

On the way home, I wondered: how does it happen? How do men like him – arrogant, sleazy, unprincipled – always end up on top?

Perhaps it is fate, after all. Perhaps we're destined to be who we are, where we are, and there's nothing we can do about it.

I park in Cabot Circus – a little too close to a pillar for my liking – and check my watch. Plenty of time to walk over and meet Lisa. I messaged her this morning to ask if she'd like to go to the Italian restaurant opposite the Hippodrome theatre, because I didn't know who else to turn to. Jemma called earlier to 'see how I was doing', and I thought that maybe she was mellowing a little. I told her about the man called Oscar who pressed a business card into my hand at the fan meet and said they needed men like me in his firm. Bold. Adventurous. Unafraid to take risks. I'd even laughed, thinking she'd laugh in response and agree that he had no idea. Or maybe she'd placate me. *Actually, I like the new you, Adam. Come back. You can see Toby whenever you like.*

She told me the podcast was a shitshow. She was fed up of being cast as the villain and constantly having to look over her shoulder. And, somehow, Dan's sister had been sucked into it. 'We need to have a proper chat soon,' she said. 'You know... about the house and everything.'

A row of hives appeared from nowhere, twining up my forearms in angry red cables. I must have chewed furiously too, because now the inside of my mouth feels rougher than the Bretti Rocks climbing wall. I told her I was busy, then hung up before she had the chance to burn me with another word.

Lisa arrives at the restaurant a few minutes after me, looking angelic in a crisp white top and billowy dark trousers. Her eyes are brown, glittering, with a thin line of chestnut pencilled above each lid, and when she raises them to meet mine, I'm reminded of the owl I saw when I took Toby to the zoo. 'You look beautiful,' I tell her, after we've embraced and taken our seats. 'Thanks so much for coming tonight – I thought you might have been put off after everything that's happened.'

'Don't be silly. You haven't done anything wrong.'

'I know, but I feel responsible.' It doesn't matter that we sent the old couple flowers and a personal apology; it still happened. Someone at the party said they'd had to break character to stop a challenger from getting 'battered' and were concerned about the repercussions. Many listeners have spoken up to say

Die Trying

they've been deeply hurt by newly unveiled truths. And Will's marriage now appears to be hanging on by a thread, although obviously I'm not accountable for that. 'Our podcast isn't a licence to cause harm. It's never been about that.'

'That's the nature of the show though, isn't it? Giving people a script and seeing how they interpret those choices. I've been surprised, actually, by how revealing it is. Everyone *thinks* they're good, but give them a die to roll and suddenly you see their micro biases. Especially towards women.'

A waiter comes to take our orders and when he moves away, I tell her that, if she's talking about men with an arrogant belief in their superiority, I know what she means. 'I hate people like that. The ones who disrespect women. There's absolutely no need for it.'

'I think a lot of them don't even realise. You know: "family" men who look at porn because "everyone does it". The ones who don't let you merge into traffic because they've got this subconscious thing about female drivers going on.' She pauses to thank the waiter, who returns with our drinks: a small red wine and a non-alcoholic beer. 'You'd be surprised how many men view women through the prism of how fuckable they are.'

Fuckable. I feel a traitorous, shameful, stirring between my legs. Lisa's doing that Lady Di thing again – rolling her brown, snowy-owl eyes up to mine – and I slide my feet forward beneath the table, withdrawing them quickly when they collide with hers.

'Listen, it's not all men, and I know women can be *very* toxic too. Oh, I probably sound bitter, because I've been in the same situation as you.' She raises her glass. 'Anyway. Here's to not dating arseholes.'

'Here's to not dating arseholes.' I return the gesture, tapping my glass gently against hers. Are we dating? What is this, exactly?

A door to the kitchen swings open, and a waiter strides out carrying two sizzling platters: chargrilled chicken legs and wings smothered in something red, a cluster of onion rings, two pork chops nestled beside four chargrilled sausages. And on top, a tomato sliced in two, hot and weeping. He disappears around the corner and returns a moment later carrying only the serviette, like a magician performing a magic trick. I think of Will and Claire, also out tonight for a 'make-up meal', and then I think of the die, sitting impassively on the studio shelf. Sometimes I wonder about all the other choices that didn't happen and whether they exist in some other universe, like unborn children. I'm about to explain Jemma's philosophy – that no one collides at random – when our food arrives, steaming, on dark-green plates. Lisa talks about her work, her family, her dog, while stirring her fork, round and round, in a sticky red sauce that reminds me of Toby's blood. When she goes to the toilet, I scroll through our *Diecast* socials. There are more uploads. More comments. The yin and yang of love and hate, blotting the screen like dead spiders. And then, two words leap out at me. *Beth Bretti.*

Tom Starling left the comment a week ago, and somehow it passed me by:

Anyone know how I can track my ex, Beth Bretti? I don't live in Bristol anymore and can't see her on socials.

I scroll through the previous comments, feeling angered on his behalf. Beth walked out on him *with another man* when he'd gone to the trouble of booking a hotel suite for her birthday. There can't be too many Brettis around here. It must be Dan's sister, Beth Hawkins. What is it with this family? Are they all parasites? I start typing a private message, and when Lisa returns from the ladies, I slide my phone back into my pocket.

'I brought my die,' she says. 'I thought we could roll to decide where to go next. *If* you want to go anywhere next.'

'I... well...'

Colour appears in Lisa's cheeks. 'It's fine, you don't have to.'

'No, it's not that I don't want to – I just can't roll outside the podcast. It's a personal thing. But I'm happy... if you're ok to do the roll, of course I'll come somewhere else with you.'

My phone starts vibrating in my pocket. I ignore it.

'I've got a few ideas,' Lisa says, fumbling in her bag. 'Wild Card – we ask a stranger. They might have a recommendation for somewhere neither of us has ever been. If it's three, we could go to a karaoke bar. Unless you're brilliant at singing, then that would be—'

'Oh, I'm not. I'm a *terrible* singer.'

She laughs. 'Four... we could phone one of those fortune-telling lines. And if it's one—'

'Sorry. I'm really sorry,' I interrupt. My phone is vibrating again, urgently, against my thigh. *Will*. 'Do you mind if I take this?'

'Go ahead.' Lisa sits down again, placing her bag close to a tiny red stain on the tablecloth. I slide my finger across the screen. Before I have a chance to speak, Will's words spill out; so quickly that it takes a moment to make sense of them.

'Mate, you need to come back, the police are here. Molly's missing.'

CHAPTER FIFTY-THREE

Molly's missing. I paid the bill, apologised to Lisa and now I'm driving along roads both familiar and unrecognisable, my headlights picking out the elbow-sharp bends just moments before I'm upon them. I'm reminded of the time I drove in darkness; the fist in my stomach that punched upwards and outwards at each of my organs in turn. I pass through a dense tunnel with trees bending to form an archway, and the distance between me and Lisa grows.

When I arrive at the Kings', the police car is on the drive, parked at an angle behind Will and Claire's Mercedes. I pull up on the road, close to the hedge, feeling horribly dazed at the sight of it. Will opens the door and gestures for me to come through to the dining room where two male police officers are sitting at the table, talking to Claire. One is older than the other, and the conversation doesn't seem to be about Molly but the awkwardness of his security belt, which he's taken off and placed on the table. 'It's not the belt that's the problem, it's my gut.' And then, to me. 'Hi. You must be Adam.'

He wants to know how long I've been staying here. How long I've known the family. What my relationship with Molly is like. His younger – thinner – colleague scribbles notes on his pad between sips of tea while Claire's mug remains on the table in front of her, untouched. 'I don't know her that well,' I tell them. 'She seems like a normal teenager to me.'

Will shakes his head, then leaves the room. I wonder if he's thinking of Abbie. The days that followed her disappearance – each one ten, fifteen, twenty feet tall. We told ourselves she'd probably gone off grid. Perhaps she had fallen and injured herself and would soon be discovered; hungry and cold, but alive. All the while we didn't know, there was hope.

Until there wasn't.

I wonder if I should sit beside Claire. She's looking up at me, moving her fingers between her throat and lips.

'We understand you were out with a female friend this evening,' the officer says. 'Can you give us some details?'

'Yes, her name's Lisa Fisher. I met her at Ciao Amici, around 7pm.'

'I'll need her contact details. When did you last see Molly?'

'I don't know. A few days ago?'

'Where?'

'Going in and out of the house. Not to speak to.'

'Have you heard her mention anything that might be relevant? Any dice games she and her friends might—'

Claire cuts in. 'You think this might be related to the *die*?'

'It's a line of enquiry we're considering. We're gathering information from her social media to get a picture of what she likes – it might help us locate her. Can you think of any other favourite places she might like to hang out? Places you've been as a family, anywhere that might have a sentimental connection?'

'No.' Claire explains that Molly has found new friends quite easily since they moved; she has no reason to go back to London. 'Will's parents don't even bother sending a birthday card. My mum lives in Canvey Island, but she hasn't turned up there.'

'Her father?'

'He only sees her for a week or so in the summer holidays, and occasionally at Christmas. They're not close.'

She gives names and contact details, and I slide off my shoes. The socks come partially away with them, and the skin on my feet looks a puckered, cowardly yellow. 'Is there anything I can do? Do you want me to try calling her?'

'No, it's ok.' Claire glances up with a hopeful expression at a disturbance in the light, but it's just Will coming back into the room. 'She won't pick up.'

There's an abrupt silence, punctuated by a ticking clock on the shelf above the TV. The bouquet of flowers has disappeared, probably dead now, crushed into a bin somewhere. The beltless officer stands to look at the black-and-white family photos on the wall. 'Apologies for asking the same questions, but has there been anything unusual in the last week or so that you can think of? Any changes in behaviour? Arguments?'

Claire rests her arms on the table. She turns to give Will a withering look, then inspects each of her upturned palms in turn. 'The podcast party has caused quite a bit of friction between us. Molly hasn't mentioned it, although I'm sure she doesn't appreciate her stepdad behaving like a teenager.'

The officer stops writing and looks up from his notepad. '*Diecast*. We're familiar with that. Did she say anything about how she was feeling?'

'Yes,' Claire says. 'She said she was angry with all of us.'

CHAPTER FIFTY-FOUR

Toby went missing in a country park when he was three. It was Jemma's idea: if we couldn't even have a family holiday due to my dickhead boss, she said, we could bloody well enjoy a few days out over the summer. It was a battle to get the time off, so – under threat of divorce – I'd phoned in sick. We were miles from home and forecasters spoke of it being the hottest day of the year, so we took plenty of sun cream, a picnic and three blankets which we spread over the grass near the play park. We rented a boat, laughing when the oars got tangled in the weeds and telling Toby off when he stood up or tried to lean over the side, but the sun was ferocious on my pale skin and, by lunchtime, I couldn't stay out in it any longer. I told them I was heading to the on-site shop to buy more water. It was several hundred feet away and I browsed for longer than I normally would, enjoying the cool caress of the air-conditioning on my body. When I took the water back, Jemma frowned at me. 'Where's Toby?'

She thought he'd come to the shop with me. He was nowhere to be seen.

The lake lay all around us, its beauty suddenly a thing of terror. And then, within moments, Jemma became unrecognisable from the person she'd been moments earlier: screaming, crying, grabbing people at random and asking if they'd seen a small boy in a blue-and-white striped t-shirt. I was about to sprint to the entrance to ask a park warden for help when someone came running over to say they'd found him. He was playing inside the small wooden ship, completely unaware of the chaos unfolding around him.

We kept him close after that. I taught him about the importance of staying safe near roads, water, strangers. I was relevant. I had influence. I had authority.

And I had it again, with *Diecast*.

Until everything turned to shit.

Molly's Instagram page is full of dozens, if not hundreds, of images: plates of food, close-ups of milkshakes set on a table against the caption *sharing with my besties*, screenshots of conversations with friends, quotes about life, clips of animals. According to the Bristol police Facebook appeal – and Claire – Molly was last seen in the city centre at 11am, coming out of Primark. After that, she caught a bus to her friend Jasmine's house in Filton, where they were joined by three more schoolfriends: Ella, Harry and Fin. Molly left shortly after 4pm, saying she was heading home.

Now, the police have gone. Will has stopped repeatedly asserting that she'll be fine; she'll have crashed at a friend's or lost track of time. 'CCTV,' he announces suddenly. 'Did we ask the police about CCTV before they left?'

'I'm sure they'll have thought of that,' Claire snaps. She keeps shuffling from one end of the room to the other, pausing to gaze at the spatter of rain that has started tapping quietly against the dark windows. The police have advised them to stay put while they co-ordinate the response, just in case Molly makes it home. *We'll be doing everything we can to find her.* I run the hot tap to drown out the sound of rain, then wash up the cups and plates. Claire loads video clips of the *Diecast* party and starts watching them closely, through narrowed eyes. 'Who's that?' she says. 'And that? Who is that man behind you? Did you say anything about our family? That woman who kissed you – who is she?'

When she eventually goes upstairs to get a tissue, Will and I sit, silent, like disgraced schoolchildren.

I glance at him. 'Is there?'

'What?'

'Anything else? Has anything else happened?'

Will glowers. 'Absolutely not. If there was something they needed to know, don't you think I'd have said? I know I was a prick, but... Jesus. I'd never put my family at risk.'

You have, though. We both have.

I suggest sharing Molly's missing person appeal to the podcast socials, something Will agrees is a good idea until several people leave comments asking how much lower we can sink. *Seriously, you're using a missing girl to try and distract people from the fact you've fxxed up? Give your heads a wobble.*

'Great,' Claire says, when she comes back downstairs. 'You've made content from our daughter's disappearance and advertised the fact there's a teenage girl out there, alone. And for the people who've said they'll go looking, what if they find her? What if they roll the die to decide whether to rape or strangle her?'

'Claire—'

'They *might*. You don't know how far some people would be willing to go. Maybe someone has kidnapped her, after rolling a die. You don't know!'

Twelve new notifications. Seven shares.

`Let's help find this missing teen.`

`Tagging my friend in the Filton area. @`**`BeckyFeeney`**` seen this girl?`

`Shared: Missing People in Bristol and surrounding area.`

`Do a six-location roll, we'll all look` 😊

'Someone must have seen her,' I say. 'The more people that look, the better. That's what the police said, wasn't it? Someone must have seen something.'

Will stands up and wraps his fingers around the back of the chair. 'I've just remembered something. Moll said she thought she heard you prowling outside her bedroom door the other week when you came in for a drink. I said she was being paranoid.'

Claire's back at the window. When she turns, I don't like the way she's looking at me.

'What? I'm *nothing* to do with this.'

'I wasn't saying that.'

Then what *is* he saying? No. Disgusting. The thought of it. The thought of him *thinking* it, and I can tell from the downward pull of his mouth that's exactly what he *is* thinking. 'I wasn't *prowling*. I went to the toilet, and when I was heading back across the landing, yes, I did hear her talking. She said you weren't interested in her anymore and she was sick of all the arguing... something about "doing it".'

'You're coming out with this now?' Will says. 'Why didn't you mention it when the police were here?'

'I've only just *remembered*. Will, if you're trying to pin this on me, you've got a nerve. You're the one who always...'

A sprig of colour appears on Will's face. *Go on*, his eyes are saying, *I dare you*. I feel it smouldering: *the party wasn't the first time you abandoned your girlfriend to chase a new thrill, was it?*

'He's the one who always *what*?' Claire's frown deepens.

'Messes up. Fucks around. Did you know Will rolled the dice the night his girlfriend died? When we were at college together? It told him to sleep with someone else, but who *puts* that kind of option to the die in the first place? She'd still be alive if—'

Will's punch lands on the side of my nose. I stagger backwards, knocking a glass to the floor where it shatters on impact. Blood rushes to my head, bringing things into sharp focus: Claire's bag, sagging open on the table, a gash of black fabric.

Lip balm, hairbrush, purse, tissues, a half-eaten pack of gum. A hot, clear liquid trickles from one nostril. 'Stop going on about Abbie,' Will thunders. '*Are* you anything to do with this? Are you?'

He's wearing the same expression Claire did a minute ago. I can see her in the corner of my eye, standing several feet away, and I don't recognise the tightness of her lips, the sharp line of her jaw. How could they *think* that? Claire picks up her phone and moves out of the room just before I land a return blow on Will's cheekbone. One for sorrow, two for joy. A moment of surprise, then his hand is at my throat, pushing me backwards until my head strikes the kitchen cabinet behind me with a thud that I feel through the soles of my feet.

Again.

And again.

A blissful ringing in my ears. My teeth snap together, landing on the grisly lump of my tongue. I wonder if the scar at the back of my head will burst open.

'YOU CAN STOP NOW.' Claire pulls Will's arm away. 'The police are on the phone. They've found Molly.'

PART THREE

CHAPTER FIFTY-FIVE

I go out to see Will the following morning, while he's taking bags to the bin store in the garden. There are swollen pillows beneath his eyes, a network of broken veins beneath the skin, and the punches I landed have left a shiny, reddened disc on one cheekbone. I probably don't look much better. After the fight, Claire told me I needed to leave, and because I wasn't sure whether she meant the house or the annexe, I went to the only space I could still lay claim to: my car. As the rain hurled itself contemptuously against the windscreen, I thought about calling Lisa. I thought about Toby. But mostly, I thought about Molly.

What happened to her?

The Kings returned to the house around 2am and shortly afterwards Will texted me to say I didn't have to stay outside. He replied to my message of apology with one of his own, saying Molly had been found at an abandoned bungalow in Portishead with a group of eight friends. The police confirmed that she was part of a Discord group with other teens who roll, and wasn't the only child reported missing last night.

'Has she said anything else?' I ask him now. A mob of dead leaves circles us, whisking away the ghostly wave of my breath.

'Not much. But the police showed us the Discord group footage and it's disturbing. The other teenagers have been on the group for a while, and they've shared uploads of themselves using the die for dares: breaking into other derelict buildings, swimming naked in the dark, even taking it in turns to lie on a train track. It's lucky no one's been killed.'

'Jesus.' Poor Molly. Claire said last night that she was angry with all of us, and no wonder. While Will and I had been locked in a bubble of our own making, she'd been crying out for attention. 'Is Claire ok? Does she think—'

'She's in pieces. Because... well, we don't know for sure, but there's a suggestion that they might have been rolling to do stuff. You know. Sexually.'

'She's thirteen!'

'I know. They said there'll be an investigation.' Will tugs at the hood of his sweatshirt. 'Look, the podcast. With everything, I don't think we'll be able to carry on—'

'Of course not. No, it's fine. Honestly. It's fine.'

'I'll have a chat with Claire. I'm sure she won't mind you staying until you've found somewhere else.'

'Thank you.'

Will drops the lid of the bin store with a clang. He pats me, once, on the shoulder. And then he returns to the house without saying another word.

I can smell the death of hope, putrifying and fetid, like the stink of stale food and rotten milk that's just been dispatched in a startling blast. We will not be preparing the next episode of *Diecast* today. We will not be buying merchandise and setting up sponsorship deals. We will not be 'catching the wave and riding it' – as Will so confidently declared less than a month ago – because it has crashed on our heads.

I find my legs propelling me to the car, and after slotting myself inside, it fleetingly occurs to me that this is the only thing I can still call my own. *Well, what did you expect?* Dad sneers, as I start the engine.

Fuck off, I think. *Fuck off, you selfish, twisted piece of shit.*

I catch a glimpse of myself in the rear-view mirror. No, I'm definitely not seventeen anymore. The hairs protruding from my nose and around my ears are growing thicker and longer, and there's a light dusting of grey amongst the dark flecks pushing through my chin. I'm starting to look more and more like my father. Am I turning into him? Abandoning my son, moving from place to place, trying to find myself through someone – or some*thing* – else, and ruining everyone else's lives in the process.

No, that cannot be. I will not walk away that easily. I will not leave my child to feel lonely and insecure, like Molly did.

All the way home, I manage to convince myself that I no longer miss Jemma, but when she opens the door – red top, black jeans: danger and darkness – something stirs. Tiny flakes of ash. She'd tried to put me off coming, saying it would confuse Toby, they were going out shortly, it wasn't a good time, but when I asked where they were going, she stumbled. It was a lie, of course.

'Can I come in?'

'I just...'

Toby is standing behind her, toy car in one hand, finger tugging at his bottom lip, looking at me with a mixture of curiosity and suspicion. As if I'm something unfathomable. 'It doesn't have to take long. I need to talk. A lot has happened, and I'm—'

'I heard.' She stands to one side, granting me access. I sweep Toby into my arms, but his body remains firm, a bollard of mistrust. 'Is this about your friend's daughter?'

'How do you know about that?'

'Matty's part of the same Discord group, along with a couple of his friends. Frankie's going *nuts*. Did you hear what they were doing?'

Toby extracts himself from my grasp. He says he wants to show me something, and runs upstairs. 'Not exactly.'

'They used a die to... well, it sounds like it might have turned into some kind of orgy if police hadn't arrived when they did. Rolling to snog, rolling to get naked... grim. I've fallen out with her about it because she's adamant that none of it was Matty's fault.'

Matty, two years older than Molly. Matty, who feels the whole world owes him a favour because his mother always bails him out. I can't deny that this knowledge gives me a small shot of pleasure. Holier-than-thou Frankie, always on hand to give Jemma advice – usually the toxic, unwanted kind.

'He was trying to make out it was all the girls' idea and he was being made a scapegoat, but your friend's daughter was the youngest there.' She takes a deep breath, folds her arms. 'The only thing we were in agreement about was the fact your podcast has caused a shitload of misery for everyone.'

'I know. I'm sorry. But Jem... you don't need to worry about that. I'm not doing the podcast anymore. I'll get a new job. I *promise* I won't let Toby down again.'

'Yeah. Thing is, I've heard that before,' One of Jemma's hands starts moving, up and down the opposite arm. I instantly think of the human lie detector's words: *you spot the leaks by contrasting normal behaviour with how they respond under questioning.* She wants to believe me, but she doesn't know if she can trust me, and that's fair enough. Actions speak louder than words. 'As you're here, though, we do need to talk about selling the house. Or at least formally seeing a—'

'I've got a calcleator.' Toby says, clattering back down the stairs. 'Seven three three spells eel.'

'That's clever.'

'You can put any numbers in.' He slips the calculator into the fabric bag hanging from his shoulder and takes my hand; all is forgiven. I follow him into the lounge where he tips the bag upside down, and a pile of plastic bricks fall onto the rug. Jemma watches me kneel beside him, her mouth a puckered knot.

'Can I just have this time?' I ask her. 'Please?'

She relents. And as I play with my son, sorting colours, pressing the bricks together and building houses without doors, Jemma's earlier words soften around the edges. I knew this was coming. And selling the house may not be such a bad thing – I'd have money, for a start. Maybe – eventually, because obviously it would be a long way off – Lisa might even want to move in. And if we were close to Jemma, I'd still be able to see Toby every day.

It strikes me that maybe the die hasn't been *all* bad. I can choose my reaction to this. I can change my perspective. I can be a provider *and* a stoic, instead of a disrupter or challenger. Maybe one day, I'll even be a confessor.

Toby abruptly stands and declares that he needs a wee. He needs a wee *now*. When he runs upstairs, I turn to Jemma. 'I know we need to sell the house and sort things out properly, through solicitors.'

'You're ok with that?'

Oh, Jemma. No, of course I'm not ok with that. I will never be ok with it. I will never drive past this house without thinking of the hours we spent trudging around B&Q for furnishings and colours, her hand a warm, reassuring weight on my arm. Or the morning we brought Toby home and spent the entire day admiring his perfect features. How tiny he looked inside the moses basket and, later, his big-boy bed. I will never hear an Abba song without thinking of her dancing in our kitchen, both arms aloft, telling me *of course* she wouldn't spill the wine in her glass before doing exactly that. 'I have to be alright with it. As long as I can see Toby...'

'Yeah.' A pause. 'I've been thinking about that, and I might not stay in Bristol. But, you know, you could have him during the holidays. Let's just see how everything goes.'

There it is again, the bludgeon, crashing straight through my ribcage, flattening my heart. I press my teeth together. Remain calm. 'Are you moving in with Dan?'

'Maybe.'

Maybe. Might not. She's uncertain. She won't commit herself to anything until I've proved myself, and it's a game. It's just a game. She's waiting to see if I can stick to my side of the bargain and give up the podcast, get a job, be a reliable father.

I can. I will.

CHAPTER FIFTY-SIX

It's been nearly two weeks since Molly was found. I've applied for dozens of jobs, as well as emailing Oscar West, the man from the *Diecast* meet who asked me to get in touch if I was interested in a job in his team at *AJBE*. Will and I put out a notice on our socials last Wednesday stating that, due to personal reasons, we would not be recording any more episodes of *Diecast*. We felt it had been 'hijacked for nefarious purposes' and were sorry for anyone who had suffered a disruption to their lives as a consequence of our movement. As predicted, the backlash was swift and brutal. Followers were disappointed; enemies were unsurprised.

Noooo! I was just getting into it. Roll again!

'Sorry for anyone who has suffered disruption to their lives'. I'd say I suffered more than that, you fucking idiots.

Healthy masculinity unless its inconvenient masculinity, apparently.

Is the die no longer directing fate, then? Because it didn't go the way you wanted?

'I thought you might want to borrow my laptop,' Will says. He's come down to the annexe with a bag of fruit and cakes and other food they 'won't possibly get around to eating,' according to Claire, but I don't want to take any more from this family than I have done already. I suspect the offerings come from a place of guilt for the accusations that were cast, as carelessly as paper dice, on the night Molly went missing.

In return, I've offered to clean their cars, run errands, mow the lawn... anything to repay their kindness while I'm trying to get back on my feet.

Will unlocks the studio door and drops the laptop on the table. 'Only because you said you were struggling to apply for jobs on your phone. It's old, and the battery life is non-existent, but if you keep it plugged in, it's fine.'

'You're a legend. Thank you.'

He picks up the die. 'Look at him. Smug little six-faced bastard. Haven't rolled again, have you?'

I laugh. 'No. To be honest, I don't really feel the need.'

'Nor me.' He puts the die back on the shelf, then moves to the table and disconnects one of the microphones with a *pop*. 'I am gonna miss this, though. You and me. The whole podcast movement. It was pretty awesome at times.'

'Are you and Claire ok now? And Molly?'

'Yeah, we're getting there. Molly seems to have bounced back – she says nothing happened against her will, thank fuck. It could have done, though, couldn't it? I keep wondering if we did enough to protect people, because there might have been other stuff...' Will turns to crack open the blind instead of finishing the sentence, and I see the same changes I noticed in my own reflection a few weeks ago. Fine lines. A shift in facial structure, like the gradual erosion of rock weathered by wind, water and time. The sense of resignation. Sometimes we make things happen, sometimes things happen to us, and that's all there is to it. Will never believed the die was connected to some other entity – fate, destiny, whatever you want to call it – but I did. Even that night, when I hurled the die against the wall after hearing Jemma and Dan having sex, I still believed. Because otherwise, what was it all for? *A reason, a season or a lifetime*, Jemma said. *Everything teaches us something. Nobody collides at random, Adam.*

Well, perhaps they do, Jemma. Perhaps you weren't always right.

'End of an era,' Will says. 'End of *another* era. What do you think Abbie would say, if she could see us now?'

I pause before answering, because the question has taken me by surprise and suddenly, she's here again, twisting her hair over one shoulder, revealing a streak of violet. Short skirt. Long, black, lace-up boots. She's shaking her head, pulling a face. I smile. 'That we're both a pair of spaniels?'

He points at me. 'I forgot she used to say that! *You're such a spaniel.* Ah, I do miss that girl. Remember her clothes? She didn't give a shit.'

'And the gum.'

'Yeah. Always chewing.' Will laughs ruefully. 'You'd have been a much better boyfriend to her than I was, mate.'

He's right; I would have been. Not much we can do about that now. And it's not even like I can blame him for what happened – he had to obey the die's command.

'I even thought... and this is how mental I was, for a while... I thought *you* might be something to do with it. That witness saying he'd seen a grey Toyota on the bridge that night, and my brain went: *Adam*. But then—'

'Didn't he have Alzheimer's?'

'Yeah.' Will raises a hand, dismissively. 'I think they discounted him as a witness almost straightaway. Anyway, I know you'd never have hurt Abbie. You were literally obsessed with her.'

Obsessed. I've heard that word a lot over the years. Is that a bad thing? Drive, passion, love – yes, and obsession – they're all sides of the same die, surely? But if we keep talking about this, I won't see Abbie in the doorway anymore, it'll be the bloated, blackened body that haunted my nightmares for months after she was found. *Cause of death: undetermined due to decomposition.*

'I still wonder, sometimes, what happened to her,' Will says. 'Was it a hit and run, like the police thought, or did she slip and... God, I just hope she didn't suffer. Maybe we'll never know.'

'No.'

He seems relieved to change the subject and so am I. We talk about our plans for the next few days: I'm meeing Lisa at the mall tomorrow, Will's taking Molly and Claire to see *Grease* at the Hippodrome. He's going to be the man they both deserve, and he might – *might* – even propose at Christmas, but I'm not to say a word. I tell him that Jemma has finally agreed to permit visits with Toby, but only for two hours a week, and only at our house for now, but it's better than nothing. A silver-plated breadcrumb. 'Not next week, though,' she said. 'It's half term, so I'm taking Toby to spend some time with my mum and dad. Might even do a bit of hiking in the Lake District while we're there.'

We. No prizes for guessing who she was going with. But until I've got a job, instructed a solicitor and sorted out the – wholly unnecessary, it has to be said – counselling, there's absolutely nothing I can do about any of it. Not until I've proved myself worthy.

I'm about to show Will the latest photo of Toby on my phone when a sudden blaze of pain starts, deep inside my right eye socket. I blink hard, twice, and when it clears, I notice there's a new message on the screen: Thank you for sending your application for the post of IT Support Technician at AJBE, a not-for-profit organisation helping veterans all over the UK. Would you be free to come to our London branch for a chat next Tuesday?

I turn the phone to Will.

'*Mate.* That's brilliant!'

My smile feels unfamiliar. 'It is, isn't it? What do you think they mean by chat? A formal interview?'

'I'll ask Claire,' Will says. 'She's an expert in this kind of thing. Hey, is this the guy you met at the podcast gathering?'

'Yeah.'

He claps a hand on my shoulder. 'There you go, then. It's obviously meant to be.'

CHAPTER FIFTY-SEVEN

The last time I was on a train to London, Will and I were heading for the *Diecast* fan meet. Now, everything is sliding by in reverse, thin splashes of autumn light sliding in and out of the clouds. The man beside me is sitting upright, both arms pausing at right angles over his laptop like a begging dog, and when I look past him to glance out of the window, I see a spreadsheet open on his screen. If I had closely-cropped dark hair and a mole close to my left eyelid, he could be my younger self: eager, studious, starting my first job at a finance company.

Everything hinges on this interview. It might be my ticket out of the annexe and into a place of my own. And if *that* happens, I'll be in a better position for overnight stays with Toby. I'll have enough money to take him out to the cinema, soft play and swimming again. I'll have my dignity back. Last night, Claire invited me up to the house for a run-through of likely scenario questions, and I'd forgotten how much I knew. I was, if anything, *over*qualified for the role. I'd taken my suit to be cleaned and pressed earlier in the day, then caught up with Lisa over tapas, and I was feeling so positive, it was as though the outcome had already been decided.

Then I woke this morning at 3am, sweating and shivering, my head a cacophony of pain. I popped a couple of paracetamol tablets, which did nothing but push it from one side of my skull to the other. At 5am, I took a brief shower and felt better for fifteen minutes, before the weight returned behind my eyes and a raging heat pimpled across my body.

Will's laptop is dead. I'd been hoping to run through the questions before the interview, but the power bank doesn't seem to be working either, despite the blinking assertion of 100% charge when I plug it into the device. I disconnect it, pushing the power bank roughly into the side pocket of my rucksack, then drop my head into my hands. How is it possible to feel this unwell? I imagine an invisible print on a handrail or door handle, a virus sneaking into my body undetected, multiplying by stealth. *My name is Adam Dowdell. I enjoy problem-solving and helping people understand technology...* fuck, I wish I could think straight. Trouble-shooting, MacOS, network configuration – what was I going to say about that?

The train slows with a high-pitched squeal, then comes to a halt. The man beside me glances out of the window then back at his laptop. There are fields for miles around; we are nowhere near London. What's happening? Why have we stopped? I can hear other sounds: coughing, laughter, the muffled scuff and thud of dance music from someone's headphones. A moment later, when the announcement comes through the speaker to apologise for the short delay, I can't help thinking about the teenagers Will talked about who rolled the die and took it in turns to lie on the train track. A sick, dragging sensation tugs at the bottom of my stomach. I anchor myself by leaning down and gripping the rucksack until the train starts to move again.

I arrive in Paddington Station just before 9.45am and follow the signs to the Hammersmith and City Line where, thankfully, a train has just pulled in. I clutch at the rail and close my eyes against the harsh overhead lights. Six stops, then a change at King's Cross. I wipe a prickle of sweat from my forehead and the young woman beside me moves her painted fingernails to another pole. So hot in here. So many bodies. I turn to look out of the window at the seemingly endless rows of cables rushing past, umbilical-like, in the dark tunnel. We rattle past Euston, Warren Street and Oxford Circus, and I sway on the post, feeling faintly vertiginous. By the time I step off the train at Green Park, my armpits and back are beacons of damp. I'm desperate for air.

Passengers spill around me. I'm jostled by elbows, bags, a suitcase on wheels. A man wearing a baseball cap turns to look at me over his shoulder and says something I can't hear.

I'm going to pass out.

I slump onto a bench halfway along the platform and remove the rucksack from my shoulder to check my phone. 10.08. Just over fifty minutes until my interview. What if this is the tumour, returning with a vengeance to finish me off? The universe, reminding me that we don't get to decide anything, not really.

A virus, that's all.

There's a message from Lisa, wishing me luck. Another from Jemma, reminding me not to come over on Wednesday because Toby won't be there.

And one from Tom Starling, the follower who was trying to get back in touch with Dan's sister. I forgot that I'd messaged him on the night Molly went missing – so much has happened since then.

Hey, thanks for reaching out! Didn't come to anything unfortunately – she's married with a kid now – hopefully not to the guy who turned up in his POS car sixteen years ago lol. Never mind, worth a shot!

Sixteen years?

It's so cold on this bench, I'm surprised my breath isn't coming out in icy puffs. I stand up, smear another sheen of sweat from my head. Amongst the words, something jars, but I can't make sense of it. He'd said previously about balloons and rose petals. A birthday gift.

Another batch of passengers has just been disgorged, and I'm gradually aware of a murmuration around me. *What's he doing? What's wrong with him?* I can feel myself burning up, a sensation of vertigo rocking me as people dart past, foreign voices joining the babble. It takes me a moment or two to realise that they're looking at me as I pace the platform, phone in hand. And my rucksack, abandoned on the bench close by, its assortment of wires hanging loose from Will's winking power bank.

A bomb. They think it's a bomb.

Within seconds I'm swept away in a hot crush of bodies, darting like rats in a collective tide of panic.

CHAPTER FIFTY-EIGHT

Jemma

'It's perfect out there. Look at the water.'

It's still early, and the weather forecast has indicated that everything could change later, but at the moment there's no sign of cloud over the looming brown bear of the mountain. We've been listening to music all the way here; not just Abba – Dan said he couldn't stand a full four hours of that – but his tunes as well: Twenty-One Pilots, Imagine Dragons, Linkin Park, Lost Frequencies; and I've had my feet on the dashboard, rocking along, enjoying the sense of liberty. 'It's a shame Beth couldn't make it. Are you *sure* she's ok with me?'

'She's fine with you. Stop worrying.'

I haven't seen her since the night of the argument, and although she sent a message the following day to apologise, I can't help wondering if the sore throat and cough they've all supposedly come down with over the weekend is just an excuse not to join us today. 'Probably Covid,' Dan speculates now. 'She said it felt like Covid, but no one tests anymore, do they? It's doing the rounds again.'

'Yeah. Maybe.' To be fair, everyone at work seems to be off sick at the moment. Perhaps it's worked out for the best. Dan and I have been able to talk – really talk – and although I miss Toby, it'll be peaceful to have a few days without him. When we dropped him at my parents on Sunday night, Mum installed us in the conservatory with a cup of tea, then proceeded to ask so many questions, I had to remind her this wasn't an interview under caution. 'Sorry. Sorry, Dan,' she laughed, and I realised she was doing the same thing I do – talking non-stop to cover feelings of awkwardness. And probably, to stop us all from focusing on Dad, who was sitting benignly on the sofa, one leg twice the size of the other. 'I hear you run a rock-climbing business.'

'Yeah. It's my passion,' he said, before I had a chance to correct her and say no, it's his parents' business, he's only been working there for a few years since coming out of the army. It didn't matter, I supposed. We were all showing our best faces.

'You ok?'

'Yeah.' I watch the scenery pass in a reel. Yellows, blues, browns and greens: water and curves of land, all winking in the morning sun. 'I'm good. Just thinking about... everything. All of it. Selling the house, moving back, living with you...'

Dan squeezes my thigh and smiles. We're spending two nights in the Lake District, then returning for another day and night in Manchester when we collect Toby, and I'm hoping we'll have time to look at a few properties while we're there. Just to get a feel for the reality of it.

The road narrows to a path with high walls and only enough room for one car to pass. I drop my feet from the dashboard as Dan slams the brakes on and the owner of the Land Rover Discovery coming in the opposite direction stares Dan down, forcing him to wrench his gearstick into reverse and shoot backwards at speed. The Land Rover passes in a scuff of mud as he flies past without any acknowledgement.

'Arsehole.'

'Knob. I should get out and clobber him with my new walking boots.'

Dan laughs. 'You did pack them, didn't you?'

'Yeah, they're in the boot. Boots in the boot.' Along with my sketchbook and pencils. I probably won't have time to draw – Dan says it's cold and windy at the summit, and ideally, we want to head back down as soon as possible – but I can take photos and sketch from those on the way back. 'Is this it?'

'This is it.'

'I thought it would be busier.'

'It's midweek, end of season. This place never gets mad like Snowden and Ben,' Dan says.

Mum says she brought me here when I was small, but I don't remember it. A patch of land, fringed with grass, leading off to a field beyond. A tiny welcome centre and toilet block. 'It's... basic.'

'What were you expecting?' Dan asks, unclipping his seatbelt. 'Costa drive-thru? McDonalds?'

'Well, no, but...'

He cocks an eyebrow. 'There might be a café at the top.'

'Better be Michelin-starred.'

He laughs. I tell him I need to nip to the loo which – unbelievably – turns out to consist of a row of toilet seats covering holes in the ground. The smell is so strong I breathe through my mouth, staring up at a spider crawling across the toilet door. A distant memory surfaces of camping in a place just like this as a child. A sensation of joy. Dad trying to melt marshmallows over a fire, where they crackled and burned, turning to hot gloop in our mouths. Water bubbling in pans. The enthusiastic *trrrp* of zips. Torchlight picking out a rabbit, a stream, a patch of closed daisies. Hannah, singing at the top of her voice.

I reach for the toilet paper and discover there isn't any. No wash basins, either. Of course there aren't; this is a mountain, not the mall. I pull up my knickers and trousers – bit tight, shouldn't have indulged in all those takeaways this week, but life's too short – and thank God I'm not on my period. What do people do here, if they are...

Die Trying

Wait – why am I *not* on my period?

Next week, I remember. It's fine. It's due next week, not this week, because it was late last month. Probably due to all the stress. Anyway, Dan and I have been careful. 'I *do* want kids,' he said, when we were in bed the other night. 'Maybe. One day.' He's scared of getting hurt again and I understand that – I found his ex on Facebook and she looked exactly as he'd described: terrifyingly smug, chin tilted in the air like someone with an agenda. Or a grudge.

No rush, I agreed. What we have now, this is perfect. Just the three of us.

The wind has picked up slightly. I return the smile of the old man sitting inside the welcome centre, and notice a silver urn with a sign sellotaped to the side of it: *Coffee/tea. £2.50. Cash only.*

'I've got change,' Dan says, when I reach the car. He's leaning out of the driver's side, lacing up his walking boots. 'Not sure I've got enough for two, but we can share, if that's ok? Actually, I think I'll take a leak while I'm there.'

'That's fine.' I catch the car keys with one hand, then open the boot to retrieve my rucksack. 'Prepare for everything,' Mum said. 'Things can change up there in an instant.'

I pull on my boots, listening to the rustle of the trees, the faint roar of a motorbike in the distance, the cheerful melody of birdsong, which falls silent the moment I try to identify it. An older couple stroll through the gate then bundle their black spaniel into the silver Toyota Yaris parked on the other side, and for some reason, I think of Adam. '*We were supposed to grow old together*,' he shouted, the night he came to Dan's door. We weren't though, were we? If being with Dan has taught me anything, it's that real love isn't about rules or ownership or control. It's about freedom from constraint. Adventure. Connection. *Fun.*

I hope Adam will be ok. He certainly seems to be trying now, and not in a creepy, oppressive way. It's hard to say whether it was our split or the brain tumour that changed him. Perhaps it was both. Perhaps now he's been through this process of self-discovery, he might be able to recognise that we *weren't* right together and it was over long before it was officially over. I hated the person I was back then – prickly, angry, cruel. The sort of woman people call 'difficult'.

The spaniel stares beseechingly at me from the rear window as the old couple pull out of the car park. My phone chimes on the lip of the open boot. I don't normally pay attention to news bulletins, but my brain is primed to respond to every notification at the moment, just in case Mum needs me. In case *Toby* needs me.

Breaking news: Police link 'social experiment' podcast to Green Park tube alert.

Surely not? I heard something about a panic on a London tube station on the news yesterday, but wasn't really listening – it flashed up close to bedtime and as far as I could tell, no one had been seriously hurt; it wasn't flagged as a terror attack. But if it's linked to—

There's a second, muffled, *ping* nearby. It's not coming from Dan's phone, because he had it in his hand when he threw the keys at me.

Weird. Did I imagine it?

I rummage through the jumble of carrier bags, rugs and spare clothing beneath my rucksack until I find a fleece-lined black North Face waterproof with more pockets than anyone could possibly need. I feel around each one before pulling out a phone.

This one is smaller, with a dark-blue metallic case. I swipe the screen, and a stock wallpaper image of the Aurora Borealis appears. *Enter passcode.*

Perhaps it's Dan's old phone. Beth said his ex had hounded him to the point where he was forced to buy a new one and change his number.

But they split two years ago: why would it still have charge?
Enter passcode.

I've forgotten to put plasters on; my boots feel uncomfortably tight. I shouldn't – I know I shouldn't – but I try a couple of combinations he uses for his laptop and phone. His *other* phone.

Password incorrect.

Password incorrect.

Maybe Dan has borrowed his colleague, Evan's, jacket, and this is his phone. He's mentioned how cold they get between sessions, how they're always picking up each other's fleeces.

I look up to see Dan talking to the man at the visitor centre, coffee cup in hand. I have no right to be suspicious. I was married when we met. I've lied and kept secrets.

I'll just ask him. There's bound to be a simple explanation.

I slip the phone into my pocket, then slam the boot closed.

BREAKING NEWS

Police investigate cause of panic in busy Green Park tube alert.

Authorities are investigating a suspicious bag found at Green Park Underground station yesterday, believed to be connected to a podcast briefly popularised for encouraging social experiments. It is not yet known whether the bag was left as part of a prank. The podcast host was seen near the bag and fled during the initial panic, but was later seen helping a man injured in the stampede. Police say he is not under arrest but is assisting with enquiries.

They would like to speak to anyone who was in Green Park Underground station at the time. Eight people were treated for injuries while fleeing the scene. An emergency alert was issued, and police initially treated the event as terror-related before standing down.

BBC reporter Jennifer Hughes said witnesses had described it as 'pandemonium'. 'There was an announcement for the platform to be evacuated and everyone was panicking, grabbing at people's clothes and climbing over each other. When we arrived outside on the street, phone alerts were pinging and everyone was running amok, with several cries of a supposed bomb.'

The Met Police have confirmed the contents of the bag to be non-suspicious.

CHAPTER FIFTY-NINE

Dan comes back, steam from the coffee rising to meet the cool air. 'Did you just get that news—'

'Yeah. I hope it's nothing to do with Adam.'

This is the moment to whip out the phone, but Dan says it certainly sounds like it could be – the report mentioned a podcast host, a suspicious article, a *stampede* – and my mind is full of other questions then. If it was a *Diecast* stunt – why? Why stop the podcast and turn up in London to plant a fake bomb, or whatever it was they'd done? It makes no sense, unless Adam hasn't changed at all, and this is yet another example of him going back on his promises.

Maybe it was the other guy, Will King.

We carry on talking about it as we start the ascent, and soon Dan's phone is thudding at my side, a gentle tap of disquiet. I'm already out of breath. Dan moves ahead, taking great strides up the rocks, and I watch his trousers fold into the shape of his buttocks, the soft swing of his ponytail against his neck. Familiar terrain. 'We'll need to be careful in a minute,' he shouts, over his shoulder. 'Have to cross the water.'

It's flowing abundantly down the rocks, forming a river on our right. *Down*, it seems to be saying. *This is the way you're supposed to go. There's a reason for gravity.*

The ground levels off slightly, before climbing again. Brown Tongue. Hollow Stones. The names sound like they've been lifted from a fantasy novel. I take sips of water from the pouch

Die Trying

at the side of my rucksack as we carry on through the cairns, where shingle is scattered on a platform of land between huge boulders. They certainly look like something from a fantasy novel; other-worldly, set below an obstacle course of dark, barrelling clouds. Up one ascent, then another. My boots are rubbing painfully at my ankles and I know, when I take them off later, the skin will almost certainly be shredded to weeping sores. Just as I think this must be it – *surely* we're at the summit? – another rocky staircase appears. One of those optical illusions where the stairs look normal, but when you look closer, it's obvious something's wrong – there's no way of getting off.

I slump against the back of a large stone, facing against the wind. My thighs are burning. 'How much further?'

'About fifteen, twenty minutes at current pace? We don't have to keep going, if you don't want to.'

My fleece is sticking to my back with sweat, but my face is so raw with cold that when I speak, my lips feel rubbery and swollen. 'I do want to.'

'I'm not even sure whether it will be safe to go all the way to the summit. Looks foggy up there,' Dan shouts. 'You could say you've done it, I'd back you up. No one would know.'

'*I* would know.' We're now so high, the enormous lake below appears as a single blue token I could fit in the palm of my hand. Dan isn't even out of breath. *Seven*, I remember his friend Evan saying. *007. James Bond.* 'We can keep going. Dan?'

'Yeah?'

'Have you got a work phone? I found one in the boot before we came out.'

Something passes over his face. Hesitation, but something else, too. Guilt? Defensiveness? It doesn't stick long enough to read, and then he relaxes. 'Yeah. Don't use it very often. It must have fallen out of my jacket.'

'Ah, right. Ok.'

It could all be innocent. Of course it could. He says we probably should push on, because the weather isn't going to get any better, and I stand, pressing my hands into my pockets. A couple pass us on the way back down, wearing matching bright yellow jackets. 'It's real misty up there,' the woman says in an American accent. 'Could bearly see Jim's face, could I, honey?'

'That's right.'

We wish them well, and they disappear into the gloom. Halfway up another steep incline, Dan offers for me to go in front.

'No, it's fine. Better if you're ahead, you know the way.'

'Sure you don't want to turn around? You look freezing.'

You could say you've done it, I'd back you up. No one would know.

A lie.

I tell him I want to keep going.

And this is the moment I look back on, afterwards. I could have left the phone in my pocket. We could have taken photos at the summit like everyone else did, wearing identical pained smiles, telling the story of how we'd pushed through, despite the weather, but it was all worth it for the view… except there isn't a view. Maybe if there was, things would have been different. Maybe I would have been so in awe at the magnificence of it, I would have decided this was all I needed to see.

But I can't see anything. Only the back of Dan's legs, the soles of his boots, a T-shaped watermark at the top of his shoulders.

I slip Dan's phone from its case and pull one finger free from my glove to attempt the passcode for a third time, just as I always knew I would.

007.

I'm stunned when the phone unlocks. Even though I suspected it, the sight in front of me – coloured icons, all the apps now with unrestricted access – fills me with fresh doubt. I should not be doing this. I should not, and yet, I already know I will. Because something has been whispering, something that wriggles and squirms and slips away when I try to put my finger on it.

Dozens of apps. Dozens of icons. All normal, it seems, until I tap on Instagram and realise this isn't his account.

Except... it is. He's using his middle name as his forename, a different profile picture.

Dan turns, briefly, to check I'm ok. The phone is concealed within my palm. I snatch another glance.

On Whatsapp, a recent conversation with Evan: `I'm genuinely not built for kids! Thought I could do it for her but he's a fucking brat.`

Somehow, my legs are still carrying me forward. A fucking *brat*? Maybe he's not talking about Toby. He can't be talking about Toby.

But who else would he be talking about? It occurs to me that he always has excuses not to play with Toby: his rotator cuff injury, stiff knees, busy 'talking to Mummy'.

I keep scrolling forward, through their exchange. *Jemma... amazing... pretty good for now... not serious.* And – devastatingly – messages about my job having 'added benefits' and 'happy endings all round', complete with dozens of laughing emojis. There are tabs open: likes and heart emojis on the Instagram profiles of women I've never seen or heard of, a banking app for Nationwide. The last message from his ex: `I'm not stalking you, I just want my Nan's money back for the wedding venue you said you'd booked, you arsehole!`

I should stop now. I should stop looking, because my hat is slipping down my head, my hair is in my eyes and I can't see for the wind, the fucking wind, slashing cold, stinging tears across my face.

'You ok?' Dan shouts.

I've fallen behind. He thinks I've had enough.

I turn around without saying a word. The straps of my bag are tugging painfully at my shoulders, and I start walking away, back down the mountain, damp scree tumbling away from my feet. I need to get away from him.

His hand lands on the sleeve of my jacket a moment later.

I react instinctively, so full of rage and shame and disbelief that I throw my arm up and away from my body forcefully, knocking him backwards. I see him clutch at the air, a cluster of stones scurrying over the edge. A dark billow of cloud overhead. It looks almost cartoonish, as if he's preparing to sit back into a chair, and then he's falling.

He doesn't shout, and at first, neither do I. I can't move. I am stuck to the spot, the wind savagely tearing at my clothes, and yet, I am hot. Hot and cold. My heart is stamping furiously against my ribcage, and I'm still holding his phone. I don't know which one I use to call the emergency services, mine or his. Does it matter? When I tell them that my partner has gone over the edge, my voice is high, the words scrambling over themselves to be heard. No, I don't know if he's breathing, because I cannot move, I do not want to see. I heard it, I heard when he landed.

I do not want to see.

CHAPTER SIXTY

Adam

One online article called it a 'fear contagion'. Another described it as 'widespread panic'. The episode now feels like a bizarre hallucination or half-remembered dream: bodies flowing in a single ribbon towards the exits, alarms bounding from the walls in short, stark bursts, station staff shouting for everyone to clear the platforms as quickly as possible. A wet mess of sound, heat and colour.

I can't remember much about being transported to St Thomas' hospital, only the part where I was hooked up to an IV drip and diagnosed with dehydration and a kidney infection and then discharged for questioning by police. By then, things had calmed down. The police had spoken to paramedics, seen CCTV and assessed the contents of my rucksack, so it was just a formality. By the time I returned to the annexe, I was utterly exhausted. I took another of the antibiotics I'd been sent home with and kept refreshing my emails, in the hope that Oscar might have responded to my apology for missing the interview with an alternative date. I called Will and thought about having a shower.

Tom Starling's message was still niggling at me. It was probably nothing. Nothing at all. Even so, I sent a reply. *POS car?*

He replied at 3.10am this morning.

```
Yeah, state of it! Headlamp out, dent on wing.
She could have done a lot better with me. I
```

had a sweet little ST back then. 0-60 in less than 6 seconds – went like shit off a shovel. Her loss! Btw, was that you or Will causing havoc in London lol?

Headlamp out. Dent on wing. I took a closer look at Tom's profile and saw that he could be anywhere between thirty and forty years of age. Multiple piercings in one ear, two in nose. Black-rimmed glasses. Pale and slightly overweight. *Team Leader at CeX Broadmead.*

I thought about messaging Will and asking his opinion, before deciding it would be pointless. He'd groan that we'd talked about all the Abbie stuff the other day. *Mate, I thought we'd put that shit to rest.*

So did I.

But in the morning, I call Tom Starling anyway.

'I didn't see him. I don't know what he looked like. Why do you want to know?'

'A girl went missing that night.' I can't believe I'm having to spell this out. 'Didn't you hear about it? It was all over the news, there was an online appeal—'

'I went to Torrevieja two days after wasting my money on that hotel room, although... hang on, is this a dice thing? It is, isn't it?' Tom laughs. He actually laughs. 'I was thinking last night about that London stunt... are you making *Diecast* live?'

There's a strange taste in my mouth. My bedsheets are soaked with sweat and I've already drunk two pints of water, but I'm still thirsty. Or perhaps it's hunger? I throw back the covers and pop another antibiotic from the blister pack. 'No, not at all. Her name was Abbie Reynolds. And if you were in Dundry at the time, it's close enough to the Basin that whoever picked Beth up might have been involved.'

'What's this about? Are you doing true crime now?'

I can see steam billowing out of the flue attached to Will's house. He's taken the day off and the family are going to Thorpe Park; someone must be getting ready in the bathroom. *Diecast detectives*. It had a nice ring to it. Will and I could carry on recording, I'd be able to stay living here; maybe we'd even be revered instead of scorned.

But it's not going to happen. We must all move on. 'No. She was someone we used to know.'

'Actually, I *do* remember hearing something about it.' A sharp intake of breath. 'Months later, though. I thought they said she drowned?'

'They don't know for sure. She had a significant head injury, so a...' I pinch the top of my nose, imagine myself sinking into cold water. *Face your fears*. 'A hit-and-run was also raised as a possibility.'

'You think it could have been the guy that picked Beth up?'

'I don't know. Maybe. Was the headlight broken, or just not working?'

'No idea. I didn't get a good look – I only noticed because I thought it was a motorbike at first. I think it was a dark colour. Silver, maybe. Or grey. Could even have been black? We were arguing, so I was more focused on that. Do you know, I paid over a hundred pounds for that hotel room? Even now—'

'Did you see the man who was driving?'

'No. Sorry. It was dark, pissing down with rain. You'd have to talk to Beth, see who she was banging at the time.'

Impossible. It was impossible. How would I even begin to have that conversation with the sister of my wife's lover? I thank Tom and he keeps me on the phone for a few minutes longer, trying to persuade me to change my mind on the dissolution of the podcast. He has ideas for how to make it better. He's going to carry on using his die every day, with or without the podcast. He wants to know how me and Lisa are getting on, because we are proof that every roll, every seemingly insignificant decision, could change a life. 'You said that yourself, remember?'

I did. I did say that. And now I tell him it doesn't always change for the better.

Beth's profile is locked, so I can't scour her socials for information on previous partners. Her husband, Sam Hawkins, doesn't have the same restriction, however, and a quick scroll through his photos and posts is enough to ascertain that they only appear to have known each for eight years.

A blown headlamp; a small dent. It could be nothing.

I make myself a slice of toast and butter, take a shower, then call Lisa. As it rings, I think about our tapas date, when she talked about her patients who sit in the chair for just five to ten minutes at a time, offering a tiny snapshot of their lives. Her Scottie dog, Millie. Her parents, now living in the seaside town of Sandown on the Isle of Wight. And then, when I dropped her home, that electric crack of a kiss.

She doesn't pick up.

I don't know what makes me call Jemma's number instead. Maybe, on a subconscious level, I feel guilty about the kiss. Maybe it's because I feel dreadful and need to hear a woman's voice. Maybe, subconsciously, something feels off about her silence, because she must have heard about what happened in London. Tom assumed it was another *Diecast* stunt, and it occurs to me that if Jemma thinks the same, I'll need to put the record straight.

Jemma doesn't pick up, though; her mother does.

'Oh, Adam,' she says.

Her voice. What's wrong with her voice?

'Have you heard?'

Peppermint on my tongue. There's a smattering of crusts on the plate beside me, like gnarled bones. I move it and and sit down on the bed. 'Heard what?'

'Dan's dead.'

CHAPTER SIXTY-ONE

Dan Bretti is dead.

After all this time, wanting and wishing it to happen, it has. Dan Bretti. Dead.

I pull up outside our house and pause for a moment before going inside. There's a *For Sale* sign stabbed into the grass, not quite straight.

Dan Bretti is dead.

Jemma's mum lets me in with a wan smile. The house is tidy – I suspect she might have pushed the vacuum cleaner around and tidied up, because everything is neatly in place. The dishcloth is hanging over the kitchen tap in the same way she places it at her house, and all the surfaces are clean. She leans forward, so close I can see a smudge of blue eyeshadow, carelessly applied, and catch a whiff of her rose-scented perfume. 'Jem's really low,' she whispers. 'I'll take Toby out, so try and talk to her, see if she'll let you stay for a bit. Her friends have been over, but I don't think she should be on her own.'

If anyone's told our son about Dan's death, he doesn't seem fazed by it. He runs into the hallway to put his jacket on, eager to show me his new Monster toy. This one has an orange belly, his other one is purple. 'Very cool.'

'Dan is gone to heaven.'

Ah.

'He didn't come down the slide with me.'

I don't know what to say. *That's a shame, never mind, I'm sure he would have done if...* well, it doesn't matter now, does it? Toby starts rattling the door handle, impatient to get outside, and Jemma's mum throws her scarf over one shoulder with a raise of her eyebrows. For a moment, I envy the simplicity, the fluidity, of his four-year-old brain.

'See you later,' she says, then calls out. 'Bye, Jemma.'

'See you later.'

When I move through the kitchen into the lounge, Jemma is sitting on the sofa, a pillow pulled to her chest, pressing crisps robotically into her mouth. She's wearing her purple leggings. 'I'm sorry.'

She licks her fingers and crushes them back into the bag. The skin around her eyes looks like it's been filled with padding.

'Thanks.'

'Did he—'

'I don't want to talk about it.'

'Ok.'

I sit down beside her, making the sofa sigh. *You again.*

After a few moments of silence, I tell her about London: the interview I'd been so looking forward to, and the kidney infection that made me feel so confused and cognitively disorienatated, I feared another brain tumour. The wires hanging from my rucksack, making commuters see connections that weren't there.

'Karma,' she says.

'Sorry?'

'That's what you're going to say, isn't it? Karma. For the way I treated you.'

'I wasn't—'

'It's ok, I've been thinking it too.' She stands abruptly, then brushes past me to drop the crisp wrapper into the bin. I can't imagine what it must have been like to see Dan plummet to his death. Was he kneeling to propose? Did he hit his head on the way down, or land on a ledge? I rise from the sofa and pick up a piece of paper from the dining room table. It's a pencil sketch of a woman in front of a mirror and behind her, dozens of heads, getting progressively smaller. I don't know what it means. I don't know why Jemma drew it, or where it comes from, the calling to do so. I'm not sure she does, either.

I follow her into the kitchen. 'What can I do? Get you something to eat?'

'No thanks. I can't, not at the moment.'

'But you need—'

'*Please*, Adam. I need to be on my own.'

She pushes open the patio doors and stands outside with her back to the house. Behind her, the curtains flap. I feel useless, helpless, out of place. I wanted Jemma back – the Jemma I loved – but she is not the same person anymore. Did I love Jemma for who she was, or how she made me feel? Even when she rejected me, her betrayal felt right on some level, because it was Dad's version of love. The pain, the shame – wasn't it everything I deserved?

I make a cup of tea and take it out to her anyway. She touches my arm, thanks me for this small act of kindness.

'You look shattered.'

'So do you.'

'I'm still getting over this infection.' I wait a beat before asking if I can stay here. Just for a day or two, or however long she needs, to help out with Toby. 'I won't get in your way.'

'We're still selling the house, Adam. I can't stay here. This doesn't change—'

'I know.'

There are pinpricks of damp at the edge of her eyelashes. I head back inside, and that's when I notice the fingerprint on the patio glass, about a foot above her head. Or more specifically, finger*prints* – two oval smudges – too high to belong to Toby, too big to belong to Jemma. Did they have sex here, against the window? Perhaps Dan left them on purpose; a calling card. I wipe them with the sleeve of my jacket, and Jemma turns to look at me, questioningly, through the window. *What? What is it?*

I shake my head. 'Nothing.' It's nothing at all.

That evening, Jemma keeps me awake by going up and down the stairs at two, then three, in the morning. I lie there in the dark, listening to the pained strings of her voice, wondering who she's talking to. At first, it feels like the prodding of a bruise – *I'm so hard for you it hurts* – but then I remember: he's dead.

Toby's Moses basket is here in the spare bedroom with me, beside the lumpy shapes sticking out of boxes – his old baby gym, a tinky-toy piano, the ghostly arm of a Harry Potter wand. Jemma *had* been serious about moving. And clearly, she wants it to happen as soon as possible. Toby even talked about it in the bath, telling me he might be living near the trams and big massive buildings. 'Do you want that?' I asked him. 'Do you want to live in Manchester?'

His answer was an emphatic *yes*, making me feel jittery and hollow. I convinced myself that Jemma must have brainwashed him into thinking it would be a good idea, and if Lisa hadn't called back when she did – *after* Toby was out of the bath, I wasn't ever going to make the mistake of leaving him again – I might have crashed into the bedroom and shaken Jemma awake. 'You'll have school holidays,' Lisa said. 'And weekends. And Facetime. Separated parents manage long-distance relationships all the time. At least he's not moving abroad.'

Lisa was right. As she kept talking, I remembered how warm the back of her head felt in my palm as we kissed. It had become like a slow-acting drug, a memory I sucked on to numb the pain. Then three words drifted into my head, as though Mum were speaking to me from the other side: *She's a keeper.*

I go downstairs to check on Jemma. She's sitting on the sofa with a glass of red wine, her face slick with tears. Her phone is upside down beside her, slipped halfway between the cushions.

'Are you ok?'

'Not really. Beth keeps calling and I don't know what to say to her. She wants to go over every detail about what happened. How it happened, what his last words were…'

I sit down, leaving a space between us, and say I know what she's going through – sort of – because I lost someone I loved, years ago. Abbie Reynolds. I told her about the chocolate I was always too afraid to give her, melting in the bottom of my bag. I told her about the oval patch of orange on her chin where she used to apply concealer, whenever a spot appeared. I told her about Abbie's terrible dancing, the tears of her parents when they appeared on TV; sadness tugging hooded pads of skin over their eyes. 'They never found out who was responsible for the hit-and-run. But this is the weird thing – I think someone Beth was seeing might have been involved.'

I tell Jemma about Tom Starling calling into the podcast to describe his random act of kindness gone wrong. 'He said they'd had a row and Beth went off with another man in a beaten-up car. It could be nothing. But it could also be a lead.'

Jemma looks pale. She presses her lips flat against the glass. 'Why didn't he tell the police?'

'Abbie wasn't reported missing until the following day. The police put out an appeal the day after *that*, and he'd flown out to Torrevieja by then.'

'Oh.'

'Are you ok?'

'I'm not… I don't feel well,' Jemma says. 'Could you get me a…'

It's too late. She throws up her wine in a single jagged splatter on the Ikea rug.

CHAPTER SIXTY-TWO

Jemma

'Come in,' Beth says. She's wearing a pair of skinny jeans and an oversized blue hoody which keeps slipping off one shoulder. 'I'd offer you a drink, but we haven't got any milk. Sam's just gone out to get some.'

I follow her into the lounge, where two biscuit-coloured sofas are set in front of a TV wall unit and fireplace. A white cat is curled up on one of the cushions, looking at me with a scowl of derision. I keep replaying what happened: the phone, the climb, the way Dan grabbed at my arm, constantly thinking that, if only he'd reached for my other arm, he'd be alive now. Those words in my ear: *Can you hear me? Are you still there? Emergency services are on their way, caller.*

If only I'd confronted him at the beginning instead of walking off. If only...

Could we have sorted things out? No, probably not. He called Toby a fucking brat, and that's something I could never get past, even without all the secrecy. Perhaps it's a good thing I found out now, before we blended our homes, our finances, our lives.

Well. He doesn't have a life now, does he? And all this stuff about Adam's dead girlfriend is too creepy to ignore. Almost as creepy as the fact that when he showed me a picture of her, I was blown away by how similar we look. Was Adam attracted to me in the first place because I reminded him of her? I used to believe in soul mates, that we came into each other's lives for a reason, but now I'm not so sure. Maybe we create these fictions to set ourselves apart. *We're not like everyone else. This is fate, this is destiny*, all that crap about it being written in the stars, when the brutal truth is that we could be with anyone. Love isn't just something you feel; it's what you choose to do, how you choose to behave.

Or maybe I was right and this *is* karma. I wish I could talk to Beth properly to see if she knew what kind of person Dan really was, but how can I, when it might implicate me in his death? I haven't even told the police I found his second phone. The investigation is ongoing, but they have no reason to suspect foul play. His original mobile was recovered with his body, so as far as they were concerned, the story I gave – about him slipping on wet scree while adjusting his strap a little too close to the edge – was true. Dan's second phone is still zipped into my jacket pocket, and the couple we passed on the mountain shortly before his fall gave a statement to say we didn't appear to be having any kind of dispute.

It *wasn't* foul play. Not really.

'I miss him,' I tell Beth now. 'I really fucking miss him.'

'So do I.'

She shows me photos of their childhood, most of which I've seen on Dan and Beth's socials, but this time she adds colour. Camping at the Gower every year as kids, where it always rained without fail, no matter which week they chose. A trip to London which resulted in Dan chasing the stranger who stole Beth's purse. The time he showed off on a zip line and ended up in A&E with a fractured clavicle. 'He clearly loved you,' I say.

'Yeah, he did. I know a lot of siblings grow apart, but we never did. We shared a lot of interests, a lot of… you know, I can't get my head around talking about him in past tense.'

'I can't, either.' The cat is still staring at me through narrowed eyes. *I see you.* I want to know more about Dan's life, I want to drink it all in, because maybe it will lessen the betrayal to hear different sides of him. *Was* it a betrayal? He hadn't cheated, he hadn't technically done anything wrong, but yes; yes, he had, because he led me to believe in a version of himself that was built on sand. But was he a killer?

No. Surely not.

'I just… there's one thing – it's strange. That night, your birthday, when Tom Starling booked a hotel and Dan came to pick you up.' I pause. 'Tom called the podcast and said Dan's car had a dent and a headlamp out. And I thought, that's not like Dan. He loves his car, he's proud… you know, proud of his image. He wouldn't drive around like that. Would he?'

Beth slides her top back onto her shoulder. 'It was a long time ago.'

'Yeah, it was, and it probably doesn't even matter, but… you know, I heard about the girl who went missing.' I keep going, not daring to look at Beth. Instead, I focus on squeezing softly at the sofa cushions: squeeze, release, squeeze, release, like I did to Adam's hand while I was giving birth. 'I love Dan. *Loved* Dan. I don't want people talking about him like he'd deliberately gone and mown someone down that night.'

'Is that what Tom said? Because if he wants to talk about that night, I *will* report him. He was getting so angry about the fucking hotel room that cost him nearly £150 and that he'd spent all day filling it with balloons, I was scared. He was trying to stop me leaving, standing in the doorway, snatching my phone off me, pushing me back inside. I bet he didn't tell your ex that. If I hadn't called Dan when I did, I think something bad would have happened. Really bad.'

What is she saying? That Dan rushed to get to her as quickly as possible? Yes, that's exactly what she's telling me, and I would have done the same for Hannah. In fact, I *had* done the same for Hannah – driving to her attacker's house with a rage so acute, I could feel it, hot as a blade.

'He wanted to come in and deal with Tom, but I told him to go, it wasn't worth it. I just needed to get out of there. And I asked, I asked about the broken light. He admitted he'd hit something; he wasn't sure if it was a deer, or...' Beth's crying now. She pulls the sleeves of her hoody over her hands, like a child. 'He said someone else was there, so whatever happened, they'd probably sort it out. Dan wasn't in a good place, Jemma. Nor was I. He wanted to report it, but he had his passing-out parade a week later. And he'd injured his shoulder, was popping a lot of strong painkillers. We waited for a knock at the door, thinking the other person would have given our details, but it didn't come. The car just sat in the garage. Eventually...'

I think of the girl who looked like me, with brown and purple hair, ripped tights, a black denim jacket. Her life severed, just like that. 'You still should have reported it. You should have reported him, too. Tom.'

'I know,' Beth says. 'Of course I know that. But we were scared. And I wasn't there, so I managed to convince myself it probably wasn't the girl Dan hit, that night. It could have been anything.'

When I get home, Adam is on the phone to someone called Lisa. The woman he met on a podcast challenge, and I'm pleased for him, because he seems genuinely happy. Although, nothing is ever what it seems, is it?

He'd injured his shoulder, Beth said. Dan's rotator cuff injury. The one he'd come to me for, the old climbing injury that 'got a bit stiff sometimes'. He talked in such detail about the gut-wrenching terror of feeling a piece of rock come away in your hand, the sensation of slamming into rock, then swinging in the harness, that I wonder now if he'd heard the story somewhere else; perhaps from someone at the climbing centre. Because Beth said he'd never been injured during a climb.

I look at my drawings on the table that Adam has tidied into a neat, rectangular stack, then down to my walking boots, pushed under the table because I can't bear to put them away. I manage three mouthfuls of the chicken fajita that Adam has left on the side for me, before bursting into tears. And then, when he comes off the phone and Toby goes upstairs to find his monster truck, I close the kitchen door and stand beside Adam at the window.

'There's something I need to tell you.'

CHAPTER SIXTY-THREE

Adam

The parts fit together now. The pattern, because there is always a pattern, even when it looks like randomness. Sometimes, you need to wait, just long enough to see it slowly coming together, like pieces of an incomplete jigsaw puzzle.

Jemma didn't meet Dan by coincidence. He was always destined to walk into her path; she into his. If I hadn't met her on the train that day, if she hadn't taken the diploma in sports massage, if I hadn't reconnected with Will and set up the podcast which led us to Tom Starling… if, if, if. Everything we've done has been a complicated tangle of the unseen, unconscious and intangible: history, genes, biological and chemical processes making our actions and impulses appear as conscious thought, having already been planted there on a subconscious level. And behind it all, fate, gently steering.

It's quite a trick the universe pulls off. Convincing us we're in control.

I don't know what to make of Jemma anymore. She's unpredictable and unreliable, seemingly normal one moment, a snivelling mess the next. Connection. Withdrawal. Discomfort. Truth. Conflict. A wild card. She runs through them all, sometimes at dizzying speed, without a die in sight. I thought I'd enjoy living at home again, but in just a few days she's resenting my presence, asking if I've moved her pencils, used all the water in the kettle, turned off the oven when she was about to put something in it. Every time I see the *For Sale* sign outside the house, I don't know whether I'm angry with Jemma for bringing evil to our door and changing all of our lives forever, or relieved that the die has finally, inadvertently, brought justice for Abbie.

I can't be angry, not really. None of this was ever truly in our power to change.

The house is quiet, apart from the gentle rattle of Toby's snoring. 'Beth said Dan told her there was someone else on the bridge that night,' Jemma said. 'Why wouldn't they have reported it? Do you think he only said that to make her feel better?'

I roll over. Lisa has offered to cook dinner for me tomorrow at her house after I've picked up some more of my belongings from the annexe. Dinner, not tea. Already I'm shedding the Jemma-isms that have become like a second language to me. I told Lisa things had been difficult, that being here seemed to be making things worse, not better. 'Come over, then,' she said. 'I'll make a curry.'

The pillow is too thin; the scent of Ocean Breeze overpowering. My hand strays to the back of my head, where the seam of my scar is still just about palpable.

Yes, perhaps everything unfolds exactly as it's supposed to.

It's almost 10am when I arrive at Will and Claire's house. Will comes down to the annexe while I'm packing my stuff into bags, and when he opens the door, I can see he still hasn't digested the news. 'You ok?'

'Yes,' I say. 'Well, apart from all the madness of the past few weeks. You?'

'I can't stop thinking about it. It's all so fucked.'

I fold my work trousers and place them next to the bag of toiletries. 'Are you going to tell Abbie's family?'

'I don't know. It's not concrete proof, and he's dead anyway, so... I don't know. I'll chew it over.'

'Ok.'

While Will is carrying my bedding to the car, I open the door to the studio; place his laptop case back on the table. The die is sitting benignly between our headphones and the microphone stand. Four. *Truth*.

I was going to leave the die here, tell Will to keep it. But now Dan's dead, I can feel it again, crackly and distant; the synergy. This is mine, the only link to the good times I had before Mum left; my only connection, once, with the ghost of Abbie. And the one question which has continued to plague me all this time: why did she die, when we always obeyed its command?

The answer to that comes sooner than I expect. I shut the boot and thank Will for everything, but instead of moving away, he steps forward and rests a fist on the roof of the car. 'I think there's something you should know,' he says. 'The night Abbie died...'

And I know. Before he says it, I know.

'The dice didn't tell me to go to Lily's. I was supposed to be with Abbie.'

I don't react. I could, but I don't. I thank him for telling me, because in a way it's as much of a relief as knowing what happened to Abbie. I wasn't wrong about the dice directing fate. All of this – it wasn't for nothing. I wasn't entirely to blame.

CHAPTER SIXTY-FOUR

Jemma

Dan's funeral is so much more painful than I expected. There are two screens at the front of the crematorium, beaming out a picture of him in the centre of his family: Mum and Dad, silver-haired and smiling, Beth and Olivia, the five of them in front of a Christmas tree. The last Christmas he would ever know. Choir music is piped through the speakers, a rousing harmonisation of four or five voices that talk of loss and love and meeting again. When Dan's coffin is carried in on the shoulders of four pallbearers, Beth lets out a shriek of grief and her mother grabs at her arm, like prisoners awaiting execution.

Unbelievable, to think of him inside.

There are songs, tears, speeches. Wry, sad, laughter when his uncle stands to talk about the climbing career of Dan's parents, who were never content unless they were in a hot air balloon or dangling from a mountain, and had passed their love of adventure to their offspring. They were so proud, he says, when Daniel joined the forces. 'Although they were living in Cornwall by then, the family remained close, and he...'

A taste of saltwater, burning my mouth. I can't help thinking of Dad, his blue eyes now peering out through drawstrings of skin, and what we might say about him when the time comes. Dan's uncle cannot manage another word and withdraws from the podium. Someone steps up to talk about Dan's short stint in the armed forces, then Evan speaks, without a hint of irony, about Dan being a free spirit. 'This world was too big for him,' he says. 'He died doing something he loved.'

I don't feel as bad when he says that, because it's true.

We step outside into a burst of sharp lemon sunlight. I could ask Dan's ex the truth about what happened between them, but what would be the point? There are more than two sides to any story, and it won't change anything. It won't do me any good to know.

In the car park, Beth hurries to speak to me. 'He loved you,' she says.

And this, in the end, is what I choose to believe.

It's a relief that Adam's moved out. The first few nights when he stayed here, there were moments I felt close to him again, and thought of all we'd lost. *Had it been so bad*, I wondered? I lay in bed alone, and couldn't decide whether it was shock or regret that pooled in a stagnant puddle at the back of my head, sloshing this way and that every time I turned over until it became impossible to sleep. I didn't know what I wanted from Adam. I don't think he knew what he wanted from me. I found myself getting annoyed with all the same things that irritated me before, and this time I think I irritated him, too.

He's staying with the woman he met on the podcast until the house sale has gone through, which will hopefully happen quickly now we've got an offer from a couple of first-time buyers. I met Lisa at the park when I went to collect Toby yesterday afternoon, and she seems nice, although it was a surprise to discover she was nothing like me. Weirdly, she looks like the photos I've seen of Adam's mum.

I run the tape along the top of the box and tap it closed with the flat of my hand. It contains several pairs of shoes I won't wear until next summer, along with my walking boots and rucksack from the hike that the police returned yesterday.

One day, I know I'll be able to open it and examine the contents. Torch. Tissues. Spare socks. Map. Plasters. It might sound odd, but I'd like to go back and attempt the climb again at some point in the future, perhaps with Toby. I don't know if he fully grasps the concept of death, but I tried to explain gently that sometimes we don't get to choose what happens, but we can choose how we treat others and keep being brave. He asked why I climbed the mountain if it was dangerous, and I had to think about that.

'Because it made me feel strong.' And free. If it hadn't been for the chatter in my head that day, telling me Dan's phone might hold the clue to something that could destroy us, maybe I'd have relished the rawness, the peace. I wasn't Adam's possession anymore.

I pause at the dining room table and pick up the card Frankie dropped off the day after Dan died. *With Deepest Sympathy.* She'd hugged me on the doorstep and I hadn't known what to say, because in my mind I had somehow managed to conflate what happened to Hannah with Matty, and I hated Frankie for protecting him. But then, over her shoulder, I spotted Matty in the passenger seat of the car, looking pale and unsure of himself; much younger than I remembered. He wasn't the boy who attacked Hannah. He's still learning the rules of life, which, it turns out, *isn't* just about adventure and fun. Sometimes, it's also about self-deprivation. Making tough choices.

Frankie and I have promised to stay in touch and visit each other during the school holidays. I'll be renting on the outskirts of Manchester to start with, and although it isn't the curating job I've been dreaming of, two days a week invigilating an exhibition in the Castlefield Gallery will give me a foot in the door. Toby's just as excited as I am. I've told him he can come back to see Adam at weekends and holidays. And he had such a good time staying with Nanny and Grandad, he keeps asking how many sleeps until we go there to live. '*One*,' I told him tonight. 'Just one more sleep, gorgeous boy.'

Die Trying

Beneath Frankie's card, my stack of drawings. I shuffle through them, wondering which box to put them in and whether they might even be good enough to go in a portfolio to take to Castlefield, when something strikes me: the change in *mood*. The first few sketches are comprised of dark, angry gashes which have been scored into the paper with such depth, it's surprising the pencil hasn't gone through. Faces; some without mouths, some without eyes. Squares, circles and spots. Windows and shadows. As I flick through them, it's like watching dawn gradually break above a dismal landscape. My latest drawing, taken from a photo on the mountain at the beginning of the hike, has been created with the lightest of touch, showing a body of water between two muscular shoulders of land. I don't remember giving it a title, but there it is, scribbled in the bottom right-hand corner. *Hope.*

CHAPTER SIXTY-FIVE

Adam

Three months later

We've taken the 9pm crossing to the Isle of Wight and it's already dark, the ferry rising and falling with the pulse of the waves. Lisa invited me to meet her parents, admitting it was early days in our relationship but, she said, if I wanted to come, I'd be welcome. The horn sounds, long and loud, and I jump, laughing at other passengers nearby as they do the same. *Nearly gave me a heart attack!* At the hot food counter, a long queue trails through to the seating area, where people are positioning bags and coats and children, settling near the windows as though preparing for a show. The smell of heat and grease is overpowering.

Whisper it: love. Lisa and I have been inseparable. I was afraid of handing over my broken heart at first, so I've been giving it to her in pieces. One at the Chinese restaurant, another as shards of morning light filtered through her bedroom curtains. She is brand new, a fascination of matching socks, low-carb meals and half drunk cups of tea. When Jemma took Toby to Manchester, Lisa cheered me up with a day out shopping in Cardiff, and it felt strange to be with someone who didn't pretend to ride on the children's electronic coin-operated cars or try on the ugliest clothes in the shop, 'just for a laugh'.

Being with Lisa feels like the real thing, a serious grown-up relationship after the chaos of Jemma.

This time, I'll get it right.

Lisa doesn't like going out on deck, but I need to get away from the mass of moving bodies. I need some air.

Outside, the cold snatches at my breath, shredding it to white slivers. The light from the ferry picks out the dark peaks of moving water, like hundreds of gaping mouths, and I'm hit, suddenly, by a blur of spray.

What is my life? Who was I? Who am I?

I don't know. I don't know. I don't know. There's only one other person mad enough to be out here – a smoker, standing with his back to the great metal wall of the funnel, hood and hat pulled tightly around his face. I return his stiff smile and keep walking until I'm at the side of the boat, where there's a curious absence of wind. If it weren't for the stink of food and diesel pumping from a vent, it would be like entering a cave.

I move to the rail and push the pad of my finger into the pips of the die. Four.

Here it is, then, pure and simple: the truth.

Abbie wasn't meant to be killed that night. I was furious with Will, furious at my father, furious with the die, and set off in the driving rain, my vision distorted by the furiously thrashing wipers. *I'm With You* was playing on the radio and it couldn't be more serendipitous, because suddenly there she was, walking towards the bridge. Mud seemed to be everywhere, spattering the windscreen, rushing in brown rivers down the side of the road and speckling the back of Abbie's tights. I pulled over and ran towards her, calling her name. The wind was tugging at her clothes, fingering her hair, and I was consumed with a sudden, irrational hatred for it. '*Abbie,*' I shouted again, and this time, she turned.

Rain was travelling down the back of my head into the collar of my new shirt. I'd bought it from Next earlier that day and ironed it carefully, hoping Dad would be impressed. I'd had a haircut, too, gelled into spikes. Abbie's face collapsed into an expression of relief, and I thought: *this is it*. The moment we would both recall falling in love. The two of us, shivering and sodden, shining in the headlights.

'Where's Will?' she asked.

The gel was running in sticky rivulets down my face, and I could taste it – soapy, stinging, a hint of chamomile. We didn't need to talk about Will. She owed him nothing. The words came out in a shout, lumpy and imperfect, tripping over themselves to be heard: 'I love you.'

Her face fractalled into patterns. Around us, the paths and riverbanks were bloated and gleaming, like the inside of a carnivorous mouth. *I love you*, I repeated, because she looked confused. And then, because her mouth had started moving rhythmically around the small white lump of gum in her mouth, I told her the truth about Will.

The chill was burrowing so deep, it felt like pain. Abbie turned and started walking away, so I followed, talking about what he was doing at that very moment with Lily. She had to see it was *us*. It had always been us. It could only ever be us.

Her feelings, in that moment, must have been overwhelming. Perhaps she wasn't ready to face them. She started to cross the road.

Then, across the concrete slab of the bridge, a second glare of headlights. The wind lifted her hair around her ears, as if to whisper a warning. Ruffles on the water. Stumps of grass, swollen from rain.

A sickening thump.

My consciousness pixellated. I was back at the car, outside, inside. What happened? Had I hit her? My hands moved to the die in the glove compartment and I was vaguely aware of a ringing in my ears, a sticky taste of chamomile on my tongue. Water, dripping everywhere. The die clattered into the footwell. Two.

Die Trying

Do nothing.
I couldn't leave Abbie.
I couldn't disobey the die.
My breath, sour from the alcohol I drank with Dad.
Do nothing.
I was never supposed to be here anyway. When I turned the key, a new song was playing, something upbeat.
I started the ignition and drove back the way I came.

The boat lurches sideways. I should go back inside; Lisa will be waiting for me, clutching a hot drink in each hand. Sanctuary. She doesn't know I've brought the die. 'Do you see it as a talisman?' she said, a few weeks ago. 'It's getting a bit much.'

I tried to explain: the die has always been right. Even when it appeared to be wrong, it was only because we hadn't seen all the pieces of the puzzle. We weren't *meant* to see all the pieces of the puzzle. Sometimes, change could only be achieved through sacrifice, and it was necessary for Lisa and me to go through all we had – the pain, the heartache – to find each other the way we did.

Abbie's gone now. She is at peace.

I seize the die in my fist. *Don't think, just do.* A juddering vibration through my feet, as the ferry pushes through the waves. The water tautens and relaxes, tautens and relaxes, as though preparing to birth a monster. I lift my arm, then throw it, as hard and far as I can. It glints in the light from the houses on the opposite coastline, then falls into the darkness of the Solent, making barely a ripple.

How do I feel? People asked the same question, after my operation. *How are you feeling?* I don't know. Relief? Sadness? Lightness. A severing... of what, I'm not entirely sure.

No discomfort. Only clarity.

I can't wait to tell Lisa.

I've come in at a different part of the ferry, a slab of heat bearing down at my crown as I open the sliding door. The North

Lounge has a smaller café – more like a desk – and the seating area is scattered with passengers and dogs. I head down the stairs to the main lounge, clutching the cold silver rail as the boat undulates. Lisa isn't in the queue for drinks. She isn't in the seating area, either. What was she wearing, when I last saw her?

Black coat, grey jumper.

The door to the women's toilet opens, dispatching a blast of sound. 'Sorry,' the woman says.

It isn't Lisa. Where is she?

I try calling her. There's a family at the table beside me – two generations, it seems – and the younger man stands to rock the fractious baby tied to his waist in a sling. *Shhh*.

Lisa's phone rings and rings, then goes to answerphone. Something's wrong.

Something is very wrong.

I cut the call. On the screen in front of me, her last message. We need to talk. I am sorry, honestly. But I don't think I'm ready for this - it's getting a bit intense.

Yesterday. Did she send it yesterday, or the day before? The days all seem to blend into one. Intense. Intense is good, isn't it? Strength, passion, flavour. 'What about the Isle of Wight?' I said. 'You told me I could meet your parents.'

'I know,' she said, when I came home from work. 'And you're a lovely guy, Adam. But...'

But. There is always a *but*. She didn't want to be with me.

Too broken.

Too needy.

Too intense.

She suggested I take up the counselling Jemma had suggested, the counselling that, months earlier, she'd agreed was probably nothing more than a smokescreen from my ex-wife. '*We can stay friends*', Lisa added, a statement that made something fold and flop inside me. Friends.

Die Trying

I took my things and slept in the car outside my old flat. This morning, a message from Will: `Thought I'd share the happy news. Me and Claire are expecting a baby!`

Lisa is not here. What have I done?

The child starts to scream. I bolt back up the steps, almost colliding with a woman clutching the hand of a toddler at the top. I tug at the door, but it resists, clinging to the gums of its frame before releasing wih a sticky *pop*.

Outside.

Always, outside.

I scan the water. It's made of glass, it won't be—

There.

That's it, isn't it? Dark and light, glinting, because... it must be.

The die. The only thing that ever made sense. It came to me – a gift, a sign – and I threw it away.

I move forward, along the side of the railings where the wind greets me like a whip, throwing chains of rain against my face. My trainers slide against the metal and I use my knees to manoeuvre myself upwards. '*Don't you just wish time could stand still so we could stay like this forever?*'

Time doesn't stand still; nor does the water. It is restless, constantly in motion, making it impossible to keep my eye on the die. It keeps dipping in and out of the pools of light in a freakish game of hide and seek.

I'll get it back, and everything will be alright.

I haul myself up, one knee on the cold rail.

A gust of wind, or perhaps an invisible hand.

I am falling.

ACKNOWLEDGEMENTS

Well, this is amazing! There have been times during the writing of this book that I felt truly lost, unsure which direction to take, and yes – a couple of times, I even rolled a die. Who knows what kind of story it would have been, had fate not lent a hand?!

Fate – if that's what you want to call it – and, of course, the incredible team at Harper North. I'd like to offer my huge and heartfelt thanks to Gen Pegg, Alice Murphy-Pyle, Jess Haycox and Millie Morton for the valuable support, advice and palpable excitement throughout the process, not to mention the beautiful cover design. Thank you to Daisy Watt for the structural edits, without which this book would be frankly unpublishable. And thanks for finding me! I am eternally grateful for that.

I would also like to thank Christine Johnson and everyone else involved in the production of this book.

Apologies to my family for having to put up with me staring at the wall, paying no attention during conversations and mealtimes, and darting off at various opportune moments to jot down scenes or ideas. Thank you for supporting me regardless. Especially my son Andrew, who stayed up with me after midnight brainstorming ideas as I approached the end of the novel. And of course, to Brad, Jess and Ethan, who continually asked: 'have you thought about looking at it *this* way instead?'

My husband bought me a huge glass die which is now sitting pride of place on the bookshelf he spent hours polishing during the long hours when I was writing. When the light catches the die at a certain angle, there's something quite unnerving about it. But unlike Adam's die, it represents solidarity and a quiet, subtle love shown through mutual acts of kindness. Thank you, Kris.

Thank you to my friends. Thank you to Nicola Martin, who designed a simply stunning website for me. Please pop by at eleanorbarker-white.com and say hi!

I remain deeply grateful to those who supported my first book, *My Name Was Eden*, particularly the Curtis Brown Discoveries Prize, Capital Crime festival, Swindon Festival of Literature and Tea, Leaves and Reads festival. I'd like to thank all the wonderful authors who offered early endorsements, and my US editor, Liz Stein, whose encouragement and guidance helped set me on this path.

Finally, an enormous thanks to the booksellers, librarians and reviewers who help facilitate the joy of reading. And, of course, to the readers. Thank you!

Harper North

Book Credits

would like to thank the following staff and contributors for their involvement in making this book a reality:

Fionnuala Barrett
Laura Braggs
Sarah Burke
Rhys Callaghan
Alan Cracknell
Jonathan de Peyer
Morgan Dun-Campbell
Tom Dunstan
Kate Elton
Sarah Emsley
Simon Gerratt
Imogen Gordon Clark
Lydia Grainge
Monica Green
Natassa Hadjinicolaou
C J Harter
Jess Haycox
Megan Jones

Jean-Marie Kelly
Taslima Khatun
Holly Kyte
Rachel McCarron
Millie Morton
Alice Murphy-Pyle
Adam Murray
Genevieve Pegg
Amanda Percival
Dean Russell
Colleen Simpson
Eleanor Slater
Megan Smith
Hilary Stein
Emma Sullivan
Katrina Troy
Claire Ward

For more unmissable reads,
sign up to the HarperNorth newsletter at
www.harpernorth.co.uk

or find us on socials at
@HarperNorthUK

Harper
North